'I'm not going ▓▓▓▓▓▓ **blurted before s**▓▓▓▓ **nerves riding ro**▓▓▓▓▓ **sense.**

He laughed out loud, shaking his head in mirth.

'Don't worry—I'm taking a break from seducing innocent young journalists, so your virtue is safe with me,' he said, his mouth quirked in a playful smile. 'I *am* interested in your body, Jess, but only on an artistic level.'

'You can't blame me for being wary when you make provocative statements. You do have a reputation for being a bit…'

'A bit what?'

She paused, searching for the right word. 'Wild.'

He gave her a bemused grin. 'I promise to be on my best behaviour,' he said, making a crossing motion over his heart. 'And if I slip up you have my permission to *lick* me into shape.'

Oh, my *God*, the images he'd just conjured in her mind.

She really needed to get out of here before she totally lost her cool.

An overwhelming urge to pack up and go home, where she didn't have to deal with these weird and disturbing feelings he provoked in her, besieged her. But she couldn't leave. Not if she wanted to keep her job at the magazine. She was going to have to brazen it out and ignore the blatant innuendos he seemed so keen to tease her into a jittery mess with.

He was a player, all right, but she wasn't about to let him play *her*.

Dear Reader

Who can resist the dangerous charms of a bad boy? Not me! Especially a disgustingly talented one with a body built for sin and the wits to win over the hardest of women. My heroine, Jess, *is* that hard woman, and Xander, my hero, certainly has his work cut out to get the better of *her*.

These two characters were such fun to write. They're both headstrong, super-ambitious and broken in their own heart-wrenching way. Thank goodness they had me to throw them together and force them to sort out their lives!

I had the pleasure of sending them off to pass some quality time on the banks of Lake Garda—a place I have a great fondness for after spending my honeymoon there. How could they fail to fall in love in such romantic setting? I challenge anyone to resist the charms of the place.

This is a story of divine inspiration, a little bit of magic and some very messy artistic endeavours. I hope you enjoy it.

Christy x

PS I love to hear from readers. You can contact me at christymckellenauthor@gmail.com or www.facebook.com/christymckellenauthor

LESSONS IN RULE-BREAKING

BY
CHRISTY McKELLEN

MILLS & BOON

Published in Great Britain 2014
by Mills & Boon, an imprint of Harlequin (UK) Limited,
Eton House, 18-24 Paradise Road, Richmond, Surrey, TW9 1SR

© 2014 Christy McKellen

ISBN: 978 0 263 24616 2

Harlequin (UK) Limited's policy is to use papers that are natural,
renewable and recyclable products and made from wood grown in
sustainable forests. The logging and manufacturing processes conform
to the legal environmental regulations of the country of origin.

Printed and bound in Spain
by Blackprint CPI, Barcelona

BK (Before Kids) **Christy McKellen** worked as a video and radio producer in London and Nottingham. After a decade of dealing with nappies, tantrums and endless questions from toddlers she has come out the other side and moved into the wonderful world of literature. She now spends her time writing flirty, sexy romance with a kick—her dream job!

In her downtime she can be found drinking the odd glass of champagne, ambling around the beautiful South West of England, or escaping from real life by dashing off to foreign lands with her fabulous family.

Christy loves to hear from readers. You can contact her at: www.christymckellen.blogspot.com, http://www.facebook.com/christymckellenauthor or https://twitter.com/ChristyMcKellen

Other Modern Tempted™ titles by Christy McKellen:

HOLIDAY WITH A STRANGER

**This and other titles by Christy McKellen
are available as eBooks from www.millsandboon.co.uk**

To the Prosecco Book Club ladies
for their encouragement and friendship.

And to Clio, my fantastic editor,
thanks for your positivity and unerring support.

CHAPTER ONE

'THE EDITOR WANTS to see you in her office.'

Jessica LaFayette glanced up from the screen of her laptop to see Claire, one of the other junior staff writers at *Spark* magazine, looking down at her with worry in her eyes and a speculative eyebrow raised.

Clearly Claire was as concerned as Jess about what sort of news was about to be bestowed on her.

There had been rumours flying about the office recently about staff cutbacks and everyone had been on tenterhooks for weeks, desperately worried that they were the one about to be summoned to the editor's office in order to be given the boot.

Okay, time to buckle up.

Smoothing a hand down her hair and straightening her blouse, Jess gave Claire a curt nod and stood up, balling her trembling hands into fists at her sides, before striding over to the editor's office.

If she lost this job she was in big trouble. She'd already raced through her meagre savings living in London as an intern for nine months, before finally securing the job here—on the proviso she made it past her three-month probation period. The thought of having to pack up and go home to live back with her parents in the burbs of Leicester, after all the excitement of finally being employed in her dream job, sent a twist of panic through her.

They thought she was crazy chasing such a competitive career, but it was what she'd always wanted to do and she'd been determined to give it everything she had.

She was stubborn like that.

It had taken her two years after leaving university to land a placement at *Spark*, two long years of living back at home with a woman who would surely place as a top contender for 'World's Most Disappointed Mother.'

Jess was *not* the daughter Ingrid LaFayette had hoped for. Instead of a vivacious, beauty—a carbon copy of herself—she'd been lumped with kooky-looking, strong-willed Jess.

No way was she going back to the raised eyebrows and tense silences that she'd lived with for longer than she wanted to remember. Life had moved on and so had she.

Pushing back her shoulders and taking a deep breath, Jess rapped on the glass partition of her editor's office before walking in.

Pamela Bradley—editor extraordinaire—looked up from her computer and waved Jess into the office with a perfectly manicured hand.

All the women who worked on the magazine rocked up to work every day looking as if they'd just stepped off a Paris catwalk—all except for Jess. She preferred to stick with her smart, comfortably fitting suits. She knew her limitations when it came to fashion—she hadn't a clue what was supposed to suit her body shape and didn't want to make a fool of herself by looking as if she was trying too hard. She was a smart, but practical, girl through and through.

'Jess, sit.' Pamela gestured towards the chair facing

her and Jess sat down on the edge of the seat, her hands folded neatly in her lap, and waited, her heart thumping hard against her chest.

'So, I read your piece on nail salons.' Pamela gave her a steely-eyed look and Jess shrank back into her seat under the confidence-wrecking force of it.

Uh-oh. That wasn't the look of unadulterated joy and respect she'd been hoping for.

'To be perfectly honest, Jess, it wasn't good enough. The pieces you've been submitting recently have been a little… How can I put this?' She put both hands onto the desk in front of her, her nails digging into the wood like talons, and leant forward. 'Dry. Lifeless. Dull.' The words snapped out of her mouth as if she found them utterly distasteful. She gave a small shake of her perfectly coiffed head. 'I expected more, Jess, when I offered you the position here.'

Fear and embarrassment wound through Jess's chest and pooled like burning acid in her stomach.

She'd blown it. Pamela had to make someone redundant and it looked as if it was going to be her head on the block.

'I c-can do better,' she stuttered out, desperate to stall the words she felt sure were about to trip from Pamela's lips.

Pamela shook her head and her mouth twisted into a dissatisfied smile. 'I gave you the job because I sensed there was some hidden potential there, Jess. You're a talented writer, methodical with an accomplished style, but your writing lacks the edge you need to make your pieces really stand out. It's *too* controlled, too stuffy.'

'I can unstuff it,' Jess yelped, feeling tears of frustration burning at the backs of her eyes.

'How do you propose to do that, Jess?'

Jess mouthed at her, totally at a loss for how to answer.

'To be frank, I think you need to stop living in that self-controlled little bubble,' Pamela continued, eyeing the immaculate, but understated, suit Jess was wearing today.

Jess smoothed her skirt down, then her hair. 'I don't understand what you mean.'

'Look, Jess, I think you're a talented writer and you could build a great career with us here, but my advice to you is that you need to find that extra something to make your work sparkle. To find the life beyond your neat little world.' She tipped her head in a motherly sort of way. 'When did you last go out on a date, for example?'

The question made Jess uneasy. 'What does that have to do with anything?'

'You're what? Twenty-five? You take life too seriously. You should be out, having wild sex and falling in love at your age. Widening your experiences.'

'Sex is overrated,' Jess muttered, thinking back to the awkward sexual experiences she'd had up till this point. She didn't get what all the fuss was about when it came to sex. It was uncomfortable and messy and she was usually glad when it was all over if she was totally honest. Neither of the guys she'd slept with had rocked her world, but at the time she'd thought she ought to put the effort in, just to see what she was supposedly missing out on.

It turned out she wasn't missing much at all.

There was a knock on the partition behind her and Jess turned to see Pamela's assistant standing there with a slip of paper clutched in her hand.

'Sorry to interrupt, but Maggie just phoned. She's stuck in Greece because of an air-traffic-controllers strike and can't make it back for her assignment today. She sounded pretty fed up because apparently she'd managed to snag an interview with Xander Heaton, that bad-boy artist everyone's so crazy about.'

Pamela sighed. 'Can't she reschedule? I really need that piece in the next issue. Xander was going to be the linchpin of the article.'

'Apparently not. He's refusing to change the date because he's about to start working on a new exhibition. He'll be at his studio in Old Street today, but he's off to Italy tonight and he never gives any press interviews while he's working. Something about killing his muse.'

'Yeah, okay.' Pamela sighed, flapping a hand in a tired manner. 'Can Marnie go?' she asked, clearly not that hopeful.

'She's off with the flu. Nearly half the office has called in sick this week.'

'I can go and cover it,' Jess said a little too loudly, her heart racing as a sudden shot of adrenaline fired round her body. If she didn't grab this opportunity quickly one of the other junior writers would and she really needed to show Pamela some of that spark she was so keen to see.

'I don't know, Jess.' Pamela flipped her a look of deep scepticism.

'Please, Pam, give me another chance to show you how I can make my writing sizzle.' Jess leant forward in her chair, clasping her hands together in a prayer of hope. 'It would be such a shame to miss out on the opportunity of interviewing him while he's in the country.'

'You think you're up to handling someone like Xander Heaton, do you?'

Jess sat up straighter, pulled taut by a thread of hope. 'Of course I am. How difficult can he be?'

She could have sworn she saw an amused smirk flit across Pamela's face.

'Okay, then,' Pamela said, finally. 'If he's working with a model, make sure you talk to her, too, if you get the opportunity—see if you can get something interesting. What he's like to work with, whether she's sleeping with him, why he picked her as his model, anything to give the piece an edge. Try and get a sense of who he is, any personal details you can draw out of him. He's got himself a reputation as a real playboy over the last year—he's turned up to pretty much every high-profile party going and caused a scene at all of them—so see if you can get some gossip about what happened there. Oh, and try and find out why he hasn't produced anything of note recently, too. His last exhibition was a real critical flop so that might have something to do with it. And most importantly, find out what he's planning to do for his next project.'

Jess was nodding so much her neck was starting to ache. 'Okay, got it. No problem.' She stood up and smiled at Pamela. 'Thank you, for giving me another chance.'

Pamela raised a severely plucked eyebrow. 'Don't waste this opportunity, Jess. If you want to keep your job on this magazine you're going to have to pull something pretty special out of the bag.'

Pamela's words rang in Jess's ears as she took the tube over to Old Street.

She made copious notes on the way, determined to remember everything Pamela had asked for.

The train had just reached Moorgate station when it slowed down to a crawl, then stopped, midjourney.

The driver's voice came over the tannoy to let the passengers know there was an electrical fault with the train, but they were hoping to get it sorted out in a few minutes.

Jess looked about her wildly; she was already running late to hit the allotted time for her interview with Xander and she didn't want to turn up there flustered and on the back foot. She wanted him to be impressed with her cool professionalism and trust her enough to spill the sort of information she needed to make her piece stand out from the ones he'd done in the past.

She'd seen pictures of him in the press—at parties with the great and good of London society, usually with some eminently beautiful woman hanging off his arm—and she knew in her bones he was going to be a challenge. If she was going to win him over she couldn't allow herself to be daunted by that famous dark charisma and overabundance of sexual confidence.

He was exactly the sort of man she usually avoided in real life. Bad-boy types who flitted from woman to woman like moths in a lighting shop were the antithesis of what she was looking for in a partner. She needed steady and safe. Comfortable. A relationship she could feel in control of.

A nervous shiver tickled down her spine at the thought of facing him, but she shook it off. She was *not* going to let his challenging reputation get to her. She was a smart, savvy, professional woman and that was exactly what he was going to see—when she finally arrived there.

She sat there for another fifteen minutes, tapping her feet and biting at a ragged fingernail until the train finally began its excruciatingly slow roll into Old Street station.

She was now officially late for her interview.

She hated being late. Hated it.

Anything that took control out of her hands like this made her so stressed she felt ill with it.

After a few more frustrating minutes of trying to figure out where she was meant to be going using the sat nav on her phone, she finally found the converted warehouse where Xander's studio was located.

Feeling sticky and jumpy after running all the way there in her heels, she stepped into the blissfully cool entrance lobby and looked at the list of names and businesses on the large brushed-metal sign. Xander's studio was just one of a collection of spaces used by a group of high-profile artists and creatives.

The place was shabby chic through and through with huge, squashy leather sofas scattered around a break-out kitchen area, all done out in stainless steel and black lacquer-fronted cupboards. Amazing murals had been painted on all the walls and Jess recognised one in Xander's famously biting style. It was a social commentary on the state of reporting in the press. An open newspaper showed a picture of a child crying, with a meat cleaver slicing through the middle of it and the word *HACK* painted in big red bloody letters along the blade.

Okay, she really needed to stop looking at that before *the fear* got to her. Did he really hate journalists that much? Would that make it even harder for her to conduct a successful interview with him?

Only one way to find out.

Gritting her teeth and smoothing down the jacket of her suit, she walked up the stairs to where Xander's studio was located on the third floor.

Taking a moment to get her breath back, she knocked

loudly on the heavy wooden door to his studio and stood back to wait for him to appear, her hands grasped tightly behind her back and what she hoped was an open and friendly smile plastered across her face.

There was the sound of footsteps from the other side of the door and Jess steeled herself as it swung open to reveal Xander Heaton, with a paintbrush in one hand and a look of tense annoyance on his face.

Jess couldn't help but stand and stare up at him as he towered over her. She'd anticipated him being some-how disappointing in the flesh, but he wasn't. He *really* wasn't.

Paint-splattered jeans hung low on his hips and a grey cotton T-shirt clung tightly to the hard contours of his chest, making no effort whatsoever to disguise the swell of muscles on his rangy frame.

Despite the hard angles of his bone structure there was something faintly boyish about him. Perhaps that was the key to his appeal? A hard alpha male on the outside with just a glimmer of a softer, more vulner-able soul inside.

There was an almost ethereal glow about him, too, as if his charisma were being overmanufactured inside his body and the excess were spilling out through the pores of his skin.

Even his just-rolled-out-of-bed, designer mess of rich chestnut-brown hair seemed to glow like a freshly shelled conker in the sunshine pouring in through the large warehouse windows.

Jess's body buzzed with longing to reach up and run her hands over his face, to feel the hard contours of his bones under that golden skin and the gentle rasp of his barely there stubble as it caught on the whorls of her fingertips.

It took her a moment to realise he was staring at her mouth with his amazing, bright, aqua-coloured eyes and giving her an impatient frown as if he was utterly nonplussed by her appearance and thoroughly pissed off about being disturbed.

She gave herself a little shake and pulled herself together. She was a twenty-five-year-old professional woman, not some love-struck teenager, and she needed to act like it.

'Hi, Xander, I'm here to do the interview with you today,' she said brightly. 'Maggie's caught up so you've got me instead.' Her smile began to falter when he didn't give up his hard frown. 'I know I'm a few minutes late, but it was totally beyond my control. The tube train I was on…' She ground to a halt as he began shaking his head.

'I have no idea what you're talking about.'

Panic rose in her chest and her blood began pumping round her body with such vigorous force she could feel the jittery buzz of it right down to her toes. 'The interview. With Maggie? She said you'd agreed to talk to her today about the new exhibition you're planning.' He continued to stare at her blankly. 'Before you go to Italy,' Jess said, gesticulating wildly now, as if she could somehow waft the memory of the interview back into his head through the sheer force of her determination.

Her rambling explanation must have sparked something in his brain because his eyes widened a fraction before his expression shut down into a hard frown again.

'Yeah, okay, I'd forgotten about that…' he shrugged '…but you missed your window. I'm right in the middle of something now.'

'But…' Jess could barely get the words past her lips in her panic.

'Sorry, sweetheart, but you snooze, you lose.' He turned to go.

'What? That's it? You can't even give me five minutes of your time?' she nearly shouted in her panic.

Xander sighed and turned back, rubbing a hand through his hair. 'To be honest, I never wanted to do this interview in the first place. I only agreed because your colleague is a friend of a friend and she caught me at a weak moment. I seem to remember I was pretty drunk.' He leant against the doorjamb and flashed her a 'crap happens' look. 'I don't have time to pander to journalists right now. I have work to do. Now, if you'll excuse me.' He shot her a wink before striding off into his studio, slamming the door behind him and leaving Jess mouthing like a landed fish in his wake.

Xander Heaton walked back to where he'd been sketching his model, trying to shake off an unsettling twinge of guilt as the look of utter dismay on the journalist's face permeated through to his conscience.

He flipped it out of his head. He didn't need distractions like that at the moment. It was hard enough holding it together without having to accommodate any old Tom, Dick or Harriet who wandered in for a bit of show-and-tell. Everyone seemed to want a piece of him at the moment and he barely had enough of himself left to keep his strung-out existence going.

His latest model—who was giving it everything she'd got to contort herself into the strange pose he'd asked her to take up—gave him a slow, seductive smile as he sat down and attempted to focus back on her.

Ah, hell. He knew he'd been playing with fire when he asked her to pose for a picture. She'd been one of a bunch of professional models he'd got talking to at a party and he'd thought she might be an interesting subject to paint. She was making it pretty clear she was interested in more than just modelling for him right now, though.

She was a beautiful woman—too young for his tastes—but she was going to be a big thing at some point, he could tell. He should be excited about working with her, but somehow he couldn't summon the energy for it today.

A wave of tiredness crashed over him. He'd been searching for inspiration for this new exhibition for months, desperately trying to drop-kick his muse into action, but for some reason he kept missing his mark. He'd ended up destroying every picture he'd painted recently, disgusted by the banal rubbish he was coming up with. Just like the picture he'd been working on before he was interrupted.

The dark-haired journalist's face slid back into his mind as he tore off the page in the sketchbook he'd been working on, crumpled it up and lobbed it at the bin.

She had enormous eyes, he reflected now, dark blue with bright, white flecks that had drawn him right in. She wasn't conventionally attractive, but there'd been a kind of spirit about her that had made his blood pump faster. Thinking back, there had been something about her expression that disturbed him when he'd said *no* to the interview. It hadn't been the usual sort of annoyance or disappointment he tended to invoke in journos when he refused to talk to them—she'd looked as if he'd just stomped hard on her life's dream and left it broken and bleeding on the floor.

He had a sudden mad urge to sketch the image that had just pinged into his head. It was brighter and clearer and sharper than anything he'd envisaged in a very long time and his sluggish blood picked up speed as a long-forgotten feeling of elation coursed through him.

Rubbing his hand over his eyes, he felt the puffiness that had taken up residence there since the insomnia had set in. It had been months since he'd slept properly and no matter what he tried it wouldn't break its hold on him.

It appeared to be making him crazy.

'Everything okay, Xander?' his model, Seraphina, asked, unfolding herself from the chair and sauntering over to where he sat with his now blank sketch pad on his knee. 'Hmm, so are you using invisible ink here, or what?' she asked.

He flashed her a look of irritation and her smile faltered.

Guilt pulled at him and he replaced the unreasonable expression with an apologetic smile to try and make up for offending her. 'Look, Sera, I'm sorry but this isn't working out.'

'What? I'm not making your creative juices flow? Do you need a bit of inspiration?' she asked, her voice laden with innuendo.

Before he could react she slipped her top over her head, stepped close and picked up his hand, pressing it to her bare breast.

He felt nothing.

Closing his eyes, he shook his head and carefully removed his hand.

He'd partied hard this year, needing an outlet for his frustration and anger after the cutting reviews of his last exhibition—where the reviewers had wondered in full public view where his talent had disappeared to—but it had all caught up with him recently.

He felt hollowed out by all the vacuous affairs with an ever-changing kaleidoscope of willing women, none of whom lasted for more than a couple of months. He'd been constantly on the lookout for something new and fresh and revitalising to draw him out of his depressed funk but he'd overindulged, leaving him feeling strung out and empty.

His work had suffered. Big time. In fact he couldn't remember the last time he'd felt a genuine urge to pick up a paintbrush, or pencils, or even a spray can and make his mark. He felt washed up, wrung out and desiccated.

Looking up at Seraphina, he was horrified to see tears had welled in her eyes. He held up a placating hand—none of this was her fault and he felt a sting of shame at hurting her. 'Look, you're a beautiful woman, but you're not what I need right now.'

'What *do* you need?'

'I don't know, Sera. I wish I did. I'll know it when I see it.'

'Fine,' she interjected, her voice wobbly and high. 'If I'm not good enough for you I'm not wasting my time hanging around here.' Pulling her top back on, she gave him one last accusatory look before storming out, slamming the door behind her.

Jess was smoothing her hair down with a shaking hand and trying to pull herself together in the loos across from Xander's studio when the door flew open and a tall, beautiful woman stormed in and slumped against the porcelain washbasin, swiping away a waterfall of tears that were making her meticulously applied make-up run.

'Are you okay?' Jess asked, grateful for a reprieve from worrying about her own problems for a moment. She wondered whether the woman was anything to do with Xander. She wouldn't be at all surprised.

The woman glanced up into the mirror. 'I'm fine,' she said, giving a shaky smile before looking away again.

Jess went into the toilet to grab some tissue and placed it on the basin next to the woman before leaning back against the wall in companionable silence. The woman nodded in surprised thanks and picked up the tissue, dabbing under her eyes.

She was incredible-looking, all Bambi limbs and delicate bone structure. Her huge blue eyes seemed to glow with life—even through the tears—and her skin… What Jess wouldn't give for flawless, soft skin like hers.

She pulled her long suit jacket around her, feeling like a massive frumpy lump in comparison.

'Are you sure you're okay?' Jess asked.

'Yeah. Feeling humiliated and rejected, but I'll survive.'

Jess snorted. 'Join the club.'

The woman looked at her in confusion. 'What happened to you?'

Jess sighed. 'I was supposed to be interviewing Xander Heaton but he blew me off.'

The woman snorted. 'Sounds like Xander. Does what he wants, when he feels like it and sod everyone else. He's a law unto himself, that guy.'

Aha, so she was right.

'What did he do to make you cry?' Jess asked tentatively. If she couldn't get an interview with the man himself, she could at least get some information from one of his disgruntled models to try and appease Pamela.

The model looked down at the sink. 'I've been stupidly excited about working with him and I've been telling everyone I'm going to be in a famous painting, but apparently I'm totally uninspiring. He doesn't think I'm attractive enough,' she said quietly. 'He was all sweetness one minute and cold as ice the next and I have no idea what I did wrong.'

A shot of anger fired through Jess's veins. Just who did the guy think he was? 'What's your name?' Jess asked gently.

'Seraphina.'

'Well, I think you're a very beautiful woman and Xander's an idiot to reject you,' Jess said, giving the woman an encouraging smile. 'From what I've heard about him you've had a lucky escape. He's not exactly known for having meaningful relationships.'

The model snorted, but managed to raise a smile. 'No, I guess not. And it's not as if he made a move on me, but I hoped he might.' She looked down at the floor. 'I just got a bit swept away by the excitement of it all and he's *so* damn hot. You can't blame a girl for falling for him.'

Jess nodded. Okay, well, that answered the *'are you sleeping with him?'* question. 'Yeah, I imagine that's easily done.' She brushed a speck of dust off the sleeve of her jacket. 'Right, well, I'd better go. I have to go back to work and persuade my editor not to fire me.'

Her stomach sank at the thought of returning and admitting she'd failed.

Seraphina gave Jess a sympathetic smile. 'Good luck.'

'You, too,' Jess said, giving the girl's arm a reassuring squeeze before leaving her alone in the bathroom—hot wrath at Xander rising like an out-of-control soufflé in her chest.

Xander was locking up the studio when the dark-haired journalist slammed through the ladies' toilet door and stalked towards him. Her cheeks were flushed and disdain and anger flashed in those huge midnight-blue eyes of hers.

She jerked to a halt, a dark frown marring her face, before turning to go on her way. She'd only taken two steps before she swivelled back to face him again. 'What the hell is wrong with you?' she practically spat.

He took a step backwards in surprise. 'What are you talking about?'

'The way you treated that woman is inhumane.'

He frowned at her hard, baffled. 'What woman?'

She threw her hands up in disgust. 'Seraphina.'

Her reprimanding tone bothered him. Who was she to tell him how to conduct himself? 'She needs to toughen up if she's going to make it as a model.'

Her eyes widened in contemptuous disbelief. 'Not everyone has rhino skin. Can't you remember what it feels like to be young and filled with hope and excitement for the future?'

There was a hint of expectation in her face, as if she wanted to hear him admit to his weaknesses out loud.

His automatic privacy barriers shot up.

Not a chance, journo.

'I don't think I've ever been filled with hope. I may have *filled* a Hope in my time, though.' He flashed her a grin and took a step towards her.

Her frown deepened and she took a shaky step away. 'Have you always been this arrogant?'

He grinned. He couldn't help it. It was too tempting not to tease her, to see that passion flash in those amazing eyes again. 'Yes.'

Shaking her head, she looked away from him, over his shoulder at the closed studio door. 'No wonder everyone's beginning to think you're just some washed-up playboy. I'm not surprised your reputation's on the rocks if that's the way you treat people.'

Indignation trickled through him. That was a low blow. He couldn't let her get to him, though; she had no idea what it was like living in his world. Perhaps she wouldn't be quite so quick to judge if she did.

The immense pressure to continually produce better and better work had been a killer to his self-confidence, and more importantly to his self-control when it came to distractions.

Not that he was about to explain that to her.

She turned back to face him and he stared into her eyes for a moment, lost in their depths. Her little show of snappy rebellion intrigued him—in more ways than one.

She was properly saucy, in a hands-off-the-merchandise kind of way. Her face wasn't classically beautiful: her nose was a little too big, her eyes set too far apart, but there was definitely something striking about her. He was pretty sure there was more going on behind that guarded expression, too, that wasn't quite reaching surface level. The suit that hung so badly on her curvy frame looked like something a fifty-year-old woman might choose to wear and the long bob of dark hair she sported dragged her already long face down. She was all buttoned up—her youth and vitality clearly being repressed and controlled.

The thought of getting beneath that well-secured façade made him want things. Things he really shouldn't be wanting right then, not when he ought to be swearing off women until he started producing some decent art for this long-overdue exhibition.

His gaze dropped to her small, cupid-lipped mouth and he wondered for a second what it would feel like to kiss her, how she would taste on his tongue, before dismissing the idea. He *really* needed to focus right now.

A flash of him sitting down to capture this intriguing contradiction of a woman in paint and pencils flitted through his head. He'd love to have her pose for him. He hadn't felt this captivated by anyone or anything for such a long time it was as if he'd been given a shot of adrenaline to the heart. His fingers itched to pick up his pencil and start sketching her face.

She threw her hands up in exasperation when he failed to respond to her last jibe. 'Okay, well, I guess I'd better leave you and your *massive ego* in peace so you can get back to work.'

Turning on her heel, she strode away from him, her shoulders pulled forward with tension and her hands balled at her sides.

'Let me draw you.' The words came out of his mouth before she reached the stairwell, stopping her abruptly in her tracks.

She turned round to face him and her look of utter confusion made him laugh out loud. She'd make a great comic actor.

'What did you say?' The words seemed to catch in her throat and she gave a little cough at the end as if to clear the blockage.

He walked over to where she was standing. 'I'm in

need of a portrait model and I think you'd make a fascinating subject.'

'You want *me* to pose for you?'

'Sure, why not?'

'Firstly, because I have a job as a serious *journalist*, and secondly, because I've seen how you treat your models and, I have to say, I'm not champing at the bit to get the same treatment.'

He startled her by lifting a hand and running it vigorously over his face before snorting with laughter. 'Okay, *Lois Lane*, but in my defence Sera was the one up for more than just modelling and I was being a gentleman for once by turning her down,' he said, resting one arm against the wall behind her so it nearly touched her shoulders. 'That's why she was so mad at me.'

She seemed to bristle at his close proximity and readjusted her stance to lean away from him. He tried hard not to let her casual rebuttal bother him.

'Okay, clearly I'm off my game and I apologise for being rude to you earlier,' he said, tipping his head to one side in an attempt to mollify her. 'Can we call a truce and start again?'

He stared at her hard, attempting to commit her face to memory in case she refused his offer and he never saw her again. The thought bothered him more than it should considering they'd only just met. What was it about her that he found so enticing?

'Okay. Truce,' she agreed, smoothing her hand down the front of her immaculate blouse.

'How about this?' he suggested, spurred on by her acceptance. 'You come out to Italy for a few days and let me draw you and I'll give you an exclusive interview.'

Her eyes widened at the—admittedly rather out of

the blue—offer. 'You want me to go all the way to Italy to interview you? Why can't we do it here, now?'

'Because I need to leave for the airport in a couple of hours and I want to be able to give you my full attention. It's Italy or bust.' He had to forcibly stop himself from dropping his gaze to her own rather impressive bust that nestled beneath her shapeless, overlarge jacket. He didn't want her to think he was asking her to do more than pose for him. He didn't need a complication like that right now, not when he'd finally started to feel the buzz of creativity that had been eluding him for so long.

She stared at him for another minute, clearly trying to process it all, twisting her hands together as she thought about it.

'What's the matter, Miss Prim, too wild for you? Perhaps I should offer an exclusive to one of your rivals instead. I'm sure it would help sell a truckload of *their* magazines.'

Her eyes widened at the challenge and he wondered for a moment whether she'd be brave enough to rise to it. He sensed from her earlier frustration that she was hungry for an interview with him, so perhaps this would push her to say yes.

He hoped so. He really wanted her to come now he'd suggested it.

She was twisting her fingers together as she thought about it, but when she caught him looking at her hands she crossed her arms defensively in front of her. 'Okay. I'll come to Italy and sit for a portrait, but I want an in-depth interview, not just the usual pat answers you reel out for everyone else.'

He raised an eyebrow. There was no way he was giving her anything *deeply* private, but he could break his no-discussing-anything-personal rule just this once. It would be worth it if it meant finally breaking his dry spell and getting this exhibition off the ground.

'Deal.' He went back into the studio and jotted down the address of the villa on the banks of Lake Garda, which he was borrowing from a friend for a few weeks while he worked on his exhibition in peace and isolation. A complete change of scene was exactly what he needed right now in order to get his head straight. He felt stifled here in London. He needed space and sunshine and fresh air.

Coming back out, he handed her the slip of paper and she took it with a shaking hand. Was she nervous? The idea of it surprised him. She seemed so put-together with her straight clothes and strident manner.

'Maybe we should formally introduce ourselves,' he said, flipping her a cheeky grin and smiling as a pink hue tipped her cheekbones. 'Xander Heaton.' He extended a hand and she put her own small, cold one into it. Her grip was firm, though, which surprised him. Usually women did that limp-handed press that left him feeling as if he were an overzealous brute when he shook hands with them.

'Jessica LaFayette. My friends call me Jess,' she said, giving him a tight smile.

He grinned. 'So which should I use? Clearly I haven't made it into the friends bracket yet.'

'Jess is fine,' she said. 'But I might withdraw the privilege if you do something else to annoy me.' She flashed him a more relaxed smile this time, a hint of playfulness flashing in her eyes.

He laughed at that. 'You have cold hands, Jess,' he said, enclosing hers in both of his.

'But a warm heart,' she said, giving him a solicitous smile before pulling her hands firmly out of his grip.

She was going to be a fascinating subject to get to the heart of. The mere thought of it excited him. She was exactly the breath of fresh air he needed.

He was finally on his way back to the big time, baby.

CHAPTER TWO

TWENTY-FOUR HOURS later Jess stared out of the wind-screen of her hire car in wonder as the incredible scenery around Lake Garda flew by.

Pamela had been bemused at first by Jess's assertions that she would get a great exclusive out of Xander if she followed him all the way to Italy for the interview, but in the end she'd agreed to let Jess go if she stumped up for the flight and accommodation herself. She was also to visit some of the towns that bordered the lake and write some short 'Best Places to Holiday in Northern Italy' pieces for the travel section while she was there. The magazine didn't have the resources to send their staffers off to 'just swan around the Italian Lakes,' or so Pamela claimed.

Jess had taken it on the chin and booked herself onto the cheapest flight she could find the next day and found a room in a rather dubious-looking two-star hotel, which was the only place available on Lake Garda at short notice that didn't cost more per day than the rent on her flat for the entire month.

The memory of Xander's challenging look when he'd asked her to come to Italy made her insides twist and swoop. In that moment before responding, she'd thought about what Pamela had said about how she needed to live a little to become a better writer, and how much she wanted to keep her hard-fought-for job at the magazine, and despite hating the idea of sitting for a picture for him—frankly it was her idea of hell to be scrutinised from all angles by a man who made her feel so unsettled—she found herself agreeing to it if it meant he'd give her what she wanted. Strike that, what she *needed*.

No way was she going to let this once-in-a-lifetime opportunity slip away from her.

Before she'd left, Pam had pulled her to one side and reminded her that Xander was notoriously difficult to interview and that she should try and stay objective. She didn't say the words, 'Don't let him twist you round his finger and into his bed', but they were very much implied.

Jess had smiled to herself; as if *that* were ever likely to happen. Flings were not her thing and definitely *not* with men like Xander.

She had more sense than that.

As the villa where Xander was staying swung into view she took a deep breath to quell a disorientating surge of jittery excitement as she took in the sight of immaculately landscaped gardens and the imposing seventeenth-century building that resided like a noble queen over spectacular views of Lake Garda.

She'd never seen anything so perfectly picturesque in her life.

She could barely believe she was here to spend a couple of days hanging out with Xander Heaton, disgustingly talented artist, womaniser and undisputable contender for sexiest man alive.

Glancing down at the neat, but unfussy, trouser suit she'd put on for travelling, she acknowledged with a sinking feeling that she was *not* going to feel comfortable in his world.

Still, she was determined to make the most of the time she had with him. She just needed to hold her nerve and not let him intimidate her.

Ah, hell, who was she kidding? She was going to be a wreck from beginning to end. The trick was not to let him see it.

She drove up to the front of a long sweep of sandy-coloured stone steps and parked up. Swinging the door open, she got out and stretched her back, which ached like hell after being cramped up for hours, first on the plane, then in the car as she'd swung it through the Italian countryside.

Looking up at the magnificence of the building, she felt another sting of insignificance.

Get it together, Jess, you have nothing to feel humbled about.

The door to the villa opened and a handsome middle-aged woman in a beautifully cut shift dress appeared. Her long swathe of dark hair swung across her back as she walked down the steps towards where Jess was standing.

'Ms LaFayette?' she asked, holding out a welcoming hand.

Jess shook it. 'Call me Jess,' she said, giving the woman a friendly smile back.

'I'm Rosa. I'm the housekeeper here. If you need anything during your stay please let me know.'

Jess stared at her, confused. 'Oh, I'm not staying here. I've booked a room in a hotel down the road. The Royal, I think it's called.'

Rosa frowned, looking flustered. 'Oh, my mistake. Well, I hope they give you a good room there.' The uncertainty in Rosa's voice made something pinch in Jess's chest. Did The Royal have a bad reputation?

Ah, whatever. She was only going to be staying for two nights, so it wouldn't matter, and it was all she could afford anyway. This wasn't a holiday, she reminded herself, it was an assignment. The first of many more, she hoped—once she'd blown Pamela away with her fun, but insightful, piece on Xander.

Another thought struck her. Had Xander given the impression she was here for more than just business? Or had Rosa just assumed she was because of his track record?

Shaking off the unnerving tingle deep in her pelvis at the thought of getting up close and personal with Xander, she smoothed down a wrinkle in the sleeve of her jacket with shaking fingers. She should really take the thing off, it was already making her hot in the intense heat of the afternoon, but she wanted to stay formal and professional to remind him she was here as a serious journalist and not someone to be toyed with. There would be no flirting and manipulating the situation by Xander.

Control, Jess, cool, calm control.

'Is Xander around?' Jess asked, determined to get this interview under way as soon as possible. Pamela had only given her a week to get the article written. They were going with a *Great Artists of the Twenty-First Century* theme and Xander's interview was going to be the showcase piece, so it had to be good. If she didn't manage to produce something whiz-bang enough Pam had suggested she'd have to pass on Jess's notes to Maggie and have her write the article instead.

No *way* was Jess going to let that happen. This was

her big opportunity to prove to Pamela she was the right fit for *Spark*.

She just needed to get Xander to trust her enough to open up and talk.

Rosa nodded. 'He's down at the villa's private beach. Just follow the path over there to the lake.' She pointed in the direction she meant.

Jess thanked her and set off to the beach, pulling the hem of her blouse down where it had ridden up over her middle and swiping a rather damp hand over her hair.

The path took her through a small grove of sweet-smelling olive trees and opened up onto a small, sandy cove with spectacular views across to the other side of the lake.

There was no sign of Xander at first, but as she looked around she noticed a movement in the clear, still water of the lake.

Jess came to an abrupt halt as Xander stood up from where he'd been swimming, gleaming rivulets of water running down from his hair and cascading over his naked chest. She watched, mesmerised, as he waded towards her, his movements agile and smooth as he powered through the water.

He glanced up and saw her standing there, tipping her a mischievous grin and giving her a welcoming salute.

'Jess, good to see you.'

She watched him advance towards her, rooted to the spot and with an unnerving pulse beating in her throat.

His golden skin gleamed in the bright afternoon light, the gentle rays highlighting every contour of his solid frame, and as he pushed his wet hair back from his angular face, making the muscles of his chest twist and flex, she had to suppress a squeak of pure delight.

There was unbridled power in his stride, as he quickly covered the ground between them, that made her insides jump and twist with pleasure.

Scuffing her toes into the sand, she gave herself a lecture on the evils of letting her overactive imagination get the better of her.

'Hey,' Xander said, when he finally reached her, flashing her a grin that made her stomach lurch with lust. Drops of water clung to his eyelashes, making them look obscenely long and lush as they framed those incredible eyes of his.

Jess swallowed, trying to loosen up her throat, which was tight with tension. Shaking her nerves off before they took too firm a hold, she reminded herself that she was here to work, and that was what she was damn well going to do.

'H-hello. This place is beautiful,' she managed to stutter out, cursing the shake in her voice. She was having immense trouble keeping her gaze on his face and not allowing it to drop to the incredible physique of his chest.

'It's a friend's holiday home. Pretty impressive, huh?'

'Yup. Impressive.' It seemed she was totally out of intelligent conversation. Not a great start for someone who was supposed to be a wordsmith for a living.

'I'm heading back up to the villa for tea and cake. Rosa makes the best summer panettone. Come and join me.' It wasn't a question and she bristled a little at his bossy tone.

'I'm not hungry. I had a late lunch.'

He gave her a slow, sexually laden smile that made her stomach swoop alarmingly. 'Well, I'm hungry.'

The gentle breeze caught her hair and blew it across her suddenly incredibly hot face. Before she could react, he took a step towards her, lifted his hand and slid his long fingers against her cheek, then tucked the rogue curl of hair behind her ear. It was such an intimate thing to do she was utterly lost for words, and, instead of speaking, she found herself staring at his mouth, totally transfixed by the fullness of his lips as they parted slightly, revealing his perfect white teeth. The heat of his almost naked body bled into her skin and she took a deep, calming breath in, only to draw the musky fragrance of his skin into her nostrils, sending her senses spinning out of control.

Every bit of her body felt energised and tingly—the anticipation of what could happen if he just leant forward a couple of inches burning like wildfire in her chest. Was he going to...?

Kiss me.

She wasn't sure for a second whether she'd said it out loud and she skimmed her gaze up to look into his eyes, hoping desperately it had only been an errant voice in her head.

His gaze flicked between her eyes, the bright aqua of his irises captivating her with their other-worldliness.

What the hell was going on here? A nervy panic rose inside her, causing a wave of jittery heat to rush up her neck. She couldn't handle this. Not here, in broad daylight, totally unprepared for what might happen if he kept on looking at her like that.

Xander must have sensed her panic because he took a step away from her, giving her the space and air she suddenly craved.

'You okay, Jess?' he said, bemused concern clear in his voice.

'Fine. I'm fine,' she managed to gasp, forcing a smile onto her face. 'Just a bit hot in the sun.' She flapped a hand in front of her face in a pathetic attempt to cool herself down. 'I have to go and check in to my hotel but I wanted to let you know I'd arrived. I'd like to make a plan for starting the interview so we can get started as soon as possible.' She kept her voice clipped and businesslike, trying like mad to pull back the professional persona she'd been so keen to promote.

'How very diligent of you. Well, to be honest, I'm not in the mood for spilling my deepest, darkest secrets right now.' He took a step closer to her and dipped his head, his gaze capturing hers as something dangerous flashed in his eyes. 'I'd like to get to know you a bit more *intimately* first.'

'I'm not going to sleep with you,' she blurted out before she could stop herself, her nerves riding roughshod over her common sense.

He laughed out loud, shaking his head in mirth.

Jess just stood there dumbly, flushing hot with embarrassment.

What an idiot she was. Of course he wasn't talking about sleeping with her. She very clearly wasn't his type if the media reports of his affairs were anything to go by. From what she'd seen in the press—and at his studio—he was more of a leggy-blonde type of guy.

And that suited her just fine. Absolutely fine. Couldn't be finer.

'Don't worry, I'm taking a break from seducing innocent young journalists, so your virtue is safe with me,' he joked, his mouth quirked in a playful smile. 'I *am* interested in your body, Jess, but only on an artistic level.'

Jess pulled her arms across her chest. 'You can't blame me for being wary when you make provocative-sounding statements like that. You do have a reputation for being a bit…'

'A bit what?'

She paused, searching for the right word. 'Wild.'

He gave her a bemused grin. 'I promise to be on my best behaviour,' he said, making a crossing motion over his heart. 'And if I slip up you have my permission to *lick* me into shape.'

Oh, my God, the images he'd just conjured in her mind.

She really needed to get out of here before she totally lost her cool.

'Come over for dinner tonight at eight,' he continued, going over to a rock where he'd left his towel and swiping it along his long, lean arms, 'and we can get better acquainted.'

He flashed her one last beguiling smile before turning and walking away up the path, the bright drops of lake water that still clung to his broad back shimmering in the sunlight.

An overwhelming urge to pack up and go home, where she didn't have to deal with these weird and disturbing feelings he provoked in her, besieged her. But she wasn't going to leave. She was determined to keep her job at the magazine, no matter what it took. She was going to brazen it out here and ignore the blatant innuendos he seemed so keen to tease her into a jittery mess with.

He was a player all right, but she wasn't about to let him play *her*.

In total contrast to the villa where Xander was staying, her hotel was the most run-down, sleazy-looking pit Jess had ever had the misfortune to set eyes on. She could have sworn she saw a rat run around the corner of the building as she parked her hire car in the tiny, litter-strewn parking lot. The thought of it made her shudder. She wasn't good with rodents. Or spiders. Or any type of insect if she was totally honest.

It looked as if they were doing building works on the place, too, judging by the mess of rubble and steel piled haphazardly against the peeling walls of the hotel, but there didn't seem to be anyone doing any actual work out there. Jess prayed she wasn't going to be woken up in the early hours by workmen banging the hell out of the wall next to her head.

A disgruntled receptionist with long, lank hair and a sweat-stained blouse checked her in and handed over her key, motioning her to walk through the rather run-down reception to a door on the ground floor, next to what appeared to be a kitchen.

The Ritz it was not.

Her room wasn't in a much better state than the reception, but at least it had a decent-sized bed and its own en-suite bathroom—even if she did have to turn sideways when in it to get the door closed.

Okay, well, it was all she needed. She was only going to put up with it for two nights. Surely it wouldn't take longer than that to get enough info to write a decent piece on Xander?

Kicking off her shoes, she flopped down onto the bed, ignoring the unnerving sway of the bed frame, and pulled her mobile out of her back pocket. Time to do some more research on the man himself.

She'd already had a cursory look through the search engines for his name, but not much of any use had come up, mostly gossip pieces about the women he'd dated and the parties he'd made a scene at. In fact he seemed to have been in a constant state of drunken debauchery for an entire year. There were a handful of articles about his last couple of exhibitions as she trawled lower, though, the last of which had been a bit of a critical flop, as Pam had mentioned.

She wondered how his colossal ego had dealt with that. Judging by the press reports on him between now and then, not very well. He'd become belligerent and withdrawn with the press and, instead of producing more work to shut his critics up, he'd thrown himself into partying and womanising instead. In fact he didn't seem to have produced a single thing since that exhibition.

Interesting.

It was a soothing distraction focusing on work after the nerve-jangling meeting with Xander and her eyelids grew heavy as she relaxed into the soft mattress. Perhaps she could get forty winks in now to power herself up before having dinner with Xander tonight? She wanted to be at her sharpest when she faced him again. She had a sneaking suspicion he was deliberately trying to unsettle her so he could avoid having to answer any of her probing questions.

If he thought it was going to be that easy to get around her he had another think coming.

A loud scuttling sound—which seemed to be emanating from under the bed—made her sit bolt upright in alarm.

What the hell was that?

Out of the corner of her eye she thought she saw something dart from under the bed and disappear behind the vanity unit on the other side of the room.

Goosebumps pricked her skin as all the hairs on her body stood up as one in disgust. Ugh! Bugs! Quite possibly cockroaches.

Her spirits sank to the floor. How was she supposed

to sleep with large indeterminate creatures running around under her bed?

Taking care not to step on any of the little blighters, she dashed out of the room and back over to the reception and tried to persuade the woman to move her into a different room.

Denied.

It appeared—incredibly—that the hotel was fully booked.

Jess sighed and went back to her room, feeling frustrated and discombobulated. She couldn't afford to move out of this hovel—her savings wouldn't stand it—and she wasn't about to leave, not when the fate of her career was in the balance.

She was just going to have to grit her teeth and suck it up.

CHAPTER THREE

WHEN DINNER TIME rolled around, Jess drove back over to Xander's villa in an even more agitated state than when she'd left it, which didn't bode well for a relaxed and fruitful interview with him.

She hadn't anticipated having to conduct her interview over dinner either. She used to hate eating in front of other people after struggling with an eating disorder for most of her teens. Thankfully things had got a lot better on that front after she'd taken herself off for counselling during her time at university. After talking things through she'd been able to work out a way to deal with the feelings of shame and self-loathing that tipped her into comfort eating when she felt stressed and she hadn't had a relapse since.

She had a suspicion that eating in front of Xander was going to be a real test of her fortitude, though. He was just so *in your face* with his off-the-scale charisma and haunting good looks.

Damn him.

Rosa opened the door to her with a smile and showed her through to the huge living room, which was furnished with only a sofa, small drinks table and fireplace. There was an amazing coloured-glass chandelier hanging from the ceiling, which looked a bit like an exploding bouquet of long-stemmed flowers. Refracted shards of light from it bounced off the walls, giving the room the feel of a disco paused in time. Jess had never experienced anything like it. 'Xander's running a little late, but he'll be with you soon,' Rosa said, giving Jess a kind smile. 'Can I get you a drink?'

'Just some water, please,' Jess said, determined to remain sharp and focused that evening, which meant no alcohol for her. She didn't tend to drink much anyway—hating the way alcohol messed with her head— and she had a horrible feeling that just a sniff of the stuff tonight would be a disaster in terms of keeping her cool and collected front in place.

Rosa nodded and gestured to the sofa before leaving her alone in the room.

Jess chose not to sit down, nerves making her too edgy to stay still, and instead wandered around the room. She took a closer look at the beautiful marble fireplace and the amazing glass chandelier, shifting uncomfortably in her six-inch heels as she waited for Xander to materialise. She'd chosen these shoes at the last second thinking the extra height would give her a bit more confidence, but they were already killing her feet, which set her teeth on edge.

She was dragged out of her funk by the sight of Xander finally sauntering into the room, wearing a light blue linen shirt, open at the neck, dark combat trousers and a spellbinding smile on his face.

He really was the perfect specimen of a man.

Even the loose cut of his clothes couldn't conceal the fact he had a killer body underneath. No doubt those lean muscles were flexing and bunching under his shirt as he moved towards her. It made her mouth water to think of it.

How would he feel if she pressed her hands against his chest?

Hard and soft at the same time.

The tips of her fingers tingled in empathy with her thoughts and there was a disturbing rush of warmth in the depths of her pelvis. She had to practically cross her legs to dull the sensation in order to concentrate.

Not good, Jess. Not good.

How the heck was she going to get through the evening? Already the butterflies that had taken up residence in her stomach were flapping about like wild things, which meant her appetite was at approximately zero on the famished to sated scale.

'Welcome to my humble abode,' Xander said, giving her a generous smile as he came to a halt in front of her.

He seemed relaxed, insouciant even, as if he was anticipating a pleasant, gentle evening of good food and lively conversation.

Her blood fired round her veins at the realisation that this dinner might not be *quite* as awkward as she'd anticipated. She just needed to keep focused and keep him on her side in order to get him to open up and talk about things that would make her article sparkle.

'Take a seat,' Xander said, motioning to the huge red velvet-covered sofa in the middle of the room.

'Okay, thank you.' Jess sank down gratefully onto the soft cushions, glad to finally take the weight off her feet, and kept on sinking. The innards of the sofa were so soft she found herself nearly doubled in two with her knees up near her chin.

Not exactly ladylike.

'I'm really pleased you decided to come,' Xander said, flopping down next to her and almost catapulting her onto his lap. 'I think we can both get something useful out of our time together.'

He gave her such a loaded smile she could do nothing but stare back at him.

'Yes, I'm sure we can,' she finally managed to mumble through lips that seemed to be malfunctioning under the force of his charisma.

He slowly dropped his gaze to her mouth and the intensity of the atmosphere stepped up another notch.

Focus, Jess, focus.

She took in a deep breath. 'This is a wonderful room,' she said, trying like mad not to go to pieces as the fresh and delicious citrusy scent of his aftershave hit her nostrils. My, he smelt good. Perhaps she *was* hungry, after all? Only not for food.

Give it a rest, Jess. You're here to do a job, keep it professional. And he's the personification of danger, remember, which is not something you need in your life right now.

Wriggling along the sofa away from him and swivelling her knees into the gap she'd left, she attempted to put a defensive barrier between them, only to watch him reposition himself, mirroring her action so that their knees were almost touching. Her breath caught in her throat at what appeared to be a deliberate move to unsettle her and she had to look away to gather her courage.

She was *so* out of her comfort zone here.

Rosa arrived with a couple of flutes of strawberry Bellini, Jess's requested glass of water and a bowl of the most enormous olives Jess had ever seen, which she placed in front of them with a flourish.

'Dinner will be served in ten minutes,' she said, giving them both a gracious nod.

'Thanks, Rosa,' Xander replied, the deep smooth tone of his voice twisting through Jess's head like music. No wonder women seemed to throw themselves at him wherever he went—all he had to do was speak and she was a gibbering wreck. Imagine the effect if he decided to talk dirty to her.

A deep, low throb began to pulse in the depths of her pelvis at the thought and her face flamed with heat. Good grief, what was wrong with her self-control? It seemed to have totally abandoned her.

Jess hurriedly picked up a Bellini and took a sip, grateful for the distraction from dealing with Xander's overwhelming presence for a moment.

So much for her no-drinking rule.

But this was an emergency—she needed something to flatten out her nerves and lull her into a more relaxed state of mind if she was going to get through the evening with her sanity intact.

Turning back, she found he was studying her, a look of concentrated interest on his face. They stared at each other for a moment and Jess's heart hammered in the pause.

Had it suddenly got hotter? She could swear they'd turned the heat up and were directing it straight at her. She was damp with perspiration under her long-sleeved blouse and even the underside of her knees was sweating.

Umm, attractive.

Thank goodness this wasn't a real date because he'd have to *swim* to get close enough to kiss her at this rate.

'You have the most expressive face I've ever seen,' he murmured, a glint of mischief in his eyes. 'I'm going to have a lot of fun drawing you.'

Jess cleared her throat and sat up taller in her seat,

anxiety at the thought of having to model for him making her body hum with nerves.

'So how exactly do these things go? Do I just sit around for a couple of hours and you produce some amazing piece of art?'

He smiled. 'Not exactly. I prefer to hang out with my subjects for a bit until inspiration hits me. It can take a while to come up with the right idea and I like to play around with things for a while before committing paint to canvas. I'll do some sketches over the next few days and see what works.'

'The next *few days*? I wasn't expecting to be here for that long. I thought we could get this all wrapped up in a day. Two max. In fact I've booked a return flight for two days' time.'

He snorted. 'A day? If only I could work that fast. No, I usually need at least three or four days of planning. But don't worry, we can make it fun.' He gave her a slow wink that made her insides flip.

'What exactly do you mean by that?' The question came out sounding curter than she'd intended, so she chased it with an awkward smile.

He snorted, the corner of his mouth twisting up in mirth. 'Why are you so nervous, Jess?'

'I'm not nervous,' she said, the squeak in her voice totally giving her away.

He laughed, the sound rumbling low in his chest. 'Is my reputation really that bad?' He leant forward in a conspiratorial manner. 'Don't worry, I'm not going to rip your clothes off and ravish you—unless you ask me really nicely,' he added with a flirtatious eyebrow raised.

Was he *teasing* her now? He was. He *so* was. And she had absolutely *no* idea how to handle it.

This was exactly why she usually avoided men like him. They rattled her so badly she could barely function.

Mercifully, Rosa returned to call them for dinner then so she didn't have to scrabble around for an eloquent response to that little zinger.

'After you.' Xander gestured towards the other end of the hall.

'Great,' Jess said, already on her feet and making a move towards the doorway he'd motioned at, desperately trying not to skid in her shoes on the smooth marble floor. She could *feel* him behind her, as if he were giving off a pulse of sexual electricity that made the hairs on the back of her neck stand to attention.

Just as they reached the dining-room door her heel caught in a small hole in the marble and she stumbled forward, her arms flailing out at her sides as she tried to regain her balance.

Xander stopped her from falling flat on her face by darting forward and grabbing her arm and pulling her against his body for support.

Taking a hurried step away from the hard wall of his chest, she smoothed down her hair, then her skirt from where it had ridden up her legs, before flashing him a grateful smile. He watched her with an amused eyebrow raised. 'You okay?'

'Fine. Thank you.' She gave him a friendly but controlled nod. 'I'm not normally that clumsy, honestly.'

Xander laughed. 'Don't worry on my account. It's not often I get to play the knight in shining armour. It's usually *me* falling down drunk.'

'I'm not drunk. I only had a couple of sips…' she began to argue, horrified he'd think she was that much of a lightweight.

He held up a hand. 'I'm joking, Jess. Jeez, I've never met anyone so bad at taking a joke.'

'I c-can take a joke with the best of them,' she stuttered, picking a rogue hair off the sleeve of her blouse before turning to stare him defiantly in the eye.

Xander shook his head and grinned back at her. 'Do you think you can make it to the table without taking another tumble? I can give you a piggyback if you like.'

'I'll be fine, thank you,' she said. 'Wouldn't want to be responsible for putting your back out.'

He laughed. 'Never gonna happen. I'm as strong as an ox. See?' He braced his arms in front of him, mimicking the stance of a bodybuilder.

Jess couldn't help but laugh at him.

'Yeah, okay, He-Man, but I'll walk, thanks.'

He smiled back, and waved a hand, encouraging her to step to it. 'After you.'

The dining room was just as impressive as the living room with an enormous, highly polished dining table sitting pretty in the middle of the room, surrounded by what looked like twenty high-backed chairs.

Another enormous chandelier, this time made from hundreds of pieces of blown glass in the shape of a flock of birds, let out a warm, low light over the room.

'Wow, the light fixtures here are amazing,' Jess said, staring at it in wonder.

'Pretty cool, huh?' Xander said, stopping next to her to admire it, too. 'Roberto, who owns this place, made it. He's sickeningly talented.'

He was standing so close to her she caught another waft of his amazing citrusy scent, which sent an energised prickle right up her spine.

'How lovely of him to let you use his place,' she said, taking a careful step into the room, away from him.

'Yeah, he's a really generous guy. We worked on a couple of projects together a few years back, before we both started getting successful. He lets friends come and stay here when they need to escape for a bit.'

'So you're *escaping* right now?' she asked, turning back to look at him.

His expression closed over. 'I need a bit of space to concentrate on a new exhibition, away from the din of the city.'

'And away from the temptation of all those parties?' she said, raising a playful eyebrow, hoping he'd bite and give her a bit of gossipy goodness that she could incorporate into her article.

'Oh, I don't know. I'm sure I can find a party round here if I really want to,' he said, moving his shoulder in a circular motion as if trying to relieve a trapped nerve.

'Have you hurt your shoulder?' she asked.

'Nah, I'm just a bit tense from being bent over drawing today. Why, are you offering to rub it for me?' He flipped her a provocative grin.

'You don't want me giving you a massage—I'm terrible at it,' she said, smoothing a lock of hair behind her ear, then flipping it back out again so it swung back to join the rest of her bob. She had a horrible urge to hide her face from him. He was so confusing with his ability to flip the conversation from something innocuous into something that made her jitter with barely contained anxiety.

He gave her a questioning frown. 'I don't believe it. How can you be terrible at massaging?'

She shrugged. 'It's just not something I count as one of my talents.'

'Hmm.' He was looking at her with such an intense, searching stare it made her insides twist.

She wasn't used to dealing with such overt flirta-tiousness. The men she'd dated in the past had been at-tractive guys, but nothing like the unwieldy package of sexual energy that Xander Heaton embodied. He was something else entirely.

Walking past her, he pulled out a chair from the table and gestured for her to sit down.

She nodded her thanks and perched herself on the edge of the leather-upholstered chair, folding her hands on the tabletop and kicking off her shoes so she could flex her aching feet under the table. She watched as he pulled out the seat opposite and dropped into it with a sigh.

'I'm curious. Why don't you give interviews any more?' she said, hoping that if she just kept firing ran-dom questions at him he'd eventually give her some straight answers.

He leant back in his chair and smoothed the front of his shirt down with long, tanned fingers.

Jess watched the movement, fascinated by the simple beauty of his hands, noting how his fingernails were dark-rimmed with ingrained paint. There was some-thing lovely about how his hands reflected exactly who he was.

A warm and tingly feeling wound through her belly—and lower—as her thoughts slid towards what sort of mischief he could get up to if he put those amaz-ing hands of his on her body.

She really needed to stop thinking about him like this; it wasn't conducive to getting the best out of the interview if all she could think about was how damn sexy he was.

'I've had some bad experiences with the press twist-ing things I've said. They take things out of context

and make me sound like an idiot.' He leant forward
in his chair. 'And I prefer to keep my private life just
that—*private*,' he said, giving her a knowing smile and
stretching out his legs under the table, his calf brushing
gently against hers. 'But I'm sure I can trust you to give
me a fair write-up, Jess, especially as I have the power
to make you look bad, too. You don't want your *bad-
hair day* hanging on someone's wall for ever, do you?'

Her breath seemed to be coming out in shorter gasps
than normal, which was making her light-headed. Sucking in a deep, calming slug of air, she carefully moved
her leg away from his and attempted to centre herself
before responding.

'You wouldn't do that.' The shake in her voice made
it clear she totally believed he *would*.

He laughed. 'Of course not. I'm only joking. I promise to be true to your character.'

She nodded slowly. 'So what happened last year
to kill your muse?' she asked casually, glancing up at
him through her lashes in the hope he'd answer without thinking.

He gave her such a *what the hell are you talking
about?* look she shrank back into her seat in disgrace.

Okay, so it wasn't the most professional way to conduct the interview, but then again she had nothing to
lose throwing out provocative questions. In fact, if she
was going to get something juicy enough to satisfy Pamela she was going to have to push the boat right out
and straight into enemy waters.

Xander must have thought he'd reacted a bit too
strongly because he flicked her a smile and manipu-
lated his body into a more relaxed posture.

'My muse isn't dead, just resting. I had a few years
where I worked pretty intensively and I needed a break.'

'So taking a break had nothing to do with the reviews you had of your last exhibition, then?'

His expression darkened and he leant forward in his chair. 'You really think I care about the opinions of a few talentless hacks? I have zero respect for people who don't have the ability to produce their own art so spend their time and energy trashing other people's work instead. They're a waste of space and not something I'm willing to talk about again, so you can cross that one off your list of *probing questions for Xander.*' The cold resentment in his voice made her shiver.

Okay, lesson learned, she wasn't going to be able to rush this. Probably best to keep the conversation bland for now and build up to the more probing questions. After all, if he wanted more time to sketch her she could afford to take things slowly and build his trust in her before slipping him the leading questions.

Xander relaxed back into his chair and attempted to shake off the unsettling avalanche of anxiety that Jess's questions had buried him in. He really needed to keep his temper under control or she'd think she was onto a juicy story about how he felt about the press's less-than-favourable reaction to his last show.

He'd relived the hurt and anger of last year's glitch in his career over and over until it had nearly driven him crazy, and he was determined to get over this debilitating fear of failing again. He really didn't need her poking at that old wound when he was finally feeling the creative buzz again.

Jess leant back in her chair and studied him for a moment and he tensed, waiting to see whether he'd been successful at closing that line of questioning down.

'What does it feel like to be voted the fourth sexiest man in England?' she said finally, a mischievous eyebrow raised.

He smiled, relieved that she'd taken the hint and changed the subject.

'Actually I hear I'm third in the UK right now and it's a real honour.'

'I bet.' She shot him a judicious look. 'Any plans to up your rating? How much sexier do you think you'd need to be to reach number one, for example?'

He laughed. 'Quite a bit.'

She snorted and picked up her water, taking a quick sip. 'If you *did* get any sexier I think most women— and probably some men—would melt under the force of your charisma.'

He gave her a lazy grin, something warm and happy growing larger deep in his belly. 'You think I'm sexy?'

Her gaze shot away from him and she put her glass down hurriedly, managing to catch it awkwardly on her side plate and spilling water onto the tablecloth. 'I can see why other people think you are.' She didn't look back at him, but busied herself mopping up the spill with her napkin.

'But you don't *personally*?'

She still wouldn't look at him. 'I have odd tastes.'

'Odd?'

'Yeah, boy-next-door types, I guess. Men I feel comfortable to be with. Men who aren't going to outshine me wherever we go.'

'I can't image anyone outshining you.'

She raised a discerning eyebrow. 'You're sweet to say that, but I'm warning you now, I can smell B.S. a mile away.'

God, she was saucy when she got all strict.

'You're really something, you know that?' Xander

said, leaning forward and putting his elbows onto the table.

There was something about the wariness on her face that made him long to get behind that tight-lipped front she put up to protect herself. He was pretty sure there was a lot going on beneath the surface with Jess and he longed to find out what was driving it. He'd not met anyone as guarded—and seemingly immune to his charms—as her in a very long time.

He liked that about her. He liked it a lot.

And he was determined to shake the real her out from under those layers of protection.

'Okay, if you don't want to talk about your last exhibition let's try some quick-fire questions,' Jess said, ignoring his attempt at flirting her into submission and hoping her *slowly, slowly* approach would yield better results. If she could keep things light and seemingly unobtrusive he might just give her something without feeling as though he was.

Although, judging by the bemused look on his face, she suspected she was going to have a tough time getting him to take *any* of this seriously.

Shoving back his chair and balancing a foot on his knee, he waved at her to begin. 'Shoot.'

She cleared her throat and sat up straighter, pen poised over her notepad in readiness. 'Okay. Beer or wine?'

He raised an amused eyebrow. 'Tequila body shots.'

Heat rushed up her neck as a vision of him licking salt out of her belly button slammed into her head. She pushed it away quickly, hoping her expression hadn't given her away. She didn't want him to know how much he was getting to her.

'Favourite animal?' she ploughed on, not looking up from her pad.

'Tiger.' He growled and she glanced up to see him making clawing gestures with his hands.

She fought to keep her smile under wraps. 'Favourite way to travel?'

'Asleep.'

She sighed. Yup, he wasn't going to make this easy on her.

'What?' he asked, holding his hands up in mock offence. 'I hate travelling—it's tedious. I try to sleep through all my journeys.' He leant forward in his chair. 'I'm guessing you're one of those people who don't believe in power naps.'

'I can't sleep during the day.'

'What, never? You should practise. It's a useful skill.'

'I'm usually too busy *working* in the day.'

He grinned. 'Yeah, well, if you sleep as badly as me you need to master afternoon napping.'

'Have you always slept badly?' she asked, intrigued by the small snippet of personal information he'd let slip.

He shifted in his chair, switching his legs over and propping the other foot on the opposite knee, obviously annoyed at himself for slipping up and offering her a lead into something else he didn't want to discuss.

'I've always had strange sleep patterns.' He didn't look at her and she wondered why. Judging by the sudden tension in his body she'd swear he was lying.

'What is it that keeps you up in the night?' she pushed, determined to pursue this until he gave her something interesting she could use in the piece.

He glanced back at her, his expression now teasing.

'Usually the hot woman lying next to me.' He shot her another grin, but the smile didn't quite reach his eyes.

'Right. So what? All the partying you've become so famous for is to help you sleep? Wouldn't it be easier to take a sleeping pill?'

'I party hard to have fun. You've heard of that, right? Fun.' He gave her a slow, lazy smile as if he knew exactly what she did for fun. She thought about all the quiet nights in and cringed a little.

'Sadly, I don't have the opportunities or resources that you do,' she said, trying to keep the giveaway clip of indignity out of her voice.

Instead of responding, he got up and left the room, leaving her staring after him.

What the hell? Was this how he was going to act whenever she started on a line of questioning he wasn't comfortable with?

Before she had chance to get up and follow him out, he reappeared, sketch pad and pencil in hand.

Her stomach did a slow dive. 'What are you going to do with those?' she asked dumbly, suddenly hot with worry. He wasn't going to start sketching her *now*, was he?

'I needed a little predinner snack and these looked delicious,' he said, his voice laden with sarcasm.

Jess bristled. 'Do you really need to start doing that right now, here at the dinner table?'

'Why not? You brought your work to the table. Why can't I bring mine?'

She had no answer for that. He had a point.

Flattening her hair down with hands that no longer felt as if they belonged to her, she shuffled up straighter in her seat.

'Look, Xander, I'm not really comfortable…'

'Don't worry, you don't need to do anything differently, I just had an image I wanted to get down before I forgot it. I have to grab these little flashes of inspiration when they strike. Unfortunately, my muse isn't something I have any control over.'

'A bit like your libido,' she muttered, staring down at the table, unwilling to meet his eyes in case he saw how awkward he was making her feel.

He didn't make any reply to her jibe, but when she flicked her eyes up to check what he was doing she noticed a small curl to his lips, as if he was trying to suppress a smile. His gaze was fully focused on what he was doing, but as she watched him move the pencil fluidly over the paper he glanced up for a second and caught her staring.

She looked away quickly, heat burning her cheeks.

Rosa appeared in the doorway with plates of food and Jess breathed a sigh of relief when Xander put down his pad and ceased the impromptu sketching session.

Taking a deep breath, she tentatively started in on the scrumptious-looking salmon, asparagus and salad that Rosa placed in front of her. Her appetite seemed to have totally abandoned her now, but she wasn't going to let her insecurities get the better of her—no way. Even so, she hardly tasted a bite of the meal as she worked her way through it. It was as if her taste buds had packed up and gone on holiday, making everything she ate turn to dust in her mouth.

She put her cutlery down after managing only half of it, defeated.

'How was your food?' Xander asked, startling her as he laid his own knife and fork onto his empty plate.

'It was delicious. I really enjoyed it. There's just a bit too much for me here,' she said, feeling the heat of her discomfort flaring in her cheeks. Looking down, she realised her hands were trembling so she hid them underneath the napkin on her lap, hoping he wouldn't notice.

'You know, I don't think I've ever met a journalist who was such an awful liar before,' Xander said, leaning back in his chair and putting his hands behind his head as he studied her. 'You looked like you were being tortured all the way through eating that.'

That did it.

The stress of attempting to stay calm around him, the pressure of potentially losing her job if she couldn't get him to play ball and his utter disrespect for her profession all collided in her head, shooting her blood pressure to maximum.

'You know what, I didn't want to believe all the gossipy reports about you being an *arrogant idiot*, but I can see now they're totally on the money.'

He stared back at her, eyebrows raised and a muscle twitching in his jaw, but didn't say a word in his defence.

Had she blown it losing her cool like that? Was that the end of this little fiasco? She felt as if the whole thing had spun out of her control and she had no idea how to claw it back.

But instead of telling her to get out of his house, he picked up his sketchbook and pencil again and started to scribble away as if she weren't even in the room.

She sat for a minute or two, waiting to see whether he'd speak to her again, but he steadfastly ignored her.

'Look, I'm sorry for losing my temper. I'm just feeling a bit…out of my depth at the moment.'

Still nothing. Not even an acknowledgement that she'd spoken.

'O-okay, then…well…' she stuttered, scrunching up

the napkin from her lap and dropping it onto the plate in front of her. 'On that bombshell, I'll let you get on with your picture and get back to my hotel.'

Perhaps once she'd had a good night's sleep everything would look rosier in the morning and they could start afresh. She tried not to shudder as she remembered the insect-infested room that awaited her.

He said nothing as she slid out of her seat, stooping to pick up her shoes. She decided against putting them back on, mainly because it would delay her leaving, but also because her poor aching feet would have screamed at her to stop torturing them if she had.

'Goodnight, Xander,' she said to the top of his head before walking away from him, not daring to look back and catch the look of amusement that *had* to be taking over that unnervingly handsome face of his.

Slumping back against his chair and dropping his sketch pad and pencil onto the table, Xander watched Jess stalk out of the dining room in her stockinged feet, her shoes swinging from her fingers at her side.

A slow burn of shame worked its way through him.

Perhaps he'd pushed things a little too far with that last comment? Judging by her violent reaction to it, *she* certainly seemed to think so. He'd found it amusing to play with her when he'd realised she was actually more nervous around him than she'd previously let on, but he really should apologise tomorrow and see if he could get her back on side once she'd calmed down.

He wouldn't usually entertain the idea of letting a journalist get anywhere close to him, but he liked Jess. There was something about her that fascinated him, something about her stoic determination not to let him get to her that made him want her more than anyone he'd met in a very long time. The thought of drawing her out of that brittle shell she protected herself with was thrilling. It did something disconcerting to him, causing a twisting heat to take him over and make him reckless—something he'd been determined not to be again until his new exhibition was in the bag, but teasing her had been such a turn-on. He'd love to see how she responded to a serious onslaught of flirting and whether he could change her mind about not wanting to sleep with him. He'd been surprised and not a little rankled when she'd said that earlier, and the narcissist in him wanted to prove her wrong. It had been a long time since a woman had turned him down, which made it a point of pride.

He knew she felt *some* sort of attraction to him because of the unconscious way she responded when she was around him. Her pupils flared when she looked his way and her body language became charmingly jerky and more drawn towards him.

So why was she fighting it so hard?

He had no idea, but he was going to enjoy finding out.

Jess got back to her hotel room in a state of nervy agitation.

Her dinner with Xander had shot her adrenaline levels into the red, but now she'd calmed down she felt utterly exhausted by it all.

Lying in her bed, she allowed her thoughts to skip over what had happened earlier. A small voice in her head started to whisper something about overreacting a bit. Hot embarrassment trickled through her as she thought about how uncomfortable she'd felt around Xander and how that had *perhaps* made her act a *little* more edgily than normal. He hadn't actually said or done anything *that* bad. He was clearly deliberately trying to wind her up—and she'd let him succeed.

Rubbing a hand across her scalp, she tried to wake up her sluggish brain. What the heck was she doing? She needed to *chill* and stop going at Xander like a harpy with a headache if she had any chance of getting him to trust her enough to talk about anything personal.

She was a smart, educated woman with good conversation skills; she could get what she needed for the article if she just stopped jumping down his throat every time he opened his mouth. No way was she going back to Pamela without something sensational to use in the magazine.

She was going to have to work harder at it, be tenacious.

It was totally doable.

As long as she could keep this crazy compulsion to get up close and personal with him out of her head.

Another scuttling sound, this time from the corner of the room, made her sit up and flick the bedside light back on. She couldn't see anything, but somehow that was worse. What if the insects crawled up the sides of the bed and found their way under the covers with her? The thought of it made her heart hammer and her skin crawl with disgust. Wrapping the sheets round her like a cocoon, she tried not to think about it and relax into sleep.

The scratching noise came again, this time from the other side of the room. Finding her earphones from her handbag, she stuffed them into her ears, connected them to her MP3 player and turned the music right up. Putting the pillow over her head, she hoped, would be enough to ward off any uninvited bedfellows.

Her thoughts drifted back to Xander and what he

would be doing right now. Perhaps he'd be in the shower, washing off the grime of the day, water and suds cascading down that impressive body of his as he soaped himself down?

The mere thought of it made her blood fire round her body again.

Her legs were twitching now as she lay there desperately trying to turn her thoughts to something innocuous so she could drift into a much-needed sleep.

Between the apprehension of dealing with Xander again and the worry about warding off the bugs, she seemed to have kicked herself back into a state of anxious alertness.

Sighing, she burrowed deeper into the covers and started counting sheep. She had a horrible feeling it was going to be a long night.

CHAPTER FOUR

XANDER HAD TO check the address of the hotel that Rosa had given him twice before he finally concluded he was in the right place. Was Jess really staying in this dump?

An unfriendly receptionist finally gave him Jess's room number and he walked along the grimy corridor and banged on her door with an unnerving sense of discomfort.

He'd woken up early that morning after a dream about Jess where she'd been buried under an avalanche of snow and he'd not been able to get close enough to rescue her. It was the most bizarre thing he'd ever dreamt—not least because he barely knew her—and the sense of loss it provoked had left a dragging sorrow in his chest that unnerved him so much he'd had to get straight up and go for a walk to clear his head.

Apparently his subconscious was feeling very guilty about how he'd treated her the night before. So, here he was, cap in hand and ready to apologise for his insensitivity in the hope he hadn't driven her away for good.

The door finally swung open to reveal a rather dishevelled-looking Jess, still in her pyjamas and with her normally immaculate bob of hair sticking up wildly around her pale face. The dark bags under her eyes made him suspect she hadn't slept well either.

Her face went from ghostly pale to beet-red in the space of a second when she realised it was him at the door and her hands flew straight up to flatten down her thatch of hair.

'Xander? What are you doing here?'

'I came to invite you over for breakfast and to say sorry for being an idiot last night.'

Jess stared at him in wide-eyed astonishment. 'Wow. Am I dreaming or did Xander Heaton just *apologise* to me?'

He snorted and leant against the doorjamb, watching in amusement as she took a stumbling step back into the room.

'It's real. Consider me humbled.'

She dipped her head and gave him a genuine smile. 'Apology accepted. Thank you for coming all the way over here. That's very decent of you.'

He batted her praise away, but acknowledged the feeling of satisfaction it brought, relieved she seemed to have forgiven him for his egotism. 'You were right. I was being an idiot.'

'Yeah, well, I wasn't exactly sweetness and light last night either,' she said, pulling her arms tightly across her chest, which only drew his attention to the large swell of her breasts. 'I'm sorry for being so narky.'

'Okay. So we're both sorry. That's great. Let's put it behind us.'

'Good idea.'

They stood looking at each other and an awkward silence crept up, making the air between them hum with tension.

'Nice place you have here,' Xander said, in an attempt to break it, shooting her a mischievous grin.

Her shoulders tensed. 'Yeah, it was the only room I could find at short notice.'

There was a loud scratching noise that seemed to be coming from inside the wall next to him.

He frowned hard. 'What the hell is that?'

She shrugged, her expression giving away her own disgust. 'Cockroaches, I think.'

The thought of her staying here in such awful conditions made him shudder. No wonder she looked as though she hadn't slept all night. A sudden overwhelming urge to protect her hit him like a hammer to the chest.

'You can't stay here. There must be somewhere else available?'

'There isn't. I looked. Everywhere else is fully booked or totally out of my price range.'

'Isn't the magazine stumping up for your accommodation?' he asked.

She shifted uncomfortably from foot to foot. 'There isn't the budget to put me up somewhere expensive. I'm just a junior staffer,' she said sheepishly, clearly worried he'd be offended that they hadn't sent their top reporter to interview him.

The flash of vulnerability did something to his insides, making him squirm in sympathy for her.

'Pack up your stuff. You're staying with me.'

She blinked at him in surprise. 'What?'

'I have four spare bedrooms at the villa. It's ridiculous for you to stay in this dump when there's so much room at my place.' He held up his hands, palms forward, when she frowned and started to shake her head.

'Rosa's there most of the time and the bedrooms have locks on the doors so you don't need to worry about me taking advantage of you.' He flipped her a grin in the hope she'd believe him. He couldn't in all conscience let her stay here any longer. The place was disgusting and he hated the thought of her having to put up with it for a moment longer when it was no skin off his nose for her to stay with him.

'But don't you want your privacy?' she hedged, rocking back on her heels.

He flapped a casual hand at her. 'There's enough room at the villa for us not to feel like we're in each other's pockets. You're going to be spending most of your time there anyway, right?'

She took a moment to think it over, staring down hard at the floor.

'I'll wait for you in Reception,' he said, moving back towards the door. 'Rosa's making breakfast so we'd better get back there soon.' He hoped his authoritative tone would tip her into action. He suspected she needed quite a bit of pushing to get past her stubbornness.

After five minutes of pacing up and down in the reception area, he finally saw her appear out of her room, now fully dressed, and walk down the corridor towards him wheeling a small suitcase, her shoulders drawn forward and her head dipped with tiredness.

The dull grey, shapeless linen trouser suit she'd put on today did nothing to express the feistiness he'd seen the previous night—it swamped her frame, diminishing her impact with its banality. Why on earth did she choose to dress like that when she had such passion inside her?

He wondered idly what her body looked like underneath those baggy layers. Soft and inviting and too tantalising not to touch, he imagined. He'd love the opportunity to find out for sure.

'Okay. I'd like to take you up on your kind offer,' she

said, coming to a halt in front of him, her chin tipped up defiantly as if she was afraid he'd think less of her for appearing so vulnerable. On the contrary, the fact she was daring enough to accept his help only made him like her more.

'Great, give me your bag and I'll meet you outside,' he said, taking the suitcase from her. She didn't stop him, clearly too tired today to put up a fight.

He waited outside by the car while she checked out, feeling the warmth of the early-morning sun seeping into his skin. Just being away from the city was already having a positive effect on him. The pace of life here was calming and he could feel the tension beginning to drain away. All he needed to do now was to utilise the growing sense of calm and the little flashes of inspiration Jess seemed to incite in him whenever she was around, and he could start to rebuild the confidence in his work he'd been missing.

He couldn't even begin to explain to himself why she had such a big effect on him, but, hell, it didn't matter, as long as the inspiration stayed around long enough for him to begin to create something he was proud of again. Already the sketches he'd done of Jess and the ideas she'd inspired in him were head and shoulders above anything he'd produced in the last year. There was finally life to his drawing again. Instead of the unimaginative marks on paper he'd had to drag out of himself up until this point.

Bizarre that she'd been the one to draw that out of him. She was nothing like the type of woman he usually hung around with, but there was something so beguiling about her.

Glancing back at the hotel, he saw Jess come out and blink in the sunlight as she looked around for him.

He gave her a wave and she walked stiffly over in those crazy high heels of hers and grabbed her case from him.

'Okay. I'll see you back at the villa,' she said, already wheeling her case off to her own car, tension clear in her gait.

'See you back there in ten,' he said, ducking into the driving seat, impatient to get back for some well-earned breakfast and the opportunity to get to know this intriguing woman a little better.

When he arrived back at the villa, Rosa had already laid out the breakfast things on the terrace. Xander flopped into a seat and stared out at the spectacular view over the lake while he waited for Jess to arrive and join him.

She was only a couple of minutes behind him and he watched as she made her way gingerly over the path that ran around the house and came to a stop at the chair opposite where he sat.

'Thank you for rescuing me from that place. You're my hero,' she said, flashing him a subdued grin and flopping down into the chair with a sigh.

Was she serious? Or was this her personal brand of sarcasm?

Man, it was unnerving not being able to read her easily. Perhaps the crux of their problem was they didn't get each other's sense of humour yet?

He chose to think she really meant what she said and smiled, relaxing back into his chair and hooking his arm over the backrest. 'Actually, it *was* pretty heroic of me. I'm *not* a morning person and I got up a whole hour early to come and fetch you for breakfast.' He chased this statement with a grin so she knew he was only joshing her.

Was that a flicker of appreciation he saw in her eyes? He was surprised by how much he hoped so.

Rosa came back and poured them each a cup of coffee, then put a plate loaded with toast and fruit in front of them. Jess frowned at it for a second before popping a piece of melon into her mouth and chewing it for rather longer than necessary before swallowing it.

'I'd like to sketch you this morning, when we've finished breakfast,' he said, before taking a long sip of the strong, aromatic coffee.

Her gaze shot to him, her eyes suddenly wild and uncertain.

'Really?' She cleared her throat, brushed some imaginary crumbs off her fingers, then smoothed her hands over her lap. 'Okay.'

He frowned at her reaction. 'What is it with you? You seem to be in a perpetual state of apprehension.'

She pushed her chair back and stood up so suddenly it made him jump. 'I'm fine. Really.' She gave him a shaky grin. 'I'm going to get settled in my room, have a shower and psych myself up before we start if you don't mind.'

He watched her walk away. Her body was rigid and her hands clenched at her sides as she moved awkwardly in her heels.

What the hell had he said wrong now?

After finding her outrageously luxurious room—which she investigated thoroughly before even taking her jacket and shoes off—Jess spent a while carefully unpacking her suitcase and hanging up her clothes in the enormous walk-in wardrobe. The soothing action of tidying was a welcome relief from dealing with the intensity of Xander's charismatic presence and she took her sweet time over it in order to stall having to go back outside again and sit for his picture.

Her small collection of clothes looked sad and limp and rather pathetic all by themselves on the enormous rail and she shut the door hurriedly on them, not entirely sure where the sudden dragging feeling of gloom had come from.

It must be down to not having slept all night.

When Xander had suggested she move in here with him, her first instinct had been to categorically dismiss the idea, but with her head feeling as if it were stuffed with cotton wool and her body aching with tiredness she'd actually been pathetically grateful when he'd insisted on it. Just the thought of spending another sleepless night in that awful hotel had made her insides clench and squirm.

She'd been surprised at his offer, considering how resistant he'd been to giving her anything personal of himself the previous night. Perhaps she'd looked so pathetic when he'd found her there he'd had a crisis of conscience?

Anyway, whatever his reasons, logically it would be a whole lot easier to stay in the same place as Xander as it meant she could get a really good feel for how he spent his days while he worked on his paintings.

She took a hot, reviving shower in the beautiful, mosaic-tiled en-suite bathroom and dressed in her most comfortable clothes: a pair of indigo boyfriend jeans and a loose, long-sleeved, white cotton T-shirt and slipped her feet into a pair of flip-flops.

Taking one last, deep breath, she went back out to the garden to find Xander, ready for the session.

Blood thundered through her veins at the thought of him scrutinising her from every angle, and flashbacks from being bullied about her weight when she was younger flittered through her mind, but she refused to feel cowed by those awful memories. It had been a long time since she'd let her eating disorder get its teeth into her, and she'd come so far since then. She refused to let it drag her under again.

Xander was sitting on the terrace with his sketch pad and pencils, making large swirling motions over the paper. He tilted his head and smiled, eyebrows raised, as she drew closer to him and she wrapped her arms around her middle and gave him her bravest smile back. She had no idea what he must be thinking right now and blood pounded in her head as her agitation increased.

Suck it up, Jess. You're doing this to save your career, remember?

If she could get through this modelling debacle, hopefully she'd have more opportunities to pump Xander for information.

The thought of 'pumping' in relation to Xander almost made her lose her cool for a second and she had to suck in a deep breath to steady herself. The low throb of arousal refused to budge from where it had nestled itself between the apex of her thighs, and she had to concentrate on putting one foot in front of the other to stop herself from swivelling on the spot and making a run for it.

She sat uncomfortably in the chair opposite him, with the lake behind her, the sun hot on her already heated skin. Her muscles were so twitchy she wouldn't be at all surprised to find she was visibly vibrating with tension.

Xander looked up and studied her for a moment, sketch pad on his knee, his bright eyes searching her face.

She wound her fingers together and placed them carefully on her lap, looking away over his shoulder in an attempt to distract herself from the discomfort of being studied so thoroughly by a man who made her insides jump and writhe as if they were filled with snakes.

'Relax, Jess. Anyone would think I was about to torture you.'

'I have no idea why you'd want to draw *me*,' she said, attempting to relax her shoulders into some sort of normal posture.

Xander laughed. 'You're much more attractive than you think you are, you know.'

She shot him a puzzled scowl. 'How the hell do you know how attractive—or not—I think I am?'

He didn't seem at all fazed by her snippy tone. 'I can see it in your body language. You don't believe in yourself.' He leant in closer. 'You know, you shouldn't worry so much about what everyone else thinks; just believe in how amazing you are.'

'That would be a lot easier if I *was* amazing.' She flipped him a grin, but he frowned, clearly unimpressed with her response.

'How can you not know how gorgeous you are?' he murmured.

The penetrating look he gave her made something awaken low in her pelvis.

Oooh.

'You need to let out the joy.' He didn't shift his gaze from her face, keeping her attention locked to him.

She laughed in lust-addled bewilderment. 'The joy?'

'You know. The place where a genuine smile comes from.'

She looked at him blankly. 'How do I find such a place?'

'Okay, think about the last time you felt happy and follow the feeling.'

She gave him a sceptical look.

'Humour me,' he said.

Sighing, she wiped her sweaty palms on the sides of her jeans. She didn't want him to see how nervous she was about being the centre of attention like this. Her pulse ticked loudly in her ears.

Sensing she was likely to lose this particular battle, and interested to see if the experiment worked, she sighed and shut her eyes, doing as he said, trying to capture the feeling of delight she'd experienced when Pamela had offered her the job on the magazine. She tried to pinpoint where the feeling emanated from, locating it somewhere deep in her chest where it pulsed low and hot.

'Okay,' Xander said. 'Now look right at me and let your eyes tell me how you're feeling.'

She took a second to centre herself, then did as he said, staring into his striking green-blue eyes and trying to communicate how she felt through the power of her expression.

'Not bad, but you need to stop worrying about what I'm thinking of you and let me *see* you.'

Heat crept up her neck. 'I have no idea how to do that.'

He was looking at her so intently she thought she might pass out. Getting up from his chair, he knelt in front of her. 'What are you hiding from?' he murmured, tucking a lock of hair behind her ear, leaving her skin supersensitised and tingling where he'd touched her.

She finally plucked up the courage to look at him and their gazes locked.

Heart pummelling her chest, Jess willed herself not

to look away this time. He was close to her, so close she could smell the fresh, citrusy smell of him, mingling with the heat of his body.

He was looking at her differently, she was sure of it. Not that she could put her finger on exactly what made her think that. It was a feeling. An unsettling, exciting, monstrous feeling she was afraid to acknowledge.

The feeling seemed to peak, swiftly followed by an overwhelming tiredness and she tried to—unsuccessfully—stifle a yawn.

Xander laughed quietly. 'Okay, I can see you're exhausted so I'm going to release you from the torture.' He sat back on his haunches.

Jess let out a loud sigh of relief. 'Thank God for that,' she murmured.

He frowned at her. 'You really don't enjoy being sketched, do you?'

She looked back at him, battling with the mixture of shame and defiance that coursed through her. 'I hate it.'

'Why?'

Sighing, she looked off towards the vast sparkling expanse of the lake, giving herself a moment to gather her wits. She wanted to tell him, so he'd know she wasn't just being freaky. 'My mum was a model in the seventies and she had this crazy idea that I would be one, too. Unfortunately, she ended up with a chubby, odd-looking child who hated being thrust into the limelight.' She laughed, hoping to sound flippant and unaffected, but instead managing to sound false and strained.

'It didn't stop her from dressing me up like a doll from the age of four and making me parade around in those awful beauty pageants you see on shockumentaries sometimes, though,' she ploughed on, unwilling to let Xander see how shaky she was about telling him this. 'I absolutely hated them, but she made me do it until I was old enough to categorically refuse. I always came last in those things and the constant look of disappointment on her face would make me physically ill.' She snorted, but still couldn't bring herself to look at Xander. 'Ever since then I've hated being looked at and judged. I prefer to blend into the background.' She shrugged, hoping she hadn't completely blown things with him. After his kindness that morning she felt as if she owed him an explanation about her reticence to be drawn. She didn't want him to think she was just being a prima donna about it.

When she finally plucked up the courage to meet his gaze her insides swooped at the expression of compassion on his face.

'So why did you agree to come here and go through with this if it meant putting yourself through so much torment?' he asked gently.

Xander held his breath, waiting to hear what would spill from those luscious lips of hers.

Say it's because you like me and want to spend more time getting to know me. The intensity of the need to hear those words shocked him.

Where had *that* thought come from?

She paused, staring back at him, a whole gamut of expressions running over her face.

'Because I need this interview with you so I can impress my editor.' She looked as though she was going to say more, but then clamped her mouth shut.

He snorted in frustration, the tension of the moment broken by her utter refusal to tell him what he wanted to hear.

His determination to win her over tripled.

Getting up, he braced himself against the arms of her chair, gathering his strength to leave without pulling her towards him and planting a reassuring kiss on those soft-looking lips first.

She was a total contradiction. On the one hand self-assured and feisty, but on the flip side withdrawn and uncertain.

'I'm going to go and work in the studio for a while and you should try and catch up on your sleep, but we should go out for dinner tonight. There's a great restaurant in Salò I want to try.' His rebellious gaze dropped back to her full, inviting mouth and he had to force himself to look away before he lost his cool and succumbed to the urge to drop his mouth onto hers, just to see how she'd react.

She gazed back at him, her eyes wide and utterly mesmerising.

'Okay, I'd like that.'

He tipped her a nod. 'Great. Let's go about eight o'clock.'

'Eight's great,' she said, nodding once.

'See you later.' He pushed himself up straight and strode away from her, forcing himself to keep his eyes front and centre and his unsettling hunger well and truly in check.

For now.

He could tell he was going to have to play the long game to get in with Jess, but the thought of it buoyed him.

He enjoyed a challenge.

After taking a long reviving nap, Jess spent the remainder of the day taking photos of the amazing villa and jotting down ideas for her article on Xander.

The reprieve he'd given her earlier had been a welcome relief, but she knew if she was going to get him to open up she was going to have to give more of herself than she'd originally anticipated. He'd responded really kindly to her confession about her hatred of being the centre of attention and she'd felt as if laying herself bare like that had actually endeared her to him.

She guessed that as an artist he needed to be able to see more than surface level, too.

But it was a dangerous game she was playing. She couldn't allow herself to get swept up in feeling as if there were more of a connection between them than there was. He was famous for his short, sharp affairs with his muses and she couldn't allow herself to get carried away and imagine there was any kind of romance to the situation.

Xander was a fantastic flirt but surely he didn't mean anything by it? He was just trying to get her to relax so she'd give him what he wanted.

He was clearly a very smart guy who played to his strengths.

After staring at her meagre collection of clothes for a few minutes, she shunned the grey linen suit—too formal—and her jeans—too informal—for the only other semisuitable thing for dinner out that she'd brought with her: a long, light wool jumper and black cotton trousers. It was a totally over-the-top outfit for a summer's evening but she hadn't anticipated needing anything for dining out. Her wardrobe at home didn't contain any decent 'going out' clothes any more anyway. Not since she'd moved to London and didn't have the money or energy to go out in the evenings.

Whatever. It would have to do. This wasn't a date, it was her job, so it shouldn't matter what she looked like.

Eight o'clock came and went and she found herself pacing the hall, her senses on high alert for any sign of Xander as she waited.

Finally, he appeared, his hair gleaming and pushed back away from his face as if he'd just stepped out of the shower. The casual, off-duty appearance did something funny to her insides. It made him more human somehow, more touchable.

As he got closer she noticed he smelt as if he'd just stepped out of the shower, too, all clean and fresh with a dark, musky undertone from some body product or other.

Even if he was the most delicious thing she'd ever encountered, she shouldn't lose sight of the fact he'd left her hanging around in the hall like a sad Muppet when he was the one who'd set the time to meet for dinner, then turned up late. She pursed her lips as he stopped in front of her, determined not to let his charisma beat her into submission. 'I was expecting you fifteen minutes ago.'

He grinned, knocking the ferocity right out of her. 'You look just like the headmistress of the school I was expelled from when you do that. Although that expression looks a lot sexier on you.'

Despite the smile tugging at her mouth, she somehow managed to raise a judicious eyebrow. 'I consider lateness to be rude, but then what else should I expect from such a *bad boy*?'

His mouth twitched at the corner but he held up both hands and dipped his head in acquiescence. 'It's a fair cop. You're right; it was rude of me to be late.'

She gave him a nod, trying to appear as if she were used to handling men like him every day.

'Let's go,' he said, opening the front door and gesturing for her to exit first.

They walked over to his car, which was parked under a small wooden awning covered in fragrant-smelling honeysuckle.

Jess was surprised and a little taken aback when Xander opened the passenger door for her and waited until she'd got in before closing it behind her. Was he on his best behaviour now she'd pointed out his rudeness? Could she really be having that much of an impact on him?

'What a gentleman,' she said after he'd walked round to the other side and slid into the driving seat.

'You don't mind that, then?' he asked. 'Some women hate having doors opened for them.'

'I don't mind at all. I consider it good manners. I'd do the same for you, though, if I got to the car first.'

He smiled and gave her a courteous tip of the head before slipping the car into gear and setting off.

'Did you book a table?' she asked.

He flipped her a grin. 'No, but they'll fit us in, don't worry about that.'

There was a queue five couples deep when they pulled up outside the vine-covered trattoria in Salò.

'Ah, bother it,' Jess said, her heart sinking. She really didn't fancy spending the next hour in such close proximity to Xander, driving round looking for somewhere else that could fit them in. Why hadn't he just booked a table?

Xander seemed blithely unconcerned as he parked the car in the trattoria's car park and opened his door to get out.

Jess followed him out into the warm evening air.

When he turned to look at her, she opened her mouth to ask him what they were going to do, but before she could utter a word he held up a hand to silence her.

'Give me a second to speak to the maître d',' he said, backing away from her towards the open door to the trattoria.

Striding confidently past the queue of future diners, he disappeared into the restaurant, leaving Jess gaping after him.

Everyone in the queue turned to look at her and she had to pull her phone out of her bag and pretend to be checking for messages so they wouldn't see how embarrassed she was.

Xander returned a minute later and beckoned her to follow him.

She hurried after him as he walked past the queue of people again, giving them all a friendly smile.

Every one of them smiled back at him. He was clearly allowed to push in front of them without causing any complaints.

Oh, to be that casually confident about things.

The maître d' met them at the door and ushered them inside to a small table at the back.

The trattoria was hot with the collected warmth of bodies and heat from the wood-fired stone pizza oven in the corner, and Jess's stomach rumbled as the amazing aromas of Italian food hit her nostrils.

'So they just happened to have this table free?' she asked after they'd seated themselves in heavy, highly decorated wrought-iron chairs and been handed menus by their waiter.

'No, but they made room for us.'

'I don't even know what that means,' Jess said, holding up her hands.

Xander grinned. 'Sometimes fame has its perks.'

Jess chose what she was going to eat quickly—a delicious-sounding chicken salad—and looked up to watch Xander as he studied the menu.

She had one of those disquieting moments where she seriously wondered whether she was dreaming this all up. If anyone had told her this time last week that she'd be in Italy, dining opposite Xander Heaton, she'd have told them to get their head checked. Even more baffling than the arbitrariness of her situation was the fact she felt as if she belonged here with him—that their camaraderie earlier had somehow taken their relationship up a level.

He glanced up and caught her staring at him.

'Everything okay, Jess?'

She flushed in embarrassment at being caught out. 'I'm fine. Just thinking how strange it is to be sitting here with you.'

'Strange?' He looked puzzled at her choice of word.

'Good strange. Not the sort of thing that ever happens to me. I live a pretty uneventful life usually.'

He leant back in his chair and considered her for a moment. 'Believe it or not, my life can be pretty dull, too. Especially when I spend a lot of time holed up on my own working on my paintings. That's why I like working with models. Having you around is a welcome relief from the usual boredom, to be honest.'

She raised her eyebrows and sat up, crossing her arms in front of her. She'd never considered his life could be like that, not when, according to the papers, he seemed to live such a hedonistic existence. 'That doesn't sound like a fun way to live.'

'It's not.'

'So why do you do it?'

* * *

Jess's question made Xander pause. It had been a long time since anyone had got close enough to ask him a question like that. He usually held journalists at arm's length when they were after personal details and none of the women he'd dated recently seemed interested in the *why*, only in what he could offer them in the *now*. But he found he wanted to talk to her about this side of him. Perhaps to prove to her he wasn't the cold-hearted playboy she clearly had him pegged as.

'It's my calling. What I feel I'm meant to be doing with my life. It makes life worth living. I think I'd wither and die if I had to go and work in an office every day.'

She smoothed a hand over her perfectly straight hair, which distracted him for a second as he wondered what it would feel like to run his own hands through it. It would be soft and silky as it slid through his fingers; he was sure of it.

'Are you worried about how your next exhibition's going to be received?' she asked, pulling him rudely out of his hair-fondling fantasy.

Get it together, Xander, for goodness' sake.

He shifted in his chair, going for relaxed nonchalance while he considered her question carefully, giving himself a few moments to formulate an evasive, but meaty answer. Apparently she was going to keep hammering at this line of interrogation and he was going to have to watch what he said in front of her.

'I'm walking on a knife-edge the whole time. There are hundreds of new faces appearing each year, desperate to step into the limelight. I have to produce something pretty damn special every time or I'll sink. That's a lot of pressure right there.'

'What do your parents think about your success?' she asked, looking down as she realigned the position of her cutlery on the table in front of her.

Clearing his throat, he put on the indifferent smile he'd perfected over the years. 'They're both dead.'

She looked up sharply. 'Oh, Xander, I'm so sorry. So you're on your own?'

'Yup. It's just me and my *massive ego* now.'

Her cheeks flushed an adorable shade of pink. 'Look, sorry about that. In my defence, I called it as I saw it at the time.'

He smiled. 'You called it right. I was being a tool.'

She pushed her knife too far back on the table and it fell onto the floor. After reaching down to rescue it, she swiped her hair away from her flushed face before giving him an embarrassed grimace and shuffling her chair closer to the table.

Their food arrived and they both tucked in, neither of them saying a word for a couple of minutes. His lasagne was delicious and it didn't take him long to make inroads into it.

Realising he was being rude concentrating on his food and not making conversation, he nodded at the half-eaten salad on her plate. 'Good?'

'Great,' she said, popping a piece of tomato into her mouth.

'So, Jess, tell me more about you. Are you married?' She must have swallowed her tomato the wrong way because she coughed and spluttered on it, her eyes watering as she fought to get her breath back.

Granted, it was more personal and direct than anything he'd previously asked and rather out of the blue, but he really wanted to know more about her.

'No,' she said finally, shaking her head and looking down at the table.

He was surprised by the relief he felt. 'Partner?'

'Not for a couple of years now.'

'Oh? Why did you split up—if you don't mind me asking?' He stood the ends of his cutlery on the table and gave her his full attention, intrigued as to how someone as attractive as Jess could have stayed single for so long.

She put her own cutlery onto her half-full plate before looking up at him. 'He was a nice enough guy, but he didn't make my heart sing.'

'You mean he didn't do it for you in the sack?'

Her attempt at a casual shrug was the worst bit of acting he'd ever seen.

'We didn't really click,' she muttered, not looking him in the eye. He wondered what she wasn't telling him. Had the guy abused her in some way? Just the thought of it made him suddenly inexplicably angry. Under that tough, shielded exterior, there was undoubtedly some deeply ingrained insecurity lurking. He'd seen flashes of it already and imagined he'd see more and more, the longer she stuck around.

'Anyway, my turn. How come you're not settled down with a partner?' she said, clearly wanting to change the subject and shift the attention back onto him.

'Serious relationships aren't my thing. I like variety. And I like sex. Lots and lots of sex,' he teased, wanting to get back to the light, flirtatious atmosphere they'd had earlier.

He wasn't sure what Jess was thinking now. Her huge, dark eyes seemed to have taken on a faraway look and her mouth was drawn back in a faintly twisted grimace as though her smile had gone wrong somewhere along the line.

He'd made her uncomfortable with his suggestive comment and seemingly not in the way he'd intended.

He really shouldn't be thinking about her like this, not when he'd promised himself he was taking a break from what the press liked to refer to as his philandering ways, but it was almost *impossible* when she looked the way she did, sitting there all buttoned up and tempting in front of him. He wanted to peel back her layers and peek at what was underneath. Hell, who was he kidding? He wanted to tear her clothes off right there in the restaurant and feast on her like a starving man.

She fiddled with the napkin on her lap, her eyes downcast again.

'I'm just going to find the bathroom,' she said suddenly, dumping the napkin on the table, pushing her chair back and going to stand up, then jerking to a stop, midrise, and sitting back down again, a look of shock on her face.

'Jess? What's wrong?'

'Um, I think my top's caught on the chair. I don't seem to be able to move.'

He couldn't help but laugh at her predicament, until he noticed the look of utter horror on her face. She tried standing up again, but the wrought-iron chair kept her in her place. Her eyes were wide with worry now.

'I'm stuck!'

He got up and scooted round to the back of her chair to find that some of the loops of her knitted top had somehow wound themselves around the swirls of the patterned metal back.

'Sit still, I'll get you free,' he said, trying to get his hands down between the narrow gap between her body and the back of the chair. He worked on the caught bits for a few moments, feeling the heat of Jess's humiliation burning into him as she sat as still as she could.

His large, clumsy fingers couldn't get the loops out from where they were caught in the iron maze, which seemed to have inexplicably closed around them.

'Jess, I'm sorry, it's no good, you're going to have to take your top off so I can get it free. I can't work in such a small space.'

He went to lift the hem of her jumper but she put her hand firmly on top of his, stilling the movement. He looked directly into her face and she shook her head hard, fear flashing in her eyes.

What the hell?

'I don't want you to see my body.' She was trembling.

He frowned. 'Why not?'

Twitching her head from side to side, she looked away from him.

'Jess? What's wrong?'

'Nothing, nothing…it's just…I can't take my top off in the middle of the restaurant.' Her voice came out all squeaky and panicked.

'Well, you're going to have to wear the chair home, then,' he said, exasperation at not being able to help her coming through clearly in his tone. 'Whatever possessed you to wear a wool top in this heat anyway?'

He stepped away as she started jerking madly away from the chair as if it would miraculously let her go if she showed enough determination.

'Jess, you're going to ruin…' But it was too late. There was a loud tearing noise as the delicate material came apart under the force of her tugging. Unfortunately some of the strands were still wound tightly around the chair back so the top still wouldn't come free.

Jess stilled, as if she'd been turned to stone, then pressed herself hard back against the chair to hide the ruined back of her top, staring up at him with such a look of abject misery it made his stomach turn over.

'Okay, this is ridiculous.' He pulled open the buttons on his shirt and took it off, ignoring the titters and murmurs of the diners around them who were clearly enjoying the show. 'I'll hold this around you while you take your top off, then you can wear it while we free your jumper.'

'Okay,' Jess said, nodding her head unhappily in agreement, managing to look as if he'd just suggested she leap across a pit of poisonous snakes for him.

He looked away as he held his shirt around her so she could struggle out of her jumper without flashing the entire restaurant, then slide her arms into the sleeves. He let go as she pulled it closed around her and attempted to do up the buttons with trembling fingers.

After a couple of frustrating moments of watching her totally fail to do up one single button, he knocked her hands away, knelt down next to the chair and did them up for her.

He could feel her eyes on his face as he worked his way down the shirt, his fingers skirting tantalisingly close to the swell of her breasts.

'Some people would suspect this was a cunning ploy to get me to take my shirt off in public,' he murmured, flipping her a grin, which she returned, albeit humbly. 'There you go.' He stood back so she could get up from the chair.

'Thank you.' She looked really grateful for his help and something lifted in his chest. He quickly released the jumper from the chair back.

'My pleasure. Shall we get out of here, before this crowd asks for an encore?'

'Yes. Good idea,' Jess said, reaching into her hand-bag and grabbing a handful of euros, which she dropped onto the table. He dropped his own share for the meal next to it and handed some of her money back to her. 'You don't need to pay for me.'

She didn't answer, just nodded and gave him a grate-ful smile. He had no idea what she was thinking; from the look in her eyes she seemed to have retreated far away into her own head.

He strode out of the restaurant, aware of the amused glances of the other diners as he passed by them, half-naked and standing out like a sore thumb, with Jess hot on his heels. He gave them all a salute as he reached the door and ushered Jess outside. She ran over to the car and he unlocked the doors so she could get straight in. He swung himself into the driving seat and burst out laughing, turning to look at her and share the joke, but she was staring straight ahead, her back ramrod-straight and her hands clutched tightly in her lap.

'Jess?'

She turned to look at him, her expression wild and her face flaming red. 'Can we go?' It came out as a hushed gasp. She flapped the front of the shirt, clearly trying to cool herself down. He frowned at her extreme reaction. It was warm in the car, but not sweltering.

He started up the engine and drove out of the car park, heading back to the villa. 'You okay?' he asked.

'I'm fine. Just hot. Is it hot in here?' She wafted the shirt forward and back creating a slight draught of air, staring hard at the dashboard.

'Not really.' He put a hand on her arm and felt the

heat of her skin sear through the cotton of the shirt. 'Jess, what's going on?'

She wouldn't look at him. 'I don't like showing people my body. I'm not comfortable with it. Never have been. I get a bit…panicked.'

He frowned, baffled. 'How long have you felt like that?'

She took a deep breath before she answered him. 'Since my early teens. I've struggled with a kind of body dysmorphia and an eating disorder since then. Bulimia.' She screwed up her face in disgust. 'But I haven't let it…you know…get hold of me since my late teens.'

Memories from the last couple of days connected together in his brain like jigsaw pieces. So that explained the baggy, unflattering clothes and her apparent discomfort when eating in front of him.

He leant back in the seat and rubbed a hand over his face. 'I'm surprised.'

'Why?'

'Because you seem so *together.*'

'It's all a front,' she said quietly.

'Takes one to know one,' he murmured to himself.

She didn't seem to have heard him, trapped miles away in her own thoughts.

They reached the villa a minute later and he parked back under the awning and shut off the engine.

He turned to look at her and waited until she looked back at him. 'Well, if it's any consolation, you're easily the most intriguing woman I've met in a long time.'

She snorted, then screwed her eyes shut in embarrassment.

'Mostly because you're smart and funny and passionate,' he said, 'but I wouldn't kick you out of bed either.'

She seemed to swallow hard. 'What?' Her voice was

raspy and appeared to barely make it out of her throat. She stared at him hard, as if she was trying to root out a lie using only the power of her cynicism.

He looked back at her, unblinking. She wouldn't win this one. Mainly because he was telling the truth.

Jess broke eye contact first and he gave himself a mental high five, feeling inordinately pleased with himself, until she turned her head and stared out of the window instead of acknowledging his proposition.

Was she turning him down?

The thought rattled through him like a cold wind. A woman hadn't rejected him like that in a very long time and it didn't feel good.

'Jess?'

She turned back to look at him, her expression confused, but wary, and he instinctively leant forward and cupped the side of her jaw with one hand, his thumb catching against the soft fullness of her bottom lip.

He wanted to kiss her. So badly.

It was an undeniable instinct, driven by a mixture of need and curiosity and a determination to not *allow* her to reject him, and frustration twisted in his gut when he realised she was fighting him and pulling away.

Releasing his grip on her, he reluctantly drew back. 'What's wrong?' he asked, holding up an open-palmed hand.

She opened her mouth, as if to respond, then shook her head hard, her long bob of hair swinging round her face, before reaching for the handle to open the door.

He watched her scramble out of the car, banging her arm on the door in her rush to get away from him.

He slumped back in the chair, staring out into the darkness, hot with anger at himself. What the hell was he thinking, coming on to her like that after what she'd just told him? God, how inappropriate. He needed to straighten himself out—fast. Getting close to Jess was going to take more than chucking a few artless, throwaway platitudes her way before steaming in full force.

He got out of the car and followed her into the villa, a little way behind to give her the space she obviously needed. She turned before she got to the staircase and gave him a strained smile.

'See you tomorrow.' It was a statement, not a question and he knew for sure there would be no invitation to visit her room that night. Perhaps it was for the best considering how ineptly he seemed to be acting around her.

The best. The best, he chanted inside his head in an attempt to convince himself of it.

'Goodnight, Jess, sleep well,' he called after her, knowing full well a good night's sleep was the last thing *he'd* be getting.

CHAPTER FIVE

JESS COULDN'T SLEEP. Again.

Her body hummed with unsettling sensations after spending the most sexually charged day of her life with the most disquieting man in the world—who she was pretty sure would have kissed her in the car if she hadn't freaked out and run away from him like that. The trouble with being around Xander was that he was such a tactile person she wasn't sure whether she'd read his intentions all wrong. Maybe he meant nothing by it.

The memory of the humiliating *jumper incident* in the restaurant made her whole body flush hot with embarrassment. Xander had been so cool to whip off his own shirt like that to protect her modesty and then she'd been cold and weird with him in the car afterwards.

He must think she was a total loon.

And what the hell had possessed her to tell him about her bulimia? It felt now as if she'd opened up the most delicate part of herself and there was a cold draught blowing in, chilling her to the bone.

Not that he hadn't been sensitive about it. In fact, he'd been lovely about that, too, which only made her want him more.

Because she *did* want him.

More than she'd wanted anyone in her entire life.

And the idea terrified her.

She knew deep in her bones it would be a disaster for her to get emotionally involved with him. He was too wild for her, too… What was the phrase? *Too hot to handle.*

She'd get badly burned; she knew it.

The most sensible thing to do would be to keep it strictly business for the rest of her time here in case she made even more of a fool of herself. But she didn't *want* to be sensible. Not this time.

Trouble was, she had a feeling her stand-offishness was all that separated her from pretty much every other woman he came into contact with and she'd be a fool to squander the advantage of his remarkable interest in her by making herself too available.

All she had to do was keep things in perspective.

Yeah, good luck with that, Jess.

Oh, goodness, this assignment was hard work.

She sighed and rolled over in bed, trying to quell the deep, vigorous throbbing between her legs at the thought of him sleeping just along the corridor.

Impossible.

Perhaps she should go and make herself a milky drink or something, in the hope it would relax her enough to let her sleep.

Rubbing a hand over her tired eyes, she sat up, shuffling to the side of her bed, only managing to increase the ache between her thighs with the friction of the movement.

Never in all her life had she felt so wildly out of control and it scared the hell out of her.

Leaving her room quietly, so as not to disturb Xander, she tiptoed downstairs to the kitchen, leaving off the light in case anyone should be alerted to her presence. She felt furtive and naughty for being there, as if she were trespassing on someone else's property, even though she was a guest in the house.

As she pulled open the fridge door to find the milk her eye was drawn to a bowl of what looked like tiramisu, sitting there innocently in the fridge.

A horrible greedy urge to take it and eat the entire bowlful gripped her around the throat.

The stress of hanging out with Xander Heaton was severely testing her rather shaky self-control.

Her hands shook and her mouth filled with saliva as she stared at the delicious-looking pudding. A tremendously powerful urge to reach forward and take it gripped her, but she knew from experience if she so much as let herself take a mouthful she'd end up stuffing the whole thing into her mouth like some crazed maniac and she really couldn't let that happen. She'd fought so valiantly over the years against the horrible overwhelming feelings of shame and self-loathing her eating disorder prompted, she couldn't let herself get pulled into that vicious cycle of binge and purge again. She'd made a promise to herself not to allow extreme comfort eating to ruin her life any more than it already had.

It would not beat her.

With a determination that she had to pull up from the very depths of her psyche, she swung the fridge door shut and walked away on shaky legs, back to her bedroom and safety.

The next morning Jess got up early and took herself off for a drive around the lake.

She needed a breather from being around Xander in order to mentally get herself in a place where she could handle the developing situation without freaking out again.

A bit of peace and calm and normality was just the ticket.

Stopping off in a few of the charming towns along the way, she took photos and made notes for the travel piece she needed to write. Each place was very different from the last—with its own unique atmosphere and character—all bordering the amazingly clear water of Lake Garda. She could totally see why the place lured so many visitors to its shores each year.

A tantalising window display in one of the women's clothes shops drew her in and she found herself trying on and buying a couple of reasonably priced tops— one white and one in a vibrant pillar-box red—a stylish, black fishtail skirt that fell to just above her knee and a couple of midlength-sleeved summer dresses. All the clothes were more fitted and flamboyant than the things she'd usually wear, but some strange compulsion made her hand over her credit card and buy them anyway. She justified the expense by telling herself she needed some more clothes since it looked as if she was staying longer and it wouldn't be professional to keep turning up in the same sad outfit every day.

After gathering as much information as she needed, she finally made her way back to the villa, feeling drowsy now in the afternoon heat.

As she pulled the car onto the driveway she could see Xander in the distance, a mug of coffee in one hand and a paintbrush in the other, standing in front of an easel set up on the lawn overlooking the lake. He must have heard the car's engine because he turned round to look her way, dropped his paintbrush onto the grass next to a pallet of paints and strode towards her, waving.

'Hey, Jess, there you are.'

He stumbled as he walked towards her, spilling coffee down his trousers.

Jess shot him a grin, glad for the distraction from the anxiety about facing him again after the debacle of the night before.

He raised a questioning eyebrow. 'What's so funny?' he said, brushing at the stain with his fingers.

She shrugged, nerves making her jittery. 'It's nice to see you making mistakes, too. It just proves even the most self-possessed people mess up. I like that—it makes me feel better about myself. If you can spill coffee all over your crotch then it's okay for me to rip my clothes off in a restaurant. Or something.'

He gave her a puzzled look. 'You're a very strange woman, you know that?'

She snorted. 'Actually I do. It's not a new observation.'

He smiled and her blood heated. There was something in his gaze she hadn't seen before. Something that made her insides flip.

'Where have you been today?'

'I went for a drive around the lake. I'm writing a travel piece too while I'm here so I wanted to get a feel of the place.'

'Man, they keep you busy there, don't they?'

She shrugged. 'I like to keep busy.'

He nodded but didn't say anything, his gaze flicking down to her mouth. She tensed under his scrutiny. He seemed to move closer to her, just a fraction, as if he were thinking about going in for a kiss and she froze with anxiety, not at all sure what to do with herself. Her lips tingled at the thought of his mouth, hot and hard against hers.

'I'm a p-professional,' she stuttered in panic and his gaze flicked back to meet hers, amusement clear in his eyes.

'A professional what?' His expression was full of barely contained laugher.

Jess straightened her T-shirt. Smoothed down her hair. 'Here in a professional capacity, I mean, so please don't feel you have to, you know, look after me or anything.'

He nodded a couple of times, still looking at her as if she was the funniest thing he'd ever encountered. 'What if I like looking after you?' His eyes suddenly lit with an idea before she could respond. 'Hey, why don't we bring a picnic down to the cove later? It should be warm enough and if we're lucky we might get a pretty amazing sunset,' he said, cocking his head while he waited for her to agree.

It sounded much too romantic an idea for her liking, but she couldn't spend the next couple of days hiding from him as she had today. She still hadn't got everything she needed in order to write the column and it would be a good opportunity to ask him some more questions while he was relaxed and happy in her company. 'Yeah, sure, that sounds like fun,' she said, not giving her cowardly alter ego a chance to interfere.

'Great. I'll get Rosa to make a hamper up for us. Shall we say eight o'clock again?'

She nodded dumbly. 'Yes. Eight.'

'Okay, then.' He was looking at her so intensely she wondered whether there was something wrong with her face.

'Listen,' he said, finally breaking the silence, 'I hope you didn't think I was being insensitive last night, after we'd talked about your…eating issues.'

He looked genuinely concerned and she felt a rush of affection for him.

'Nah, don't worry about it. I think we were both a bit freaked by what happened in the restaurant. I don't suppose it's often you have to strip off to save your date from dying of embarrassment.'

He laughed. 'As I'm sure you've noticed, I don't have a problem with stripping off.'

Jess felt the inevitable warmth creep up her neck at the thought of his naked, toned torso in such close proximity to her. 'Yeah, well, you don't need to rein that in on my account,' she said, flashing him what she hoped would come across as an affable smile. She wanted to show him she did still have *some* vestige of control in the flirty-banter stakes.

He raised a dark eyebrow and tipped his head in appreciation. 'Noted,' he said, before turning away and walking back to his easel.

Jess paced the floor of the hall, waiting for Xander to turn up and collect her for their picnic tea.

She'd put the pillar-box-red top and pencil skirt on for tonight, then taken the whole ensemble off again. Then a minute later put it back on, telling herself it was a positive step in the right direction to push herself out of her comfort zone.

To *unstuff* herself.

But then again, she needed every ounce of confidence tonight if she was going to get through the evening with her pride intact.

She'd been about to take it off again when she'd caught sight of her wild-eyed reflection in the mirror.

She was turning into a complete loony.

Whatever was happening between her and Xander

was making her lose her mind. She was ninety per cent sure it wasn't all in her head. Okay, maybe eighty, but he'd definitely kicked his flirting up a notch recently.

What the hell was going on? She could have sworn he would have kissed her last night if she hadn't broken the atmosphere by flapping about like a headless chicken. Or was that just a figure of her overactive imagination? In the past she'd been prone to reading more into a situation than was actually there, and it had made her wary about taking anything for granted when it came to men and relationships.

Another thing she hated—making a fool of herself.

Not that she hadn't already managed that in the couple of days she'd been here.

When he finally turned up at five past eight, looking, oh, so divinely edible, she was so nervous the first thing she said was, 'You're late. Again.'

Despite her snippy tone, he gave her an amused grin. 'Are you going to spank me with your ruler, Headmistress? Because I'll take whatever punishment you choose to dish out.'

She took a shaky step back away from him, but kept her gaze locked with his. 'Don't be so facetious,' she murmured, her body tense with the sudden desire to throw herself at him and consequences be damned.

He took a step towards her, closing the gap between them. 'Ooh, yeah, keep using those long words on me, too. I like that.'

She slapped him gently on the arm. 'You're incorrigible.'

He slapped her back, a seductive eyebrow quirked.

Narrowing her eyes in jest, she did it again, feeling the rock-hard muscle of his triceps vibrate under her touch.

Before she could react he wrapped his hand round hers and, trapping it there against him, walked her backwards until her back hit the wall. The heat from his body radiated over her skin, sending zingy electric currents through her limbs.

'This is just like being back in the school playground,' she barely managed to struggle out. Her tongue felt like a lead weight in her mouth and her lips were tight with tension.

He moved his body closer to her and a flood of longing flashed through her. 'Did you like playing kiss chase at school?' he murmured, dipping his head so he could look directly into her eyes. His pupils looked huge against the bright aqua of his irises.

'Of course,' she said, her voice husky and broken. 'And I'm guessing you were always the first kid to suggest playing it?' Staring defiantly back, she attempted to hold her nerve, determined not to be the one to look away first. He was teasing her, trying to trip her up and get her to admit just how much of an effect he had on her. He wasn't going to win, though; she wouldn't let him.

He shifted even closer, bringing with him a waft of his fresh citrus scent.

It was no good—she just wasn't as good at this game as he was. She closed her eyes as an onslaught of lust nearly brought her to her knees.

'Somebody has to take control,' he said quietly.

She glanced up at him, straight into those unfathomable eyes. 'I'd have fought you for it,' she practically whispered, her throat tight with tension.

He smiled in a way that made her whole body ache with longing.

His hand was still trapping hers against his body and

she could feel the faint pulse in his fingertips. Or was that her own pulse that seemed to have taken her over? She throbbed to the beat as it concentrated deep in her pelvis. She was so turned on she felt faintly queasy.

Taking a deep breath, she swivelled to one side so he had to release her from his grip. 'Shall we go?' she said.

His expression flashed with a mixture of surprise and something else. Disappointment?

'Okay, if you like,' he said, his voice rumbling low in his throat. 'I'll grab the food from the kitchen.'

He came back a few moments later with a hamper and a folded square of material, which she assumed was a picnic rug.

Jess reminded herself not to get too excited about how special this all felt. Xander had probably done things like this a million times before with a million other women.

He turned to smile at her. 'Okay, we're set.'

She nodded in agreement and joined him as he walked through the large patio doors, which opened onto the rear garden of the villa, and traversed the path that led down to the cove.

They walked in silence through the muted evening light, Xander cradling the picnic hamper close to his chest. The air was balmy and close with a threatening rainstorm, the atmosphere electric with the promise of a much-needed purge of humidity.

They picked their way over the warm sand of the cove to the far side, just back from the water, where they had a spectacular view of the opposite shore of the lake, which was beginning to glow and twinkle with colourful lights as the sky darkened.

'I hope it doesn't rain on us,' Jess said, gazing at the ominous-looking clouds in the distance.

'We'll be fine for a while,' Xander said, putting down the hamper and flapping open the thick rug, smoothing it carefully flat before gesturing for Jess to sit down on it.

Once she'd made herself comfortable—yanking down hard on her skirt so it covered as much of her legs as possible—he dropped down next to her, so close she could feel the heat of him radiating towards her.

Pulling out cartons of cold meats, salad, olives and a wealth of other local delicacies, he laid them out carefully on the rug and handed her a plate.

'Dig in,' he said, motioning towards the feast in front of them.

While Jess picked out a few things for her plate he reached into the hamper and came out with a couple of oil-fired lamps and lit them with a long match. They cast a soft glow over the area where they sat.

If she hadn't thought it ridiculous she would have assumed he was deliberately setting up a romantic atmosphere. As it was, she was so nervous she could barely eat a thing. Xander didn't remark on it, though; he must have thought talking about food and eating was a no-go area after her confession the night before.

It was kind of him—thoughtful—and she felt a glow of affection towards him.

'You know, you're nothing like I expected you to be.'

He raised a questioning eyebrow. 'No?'

'The press make you out to be some badly behaved lout, but they've clearly got you pegged all wrong.'

He frowned in mock disgruntlement. 'Don't say that. I was rather enjoying living up to my bad-boy reputation.'

She laughed. 'What was it that made you so wild in your youth?' she asked casually, holding her breath as she waited to see whether Xander trusted her enough yet to tell her something that personal about himself.

Those beautiful eyes of his seemed fathomless as he stared at her, his gaze raking her face for signs of… what? A set-up?

Her heart whammed against her chest like a malfunctioning metronome as she waited to see whether he'd answer her question. She needed some interesting backstory to make the story shine, but somewhere in her brain a small voice told her she really wanted to know for herself. She wanted to think the best of him, because despite the arrogance—which she was beginning to suspect was actually a defence mechanism—she really liked him. And not just because he was so gorgeous, but because she sensed there was a whole lot more to him than he ever let anyone else see.

The optimistic side of him must have won because he leant forward, his gaze capturing hers, and said, 'What do you think it was?'

A slow trickle of excitement percolated through her veins as she realised this could be it—he was letting her in. 'Did you have a tough upbringing?' she asked, desperately hoping she hadn't read him all wrong.

He folded his arms across his broad chest, making the muscles in his shoulders and arms bunch beneath his T-shirt. He looked down at the flickering candle between them. 'You could say that. My parents never intended having a child. I was an accident—which my father liked to remind me of every chance he got.' He looked back at her and she was shocked to see insecurity in his expression—something she'd not encountered before. 'My mum died giving birth to me.'

His voice had taken on a steely edge, which sent a shiver of horror through her. 'I paid my way in that family by spending most of my childhood working to keep myself fed and clothed—until my dad kicked me out when I was sixteen. He'd spend most of his time down the pub or the betting office, so I hardly saw him anyway.' He leant back on the rug, anchoring his arms behind him and readjusting his body before looking at her. There was nothing on his face but a blank expression now, as if he'd drawn down the shutters.

'How awful for you.' She could picture him as a child not being allowed to do the things that normal kids did—not being allowed to *be* a child—and it made her chest ache.

He shrugged. 'It was tough at times. I got into a lot of trouble, for shoplifting and fighting and then for my graffiti and got myself a bad reputation. The teachers wrote me off after a few years of failing to straighten me out.'

She'd known children like that when she was at school. Loners. Lost souls. People who had difficulty fitting into what everyone else thought of as normal life because they'd never had the opportunity to experience it.

The atmosphere had dropped dark now and she wanted to pull it back before the hard pressure behind her eyes became real tears for him.

'But look at you now.' She managed to catch the wobble at the end of the sentence and turn it into a gentle clearing of her throat. 'Everyone wants to own a piece of the great and talented Xander Heaton,' she finished on a deeply concentrated frown as she battled to conceal her need to jump into his lap and rub herself all over him.

'And which piece are you after, Jess?' he asked, leaning forward now and giving her a seductive grin, the heavy atmosphere of the last couple of minutes evaporating into the air around them.

He was king of the suggestive comment, this guy.

All she could think about now was exactly which bits of Xander she'd like to get her hands on. Her mind flew to an image of his magnificent body, prostrate on her bed, with him wearing only a sheet and that mesmerising smile. She pictured herself leaning over him, lowering her lips to his as she attempted to kiss away all the pain that kept him so distant from the rest of the world....

'Jess?' He was frowning at her now as if he was afraid she'd walked through a door marked 'crazy' and wasn't coming back.

'Yeah?' She slid her hands over her hair in an attempt to straighten herself out. Neat hair, neat mind.

'You okay?'

'Fine.' She stared out across the lake, attempting to bring herself back to reality.

'Did you go to college or university to study art?' she asked to fill the uncomfortable silence.

Putting his plate down, he leant back on his arms and looked out across the water. 'Nah, I'm mostly self-taught. I left school when I left home at sixteen without any qualifications so no college would have touched me with a bargepole. I messed up a lot at school because of having to work late into the evening and being too tired to concentrate. Then I started skipping a lot because I couldn't keep up with the lessons and ended up feeling stupid, and I *hated* that. So when I left I didn't exactly have a bright and shiny future ahead of me.

'Art was the only subject I enjoyed at school. It was the one thing I felt I was actually good at, and I had an amazing teacher who really encouraged me. Unfortunately I wasn't in the right mindset at that age to put enough work into my lessons—I didn't think for a second I could make any money out of it, and that's all that concerned me at the time—so it just became a hobby. After I left school, I used to go out in the dead of night with a crew and paint or spray the walls of public buildings with my pictures as a kind of release from the boredom of my existence. Art helped me channel the rage I felt that I didn't feel able to express in words.'

Jess experienced a swell of outrage for him. 'I can't believe no one at the school realised you needed more help and support.'

'Yeah, well, it was an underprivileged area and there were other kids a lot worse off than me. And to be honest, I wasn't interested in their help. I wanted to prove to myself I could manage on my own.'

Jess thought about her own cushy upbringing. Despite the feeling of never managing to become the daughter her mother wanted, she'd never had to worry about coping without enough food or sleep.

Shame washed over her in a hot wave, prickling at her skin, as she realised she'd allowed herself to prejudge Xander, before finding out the reasons for him acting the way he did. It wasn't because he got off on it and enjoyed the notoriety—although that obviously played a small part—it was because he was trying to live his life at triple the speed to make up for what he'd lost in the past.

She couldn't fault him for that.

'You're incredible,' she blurted. 'Look at what you've done with your life. You've made it count with no support and no qualifications.'

'Yeah, well, I'm stubborn like that,' he said on a smile.

'It's impressive.'

'Thanks.' He readjusted his position on the rug, drawing his body closer to her.

An intense longing shot through her, taking her right to the edge of her comfort zone. If she'd thought she'd wanted him before, it was nothing to how much she wanted him now. These insights into his character both fascinated and terrified her—she could totally see why he kept himself so emotionally distant from his partners—but did that mean he'd never be able to settle down with one person?

From what he'd said the night before, it certainly sounded as if *he'd* decided that was the case.

But was there scope to change his mind?

Don't even think about it, Jess.

'What did your father say when you became so successful?' she asked, trying to steer her thoughts back to safer ground. 'He must have been proud of you for what you've achieved?'

Xander barked out a harsh laugh, making her jump. 'Are you kidding? He never turned up to see any of the stuff I've showcased. He thought art was a waste of time. He thought *I* was a waste of time.'

'So you never reconciled things with him? Even after you left home and made it big?'

'You could say that. The last time we laid eyes on each other he told me he wished I hadn't been born because then my mother would still be alive.'

'Oh, my God, Xander, that's awful.'

He shrugged, clearly going for cool nonchalance, but as she continued to look at him he turned away so she couldn't see his face any more.

'But he raised you. He must have cared about you in some way,' she said, quietly.

'It was a long time ago, Jess. I barely even think about it any more.'

He was lying; she could tell. It was obvious from the clip in his voice and the way his body had become rigid with tension.

She put a hand on his arm but he pulled it away and threw his plate back into the hamper.

'Is this the kind of thing you're after to impress your editor?' he asked, his voice tinged with scorn.

Clearly she'd hit a nerve.

She shook her head quickly. 'I want to try and understand what it is that drives you, to round the piece out and give a fair and honest representation of you as a person.'

'Am I not interesting enough to write about without you feeling the need to expose my deepest, darkest secrets?'

'Of course you are.'

Tears welled in her eyes and a thud of shame landed in her stomach as he turned back and she saw pain and disappointment in his expression.

'I won't write about any of that, I promise. I'm sorry for prying. It wasn't to get some salacious gossip out of you; I was genuinely concerned.'

'Well, you don't need to be. I've coped fine without your pity up until this point.'

They gazed at each other in silence for a moment, before Xander turned away to look back out across the lake.

Now she was beginning to see the real Xander she felt a desperate urge to keep that side of him as protected as he did, to keep that side of him just for her.

What was happening to her? She'd been so determined not to fall for his charms when she first arrived here and now all she could think about was how to get closer to him, even though she knew there was little chance he'd ever be interested in a real relationship with her.

How could she want someone and some*thing* that terrified her so much?

She picked at her food some more, eventually laying the plate down on the rug in front of her in defeat. It had been delicious, but she just couldn't bring herself to eat any more of it, not when her stomach felt as if it were full of rolling marbles.

'You had enough?' he asked, nodding at her abandoned plate.

'Er, yeah.' She was glad he couldn't see how flushed her face was in the growing darkness.

After packing the remainder of the food back into the hamper in silence, he lay down on the rug and gazed up at the sky.

Jess couldn't stop looking at him, thinking about how his powerful body would feel under her hands and how overwhelmed by his enigmatic presence she was, despite her determination to keep herself emotionally distant. He did something to her she couldn't explain.

Turning his head, he caught her gawping at him.

'Sorry for flipping out like that. Don't take it personally—I'm just in a bit of a funk today,' he said.

Shaking herself out of her trance, she fumbled around for the wherewithal to get herself back under control.

'I can understand why you don't feel comfortable talking to journalists about your past. It must have been really hard growing up like that.'

He sat up, turning to fully face her and brushing his hands together before carefully laying them on his lap. 'Yeah, well, in my experience some journalists make it their life's work to root out your most embarrassing secrets just to sell a few papers and get their byline next to the story.'

'You have some *embarrassing* secrets? Can you tell me about *those* so I can cash in and make my fortune?' she said, willing a gleam of mischief into her expression.

He raised an eyebrow at her, but smiled. 'I'll tell you mine if you tell me yours,' he said, leaning forward so their eyes were on a level.

The smile dropped from her face as she struggled to deal with his sudden closeness. That feeling was back, the one from earlier, when she'd thought he was going to kiss her.

His gaze flicked from her eyes to her mouth and the surge of need to be kissed nearly made her crumple in a heap. She throbbed with it.

As if sensing her desperate want, he leant in farther, his seductive gaze locked with hers, closing the distance between them.

Her breath came shallow and fast from her lungs and her heart raced in her chest as his mouth came so close to hers she could feel the whisper of his breath on her lips.

She was frozen. Captivated. Caught. She dared not move a muscle in case she turned to dust in front of him.

'What do you want from me, Jess?' he murmured against her mouth so she felt the vibration of the sound on her skin and right down to her toes.

Closing her eyes, she grasped for a thin thread of courage to say what she wanted out loud, but the words wouldn't come. They were stuck hard in the back of her throat.

Say it, Jess. Stop being such a coward and say it.

'I want to touch you,' she whispered. 'I want to know what your body feels like.'

Opening her eyes, she saw he was looking at her intently. There wasn't a trace of the condescension she'd expected to see, only acceptance and approval.

'Go ahead.' He drew back quickly from her, leaving a chasm of cool air where he'd once been and tugged his shirt over his head, revealing his amazing body.

Taking a deep, shaking breath, she stared at him in shock for a moment, her brain taking a second to catch up with the sudden and stupefying turn of events. Had he really just offered up his body for her to fondle?

Please let it be so.

'Go on,' he urged, taking one of her trembling hands in his and placing it against his warm chest.

His skin almost glowed in the lamplight, and it felt as soft as she'd imagined, more so if that was possible, and the hard muscle underneath moved gently under her touch as he readjusted his position.

Putting his hand over the back of hers, he lay back on the rug, pulling her with him so she had to kneel up and lean over him.

He nodded at her as if urging her on and she slowly moved her hand down his chest to the top of his stomach where the muscles swelled against his skin like perfectly formed moguls.

'Is it everything you expected?' he murmured, giving her a slow smile that made the blood rush and fizz between her legs.

'Uh-huh,' was all she managed as her whole body shook with the effort of not collapsing against him.

'Okay, my turn.'

Before she knew what was happening, he sat up, grasping her shoulders and flipping her onto her back underneath him, trapping her legs between his knees and her wrists in his hands.

'Just say the word, Jess, and I'll let you go.' He leant in closer. 'But please don't,' he begged. 'I think I'm going to go crazy if I don't get to touch you.'

She just stared up at him, befuddled and entranced by the fact that *she had the ability to drive him crazy.*

Had the world gone mad? Since when did she get to hold the cards with a man like this?

Since now, Jess.

He took her silence as consent and released her wrists so he could use his hands to stroke along the tops of her shoulders, before sweeping down and pushing up the sleeves of her top to uncover her arms.

It had been such a long time since she'd been touched like this that her body nearly melted with joy.

His touch was feather-light and slow, his fingertips sweeping over every inch of her bare arms, tracing the lines between her muscles and pausing on one of the many dark moles on her skin.

'I love this mole here,' he said, quietly. 'It's such a perfectly round shape. Beautiful.' Moving on down her arms, he dipped his fingers into the well of her inner elbows. 'Your skin is so soft,' he said, swirling the pads of his fingers around the sensitive skin there until she thought she'd go crazy with it.

'You have an amazing body, Jess,' he said, his gaze moving down to take in the swell of her breasts as they pushed against her new—lucky—red top. 'I've been thinking about it all day.'

Had he *really*?

Shuffling down her body, he moved one of his knees to release her legs, pushing it instead between her thighs to open her up to him.

Her heart raged in her chest as she realised what he was about to do, his hand dipping down to caress the soft skin of her inner thigh that her skirt didn't cover.

'Wait,' she whispered so quietly he couldn't have heard her.

Both of his hands were between her legs now, making gentle stroking sweeps up from her knees to the soft plumpness of her inner thighs, his thumbs drawing erotic figures of eight across her flesh.

Great crashing waves of need flowed over her, making the space between her legs ache and pulse with the demand to be touched.

Any second now, he'd move higher, to the line of her knickers, then higher... The thought brought her crashing back down to earth.

'No.' Her voice was loud this time, loud enough to make him pause in what he was doing.

'Jess?' His own voice was ragged and low and not at all steady. 'What's wrong?'

Shuffling back away from his touch, she pulled her skirt down hard to her knees before scrambling to get up. Her legs were like jelly as she backed away from him, stumbling on the uneven ground.

'Jess? Where are you going?' His voice was filled with genuine shock and concern.

'I have to... I need to...' She couldn't form the words. They wouldn't come. She had to get out of there but she couldn't tell him why. She just couldn't. It was too humiliating.

Xander stared after Jess's retreating figure until she was swallowed up by the darkness.

He'd never been so frustrated in his life. His hands shook with the need to touch her again and the hard press of his erection against his trousers was almost painful.

He'd thought he was starting to get through to her, to help her realise just how sexy and attractive she really was, but she'd thrown up her wall again and he'd run right into it.

Goddamn it.

Perhaps he'd pushed her too hard too soon? But he couldn't see how that could be the case. He'd been taking it *way* slower than he wanted to and she'd been there with him right up until the end.

The eating disorder had obviously had a huge psychological effect on the way she saw her own body, because from what he'd seen she had a fantastic figure, all soft curves in the right places but toned and sculpted from regular exercise. Out of bounds, though, obviously.

He knew he should leave it at that. He shouldn't be doing this with someone like Jess when he had nothing more than his body to offer her, but he couldn't stop himself. Didn't want to. He felt some deep connection with her that he'd never experienced with anyone before and he wanted to explore it more. Despite her reluctance.

Was she afraid of what was happening between them and protecting herself? He couldn't blame her; he didn't exactly have a great reputation when it came to women and relationships.

But Jess wasn't like the other women he'd dated.

This felt more special, more real. Partly because he was having to work hard to get her to trust him, but also because he wanted her to understand where he came from.

He wanted her approval.

And he wanted to go after her—like nothing he'd

ever wanted before. He sensed she was worried about what was happening between them and he wanted to reassure her that there was nothing to be afraid of.

Jumping up, he pulled his shirt back on before heading off in the direction she'd disappeared.

There was no way in *hell* he was giving up on her now.

CHAPTER SIX

SHE WAS SUCH a coward.

Jess slammed the door to her room hard in frustration. What the hell was she doing running away from Xander like that?

Truth was, she'd never had a one-night stand in her life and the thought of it petrified her. Especially with someone as *intensely male* as him.

She was scared of not being able to give him what he expected from her.

He must be used to bedding sexually confident women with their lithe, toned bodies and dexterity in the bedroom and he was going to be mightily disappointed when he found out how useless she was in bed.

A loud knock at the door made her jump in fright.

That couldn't be him, could it? Surely he'd realised by now she wasn't the type of woman he should be wasting his time with? He'd given her so many opportunities to take him up on his sexual invitations and she'd blown every one of them. He must be mightily bored with her inability to take the initiative by now.

She paused on the way to answer the door as an uncomfortable notion struck her. Perhaps he thought she was playing hard to get?

Had she really given him that impression?

She thought back to all the teasing and flirting she'd allowed herself to indulge in over the last couple of days.

Yup, she probably had.

Swinging the door open, she found him standing there with his thumbs casually hooked into the belt loops of his jeans, like some vision from an advert for sex. Pushing her shoulders back, she attempted to convey cool control, all the while shaking in her shoes.

'What do you want?' she asked, her voice low and husky with nerves.

'I want *you*,' he said quietly and she sucked in a sharp breath as he suddenly advanced towards her, placing a hand each side of her jaw and pulling her towards him, his mouth pressing hard against hers before she could stop him.

His lips crushed her mouth, soft, yet hard with hunger as he forced her lips open so he could slide his tongue between them. He tasted delicious, like the most delectable main course and the sweetest dessert all wrapped up in one sensational feast.

Sliding his hands under her buttocks, he lifted her up against him and she felt the rigid length of his erection press against the agonisingly sensitised nerves between her legs.

She groaned low in her throat as he slammed her against the wall and pushed against her, increasing the delicious friction between their bodies.

'I want you like this, Jess, just like this, fast and hard against the wall,' he murmured against her mouth, his fingers slipping into her hair, holding her captive. 'Then afterwards, slow and long…sliding into you over and over again.'

She nearly stopped breathing as the sound of those

words washed over her, drenching her to her quivering bones. But she couldn't let him expect that might happen.

She *couldn't*.

Putting both hands against his shoulders, she pushed him away from her hard.

He stumbled back, catching himself before he fell against the bed and staring at her with a bewildered expression.

She wanted to cry.

'I'm sorry,' she said. 'I'm so sorry.'

'Jess, what is it?' Xander took a step towards her but stopped his advance when she shrank against the wall.

'I...don't want to disappoint you,' she said so quietly he almost missed it.

He stared at her, baffled. 'You won't.'

Moving towards her again, slowly this time, he wrapped his hands around her upper arms and manoeuvred her over to the bed, pushing her down gently to sit on it and kneeling in front of her between her thighs.

Their eyes were on a level and she gazed into his as he drew closer to her, their lips only centimetres apart.

'This is just another barrier you're throwing up.' He put a hand under her chin and forced her to look at him. 'I know you want me, Jess. I can see it in your eyes.'

She stared at him, her eyes wild. 'I don't think it's a good idea, Xander.'

He snorted and pushed himself up to standing, moving away from her. He'd never met anyone so wary about sleeping with him. Perhaps his damn reputation was getting in the way here? She seemed pretty hung up on how he ran his sex life.

'Are you scared of me?'

The question seemed to shock her. Scrambling backwards onto the bed, she curled her arms around her drawn-up legs, staring at him, frowning hard. 'Of course I'm not scared of you.'

'Then what is it?'

'I just don't need any more complications in my life right now.'

'Why does this need to be complicated?'

'I'm not the sort of person that sleeps around for fun, Xander. It's not my thing.'

'How can having a night of hot, meaningless sex with me not be your "thing"?' he said. 'It seems to me you're severely lacking *something*, because you're clearly not happy.'

She frowned hard. 'I don't need sex to be happy.'

He threw her a scathing look.

'I don't,' she said, giving herself away with the wobble in her voice.

'So you're totally fine without any affection, are you? Without allowing yourself the odd night of crazy, random fun, just for the hell of it?'

'Yes.' She tried to push her shoulders back and give it some front but she was obviously too tense to make it work and sank back into her crouch again.

She looked younger, smaller and more vulnerable like that and a sudden raging need to protect her came out of left field. He sat back down on the end of the bed so he wasn't towering above her any more.

'Why did you say you're worried about disappointing me?'

She huffed out a sigh and shook her head. 'Come on, Xander, you know what I'm talking about.'

Twisting onto his knees, he moved up the bed and

slid into the space next to her, close enough to smell the heady scent of her perfume.

'I'm not even *remotely* like the women you usually date.'

'Perhaps that's why I like you so much.'

'You *like* me?'

'Believe it or not, I like your company. You're the most genuine, interesting, *surprising* person I've met in a long time. And correct me if I'm wrong, but I think you've got a thing for me, too, despite your misgivings,' he said, flashing her a grin. He was being totally honest with her here and he hoped to God he hadn't read the situation wrong.

He really wanted this thing between them to grow and develop. She was all he could think about at the moment and he wanted her. Badly.

The corner of her mouth twitched up into a smile. 'Okay, I admit, I like being around you. You can be good fun when you're not trying to trip me up with your *massive ego.*'

The little minx.

Before she could react, he moved towards her, pulling her arms from around her body and hooking one knee over her legs, while simultaneously trapping her wrists against the bed behind her—imprisoning her beneath him.

'Maybe you should let go of that disabling control and do something crazy for once. Just for the hell of it,' he murmured, gazing down at those captivating eyes of hers as he dipped his mouth towards her.

'Wait. Xander.'

He paused midway to her lips and waited for her to finish her sentence, feeling her breath hot and sweet on his skin.

She screwed up her eyes, as if she had to pretend he wasn't there in order to get the words out. 'I don't find it easy to orgasm. I'm too self-aware.' Her cheeks flushed with mortification. 'I'm useless in bed. That's why I'll disappoint you.'

When she opened her eyes, all he could do was stare at her in disbelief. 'Who on earth told you that?'

She looked up at him, barely able to meet his gaze. 'The last guy I had a relationship with. But I've always been unsure of myself where sex is concerned,' she rushed on. 'I don't exactly have a lot of experience.' She looked away from him again, her face pale now.

He stared at her in silence for a moment, feeling inexplicably angry. 'What a jerk.' No wonder she was so afraid of letting him get physical with her. Who said things like that to someone they were meant to care about? Even though he'd never allowed himself to get emotionally close to any of the women he'd slept with, he'd never dream of being so callous and cruel to them. The guy clearly hadn't bothered to get to know Jess very well if he couldn't see how saying something like that to her would destroy her fragile confidence.

'I guess my inability to enjoy sex with him must have fed into his deepest insecurities about not being man enough or something,' she said, looking at him now with shame in her eyes.

'Clearly he *wasn't* man enough.'

She gave him a tentative smile back and something tightened in his chest.

'Yeah. Maybe.'

'Jess, listen, I hear what you're saying, but I don't want to walk away now, leaving you believing you'll never enjoy or be good at sex. Give me the opportunity to change your mind.'

He wanted to give her this—a chance to step out from behind that cloud of doubt that followed her around and to feel the sunshine on her face for once. He knew his strengths and weaknesses, and while he couldn't offer her a hearts-and-flowers relationship, he was more than qualified to show her a good time in the sack.

'You like a challenge, don't you?' she said, the corner of her mouth twitching.

He put a hand up to her face and stroked her cheek with the backs of his fingers.

'Trust me, Jess, you won't regret it.'

Jess stared at him and thought about how much she wanted to let herself have him—have this—and how she needed to start taking risks in her life if she was ever going to start really *living*.

'Tonight doesn't have to mean anything, Jess. Just think of it as a blip in the timeline. A chance to step out of yourself for a few hours. You can button yourself right back up again afterwards if you want.' He shot her a playful grin. 'Give me the chance to prove to you that sex can be more fun than you think.'

Her blood pulsed hard through her veins, the crazy adrenaline rush making her head spin. There was a good chance she'd go loopy if she didn't let this happen. The regret would stay with her till her dying day.

After all, she'd come here determined to get some new experiences out of the trip and he was offering her something incredible—a no-strings night and his heavenly body on a plate.

Her deeply ingrained insecurities waged war with her libido.

She wanted to, but the thought of him seeing her naked terrified her.

'You can't take all my clothes off and it has to be dark,' she stated, wondering if she was pushing things a bit too far. Surely he'd get fed up with it all soon and get up and leave. That was what most men would do.

But Xander wasn't most men.

He raised an eyebrow. 'You're determined to throw every single obstacle in my way, aren't you?' Lifting a hand, he trapped a curl of her hair between his fingers and gave it a gentle tug before wrapping it around her ear. 'It's a good job I relish a challenge.'

He leant across and turned off the lamp next to the bed, plunging the room into darkness.

He wasn't giving her any time to back out.

She felt him shift his position on the bed next to her and wished for a second she hadn't insisted on turning off the light. Suddenly a layer of control had gone. If she couldn't see him, she couldn't pre-empt what he was going to do and stop him.

Man, she was strung out. There was no way he was getting an orgasm out of her tonight. The thought made her even more tense. A vicious circle.

He obviously sensed her growing panic because he laid a hand gently on her foot. 'Jess. Relax. It's going to be okay.' Xander's words twisted through her head and she clung onto the sound of his voice to steady herself.

Pushing herself up onto her elbows, she tried to locate him in the gloom. She could make out the general shape of him, but no details. 'I apologise in advance if it takes me a while to…you know,' she said quickly, before the insecurity won and muted her.

'Don't worry, we have all night.' Her whole body responded to his seductive tone with an intense shiver from her ears right down to her toes. 'Trust me, okay? Just trust me. This is about *you* tonight. I don't want you to worry about me. I want to do this for you. I'm going to enjoy it.'

Oh. My. God.

'Lie back,' he said, skating his hands gently, oh, so gently, up her thighs.

It would be so much easier if she just got up and left right now, but she couldn't do it. Didn't want to. Wouldn't let herself. Not this time.

He had her pinned there with the sheer force of his magnetism.

Moving his hands slowly under her skirt to the apex of her thighs, testing her reaction inch by inch, he eventually encountered her knickers.

Biting down on her lip to stop herself from asking him to stop, Jess allowed him to slide his thumbs inside the leg holes, close, so close to where her body throbbed and buzzed with the heat he'd continually triggered in her ever since she'd arrived here.

Closing her eyes, she raised her hips and let him slide her knickers down her legs, feeling the pads of his fingers trail from the tops of her thighs, right down to her ankles, his touch leaving a burning trail along her skin.

Sucking in a breath, she waited—the anticipation of his next move making her blood pulse hot and fast through her body.

'Tell me what you like, Jess. Where you want to be touched.' His voice rumbled through her.

'I don't know. I don't know what I like,' she whispered, so glad he couldn't see how hard she was blushing. She was amazed he hadn't commented on how hot it was in the room—how she seemed to be giving off more heat than the national grid.

'Okay, let's experiment. You tell me when I'm hitting the right spots.'

Before she had chance to process what he'd said, she felt a movement of air on her legs and the bed dipped underneath her. A second later, his breath tickled the now hypersensitive skin of her inner thigh before he dropped his head to kiss her there, right below the juncture of her thighs.

She jumped in shock at the intimacy of it all, struggling for a second with the realisation of exactly what he was about to do to her. He didn't comment on her reaction, just moved his kisses lower, down towards her knees, as if he realised he'd gone in a bit too hot and heavy. He was reading her body like a pro, shifting his position and the intensity of his kisses depending on how she reacted. He spent a while working his way from the tips of her toes right back to the tops of her thighs, his slow exploration ratcheting up her need to be touched in a way she had no words to describe. They wouldn't come, refusing to allow her to ask for the pleasure she craved.

Seeming to sense her struggle with herself, Xander finally moved higher, between her thighs, then higher again, slowly and so gently, until he hovered over where she ached to be touched, his breath tickling her, teasing her.

He was waiting for her to say the words, to give him permission.

Gripping the bedspread hard between her hands for courage, she screwed up her eyes in concentration and forced the words to leave her throat. 'There. Just there. Yes.' She sounded so guttural, so desperate, it shocked her.

Her reward for finally allowing the words to come

was worth every ounce of effort. He stroked his tongue gently over her and she responded without thinking, raising her pelvis off the bed and pressing herself into him. Clearly taking that as a positive response, he spread his fingers against her thighs, pushing them wider—a gentle flow of movement that made her whole body throb and ache.

He dipped his head to her again and kissed her there hard. 'I love your body, you smell so good, taste so good,' he murmured against the sensitive nub of her clitoris, the vibration upping the intensity of the feeling.

Oh, he *so* knew what he was doing.

He worked his tongue against her, taking long leisurely sweeps, only touching her directly there for a second before moving on.

It was torture. Sweet torture.

Moving his hands up her body, he found the hem of her top and slid his fingers beneath it, finding the hot skin of her stomach. She sucked it in quickly, distracted from the roving path of his tongue for a second.

He sensed her withdrawal and removed his hand, placing it instead under her buttocks, pushing her upwards, harder against his mouth until she forgot all about her insecurities again.

Her breath tore against her throat and she gasped as each stroke of his tongue took her closer, closer than she'd ever been before to an orgasm with someone else.

But she needed more. *Something* more.

As if sensing her hesitation, Xander pulled away from her and she felt him shuffle his way carefully up her body until his dark shadow loomed above her.

'You are easily the sexiest woman I've ever met,' he said in such a guttural voice she felt a jubilant thrill deep in her chest. 'I love how you respond so honestly to me, even when you don't know you're doing it.'

Dropping his head slowly until he found her mouth in the dark, he kissed her gently, skimming his tongue across her lower lip. Moving a hand back between her thighs, he slid his fingers over her swollen folds, parting her there before sliding downwards slowly, so excruciatingly slowly. She gasped against his mouth as his fingers penetrated her, delving deep inside, opening her up to him.

A groan escaped from low in her throat and she instinctively opened her legs wider to give him better access.

His fingers slid deeper, the silkiness of her arousal allowing him easy access, and he pulsed them inside her, finding a spot that made her jump and twist with pleasure when he pressed hard.

Slicking his thumb against her clitoris, he kept up the pressure of his touch, and she moved, unthinking, against it, forcing herself to relax into the moment and just feel.

She wanted to be able to do this. So much. And Xander didn't seem at all concerned about how long it was taking her to get there.

Turning her thoughts away from anything but how he was making her crazy with only the amazing dexterity of those beautiful hands of his, she rode the movement with him, breathing in the enticing tang of his scent as he hovered his mouth above hers, the intensity of it all making her head spin.

Focus, Jess, focus on the pleasure. Find the joy.

As she relaxed into the rhythm of their movement she became aware of a concentrated pressure building inside her where his fingers twisted and pulsed. It started as a slow tingle, steadily growing into a great throbbing spasm, which intensified second after second, keeping her on the edge of reaching something amazing, for what felt like *for ever*.

'Let go, Jess,' Xander whispered against her mouth, the words vibrating on her lips, and suddenly, without warning, the feeling seemed to break and implode inside her, the rush of intensity taking her breath away.

'Whoa…whoa…*whoa*!' She writhed and twitched in ecstasy, completely out of control of her body's movements as a great thundering orgasm twisted through her, emanating from deep inside and radiating out until she felt it to the tips of her fingers. Blood roared through her head, and exquisite pleasure chased around her body as wave after wave of intense sensation flowed through her.

It took her a while to return to reality as she lived through the aftershocks her body seemed intent on throwing at her.

Xander hadn't moved, but now she felt him lean across her, his hard body pressing against the tips of her breasts, his breath tickling her ear. There was a click next to her head and the bedside light flickered on.

He hovered above her with the smuggest smile she'd ever encountered splashed across his handsome face.

She stared up at him in incredulity. 'What did you *do* to me?'

'I found your G spot.' He flopped onto the bed next to her.

'Wow. I've never come like that before,' she said, sitting up and pulling her skirt back down, smoothing her hands over it to flatten it out. She was finding it hard to look at him. All her barriers had been smashed to smithereens and she didn't know how she was supposed to act any more.

'Well, congratulations,' he murmured. Leaning forward, he put a hand to her chin and tipped her face towards him. Quickly closing the gap between them, he kissed her gently on the lips. 'It just takes a bit of patience. I'm guessing the men you've slept with in the past were more interested in their own pleasure than yours.'

She thought back to the last guy she'd slept with. She hadn't liked the way he'd touched her, all urgent and hard, as if he'd wanted to get her pleasure out of the way quickly so he could focus on his own.

'You could say that,' she said. 'The last sexual relationship I had started off as uninspiring and went downhill from there. I ended up faking my orgasms just to get it over with so he'd leave me alone.' Pulling her legs towards her chest, she wrapped her arms around her knees and hugged her legs tightly against her body.

It had been easier to lie to the guy, but she'd felt disappointed and angry with herself afterwards. She knew it was a psychological block she had about relaxing enough to let her body respond how it should and she'd reconciled herself to the belief that she'd never be able to let herself go enough.

Until Xander came along with his dogged determination.

How completely and utterly bizarre the whole situation was. It was as if she'd just tumbled down the rabbit hole and found herself in a new, completely baffling world.

Her expression must have reflected some of her bewilderment because Xander frowned and put a hand on her shoulder. 'Are you okay?'

His show of concern made her chest constrict. He seemed to be genuinely worried about how she was handling it all.

She gave him a smile, which she hoped transmitted more poise than she felt right at that moment. 'I'm fine. Thanks.'

He grinned. 'So it *is* possible for you to orgasm with someone else in the room.'

She snorted and shook her head in amusement at his awe-inspiring confidence. 'Yeah, okay, you were right, apparently you *are* a sex magician.'

'A sex magician.' He smiled. 'I like the way your mind works, Jess.'

She felt light-headed and discombobulated by it all— and suddenly, overwhelmingly tired. A yawn pushed against the back of her throat and she tried in vain to suppress it.

Xander grinned in amusement. 'Okay, I'm going to let you sleep now.'

Before she could say anything he rolled away from her, off the bed and onto his feet in one fluid movement.

'See you in the morning, Jess.' He blew her a kiss. 'Sweet dreams.'

She watched his retreating figure until he'd pulled open the door and disappeared through it, letting it click closed behind him.

She wasn't sure whether to laugh or cry.

Her whole world had been tipped upside down and she felt suddenly very lost and alone and horrifically guilty about not giving him any pleasure back.

No wonder he'd got up and left.

And she didn't know what to do next.

Now she'd allowed her hard-clung-to control to slip

she was in some kind of crazy limbo, not sure which way to turn.

Xander had made it pretty clear he was all about the here and now and that tonight was just a bit of fun for him and she didn't know what to think about that. On the one hand she didn't want that to be it for them— now she'd toppled over the line she wanted more time to explore this brave new world with him—but on the other, she had a horrible feeling she wouldn't be able to be as casual about sex with Xander as he apparently could be with her.

Could she risk it?

If she decided to walk away now and keep her sanity—and quite possibly her heart—intact, she'd need to go first thing in the morning, before things became awkward and uncomfortable for them both.

But could she bring herself to do that?

Based on his reputation she'd be a fool to think anything long-term could come out of this, but, damn it, she couldn't just walk away now, leaving things hanging between them.

She wanted more.

Flopping back onto the pillows, she rubbed a hand over her drowsy eyes.

Sleep, that was what she needed right now. The crazy whirl of emotions had exhausted her and she could barely think straight any more.

Yes, sleep now.

There would be time for decisions in the morning.

Xander paced around his bedroom, weirdly adrenalised from the effort of walking away from Jess when all he'd wanted to do was bury himself inside her and stay there all night.

To lose himself in her.

Giving his face a vigorous rub to get the blood flowing, he stared at his eyes in the mirror and tried to pull himself together.

He'd never done that before—put someone else's needs before his own—and he was amazed by just how fantastic it felt. He was making a positive difference to her life, helping her find something she'd been missing for too long, and the thought of it warmed him.

Xander Heaton, Sex Therapist. Who'd have thought it possible?

It had been hell on earth to walk away, but he was glad he'd done it. He could see they needed to take things slowly so she could keep some vestige of control. Judging by the way she'd closed herself up again afterwards, she evidently needed space away from him now.

So did he if he was honest.

He couldn't put his finger on exactly why he felt so unsettled by what had just happened between them, but it unnerved him something crazy.

Perhaps it was because he liked her so much. The lovers he'd had in the past had been very sexy, engaging women, but he'd never enjoyed being with them the way he enjoyed being around Jess. There were so many layers to her that he got the feeling he might never get to the heart of who she was.

She fascinated him.

And he was having *fun*. He seemed able to push away the anxiety that had plagued him for the last year when she was around.

She calmed him—and he needed that right now. It would be good for him to have her company here while he worked on his exhibition.

He just needed to find a way to persuade her to stay.

CHAPTER SEVEN

JESS SLEPT BADLY, despite her exhaustion, trying like mad to put the thought of what had happened with Xander out of her mind until the morning.

She failed spectacularly, of course. He was all she could think about.

He'd made her feel like the most important, fascinating, *sexy* woman on earth for those few short hours and she knew she wanted that feeling back, *so desperately*. She could almost taste the tang of need like a physical reaction in her taste buds.

The fact he'd seemed to genuinely find her a turn-on had helped something begin to shift in her head. It wasn't as though she suddenly felt like throwing off all her clothes and running around in the nude, but his gentle attentions and the stream of compliments had made her start to think about her body in a different way.

Rolling out of bed, she walked over to the cheval mirror in the corner and stood naked in front of it. For the first time in a very long time she looked at herself—*really* looked—studying the places he'd mentioned he liked so much, running her fingers over the dips and swells of her figure and tracing the lines of the muscles that delineated her body.

She was surprised by how different she felt this

morning, after finally allowing herself to release the brakes on her control and discovering that the earth hadn't crashed around her ears. It was as if she'd uncovered something new and secret and hidden about herself, after all these years.

Something that Xander had seen all along.

After showering, she dressed quickly, her body humming with a strange excitement.

She needed to see Xander, if for no other reason than to prove to herself he was real and she hadn't just dreamt it all up.

He was in his studio, stripped to the waist and engrossed in what he was painting on a large canvas. There was a dark smudge of paint on his left cheek, as if he'd absent-mindedly swiped at his face with dirty hands as a child would.

There was something so pure and human about that, something that made her chest contract with acute sadness for him. He was alone in the world and carrying around such a heavy load of pain and anger it made her want to cry. No wonder he couldn't settle down if he'd never known what it felt like to be loved. She so desperately wanted to show him how it could feel, but she was terrified she wasn't strong enough or bright enough or alive enough to get through to him.

Was she brave enough to at least give it a try?

She still hadn't figured out what she was going to write about him for the magazine. That really ought to be her top priority, *not* working out how to get him into her bed, but she couldn't think about that right now, not when Xander was standing in front of her looking like all her best birthdays rolled into one.

Her heart raged in her chest as she realised this was her opportunity to ask for what she really wanted. To make love to him. Feel him move inside her. Breathe in the clean scent of his skin and slide against him, over and over again until they were breathless. Something she'd been aching for all night.

No, strike that, since the first moment she'd set eyes on him at his studio in London.

As she walked towards him he looked round at her and gave her a tentative smile as if he wasn't sure how he should act around her today. 'Good morning,' he said, his voice low and sweet.

Without saying a word, she put out a shaking hand and pressed it against the rock-hard muscles of his chest and felt his sharp intake of breath. Encouraged that he hadn't slapped her hand away, she took a step closer to him and forced herself to look up into his face.

He stared down at her with an open, questioning look in his eyes. Summoning all her courage, she pushed up on her tiptoes and leant in towards him, her lips tingling in readiness for the feel of his mouth against hers.

His breath was coming out in shortened gasps and she felt it whisper against her skin for a moment before their lips connected.

A low, almost animal sound came from deep within his chest as she slipped her tongue against the ridge of his teeth. Opening his mouth against her tentative invasion, he flexed his tongue against hers and she tasted the sweetness of him, her body reacting immediately to a desperate need to be enfolded in his arms and held close.

He let her take control as she slid her fingers into his hair and drew him even closer. Leaning into him, she felt the solid ridge of his body press against her from pelvis to chest.

He wanted her, she noted with a breathless sort of glee—she could feel it in the tension of his muscles and, more to the point, in the hard bulge at the front of his trousers.

With shaking hands, she fumbled with his belt, her clumsy fingers making slow work of unbuckling it.

She didn't allow herself to stop to think about what she was doing. She couldn't. If she let anything other than her determination to feel him inside her flit through her head she'd stall and the moment would be lost for ever. And that meant never being able to have what she so badly wanted.

To indulge her fantasies for once in her life.

To let go of her anxiety and just take what she wanted.

And she wanted this. So much it hurt.

She was *going* to take it and decorum be damned.

The buckle finally came apart and she popped the button on the front of his trousers and slid her hand inside them, under his underwear, until she found the hardness of him. She drew away and looked up into his face.

His eyes were hazy with a need she felt sure must be reflected in her own.

'Don't stop,' he growled, his voice so low she could barely make out the words.

Wrapping her hand around the length of him, she moved her fingers from base to tip, catching the velvety soft head with her thumb and feeling the slickness of his arousal coat her fingertips.

'Ah, hell, Jess, that feels so good.' His fingers wound into her hair, pulling her mouth towards him and kissing her so thoroughly she thought she might die from the pleasure of it.

His hands skimmed beneath the hem of her dress and slid up her thighs, his fingers tugging at the elastic of her knickers so hard she felt it ping and give as the seam ripped and the scrap of material fell to the floor.

'Oops, sorry,' Xander said against her mouth, not sounding in the least bit sincere.

She giggled as he kissed across her cheek and gently tickled the sensitive whorl of her ear with his tongue, but soon stopped as she felt his fingers find the slick heat between her legs.

Pressing against his hand, she felt the beginnings of an orgasm stir deep in her pelvis and the need to have the hard length of him inside her grew even more intense. She'd been picturing this situation in her head all night and now that the possibility it might actually happen had arisen she could barely wait. She felt greedy for it.

'Xander...'

'Yeah,' he groaned, as if sensing she was about to cut their encounter short and readying himself to be a gentleman about it.

'Do you still want me hard and fast against the wall?' she asked, forcing herself to look him directly in the eye. If this was the last chance she was going to get to test out just how brazen she could push herself to be, she wanted to go all the way.

'Hell, yeah,' he breathed in relief, reaching a hand round to grab his wallet out of the back pocket of his trousers. Releasing his hold on her, he located a condom before dropping the wallet onto the floor next to them.

He didn't move his gaze away from hers as he waited for her to step back so he could strip off his clothes.

She'd never seen anyone get undressed so fast.

He stood there naked in front of her, the heat of his body radiating outwards, warming her skin with its fiery intensity. Taking a deep breath, she allowed her gaze to travel down the magnificence of him, taking in every beautiful dip and curve.

Her gaze returned to his and locked for a moment as he checked with her silently that she really wanted this.

'Yes,' she said, and he gave her a smile of such unadulterated pleasure she nearly came on the spot.

He took a moment to sort out the condom, before returning his gaze to hers, his eyebrow raised in a seductive challenge.

'You ready for me, Jess?'

'As I'll ever be,' she replied, suddenly horrendously shy about what was about to happen. But before she had time to dwell on it, he stepped forward, and, putting a hand on each of her upper arms, walked her backwards until her shoulders slammed against the wall. His mouth came down on hers immediately and she was lost in an electric storm of need, her body throbbing with want, want, *want*.

His body enveloped hers, pressing into her with a power she'd never experienced before. She *knew* she was wanted because she could *feel* it in him.

His hands raked up under her skirt again, bunching it up around her waist, exposing her to his exploring fingers. He moved them against her, then inside her until she thought she'd go crazy with it, bringing his mouth hard down onto hers at the same time, the dual stimulation sending her senses into overdrive.

She was so on the edge it wasn't funny.

'Now, Xander, I want…' she gasped.

He waited a moment for her to continue, then stilled his movement until she looked back into his eyes. 'Tell me what you want, Jess.'

'I want you. Inside me.' The words left her lips as though they'd been primed and were just waiting for the opportunity to finally be said. It was easy, so easy now she'd given herself permission not to care about anything other than what was happening between them at that moment.

He didn't need anything more from her. Sliding a hand down the inside of her thigh, he hooked his wrist under her leg and drew it up against his waist. The rigid tip of his erection penetrated the slick opening to her a second later, and she gasped with pleasure as he slowly slid inside her.

They began to move together, Xander pressing her hard into the wall to support them both as he thrust, filling her completely and hitting a sweet spot over and over as their bodies crashed together. They kissed hard, their mouths swollen and hungry as their tongues delved, tasting each other. Grasping the buttoned-down front of her dress, Xander pulled it apart hard, ripping the delicate buttons away from the material so they pinged and bounced across the room. The material gaped at the front, exposing her breasts, encased in the lacy bra she'd chosen to wear on a whim that morning and she didn't even think to react as he pushed aside the cups to expose the hard peaks of her nipples to his searching fingers.

Jess thought she might go crazy from the pulsing heat between her legs and the gentle rasp of Xander's touch on her exposed nipples. But she wasn't there yet; it wasn't quite enough.

'Xander…I need… I need…'

Seeming to sense her frustration, he dipped his hand between their bodies, sliding the pad of his fingertip against her clitoris, mimicking the movement of his thrusts inside her.

Gripping the bulk of his shoulders for support, Jess

closed her eyes and allowed the delicious friction to build and intensify, sending waves of exquisite pleasure radiating out from deep within the centre of her, teetering on the edge of an orgasm for utterly crazed moments, before finally breaking into a rush of the most intense pleasure she'd ever experienced. A low guttural moan grew from the base of her throat and vibrated in the air around them as she totally lost control.

It only took Xander a couple more thrusts before he joined her in her electric ecstasy, pounding into her hard as he came, his breath hot and fast on her neck as he surged into her.

They remained like that for a while, both gasping for breath as they came back down to earth.

Finally able to relax her fingers enough to release her grip on his shoulders, Jess put her palms against his chest and pushed gently until he dipped and slid out of her. He took a step away so she could put both feet back on the ground.

They stood and looked at each other for a beat, their breathing still low and rough from their exertions, before they pulled themselves together.

Xander disposed of the condom while she readjusted her clothes, trying in vain to reclose the top of her dress where it now gaped open after his callous treatment of it.

'You owe me a dress,' she said, raising a mock-stern eyebrow.

He laughed. 'I think it looks better like that.' He ran a hand over her hair, smoothing it against her head. 'Let's lie down before we fall down,' he said, cocking a suggestive eyebrow. Taking her hand, he led her out of the studio and into his room.

He flopped down onto the bed, pulling her down

next to him, his naked body gleaming in the soft, late-morning light.

She couldn't tear her eyes away from the magnificent strength of him as he lay stretched out next to her. Her gaze raked him from head to toe, only snagging momentarily on the deep V where his hips joined his body, and lower...

He raised a questioning eyebrow as their gazes met again and she tried in vain to quell the rush of heat that travelled up her neck to burn her cheeks.

'Like what you see, Jess?'

'Absolutely,' she said, brazening it out. 'I can barely believe I've just "made it" with the third sexiest man in England,' she said, giving him a wide grin.

'Now do you believe the hype?' Xander joked, one discerning eyebrow raised. He nodded down to where the source of her most recent pleasure lay nestled against his thigh.

'Well, I guess there is some truth to those rumours.'

'You're very kind.' He chuckled, giving her such a sexy, playful look she wanted to lock him up and keep him all for herself for ever.

They lay together, limbs wrapped around each other, drowsy and sated in the growing heat of the morning.

Xander shifted onto his side, propping himself up onto one elbow. 'Why don't you stay on a while longer? It seems a shame to cut things short now when there's so much fun still to be had.' He raised a provocative eyebrow. 'I'm going to need *something* fun to do after a gruelling day of being all artistic.'

'*Something* fun to do?'

'Okay, some*one* fun to do.' He grinned.

Her heart hammered hard against her chest as she realised he was actually serious. 'I don't know, Xander—won't you need to concentrate on your exhibition?'

'Not in the evenings.'

Where had this sudden panicky feeling come from? She'd been all right brazening this out when she'd thought it would be a one-off and she'd be back home the following day, before she had chance to get too attached.

'I don't think I can. Pamela, the editor at the magazine I work for, is expecting me back at work tomorrow.'

'Can't you tell them you're ill or something? I'm sure she can cope without you for one more week.'

There was a weird rushing in her head that was making it hard for her to concentrate. 'I can't do that. What if she finds out I'm lying? I'll lose my job.'

'How would she find out if you're stuck in Italy, unable to travel? It's not as if she's going to jump on a plane with a cold compress and a bowl of chicken soup.'

Her heart was beating so fast she felt sure he must be able to see it pulsing against her chest. 'I don't feel comfortable with lying, Xander.'

'Don't you think you deserve some fun? Why are you so hard on yourself? It's like you don't believe you deserve to be happy or something.'

She sighed, rubbing a hand over her face.

He was right. She was a mess.

'I don't know why—I've always been like that. I have a highly developed guilty conscience and I get over-anxious about things sometimes. My mum always made me feel like it'd be the end of the world if I did anything to show her up and I guess it's just stuck around in my psyche. She expected perfection and I failed to deliver.'

He gave her a puzzled frown.

'I know, it's weird. Not something most people can understand.'

'Well, I think it's about time you came and joined me on the dark side.'

She laughed and shook her head. 'Why are you so intent on corrupting me?'

'Because it's fun to see you coming to pieces.' He ran a finger from the deep hollow in the base of her neck, down between her partly exposed breasts to where her belly button lay hidden beneath the cotton of her dress. 'Especially when I'm the one that gets to make you come.'

She put her hand over his, stopping him from continuing his path.

He closed his eyes and took a breath. 'Look, I'm not going to pressure you into this. If you don't want to stay, that's fine, but you should consider doing something wild and totally selfish, just for once.' He rolled away from her and got up, pulling on a pair of trousers. God, he looked sexy, half dressed like that with his hair all mussed and falling over his eyes.

Dishevelled and dangerous.

She suddenly wanted to stay. So much.

'I have to go and speak to my agent about the arrangements for the exhibition. Come and find me if you change your mind.'

He gave her one last heated look before turning and leaving the room, pulling the door closed behind him.

The ensuing silence of the room filled her head until she thought she'd go crazy with it.

The thought of never seeing him again left her feeling empty. Totally and utterly empty. He was right: she should allow herself to do something completely crazy for once. She was sick and tired of worrying about doing the right thing all the time. After all, Pamela said she needed to *live a little* if she was going to become a better writer.

Returning to her bedroom, she retrieved her mobile phone from the nightstand, readying herself to put on her most ill-sounding voice, and called through to the magazine.

'Pamela Bradley.'

Just the sound of her editor's voice made her stomach twitch with nerves.

'Hi, Pamela, it's Jess.'

'Jess, are you on your way back?'

She took a deep, steadying breath. 'Er, actually, I think I've picked up that flu that was going around the office before I left for Italy.' She gave a fake cough, willing Pam to believe her. She was so nervous about lying her palms were sweaty and her body felt hot and tingly. She'd never played hooky in her life and it made her really uncomfortable to lie like this, but the draw of spending a little more time with Xander fortified her.

'I can work on the story from my bed,' she rushed on into Pam's silence, feeling her cheeks flame as guilt swept through her. 'I only need a few more days to get it nailed down, then I'll email it over. You're going to love it, Pam. He's such an interesting subject to write about,' she said, inordinately relieved Pamela couldn't see how red her face was.

Liar, liar, pants on fire couldn't have been more appropriate at that moment.

There was a long pause, then a sigh. 'Okay, Jess, but make sure you hit your deadline. I need this piece in on time otherwise you're going to find yourself right at the top of the redundancy recommendation list.'

Jess swallowed hard. 'Okay, Pamela, I'll get it to you on time, I promise.'

She cut the call and put her phone carefully back onto the nightstand, feeling something she hadn't felt since childhood.

Naughty.

She'd never even contemplated playing hooky before she met Xander—never lied to get what she wanted. Even the thought of doing something so against the rules she lived by would have given her the heebie-jeebies before she met him, but now she'd crossed the line she was amazed by how enlightened she felt. How alive. As if her sluggish blood had woken up and decided to have a drag race around her body.

She guessed it was something to do with endorphins, this crazy recklessness, some mad chemical reaction. It was certainly like a drug, this throbbing, screaming urge to break out of her normal, dull existence and do something crazy for once.

Her usual control seemed to have abandoned her, at least for a short while, and she felt buzzed and high on life, as if there was a world of possibility out there for her—something that had hidden from her conscious-ness up until this point, something that had only ever happened to other people.

Xander had unearthed a part of herself she never knew was there. She wasn't sensible, dependable, un-remarkable Jess when she was with him; she was ex-citing, stimulating, *wild*.

She was out of breath when she returned to Xander's studio. He opened the door with an expectant smile.

'I don't have anything planned for the next week,' she gasped. 'So I'm all yours.'

He grinned. 'All mine. I like the sound of that.'

CHAPTER EIGHT

THEY SPENT THE first couple of days in and out of bed together, taking time out for a couple of hours here and there so that Xander could squirrel away in his studio to work on the exhibition and Jess could explore more of Lake Garda, gathering information for her holiday piece.

Each time they made love, Jess would allow him to reveal a little more of her body until she was almost comfortable with him seeing her naked.

It was a revelation.

The whole thing was also a huge step away from reality—something Jess had to keep forcibly reminding herself about.

Every now and again a little bubble of hope that they could turn this fling into something more rose in her chest and she'd have to stamp on it hard to stop herself from getting carried away with the idea.

She needed to keep this thing in perspective. It *wasn't* real and she was going to have to wake up soon and rejoin the real world. This was a holiday from life, pure and simple.

Attaching any kind of emotion to it would be an utter disaster.

* * *

Partway into the week, Jess woke to find Xander had got up before her for once. After getting dressed and grabbing some breakfast, which Rosa served out on the veranda, she went looking for him.

The sun was already beating down and she wanted to go for a swim in the lake and hoped she might be able to persuade him to go with her.

He was in his studio, flinging paint from a brush onto a large canvas on the floor. More tarp-covered canvases were propped up against all four walls and his art table was laden with tubes of paint and sketch pads. She wondered what she would see if she peeked underneath the tarpaulins. He'd refused to let her look at what he was working on, saying he never let anyone see an unfinished painting, and she was slightly nervous about whether he'd used any of the sketches of her.

'Will you come for a swim? It's so hot today,' she said, moving closer to the art table and glancing down to see if she could see whether any of his sketch pads were open.

They weren't.

'Not right now. I'm in the middle of this. You go.'

He turned away again, and swiped at the canvas, already lost in his secret little world. The rejection stung. Was she really going to let him get away with ignoring her like that?

No. She certainly wasn't.

Picking up a paintbrush from the table, she dipped it in a discarded palette of rich, purple paint. It was gloopy enough to hang onto the brush for a second or two before dripping back down into the pool of shiny, slick liquid. Turning back to him, she raised the brush to ear level, then brought it forward quickly, flicking the paint towards him. It landed with a splatter against his golden skin, a line of dots making their unsubtle way from his shoulder blade to his hip.

He swivelled round and looked at her, startled. 'What the hell was that?' he said, raising a challenging eyebrow.

She grinned. 'I thought I'd paint you for a change. You look good in purple, but then you look good in everything.'

He huffed out a laugh before turning back to his easel.

Outraged at his snubbing, she moved round so she was standing facing him, just behind the easel. She flicked another splodge of paint, which caught him on his chest this time, right above his nipple.

His eyebrows shot up as he lifted his head slowly to look at her again. 'Are you sure you want to start a paint fight with me, Miss Prim? How will you ever cope with getting paint on your perfectly clean and pressed clothes?'

'You wouldn't dare,' she teased, delighted she'd been able to capture his attention.

'You're playing a dangerous game, Jess. Don't think I won't retaliate. I have a whole palette of colours here with your name on it. Just try it one more time.'

She gave him a slow, taunting smile, her blood pumping fast through her veins as an urge to see exactly what he had planned caught her by the throat.

Her hand quivered by her side.

She really should put the paintbrush down and go for a walk or something to relieve this crazy impulse to keep pushing him. It was madness, this whole thing.

He was watching her, his eyes narrowed with suspicion. Anticipating her next move.

Did she dare?

Yes, she did.

Turning back to the table, she loaded up the brush with paint again, then twisted back, holding it aloft.

'Je-e-ess.' Xander's voice was low with warning, but she caught the lilt of amusement.

The look in his eye made her insides flip, but some craziness compelled her to bring back her hand and let the paint fly through the air in his direction.

This time he dodged it and it sailed past him, splattering the floor behind where he stood.

With a dangerously predatory grin, he advanced towards her, loaded paintbrush held aloft.

Adrenaline-fuelled blood pumped through her as her fight-or-flight instinct kicked in. In her real life she'd be putting her hand up to stop this right now, to save her clothes as well as her pride, but this time she didn't want it to stop. She wanted to experience the heady rush of excitement as she let whatever might happen happen. She ached to feel his hands on her, his body pressed close to hers again, their skin slippery and messy with paint.

Where had this wild abandon come from? She hardly recognised herself.

He was almost upon her now, his bright aqua gaze trained on her face.

'No, no, Xander, wait,' she stuttered, feigning fright.

'What's the matter, Jess—can't stand to get down and dirty with me?'

She took the opportunity in his pause to tease her to sneak in another crafty flick of her brush, sending the paint higher this time so it landed squarely across his nose and cheeks.

He stared at her in utter disbelief for a nanosecond,

before letting out a low growl and flicking his own brush at her over and over again, covering her T-shirt, her jeans and her hair in bright magenta paint.

Tipping back his head, he laughed at the mock horror on her face. 'You look good in hot-pink, Jess. You should wear it more often.' He took a step towards her and her stomach did a slow roll with excitement. 'But I have to say, I think you'd look a lot better in just the paint.'

She held his gaze as he stared her down, the dare behind his words overt in his expression.

'Okay.' Before she lost her nerve, she pulled the ruined T-shirt up over her head and dropped it on the floor next to her.

Xander's brows shot up in surprise. 'What's this? Not going feral on me, are you?' he asked, his voice catching as she reached round and unhooked her bra with shaking fingers, letting it fall to the ground beside her. Closing her eyes, she willed her erratic breathing to normalise. She could swear she felt the heat of his gaze sweeping her upper body, taking in the fullness of her breasts and the hard jut of her nipples as she stood there in front of him.

Totally exposed.

Totally vulnerable.

Something cool and soft swept over her left breast and she gasped in shock at the alien sensation.

Snapping open her eyes, she saw that Xander was running the tip of his paintbrush over her skin, circling the bud of her nipple in slow, seductive strokes. She shivered with pleasure as he flicked it upwards, then began to make wider sweeping circles around her breasts.

Her skin felt so sensitive she trembled every time he moved his brush to a new area.

Without moving his gaze from her face, Xander backed away to where his easel stood propped up in the middle of the room. Reaching down, he grabbed his palette loaded with paint and walked back to where she stood.

By now she was shaking with nerves, but she made herself stand there, rooted to the spot, unflinching as he tested her nerve.

Without saying a word, he unpopped the buttons of her jeans with his spare hand and slid them down her legs until they pooled in a heap at her feet. Next, he slipped his cool fingers into the waistband of her knickers and slid those down, too, with slow, excruciating care, until she stood naked before him.

His gaze glided up and down her body and she shifted on her feet, but steadfastly kept her arms at her sides, allowing him to look.

'Beautiful,' he murmured, his voice low and deep.

He covered her body in paint, keeping his strokes long and slow until she thought she'd go crazy with it. She wanted to feel him, sliding against her skin, the paint lubricating their movement, so she reached for him, pulling his T-shirt over his head, and he helped her undress him, casting off the remainder of his clothes.

After slicking her hands over her paint-covered body, she pressed them against his chest, leaving a stark handprint over each pec, delighting in his sharp intake of breath as she then swiped her palms over and over his nipples. Looking up into his handsome face, she caught his eye and grinned, then swiped more paint across his stomach and down his arms, laughing at his comical expression, until he stopped her by pulling her close and kissing her hard, skin sliding against skin, making a sucking sound as they came apart and pressed back together.

Jess laughed in glee. 'You're going to have to come for a swim now to wash all this off.'

Xander raised an eyebrow. 'Later,' he said, his voice seductively low. 'Once we've explored just how dirty we can get.'

Xander woke early again the next day and got up to see the sun rising on the other side of the lake, spreading its soft rays across the water and tipping the buildings with a warm honey-coloured glow.

Looking back at the bed where Jess lay, the sheet barely covering her naked body, he felt a harmony he hadn't experienced in a very long time. She looked so peaceful, so content, so relaxed for once.

Moving quietly over to the bed so as not to wake her, he tugged gently on the sheet until it slipped off her, revealing her beautiful, voluptuous form in all its glory.

He could only just make out the profile of her face in the gentle glow of the morning light. Her arms and legs lay splayed towards each corner of the bed as if she'd been tied down, her spirit trapped in the amazing body she'd loathed so much. As he moved towards her his tired eyes played tricks on him in the low-level light and a double image of her appeared in his vision, as if that fighting spirit of hers had risen like a dark angel from where she lay trapped and was hovering above her body.

He had a moment of pure, clear inspiration as his imagination twisted the image so her spirit was floating above her fully clothed and trapped human form as she lay bound to the bed.

It was the final image he needed for the exhibition.

A picture of her naked spirit, stripped of all her inhibitions. Beautiful and real and breaking free.

Hands shaking, he picked up his sketch pad and pencil, sat in the chair at the end of the bed and began to draw.

In that moment, he wanted things to stay like this for ever, but he knew, with a sinking feeling in his chest, that life wasn't like that—he wasn't like that—and when the time came for her to leave he would say goodbye without putting up a fight.

He really needed to pull himself together and focus his attention on finishing his pictures for the exhibition now or he was never going to hit his deadline. He couldn't go on the way he was, unfocused and unprofessional, or it would be the end of his career as an artist. People would forget about him, and he really couldn't allow that to happen.

The thought of running out of money and having to work a real job again, like the soul-destroying ones he'd done to stay alive as a teenager, filled him with cold dread. He was terrified by the idea of not feeling special or revered any more—of being ordinary again.

He couldn't let this thing with Jess get in the way. Whatever had happened between them didn't feel like the usual artist-muse relationship, and it made him uneasy. This fling with her had rejuvenated him but he needed to step away from it now.

This was the beginning of the end.

On their last morning together, he sketched her as she sat on the terrace sipping a cup of coffee, looking out across the lake. She looked so beautiful—her amazingly expressive face alive with the vitality that had first drawn her to him. She seemed like a different woman from the one he'd met only a couple of weeks ago. She was taller, brighter and somehow more real.

She'd found her joy.

When she turned and smiled back at him, her perfect white teeth flashed between her lips. Even her smile was more relaxed since he'd first met her.

Was that because of him?

He felt a swell of pride at the thought. He'd never made anyone *less* stressed before.

The intimacy of the atmosphere tugged at his chest. The thought that this was just a fleeting moment in his life made him clench his jaw, and a low throb began to beat in his temple. Why did that bother him so much? What was this feeling? He wasn't entirely sure. He'd never experienced it before, but he sure as hell didn't like it.

He'd been bored and frustrated when he'd asked Jess to come to Italy. It had been a spur-of-the-moment thing—just for kicks—but he'd underestimated her ability to get into his head. To find out what it was that drove him. To discover his deepest, darkest secrets. And he'd let her probe and push until all the bad memories that he'd buried for so long had begun to rise to the surface.

He didn't want to feel like this. After spending the majority of his life pushing that anxiety and fear of rejection away, he didn't want to have to face it now. He wanted things to stay the way they were: light and free and easy.

He realised she was staring at him in confusion now and he adjusted the scowl on his face into a smile.

The apprehensive expression in her eyes made him wonder what she was thinking, but he didn't want to ask. Didn't want to know. Ignorance was bliss.

In retrospect, it had been a crazy move to ask a journalist to come and stay, then invite her into his bed. Of course she was going to push and push at his defences until she found a crack to get her nails into.

It was her job.

He needed to remind himself of that.

She shifted in her chair, putting her coffee cup down onto the table with a shaky hand. 'I guess I should go and write my article. Pamela's going to kick my butt if I send it in late and I haven't even started it yet,' she said, awkwardly rising from her seat so that she banged her leg on the table.

Was she feeling the same tension that he was?

He shrugged off his concern and nodded at her stiffly. 'Okay. See you later.'

Jess sat in the middle of the bed with all her notes spread around her. She was hyperaware that this was the last day they had together, but she had to get this article written. This was why she'd come here, after all.

Xander had seemed to become increasingly distanced from her over the last couple of days, which had unsettled her, and she'd thought the best thing to do right now was to get away from the intensity of their situation for a while and try and get her head straight.

This piece on Xander had to be the very best thing she'd ever written or there was a very good chance she'd be booted off the magazine as soon as she got back.

As she scanned over and over all the notes she'd written since she'd arrived a stultifying fear started to grip her. What if she couldn't do it? The words began to blur together and the more she read, the more panicked she got.

After about half an hour of trying and failing to write

one single usable sentence, she gathered up every piece of paper, shuffled them into one tidy sheaf, then threw them across the room in frustration.

She watched as they floated down like overlarge snowflakes and settled onto the cold, tiled floor.

This was ridiculous. How the hell was she ever going to be able to write a thing? Closing her eyes, she took a moment to think back over the time she'd spent here with Xander, about his passion and fears, and his determination not to be beaten down by them and finally how he'd made her feel by including her in his life. How he'd brought out a side of her she'd never known was there.

A deep, bolstering warmth pulsed through her.

Pulling her laptop towards her, she let her fingers move over the keyboard, writing whatever came into her head without letting conscious thought intrude, without giving in to her fear about whether what she was writing was any good or not. Instead, she concentrated on how Xander made her feel about herself.

And the words began to flow. It was as if she'd finally keyed into something—opened a previously locked door in her brain; now all these intense thoughts and feelings, which she'd been suppressing for so long, began firing round her brain.

She wrote and wrote and edited and wrote some more until there it was—the best thing she'd ever written. Reading it back, she had tears in her eyes. It had warmth and humour and, best of all, fire and life. She knew in her gut that Pamela was going to love it—that it might just save her career.

She also knew without a doubt that she was totally and utterly in love with Xander.

And that she'd failed to follow the most basic rule

of all: don't fall for a guy who's incapable of loving you back.

Somewhere in the back of her brain she'd harboured the hope that the time they'd spent together had meant more to him than any of his previous nonrelationships, and that this time he wanted more.

That he wanted her as she wanted him.

But she knew she was kidding herself—just look at how detached he'd been with her this morning. This relationship was only ever a temporary thing for him. For both of them. A whimsy, a folly, a lark.

What had he called it?

A blip in their timeline.

He'd made that very clear.

She had to pull herself together.

Not giving herself time to fuss and start fiddling with a word here and a word there, she attached the document she'd just written to an email to Pam and hit send, and it was gone—her future—off into the ether.

Her time here was finished.

All she had to do now was say goodbye.

Feeling as if her feet were made of lead, she searched the house for Xander, finding him painting madly away in his studio, in what seemed to have become his usual zoned-out state over the last couple of days. She watched him for a few minutes, taking in the graceful fluidity of his movements as he swiped his brush across the canvas. He was frowning hard in concentration, his handsome face shuttered and drawn as he poured his soul onto the canvas.

He barely glanced up as she moved into the room.

She understood his utter absorption in what he was doing—she'd felt the same about her writing—and it was amazing to see him in such a frenzy of excited activity after being so agitated about not being able to make the magic happen before now. She liked to think she had something to do with that, in some small way.

Finally, he glanced up from what he was doing and noticed her standing there.

'Hey, Jess, how long have you been there?'

'Only a couple of minutes,' she said quietly.

He nodded distractedly. 'The exhibition's taking shape. It's all coming together.' The look in his eye was almost manic.

'Well, I'm really pleased for you,' she managed to force past the lump in her throat.

'Jess?' He was looking at her as if he was worried she was about to cry—which was pretty much on the money.

Pull yourself together, woman.

She didn't want him to see how upset she was about the inevitable end of their time together.

Glancing away, she smoothed her hair down against her head and fought against the growing tension in the back of her throat. She couldn't look at him any more. If she did he'd see just how much she was struggling to keep it together.

'I finished my article,' she said, attempting to keep the misery out of her voice.

'Oh, yeah?' He looked at her, his eyes blank, his mind obviously still on his painting.

'Don't worry, I gave you a good write-up and I didn't include anything too salacious.'

He smiled. 'Great, that's great, Jess. Congratulations.'

He looked back at his painting as if he'd said all there was to say.

She was being dismissed.

So this was it, then. The end of the affair.

'Okay, then, I guess I'd better let you get on with finishing your picture. Will you let me know when you're exhibiting? I'll leave my contact details on the hall table. I'd love to finally get to see what you've been working so hard on.'

He looked up at her again, the hazy look in his eyes clearing as if her words had finally penetrated through to his brain.

'Hell, Jess, sorry, I was right in the middle of a thought here. Yes, of course I'll let you know.'

There was a steely look in his eye now, as if he'd hardened himself against her.

A hot wave of despair crashed over her.

She needed to get out of there before she made a fool of herself and did something stupid and crass like asking him to be her *boyfriend*.

'Okay, then. Well, it's been a blast. Good luck.' Without waiting for a response, she turned on her heel and walked away from him, before he could see how much she wanted him to ask her not to go.

All the way through packing her suitcase she wondered whether he'd come and stop her.

As she walked down the corridor, then out of the villa, then got into her car, with her heart hammering against her chest, she wondered whether he'd come running up at the last moment and say, 'I want you to stay.'

Then as she drove the car slowly out of the driveway and crept down the lane to the main road, her breath short and a hard pressure behind her eyes, just waiting to spill over into tears, she wondered whether she'd see him in her rear-view mirror, running after her car.

But she didn't.

He wasn't coming. He was letting her go.

CHAPTER NINE

XANDER SPENT THE next couple of days trying to convince himself it was a good thing that Jess had gone. He needed to concentrate on getting the paintings finished and having her around would have been disruptive.

But he couldn't convince himself.

The loneliness bit at him, sinking its teeth deep and leaving him on edge and distracted.

After a couple more days of failing to summon the energy to finish the final painting he decided that Italy and seclusion weren't working for him any more. He needed sparkiness and life again and that meant going back to London.

As soon as he arrived back he went straight out to a party some friends were holding at a bar in Sloane Square, expecting the buzz of the city to perk him back up, but it didn't work.

He felt tired and drained and ended up going home unfashionably early, telling his friends it was because he'd expended so much energy on his art recently, but even as the words left his mouth he knew that wasn't the real reason. Normally when he was excited about a piece of art he was working on he was full of adrenaline—wanting to talk about it with everyone he met—but he felt protective about this exhibition for some reason.

He couldn't quite put his finger on why.

Jess had returned to London in a state of bewildered confusion.

Walking back into the buzz of the *Spark* office had been a shock to the system after the peace and tranquillity of Lake Garda and it took her a few days to get back up to speed with the London pace of life.

To her annoyance she'd found Pamela was off sick with the flu when she first arrived back and so hadn't even looked at the piece she'd written yet—perhaps it was karma catching up with her for playing hooky. The thought that she could have stayed for a couple more days with Xander flittered through her mind, but she knew that would have only prolonged the anxiety of having to say goodbye.

Despite her determination to get over Xander and move on with her life, she was having an awfully hard time getting him out of her head.

Spending time with him had been life-changing—letting loose without the fear of being judged had excited her more than she'd ever felt possible and she'd loved being touched and explored and worshipped, and having his delighted permission to do the same back to him. He'd woken something inside her that had been slumbering for years.

For the first time in her life she'd felt desired, sexy. Beautiful.

She found she was walking around now with her head held higher, making herself look at the world around her instead of staring down at the floor as she had before she'd met him. He'd opened up a whole world of possibility in her mind. Sex *was* something she could enjoy, and while it wasn't the be-all and end-all, it added an edge of excitement to her life that had previously been missing. Now she'd experienced great sex, she could barely believe she'd gone without it for so long.

The world seemed full of new possibilities, alive with promise.

But on the flip side, no Xander making her heart race and her blood pump with excitement just by being close.

She realised, of course, that she'd run away from him again, only this time he hadn't chased her. Perhaps he'd thought there was no point, that she didn't want him to ask her to stay? He wasn't a mind reader, after all, so how could he have known what she wanted?

She should have told him how she felt.

If she'd learnt anything over the last couple of weeks it was that she needed to put herself out there, to open herself up to new experiences if she wanted the opportunity for something good to happen. She couldn't just sit back any more, with her head in the sand, and wait for things to happen *to* her.

Pamela finally came back after a couple more days off sick and Jess waited, nerves jumping, to be summoned into her office.

'Well, Jess, I've read your piece on Xander Heaton,' Pamela said as Jess perched carefully on the edge of the seat facing the editor's desk. Jess managed a smile despite her jaw being clenched with anxiety.

She just wanted it to be over with so she could move forward. If Pamela still thought she couldn't cut it at *Spark* and she had to go back home and start again she wanted time to come to terms with the toe-curling horror of it.

'Well, you did it, you impressed me,' Pam said, and

Jess felt a lightness in her chest battle with the heaviness that had been keeping her company since she'd left Italy. 'This is exactly the kind of writing I'd been hoping to see. I don't know what happened out there, but whatever it was it's had a big effect on your style. I like it, Jess, well done.'

It was a big deal to her to hear that kind of praise from someone as tough as Pamela, and her eyes welled with grateful tears.

'So I get to keep my job here?' she asked breathlessly.

'Absolutely,' Pam replied.

Jess breathed a huge sigh of relief. At least that part of her life was on the right track again.

'The only thing it needs before it can go in the magazine is a mention of what he's working on at the minute,' Pamela said as Jess began to stand up, thinking she was home and dry.

She went hot, then cold in the space of a second. 'I—I don't know what he was working on,' she stammered. 'At least, he never let me see the pictures. He was really insistent about that.'

The look of displeasure on Pamela's face made her stomach sink.

'Well, you'll just have to go and see him and tell him you have a couple of follow-up questions. See if you can get a gander at the pictures while you're there,' her boss said flippantly, as if that would be the easiest thing in the world. 'From the tone of the article it sounded like you got to know him pretty well.' She raised a discerning eyebrow. 'Use your influence, Jess.'

Her chest felt tight and her lungs seemed to be having trouble drawing air. 'You want me to go all the way back to Italy to find out what he's working on?'

Pam gave her a withering look. 'Don't you read the

gossip columns? He's back in London. Although they're all chatting about the fact he left a party early for once instead of indulging in his usual bad behaviour.'

'Xander's b-back in London?' Jess managed to stutter through frozen lips.

When she'd thought he was still in Italy it had been easier to keep her heartache under wraps, but it felt as if he were close enough to touch now—close, yet still so far away.

Pam sighed and looked at her as if she thought she was talking to a total idiot. 'Yes, Jess. So get your hide over there and source what we need so I can put this issue to bed.'

Sliding off her chair and standing up on jellylike legs, Jess gave her editor a stiff nod. 'Okay, Pam, I'll see what I can do.'

Jess stood outside the door to Xander's studio, her body quivering with nerves and her heart in her mouth.

She had no idea how she was going to play this. She also didn't know how he was going to react when he saw her again. They hadn't exactly parted on bad terms, but there hadn't been a fond farewell either.

Perhaps this was fate or serendipity, or whatever you wanted to call it, handing her an opportunity. Perhaps when he saw her he'd realise how they were meant to be together and ask her not to leave again.

Perhaps.

Only one way to find out.

Before she lost her nerve, she lifted her shaking hand and banged hard on his door, hoping he was in there.

After a couple of seconds the door flew open to reveal Xander in all his splendour, regulation paintbrush in hand and a look of acute surprise on his face when he clocked that it was her on his doorstep.

'Jess!' His beautiful voice rumbled through her, waking up every nerve ending and sending a rush of pure longing south through her body. He was even more gorgeous, more virile, than she remembered. It had been less than a week since they'd last seen each other, but to Jess it felt like a lifetime since she'd been allowed to touch him.

She wanted him back. So badly it physically hurt.

She needed to be cool here, collected and poised. No way was she going to go to pieces and make a fool of herself.

Opening her mouth to speak, she froze, totally at a loss for what to say now she was standing there in front of him again.

Say something, Jess. Anything.

'I love you,' she blurted, her brain too late to catch up with her mouth and circumnavigate the damage she'd just wreaked.

He just stared at her with those mesmerising eyes of his and didn't say a word. There wasn't even a flicker of emotion on his face.

Her heartbeat accelerated as she waited for something—anything—to give her a clue about how he felt about her laying herself on the line like that.

There was a sound of heavy footsteps behind her and, grateful for the distraction from her humiliation, she broke her awkward eye contact with Xander and turned around to see a thickset, silver-haired man reach the top of the stairwell and raise a hand in greeting to them both.

'Xander, glad I've caught you in. I've been speaking to the guys at the Brick Lane gallery and they have a couple more questions about how we want to set the exhibition up. I was in the area so I thought I'd drop in for a quick chat about it.'

Jess heard Xander clear his throat behind her. 'Sure, Paul, yeah. Tell you what, come down to the kitchen with me while I make a drink for my guest and we'll chat on the way.'

Jess's skin prickled as she felt him move from behind her and she watched in stultified silence as he walked towards his visitor.

He turned back to look at her, his face still devoid of any emotion.

'Jess, why don't you wait in my studio? I'll be back in a minute and we can talk,' he said levelly.

She gave him a nod and a tentative smile, then watched him disappear down the stairs after his visitor.

Stumbling into his studio, she closed the door behind her and put her head in her hands. She stared at the floor in horror, utterly incredulous that she just *told him that she loved him*.

Well, at least no one could accuse her of beating around the bush.

What must he be thinking right now? And what was he going to say when he finally came back into the room?

Her heart thumped against her chest as she considered the possibilities. Rejection or acceptance. Whichever he chose, it was going to turn her world upside down. Again.

She paced the room for a minute trying to get her head together, managing to knock into one of the paintings propped against the wall and jumping back when it fell flat against the floor with a clatter.

Picking it up, she propped it back against the wall

and knelt there for a moment, breathing slowly and deeply. As she stared at the back of the painting it suddenly occurred to her that she was alone, in Xander's studio, surrounded by his exhibition paintings. Well, she might as well get what she'd come here for while he was out of the room. Even if he gave her the brush-off she could still go back and give Pamela what she needed for the article before heading off home to crumple into a sobbing heap.

She walked unsteadily over to where his largest paintings stood, their paint-stained tarpaulins hiding them from sight. Her hand shook as she pulled up the bottom of one of the tarps to reveal the painting underneath.

Her heart rattled in her chest as she stood there, staring at it, hardly able to believe what she was seeing. It was a picture of her, standing naked, covered in paint with an embarrassingly provocative look on her face.

She could barely breathe, the horror of what she was seeing making her chest contract painfully.

Turning round, and with a sense of impending dread, she lifted up the tarp on the painting propped against the easel in the middle of the room. It was another one of her, lying trussed up to his bed, fully clothed in her linen suit and another image of her naked body above that in some subversive sexual pose.

He'd taken their most intimate, most intensely personal moments and was intending to use them for commercial gain.

The thought of these pictures being displayed in public view, her face clearly recognisable, made her want to vomit.

He didn't care about her at all; he'd been using her.

* * *

Xander somehow managed to deal with his agent's jovial banter and answer his questions about details for the exhibition while Jess's declaration that she *loved him* whirled like a tornado around his head.

He'd been amazed and strangely uplifted to find her standing there at his door, and seeing her again had brought home to him just how much he'd missed her company. But her announcement had thrown him for six.

Even though she'd clearly let it slip by accident—in her usual impulsive fashion—he could tell from the look in her eye that she meant it.

And it scared the crap out of him.

For the first time in his life he had no idea how to deal with a situation. Usually he'd just blow a woman off if she suddenly announced she was in love with him, but he didn't want to do that with Jess. She meant more to him than that.

He just wasn't sure how much more.

They needed to talk about this, that was for damn sure.

After finally getting rid of Paul, he walked back into the studio to find Jess standing in front of the final painting he'd been working on for the exhibition—the one of her sexual epiphany. His first instinct was to stride over there and pull the tarp back down and yell at her for peeking, until he saw the look of bewildered disbelief on her face.

'You sketched me naked? While I was asleep?' She sounded so shocked, so hurt, it stopped him in his tracks. He approached her with his hands held out in a placatory gesture, as a dark, disturbing burn wove through his chest and pooled in his belly. 'Jess, it was amazing. I had this moment of clarity—I haven't been this excited about a painting in a very long time.'

She stared at him, aghast. 'You thought it would be okay, when you knew how much I hated showing my body? I haven't exactly been coy about that, Xander, but you thought you'd go ahead and do it anyway without me knowing about it?'

A cold shiver tickled down his spine. 'I thought maybe you'd got past the worry about how you look naked.'

'You thought you'd fixed me?' she interrupted. 'That after you'd thrown a few orgasms my way I'd suddenly love my body enough to have you expose it for *all the world to see*?' Her voice was shaking now. 'It was meant to be just for you, Xander. I never would have let you seduce me if I thought you were going to do something like this. You exploited my trust.'

'Jess, you're overreacting…'

'Do you have any idea how humiliated I feel right now? I trusted you. I thought you were a good guy—a messed-up egomaniac, but a good guy at heart. But this was only ever about the art, wasn't it, Xander? For your own benefit. For your *career*.'

He was floundering now, at a loss how to explain himself. 'But you look so amazing.'

'That's not the point, Xander,' she said, giving him such a cold look he had to take a breath to steady himself.

Frustration twisted his guts. 'You want me to pull the picture from the exhibition? It's the best thing I've done in years, Jess. You inspired it. You should be proud.'

'Proud!' She spat the word out. 'Proud for everyone to know I was just another of your saps that you slept with to get what you wanted, then tossed aside? Judging by the fact you thought it was okay to produce pictures like this of me—' she jabbed her finger towards the canvas '—I don't think there's any chance you could love me back in the way I need you to. I thought perhaps you understood me, that our time together meant something, but apparently I was wrong. I was naive and stupid to think I could be the woman to tame you. This was never about me, Xander, was it? It was always about you and your *art*.'

He couldn't answer. He couldn't even get his response to that straight in his head. He hadn't been looking for a relationship and this thing with Jess had just come out of the blue and now his creativity seemed to be peaking he was afraid to let anything get in the way of it. Thinking about someone else right now would take precious mental energy away from his work and he couldn't afford to let anything damage his muse again. Not even Jess.

He needed to prove to the world he was back, bigger, badder and stronger than ever. He'd won against the disabling inertia that had held him hostage for so long. He could prove his earlier talent hadn't been a fluke and stick two fingers up at all those naysayers.

To not let his father have been right about him.

Jess stared at him angrily for a beat longer, waiting in vain for him to pull himself together enough to answer her. When he failed to open his mouth, she turned on her heel and stormed out, slamming the door of the studio hard behind her.

He slumped into a chair, unable to process all the thoughts raging through his brain. He wanted her to be pleased and proud of his pictures, to tell him what good work he'd done, but instead she'd been more concerned about how she looked in them.

A disabling indolence kept him in his chair and he sat, staring into space as the silence echoed in his head.

Over the next few days he began to hate looking at his last painting of her, the initial joy of creating it marred by the pain and distress he'd caused.

After a couple more days of staring into space, he tried calling her, first on her mobile, only to be sent straight to voicemail, then at her magazine, only to be told she wasn't available and could they take a message?

He left numerous messages asking her to call him, becoming more and more irate when his phone remained steadfastly silent.

She'd cut him away like the bloodsucking leech he was.

It wasn't the first time a woman had walked out on him, but he'd never liked any of the others enough to care that much before. He liked Jess, though, an awful lot.

She'd twisted herself into his thoughts and he found himself on edge and preoccupied by the hole she'd left by her desertion. He barely knew her, but she'd done something to his psyche by forcing him to think about someone other than himself for once—as if she'd opened up a gaping chasm in his consciousness, which he was having trouble knitting back together.

He should have been honest with her about how he really felt, instead of treating her like some*thing* fun to do. He cringed at the memory of telling her that.

But he'd been scared. It was his standard defence mechanism, to keep his lovers at an emotional distance so he'd never have to deal with more of the painful feeling of rejection he'd been living with since he could remember.

His whole life had revolved around getting people

to buy into the image of the bad-boy loner he wanted them to see rather than the *real* him and he seemed unable to drag himself out of its deathlike grip.

Without meaning to he'd let Jess glimpse the real him, but when she'd pushed for more he'd thrown up his barriers, keeping their relationship purely physical, keeping her out.

Using her for his own ends.

He'd unequivocally demonstrated that his career was the most important thing in the world to him and that she'd meant nothing. He'd used her to fix himself, drained their relationship of everything good, then spat her out. Because he was a selfish idiot. His father had been right, after all; he didn't deserve to be loved, not when he acted the way he did. He took everything he wanted and gave nothing back.

He was pure, unadulterated greed.

If he was ever going to be good enough to be the right man for Jess he needed to learn how to let go of his anger and jealousy and fear and give her back what she'd given to him.

Humility and kindness and altruism. To learn how to give for the sake of giving, instead of looking for what he could get out of it.

He'd drawn himself into such a hard shell nothing had been able to penetrate it. Until Jess had come along and started tapping at the seams.

She'd been absolutely right about how distanced he'd allowed himself to be from everyone else, how hyperfocused he was about how things affected *him*. He'd completely overlooked how he'd messed up everyone else who came into contact with him, just so he could get what he wanted.

He'd been alone for so long he had no idea how to

let someone else into his life. How to care about them and let them care for him. Deep down he accepted now that he'd thought of himself as unlovable, after having it rammed home over the years through his dad's total lack of interest in him. He'd never admitted to his father how that had made him feel, he'd just shrugged it off as how things were, but he should have been braver. He should have stood up for himself instead of shutting himself away.

And now Jess had given up on him, too.

He wanted her back so much it made him ache, but how could he ever make her believe he meant it?

It was time to face up to what kept him so distanced from everyone else in his life.

He needed to let go of this feeling that he still had something to prove to a father who had never cared about him. The old man was dead and he needed to move on with his life now.

Then he needed to find Jess and convince her that he was sorry and that he was worth taking a risk on.

After days of not being able to face going in to his studio and hiding away from the world in his flat, he finally made the journey back there. Picking up a scalpel from in amongst the mess of paints and modelling equipment on his art table, he walked over to the painting of Jess. It was the piece of work that could prove he wasn't the flash in the pan that he, and pretty much everyone else in the world, it seemed, had feared he was.

Raising the scalpel, he brought it down hard across the canvas, cutting a large gash from corner to corner, then another, and another, until all that was left was a frame with colourful strips hanging from it like ragged paper garlands.

It was time to start again.

CHAPTER TEN

AFTER A FEW of weeks of going through the motions of getting up and going to work in a stultified daze, Jess finally began to come out of the emotional coma she'd put herself in in an attempt to block the pain and humiliation of how Xander had used her.

He'd tried calling her a couple of days after she'd first stormed out, which she'd ignored in her anger at him, but she hadn't heard from him since. He'd obviously given up on her now and she didn't expect ever to hear from him again. But then, why the hell would *she* be any different from the tens of women he'd already used up and cast aside? He'd probably moved on to a new love affair already.

She wouldn't know. She hardly looked at social media any more for fear of seeing something about him and a new lover that would bring back the flood of heartache she was only just starting to break through.

It was for the best. They would never have worked as a couple anyway. He was too self-involved, too wild, too ephemeral in nature for her and she couldn't match that.

Pulling off her coat and slumping into her chair at her desk, she was just about to turn on her computer when she noticed an envelope next to her keyboard, addressed to her at the magazine. The handwriting was loopy and messy and something about it made her heart beat a little faster. Tearing it open, she took out a piece of shiny black card and stared at it for a moment. It appeared to be blank, but when she went to flip it over something caught her eye. She tipped it back slowly until the fluorescent overhead lights in the office shone up the words: *Out of the Shadows. A new exhibition by Xander Heaton.*

Her heartbeat accelerated, sending a rush of adrenalised blood to her head, making her feel for a moment as if she might pass out. Taking a few deep breaths, she waited until the pounding in her head had calmed down before looking at the invitation again.

There was an address for a gallery in Brick Lane and a date and time for the following week in neat print below it.

Xander's exhibition.

Her naked body about to be exposed to the whole world.

The invitation slipped out of her trembling fingers and fell onto the floor. Looking down, she saw there were words scrawled on the back of it in the same looping handwriting that was on the envelope. Leaning down to peer closer at them, she made out the words, 'Jess, please come. I need you to see something. Xander'.

She stared at it for a few moments, the rushing sound in her ears blocking out the noise of the office. Sitting up, she jumped in shock when she realised Pamela had appeared out of nowhere and was standing over her, waiting for an answer to a question she'd totally failed to hear. Looking up to see her boss's imperious expression, she had to quell the nervous impulse to leap up and dash off to the sanctuary of the loos. 'Sorry, Pamela, I missed that.'

Pam shook her head, clearly unimpressed by Jess's lack of focus. 'I said, did you get an invitation to Xander Heaton's exhibition, too? He sent one to me asking me to make sure you came along. You must have made quite an impression on him.' She raised a perfectly plucked eyebrow.

'Ah, yes, but I wasn't going to go. I have a thing that night.'

Pamela's other eyebrow shot up to join its counterpart. 'Cancel it. You should attend. We could do a great follow-up piece on him for the magazine. Your interview's been syndicated to a lot of influential sources already and you're in a position to exploit your relationship with him to get a good exclusive interview afterwards. Am I right?'

Jess sighed. There was no way Pamela would let her get away with missing the exhibition if she thought the magazine had something to gain from it.

Well, she was going to have to face the horror of being recognised as the model in his paintings some time. It might as well be sooner rather than later. At least it might be a friendly crowd at the exclusive first showing of his work. She could write the piece, then go and hide away under a rock until all the fuss had died down.

She gave her editor a tight smile. 'Sure, Pamela, I'll be there.'

'Good, good. Make sure you work all the angles, Jess,' Pam said, waving a hand in the air as she stalked off, unquestionably on her way to terrorise another poor member of her staff.

Xander couldn't ever remember being this nervous before a showing of his work, and for once the nerves weren't about what the critics might say about it. It was all down to what Jess would think.

Everything he'd done here was for her, after all.

After she'd refused to pick up or return his phone calls he'd realised it was going to take more than words to prove to her he was sorry and that he cared about her and wanted to make a go of a relationship—something he'd never been interested in before. Unfortunately, his reputation for being such a playboy didn't do him any favours in that regard and he'd clearly fed directly into her insecurity about taking a relationship with him seriously with his selfish disregard for her feelings.

He missed her so much.

He couldn't go on the way he was, isolated and casually using people before casting them off like pieces of rubbish.

She'd shown him how incredible it could feel to fall in love with someone and now he'd experienced it he was damned if he was going to let her just walk away.

Because he *was* in love with her, he realised. This aching hole in his chest he'd been living with for the last two months was exactly Jess-sized.

The front door to the gallery swung open, bringing him back to the present and letting in a draught of cool evening air. He looked round to see who it was.

Jess.

He'd sent an invitation to her editor as well in the hope it would force Jess to come, but had made the time on Jess's half an hour earlier.

He wanted her to see what he'd done for her first without being interrupted.

Apparently this exhibition opening had turned into a hot ticket after Jess's article on him for *Spark* magazine had been so well received. He'd been humbled by her descriptions of him and impressed by how she'd woven in his background with real sensitivity, making him sound like the kind of guy he'd always wanted to be—intelligent, passionate and talented.

She'd let the piece run, showing him in such a good light, despite how he'd treated her.

He knew he didn't deserve to even lick her shoes, but he wanted to become a man who *did* deserve her, and only she could help him with that.

If she could forgive him.

She stood in front of him now, head held high, looking so beautiful and bold he wanted to pull her against him and kiss her hard, to let her know just how much he wanted her back. How amazing she was. But he knew he couldn't do that—he needed to be more subtle, to prove to her this wasn't just about sex.

'Where is everyone? Did I read the invitation wrong? I thought it started at seven thirty,' Jess said, staring at him defiantly, her arms folded across her chest. He could see she was trying to brazen it out, but her awkward stance and the slight tremor in her voice gave her away.

Maybe there was hope? The thought made his blood buzz with adrenaline.

'You're on time. This is a private viewing, just for you, before all the other guests arrive. I wanted you to be the first to see it.'

'So I have time to run away and hide before they all arrive?' she asked, an eyebrow quirked, clearly trying to keep her voice controlled, but failing spectacularly to hit the right note of nonchalance and sliding right on through to utter terror.

He put a reassuring hand on her shoulder, feeling the heat of her skin burn through her thin cotton top. His mind flicked back to the memory of how the heat of her body felt against his and he almost lost his cool.

'I'm really hoping you won't want to run,' he said, begging with his eyes for her to give him another chance.

'You know, I don't know if I can bear to look at it again, Xander.' Taking a step backwards, she broke his hold on her and gave him a wobbly smile. 'But I wish you luck with the exhibition. I'm sure everyone's going to love it.' She turned to walk away, but before she could take a step he slid his fingers around her arm and twisted her back round to face him. No way was he going to let her walk away before he had chance to at least apologise.

He pulled her hard towards him, drawing her mouth so tantalisingly close he could feel the heat of her breath on his lips. 'Jess, please. Don't leave. I did all this for you. Not for my critics. I wanted you to know how much I miss you. How much I care about you. Please don't walk away now.'

He felt her falter and relax a little against him and he pressed on quickly before she could gather herself enough to leave.

'This is my apology to you. No one has ever given me that much of themselves before, Jess, and I can't believe I took advantage of you like that. I was so scared I was actually as washed up as everyone suspected, I lost sight of what was right and wrong. You trusted me and I treated that trust as if it was nothing. It was a cowardly, selfish, pathetic thing to do. I understand why it upset you and you were right to call me on it.'

She stared at him, her eyes wide with confusion. 'Okay. Well, thank you for apologising.'

'I destroyed that painting you saw, so you don't need to worry about it ever appearing.'

Releasing her arm and digging into his pocket, he pulled out a handful of long painted ribbons of canvas. 'This is all that's left of that painting and the one of you covered in paint.' He handed them to her and she stared down at them, her eyes widening in surprise.

When she looked back up into his face, her bottom lip was trembling and her eyes were shining with tears.

'What do you want me to say? That I'm pleased you tore your work apart?'

It was hell being this close to her without being allowed to enfold her in his arms and hold her close, to soothe all the pain away, but he knew he couldn't do that right now. The weight of his reputation for short, intense affairs with his muses lay heavily between them. He'd given her no reason to believe she was any different from the tens of women he'd already used up and cast aside.

'Let me show you what I replaced those pictures with,' he said, walking over to the light switches on the wall and flicking them up so the room was flooded with light.

He heard Jess gasp as she saw what he'd been pouring his heart into for the last month.

It took Jess a few moments for her eyes to adjust to the light before she could fully focus on what was in front of her.

There was a sculpture, made up of what looked like a multicoloured canvas stretched across a man-shaped frame, sitting in the middle of the room beneath four white spotlights. His posture was tensed as if ready to jump up and run forward, his hands gripping his knees, but, eerily, there was a flat picture where the contours of his face should be.

She walked towards it on shaking legs, utterly captivated, and as she peered closer she realised the flat piece had a self-portrait of Xander's face painted on it, showing an expression of such pain in his eyes it nearly broke her heart to look at it. The word *loser* was painted across his forehead in dark purple paint.

Dragging her gaze away from the face, she peered more closely at the rest of the sculpture and realised with a shock that the multicoloured body was made up of hundreds of tiny paintings.

Of her.

In some of them she was smiling, some looking confused, some looking insecure. In fact, he seemed to have captured every possible emotion she'd ever had in her life. As if he *knew* her. As if he'd seen inside her and understood exactly what made her tick.

There was something metallic and shiny protruding from the chest of the sculpture, as if it had been dragged out of his body and was hovering in mid-air before him.

Taking a deep, shuddering breath, she dropped to her knees to study it more closely and realised it was a small metal cage, in the shape of a heart with fine filigree letters trapped inside it.

She peered closer, barely able to focus through a bewildering haze of emotions.

It was the word *Jess*.

It was Xander's own personal love letter to her.

She felt his footsteps behind her as they made the stripped wooden floor bounce. Swivelling round, she stood up and faced him, at a total loss for words.

He didn't say anything, just took her hand and gently led her out from under the spotlight into a room at the back of the gallery, motioning for her to sit down on a cream leather sofa set back against the wall.

She sat on the edge and watched him lower himself down next to her, her whole body shaking now. She had no idea how to deal with all this. After convincing herself she needed to put her fling with him down to a freak anomaly in the short history of her life, she'd never expected to see him again, let alone have to deal with something as surreal as having a piece of his art dedicated to her.

'Did…did I imagine the life-size naked model of you, made up of images of my face?' she asked, her voice faltering as she tried and failed to pull herself together.

He breathed out slowly, as if centring himself.

'I need to explain something to you.' He ran a hand over his face, then repositioned himself on the sofa so his body was twisted towards her. 'When I was younger my art was the thing that saved me from complete melt-down. I did it as an outlet for all the anger and shame I carried around with me. I never expected for a second I could make the sort of money I have from it. After years of being shoved into the category of *troublemaker* I was totally amazed when people began to talk about me in terms of having talent as an artist instead of just being a public nuisance with my "graffiti". Before I realised what was happening, my career began to gain this crazy momentum and I was suddenly propelled into the lime-light. People were interested in what I had to say, like it meant something important to them. It was a revelation. Instead of being a problem and a drain on the system, I was someone people wanted to be associated with.'

'And, boy, did you associate with them.' She gave him a tentatively playful smile, which he returned.

'Yeah, I know, I turned into a massive tart. Believe it or not, I was pretty freaked by all the attention to begin with. Suddenly women who wouldn't have given me the time of day before were throwing themselves at me left, right and centre. After the first few had been and gone and more were lining up right behind them, I went a bit wild with it. It felt like an opportunity to make up for all the lost time in my youth when everyone else had been out at parties and clubs and I'd been working my butt off just to keep myself alive.'

He ran a shaking hand through his hair and Jess had to force herself to let out the breath she'd been holding, her throat tight from trying not to cry.

'I was living the dream, until it all began to fall to pieces,' he continued. 'The critics got hold of me and tore my last exhibition to pieces, which wouldn't have been such a big deal on its own, but it was meant to be a slap in the face for my old man. Not that he ever got to see it. He died before I got to prove he was wrong about me being a waste of space and I've been carrying this rage around with me ever since. Until you turned up and helped me channel it into something positive.'

'Xander...I don't understand what you want from me. I thought you didn't *do* relationships?'

'I thought so, too, until I met you. I want to make this work between us, Jess. I want a real relationship with you, not some meaningless fling. You've made me re-evaluate everything I thought was important in my life. I don't want to be alone any more. I want to wake up in the morning and see that amazing smile of yours and know it's for me. That I've made you happy. That I'm worth more than my father told me I was.'

'You are. Oh, Xander, you are.'

'I laid myself bare for you. That's all of me, Jess.' He put a hand up to her face and stroked his fingers against her cheek, before sliding them into her hair and cupping the back of her head, drawing her mouth closer to his. 'After tonight the whole world's going to know how I feel about you.'

'I can't believe you did that. For me,' she murmured, the heat of his mouth driving her wild.

'Yeah, well, apparently being in love can make you do crazy things.'

'You love me?' The words came out as a gasp.

He smiled. 'Isn't it obvious? I didn't think I was capable of subtlety.'

Laughing, she pressed her mouth against his, basking in the familiar taste of him, the tantalising smell of his skin.

'I think you should move in with me,' he said, drawing back to look her in the eye.

'What?' she whispered.

He grinned. 'What's the matter, Miss Prim, too wild for you?'

She huffed out a laugh. 'I can handle wild. In fact I'm giving up on trying to control everything around me. I don't want to be sensible any more. I want fun and craziness. And to experience the ups and downs. With you.'

'It's going to be quite a ride, Jess,' he said, raising an eyebrow in challenge.

'Bring it on,' she said, leaning forward to plant a firm kiss on his lips.

The sound of the gallery door opening brought them

back to the present and Jess pulled away to look him in the eye. 'It sounds like your admirers are arriving.'

He looked at her with such sexual heat she thought she might melt into a puddle at his feet. 'They can wait,' he said, kicking the office door shut and enfolding her in his arms. 'Tonight is all about you, after all.'

* * * * *

Her insides were doing weird things at his touch, and the temptation to touch him in return was immense.

She tried to kill the fantasy by imagining his reaction. Shock? Embarrassment? Then she remembered the feel of his lips on her fingers as he'd taken the sticky candy from them, and she couldn't help thinking that maybe, just maybe, he'd reciprocate. Bend down and kiss her. Tangle his big strong hands in her hair and tip her head back to get better access to her lips…

'Melissa?'

Brought back to earth with a thump, she realised he was holding the car door open for her.

'Sorry,' she said, sliding into her seat quickly.

'You're a complete daydreamer, aren't you?' he asked, looking rather amused as he got into the driver's seat. 'What were you thinking about?'

Ha—wouldn't you like to know? Melissa felt like saying. 'Just stuff,' she said after a pause.

'Random stuff?'

'Oh, very random.'

His lips quirked up at the corners as if he was trying hard not to smile.

Melissa had a nasty feeling that he knew exactly what she'd been thinking about.

Dear Reader

This is my fifth book for Harlequin Mills and Boon®, and I came up with the plot during a road trip from Mumbai to Goa. I scribbled out the outline while my husband drove and my kids dozed in the back seat. Then, three months later, with a deadline looming up ahead, I tried to make sense of the squiggles on the page. My laptop obligingly crashed when I was halfway through writing, and I finished the book on the trusty old laptop that I wrote my first book on. Zero battery life and clunky keyboard vs sleek lavender keys and flashing hieroglyphs where my manuscript used to be—well, the clunky laptop wins every time.

Melissa and Samir, the two lead characters in this book, are very different from each other. Melissa is pretty in an understated, elfin kind of way, and she has a wicked sense of humour. People often write her off as a quiet, rather mousy girl—it's only when they get talking to her that they wonder why they've never noticed the mischief in her eyes, and her melting smile.

Samir, on the other hand, is strikingly good-looking, very successful, and perhaps just a little arrogant. He's used to women chasing after him, and he's had his share of relationships—still, he gives the impression of being cold and aloof. He's instantly attracted to Melissa when he meets her, but he holds back so that *she* ends up making the first move. Both of them are carrying baggage from previous relationships, and it takes them a while for them to recognise that it's more than sheer physical attraction holding them together.

I've set the book in two of my favourite places—Mumbai and Goa—and I hope I've managed to capture the essence of both. Now all I need to do is explain to my indignant kids why this book is dedicated 'just to Papa'...

Happy reading!

Shoma

TWELVE HOURS
OF TEMPTATION

BY
SHOMA NARAYANAN

Published in Great Britain 2014
by Mills & Boon, an imprint of Harlequin (UK) Limited,
Eton House, 18-24 Paradise Road, Richmond, Surrey, TW9 1SR

© 2014 Shoma Narayanan

ISBN: 978 0 263 24616 2

Harlequin (UK) Limited's policy is to use papers that are natural,
renewable and recyclable products and made from wood grown in
sustainable forests. The logging and manufacturing processes conform
to the legal environmental regulations of the country of origin.

Printed and bound in Spain
by Blackprint CPI, Barcelona

Shoma Narayanan started reading Mills and Boon® romances at the age of eleven, borrowing them from neighbours and hiding them inside textbooks so that her parents didn't find out. At that time the thought of writing one herself never entered her head—she was convinced she wanted to be a teacher when she grew up. When she was a little older she decided to become an engineer instead, and took a degree in electronics and telecommunications. Then she thought a career in management was probably a better bet, and went off to do an MBA. That was a decision she never regretted, because she met the man of her dreams in the first year of business school—fifteen years later they're married with two adorable kids, whom they're raising with the same careful attention to detail that they gave their second-year project on organisational behaviour.

A couple of years ago Shoma took up writing as a hobby—after successively trying her hand at baking, sewing, knitting, crochet and patchwork—and was amazed at how much she enjoyed it. Now she works grimly at her banking job through the week, and tries to balance writing with household chores during weekends. Her family has been unfailingly supportive of her latest hobby, and are also secretly very, very relieved that they don't have to eat, wear or display the results!

Other Modern Tempted™ titles by Shoma Narayanan:

THE ONE SHE WAS WARNED ABOUT

To Badri

CHAPTER ONE

'BRIAN'S SELLING THE AGENCY.'

The words didn't sink in at first because Melissa was busy squinting at her keyboard. Damn the *O* key. It was jamming up again. The last line she'd typed read as if it had a particularly nasty swear word in it—the difference a single missing *o* could make was amazing.

'I need a new keyboard,' she said. 'Unless… *What* did you say?'

Pleased at the impact she'd created, Neera plopped her lush backside onto Melissa's desk and beamed at her pretty young friend. 'It's true. He's going to announce it today.'

Melissa stared at her in dismay. Brian Mendonca had set up the tiny advertising agency thirty years ago, and it was more like an extended family than a workplace. Melissa herself had been working there for a little over two years, and she loved the place.

'Who's buying it?'

'Maximus Advertising. They're expanding…and Brian wants to retire and go back to Goa, apparently.' Neera looked over her shoulder and then leaned down. 'Don't look now, but the guy who's taking over is with

Brian right now. He's pretty hot, actually, can't be very old…'

As Melissa instinctively turned, Neera tugged her back, and all she caught a glimpse of was a tall man walking out of the main entrance of the office with Brian.

'His name's Samir Razdan,' Neera reported two days later.

Melissa abandoned the ad she was working on to search the internet for the name.

'Impressive,' she said. 'Studied in the US. He's been working for only ten years and he's already Maximus's corporate strategy head. Looks pretty arrogant, though—like he thinks he's a lot smarter than anyone else.'

The picture on the Maximus website showed a strong-featured man in his early thirties—even the grim expression in his eyes didn't detract from his good looks.

'Shh…' Neera muttered, and Melissa turned to see Brian bearing down on them with the subject of the photograph in tow.

The man was magnificent in real life. There was no other word for it, Melissa thought as she stared at him. Well over six feet in height, he towered over Brian—and the contrast between Brian's rather pudgy middle-aged form and Samir Razdan's perfectly proportioned physique was striking.

She hadn't had enough time to switch screens, and her browser still had the Maximus website open. Melissa wondered if he'd overheard her remark.

'Meet some of the most talented people on the team,'

Brian said, beaming at both of them. 'Neera is our creative head, and Melissa's our star copywriter.'

'It's so nice to meet you,' Neera gushed, holding out her hand.

Samir took it after a second's hesitation and said, 'It's a pleasure.'

His tone was formal, almost dismissive, and Melissa immediately felt her hackles rise. Neera could come across as a bit silly at times, but she was brilliant at her work and Samir had absolutely no business looking down at her.

'And this is Melissa,' Brian said fondly, and his expression suggested an indulgent grandfather introducing a favourite but slightly unpredictable grandchild.

'Hi,' Melissa said coolly, giving Samir a slow once-over. She didn't stand up—even in her two-inch heels she would probably only reach his chin. And Brian hadn't *said* that Samir was taking over the company—there was no need for her to spring to attention.

As her eyes drifted over his body she couldn't help noticing how broad his shoulders were, and how perfectly his formal blue shirt and grey trousers fitted his athletic frame.... For a few seconds she actually felt her breathing get a bit out of control. Then she gave herself a mental slap. Getting distracted was *not* supposed to happen. The 'once-over technique' was something her sister-in-law had taught her. Used to ogling women themselves, most men were made profoundly uncomfortable by an attractive woman looking them over as if she found something lacking.

Okay, so that was *most* men. When her eyes met Samir's again he didn't look the least bit fazed—if anything, there was the merest hint of a twinkle in his eyes.

'Your star copywriter, you say?' he said to Brian.

'Yes, one of her ads has been nominated for an award this year,' Brian said. Clearly eager to undo the damage his protégée was hell-bent on doing, he went on, 'I'm expecting it to win silver at the very least—if not gold.'

'Impressive,' Samir said, and Melissa had no way of knowing if he was being sarcastic or not. 'Well, I'll see you ladies around.'

His eyes flickered for a second towards Melissa's computer screen. The Maximus website was still open, with Samir Razdan's picture occupying pride of place at the top right-hand corner. The man himself didn't react, however, giving the girls a polite nod and continuing towards the exit.

'He seems pretty nice,' Neera said as the doors closed behind him.

Melissa stared at her in disbelief. 'You can't be serious!' she said, turning to the elderly Hindi copywriter who sat next to her. 'You saw him, Dubeyji, what did you think?'

'He's a good businessman,' Dubeyji said a little sadly. 'Doesn't let people know what he's thinking. But I'm sure he'll get rid of the old fogeys like me. I know how Maximus runs—it's like a factory. We'll just be a little insignificant part of their operations. They wouldn't even have looked at us if it wasn't for the awards we've got recently.'

'He's right,' Melissa burst out, getting to her feet in agitation. 'It's not about this Razdan guy. Maximus will probably sack half of us, and the rest will have to go work in one of those hideous blue glass buildings and wear access cards and queue up for lunch at the cafeteria…'

'And hopefully we'll get paid every month,' said Devdeep, the agency's client servicing head, as he strolled up. 'Melissa, we all love Brian, but creative freedom is a bit of a luxury when we're losing clients every day.'

'He's great at what he does,' Melissa said hotly. 'None of us have one tenth of his talent and—'

'I agree,' Devdeep said. 'The point is the world's moved a little beyond print advertising. I know TV might be a bit much for an agency this size to handle, though we could have done it if we'd expanded at the right time. But there's digital advertising and social media—let's admit it: we've lost some of our best clients because Brian doesn't hold with "all that new technology rubbish".'

'He's right,' Neera said. 'Melly, if Brian continues to run this place we'll all be out of jobs within a year. Awards or no awards. He's a bit of a…well, not a dinosaur, exactly, but definitely ancient.'

'A mastodon, maybe,' Devdeep said, giving Melissa an irritatingly superior smile. 'Or a woolly mammoth.'

'Remind me not to ask you guys to bat for me *ever*,' Melissa muttered, and turned back to her computer to pound savagely at the keys.

She was unswervingly loyal to Brian, and she didn't understand how everyone else wasn't the same. Brian had done so much for each of them—Melissa knew that he'd given Devdeep a job when he'd been sacked from another agency, and that he'd advanced Neera a pot of money to pay for her mum's bypass surgery a year ago. Their criticising him was a bit like a bunch of Kolkata street kids saying that the Sisters of Charity could do with a make-over and a new uniform.

'I thought you hadn't yet told your staff about the buy-out?' said Samir.

'I haven't,' Brian replied. 'But it's a small office—the finance guys guessed something was happening and the word must have spread.'

'Evidently,' Samir agreed, his voice dry. 'I'd suggest you talk to them. Those women were looking a bit jittery.'

Or at least one woman had been—the other had been anything but. For a few seconds his mind dwelled on the coolly challenging way in which she'd spoken to him. She'd known who he was, and it hadn't fazed her in the least.

As it turned out Brian didn't have to speak to the team as Devdeep had called everyone into a room and was in the process of giving them a pep talk. Brian didn't object—he was already looking forward to a life of retirement, and anyway, Devdeep would be managing the bulk of the agency work until the sale went through.

Samir Razdan was a corporate restructuring expert, not an adman—there was even a chance Devdeep would get to head the agency once Samir got it fully integrated into the Maximus empire.

'It's all very well for you,' Melissa told Brian crossly as he dropped her at her hostel in Colaba that evening. 'You and Aunty Liz will have the time of your lives, going off on cruises and world tours, while all of us slog away for Robot Samir.'

Brian gave her a quizzical look. 'You met him for

all of five minutes,' he pointed out. 'Surely that's not long enough to start calling him names?'

'I looked him up before that,' she said. 'He's a businessman through and through. I don't think he has a creative bone in his body. He won't do the agency any good, Brian, he'll only try and squeeze out the last possible rupee of revenue he can. And you can tell a lot in five minutes—he's pretty cold-blooded, and he obviously thinks he's God's gift to womankind.'

'Ah...' Brian said. 'So that's it. Paid more attention to Neera, did he?'

Brian was in his mid-fifties, and he still admired the fair-skinned, luscious beauties of his youth—Neera was a pretty fine example of the type.

'No,' Melissa said, exasperated. Apart from trivialising her concerns about the takeover, it wasn't even true. Samir had hardly noticed Neera, and while he might not have been bowled over by Melissa she'd at least caught his attention.

Unbidden, her thoughts drifted back to the second their eyes had met...then she shook herself angrily. Brian's habit of reducing everything to a simple manwoman equation was as annoying as it was infectious.

'Look, I'm sorry I took off at you,' she said. 'It's just that you and Aunty Liz have been like family to me, and I don't know... I'm just a bit...'

The car had stopped outside the working women's hostel where Melissa lived, and Brian reached out to give her a clumsy pat on the shoulder.

'Sorry,' Melissa said again, taking in his anxious expression. 'Don't worry, I'm not about to start howling. Just...stay in touch, OK? Even when you're off living the high life,' she added as she climbed out of the car, smiling at him before she closed the door.

'Yes, of course.'

Overall, Brian looked rather relieved to be rid of her, and she couldn't blame him. Emotional scenes weren't really his thing.

'I'll ask Liz to call you. Fix dinner with us this Sunday, maybe, and we can talk things over.'

He was about to drive off when something struck him and he rolled the window down. 'Don't judge Samir too hastily, OK? He's a great guy—just a little reserved. Wait till you get to know him better.'

Melissa waited while he drove off and then walked into the hostel, uncharacteristic tears pricking at her eyelids. She was distantly related to Brian's wife, and two years ago, when her family had turned against her, Liz and Brian had brought her to Mumbai, given her a job and helped her settle down. Brian insisted that she'd more than repaid the debt with the amount of hard work she'd put in since joining the agency, but she felt more grateful and connected to the couple than she had to anyone else in her life. Brian's announcement had come as a shock—it felt as if her last source of emotional support was now gone.

Three weeks later, when Samir moved into the Mendonca Advertising corner office, he found himself automatically looking for the dusky elfin woman he'd met the first day he'd visited the office. Brian had spoken to him about her later, and he was intrigued by the few things that Brian had let drop. He didn't see her for the first week, though, and it was only at the beginning of the next week that he thought to ask someone where she was.

'Is everyone in the office, Devdeep?' he asked.

Devdeep wrinkled his forehead. 'Yes, I think so,' he said. 'Was there someone you'd like to meet in particular? Because I've already lined up discussions with the team heads, but I can rejig them if needed.'

Distracted for a second by a vivid mental image of jigging team heads, Samir shook his head. 'No. There were a couple of women Brian introduced me to the first day I was here. I can't see either of them around.'

'Ah, Neera and Melissa,' Devdeep said. 'Neera's not well, but Melissa should be around—actually, she should be here already. I'll speak to her about it. She's normally never late.'

Samir heroically resisted the impulse to tell Devdeep not to get his panties in a twist and said instead, 'Don't worry about it. I was just wondering if she was on leave today.'

Ten minutes later he was left in no doubt as a pink-cheeked Melissa bounced into his office.

'Devdeep said you were looking for me,' she said. She'd already had a bit of a spat with Devdeep, and she was all set to do battle. 'I got little delayed because there wasn't a single cab on the roads today. There's some kind of a strike. I'd have called and told someone if I'd known you needed to talk to me.' She came to an abrupt halt, realising that it sounded as if she was making excuses. *Damn*, she'd wanted to come across as being completely cool and in charge of the situation.

Samir waited patiently till she was done. 'I asked where you were because I was looking around for familiar faces,' he said. 'I didn't see you all of last week.'

She was even prettier than he'd remembered—large, expressive chocolate-brown eyes in a piquant little face framed by masses of spun-silk hair. Right now, she looked defensive, and a lot less fiery than when he'd first met her, and he smiled at her reassuringly. The last thing he wanted was to terrorise the junior members of what he suspected was already a very apprehensive team.

Unfortunately Samir's reassuring smile had the effect of making Melissa's knees go just a little wobbly, and she took a few seconds to regroup before she said, 'I was in a creative writing workshop last week. Brian suggested it, actually—he felt that it'd help with my work.'

'That's OK,' Samir said, but Melissa still hesitated.

'I paid for it myself,' she volunteered.

At that, Samir looked up. 'I think it would have made more sense for the agency to pay if Brian asked you to take the workshop,' he said crisply. 'I'll speak to someone about it. And at some point I'd like you to take me through what you do—I'll drop you a line and schedule a time. Is there something else you'd like to talk about now?'

Melissa's slightly belligerent expression had vanished, but she still looked as if she wanted to get something off her chest.

'Um, he mightn't have told you, but it's Devdeep's birthday today,' she said. 'Brian's secretary normally orders a cake, but this time she wasn't sure what to do, so…'

'She can order a cake,' Samir said. 'You know what? It'd help if you could spread the word—for now everything continues as usual. I'll be making changes, but they'll take time, and they'll definitely not be about things like birthday cakes and what time people land up in office.'

Melissa's eyes narrowed, but she didn't say anything, whisking herself out of his office instead. In spite of his brusqueness there was a magnetic pull about Samir that was difficult to ignore. OK, *magnetic pull* was a really cheesy way of putting it, but that was how it felt. He was dressed casually, probably with the intention of blending in with the agency staff—but even in a linen shirt and faded jeans he exuded an aura of sheer masculine power that was difficult to ignore.

'He said you should order the cake, Kash,' she told Samir's secretary on her way back to her desk. 'Tell me when it's here and we'll set up the pantry for a party.'

Devdeep was dreadfully embarrassed by the fuss.

'He'll think we're completely flaky,' he protested, when Melissa and Kash told him.

'Nonsense, even the president celebrates her birthday,' Melissa said briskly. 'Samir won't think you're flaky at all, and if he does we'll put cockroaches in his room and spit in his water jug.'

'Thanks for warning me,' a dry voice said behind her, and Melissa jumped.

There he was, standing right behind her—all six foot two inches of scorching hot masculinity—and for the first time in her life Melissa found herself completely tongue-tied.

Devdeep turned a bright purple and said, 'She was just joking, sir, of course we'd do nothing of the sort.'

'Joking, was she?' Samir gave her a long look that didn't betray an iota of what he was thinking. 'Many happy returns of the day, Devdeep. And you can call me Samir. I haven't been knighted yet—and "sir" is a bit over the top, don't you think?'

Devdeep was still in the midst of a rather incoherent reply when Samir interrupted.

'Can I speak to you for a bit, Melissa?'

'If you were trying to put him at ease it didn't work,' Melissa muttered once they were out of earshot. 'Soon he'll be thanking you for allowing him to breathe the same air as you.'

At that Samir finally laughed. 'I can see I've been set up as a bit of an ogre, haven't I?'

Melissa looked him squarely in the eyes. 'No, you haven't,' she said. 'Brian decided to sell you the agency, and we trust his judgement. But you sitting in your room and poring over financial statements day after day isn't making people feel very confident.'

'Right,' Samir said. 'I guess I should have explained that I'm only handling the take-over—I'll have someone else actually managing the agency once I've got it fully integrated into Maximus. Look, Brian told me I could trust you to call things as they are. And that you'd be discreet even though you're one of the younger members of the team.'

Melissa nodded in what she hoped was a suitably responsible and discreet manner. So far in every interaction with Samir she'd come across as being a lot more immature and irresponsible than she actually was, and she was keen to correct the impression before he wrote her off as a complete airhead. Staying calm and focussed was difficult, though, with the completely unexpected effect that he was having on her.

'So it'd help if you told me exactly what people are

worried about,' he said, leading the way into his room. 'I plan to address the team tomorrow, but I want to get my bearings first.'

'The older guys think you'll sack them,' she said bluntly. 'Especially the copywriters who work on regional languages. And people like me are worried that we'll no longer be doing the kind of work Brian trained us for—we'll just be churning out run-of-the-mill advertising. And a few, like Devdeep, just want to know how they can impress you and get promoted as soon as possible.'

Samir raised an eyebrow, and she went on.

'I'm not criticising him. He's probably the most sensible of the lot, and he has a wife and two kids to think of. It's just that for the rest of us there was a reason we joined Mendonca's, and the reason's now gone.'

'The work you're talking about,' Samir said. 'Could I see some of the things the agency's done in the past?'

'It's all around you!' Melissa exclaimed, but then the bare walls of the room registered. 'It's been taken down,' she said in surprise. 'Brian had all our best work framed and put up on the walls. And there were the awards and certificates we won…'

She sounded distinctly upset now, and Samir found himself explaining.

'I can't work in clutter,' he said. 'I didn't really look at the walls last time I was here, but I asked for the office to be cleared out completely before I joined. I assume Brian took the ads home.'

He was probably right—Brian had been inordinately proud of the collection of award-winning ads his walls had been plastered with and it was more than likely he hadn't wanted to leave them behind. It felt a little as if the soul of the agency had been torn away, Melissa thought, and then gave herself a quick mental shake. Brian was gone, and agonising over the past wasn't going to do her any good.

'There are soft copies of everything saved on the common drive that we all have access to,' she said briskly. 'I can show you if you like.'

She went around to his side of the table so that she could show him where the ads were stored. As he turned the laptop, his hand touched hers briefly, and she pulled away as if from an electric shock. His lips tightened imperceptibly, making her flush. For a few seconds she'd forgotten that she was dealing with a rather dangerously good-looking man, and the sudden jolt of attraction had made her react stupidly.

'So, the ads are here,' she muttered, pointing at the screen. 'I'll...um...leave you to it, then.'

He looked up. 'Which one is the ad you wrote—the one Brian said was nominated for an award?'

'It's in the Robinson folder,' she said. 'The third one.'

He pulled the ad up onto the screen and looked at it silently for a while. It was a text-only ad for a range of baby products, and she'd written it from the point of view of a first-time mum. It was charming, and a little whimsical, and it wasn't really an ad in the traditional sense because it didn't talk about the products at all—it just said 'Happy Mother's Day' and the brand name at the end.

'Interesting,' Samir said. 'Any idea on how it impacted sales?'

Melissa stared at him as if he'd suddenly grown a second head. 'It doesn't work that way,' she protested. 'Ads like these make customers connect with the brand. There's no immediate effect on sales.'

'Right…' he said, but he was evidently not convinced. 'Always helps to have sales figures, though.'

It took all Melissa's willpower not to snap at him. 'I work on the creative side,' she said finally. 'It's the client servicing guys who work on the numbers.'

'You're not curious enough to ask for them?'

'I did ask!' she said. 'The sales figures were good, but I've forgotten exactly what percent they went up by. Devdeep would have the details.'

Samir didn't react, and she wondered if he'd even heard what she'd said. He was gazing intently at a spreadsheet now, his brows narrowed in concentration. In spite of her annoyance, one part of Melissa's brain noted that he managed to look very, very hot in an intense, brooding kind of way. Even when he clearly found his spreadsheet more fascinating than her ad.

She moved towards the door in what she hoped was an unobtrusive manner, and her hand was on the doorknob when he looked up, his rather stern features lightened by a genuine smile.

'It's a great ad, by the way,' he said. 'I can see why Brian thought so highly of you.'

The smile made his eyes crinkle up at the corners— suddenly he seemed a lot more human and approachable, like a movie star morphing into the local college football hero. Except that he was far more potently male than the average college heartthrob, and Melissa felt her breath come a little faster.

'Thank you,' she said, all her usual poise deserting her. 'I'll…um…I'll see you around, then, OK?'

She slipped out of the door, but it was a few minutes before Samir went back to his spreadsheet.

CHAPTER TWO

'WHERE IS EVERYONE?'

Melissa looked up. 'Devdeep and Shivani are in Goa for the ad awards,' she said. 'The rest of us are all here. As in they're around,' she added as Samir surveyed the empty cubicles and raised an eyebrow. 'They've gone for breakfast, I think.'

Samir had been travelling, and it was a week since she'd last seen him. He looked tanned and fit and almost good enough to eat.

His brow creased in a frown. 'If you wrote the ad why aren't *you* on your way to Goa? Didn't Devdeep think of taking you along?'

'He did.' Melissa bit her lip. She didn't like Devdeep much, but the poor man wasn't to blame for this particular situation.

'And you decided not to go?' Samir sounded positively incredulous now.

There was no way out of this other than admitting the embarrassing truth. 'I…um…I have a slight phobia about flying,' Melissa said in a rush. 'The trains were booked solid because it's a long weekend, and Devdeep said that going alone on a bus might not be safe.'

'And a bullock cart would take too much time, I assume?' Samir said, his lips twitching. 'How about cycling to Goa? Did you consider that?'

'Very funny,' Melissa said crossly. 'I did want to go. I'm just trying to tell you that it didn't work out.'

Too late, she realised that snapping at the new agency head was probably not very bright of her. Luckily, he looked more amused than offended.

'You could come with me,' Samir said, taking even himself by surprise. 'I'm driving down—I'm leaving early tomorrow morning and I can pick you up. Where d'you live?'

'Colaba,' Melissa said, trying not to gape at him. 'But are you sure?'

'Yes, I am,' Samir said, though he was wondering whether he'd suddenly gone quite mad.

There was no way Melissa could know it, but he never volunteered to spend time with a woman—let alone thirteen hours closeted with one in a car. For a second he wondered whether he should retract the offer, but there was no way he could back out of it without coming across as being incredibly rude.

Oh, really, Razdan? he said wryly to himself as he took down her address and mobile number. As if the fear of being thought rude had ever stopped him in the past.

Melissa was ready on the dot of six, perched on her bed. It had taken some time to decide what to wear—too dressed up and he might think she was making a play for him—too casual and he mightn't want to be seen with her. She'd finally settled for denim cut-offs with a long-sleeved white cotton shirt and sat down to wait.

Her phone rang at a quarter past six, and she picked it up, her heart suddenly beating a lot faster.

'Hi,' she said tentatively.

'Ready to leave?' he asked, not bothering to return her greeting. 'I'm in a black car, right outside your hostel gate.'

And what a car it was. Melissa found it difficult to take her eyes off the sleek, powerfully built machine. Then she saw Samir, and her mouth went dry with longing. So far she'd only seen him in office clothes—in an open-necked T-shirt and cargo shorts he looked even hotter than he did in formals.

She took a deep breath before she crossed the road to join him. Letting him know how much he affected her was a bad, *bad* idea.

'Thanks for doing this,' she said politely as she got into the car. 'I'm really looking forward to the awards festival, even if we don't win anything.'

'You're welcome,' Samir said.

She looked very young and appealing, with a little rucksack slung over one shoulder, and her hair held back with an Alice band, but there was something innocently sensual in the way she twisted her slim body around to toss the rucksack into the backseat. Her hair fell over her shoulder, and he caught a whiff of a fresh floral scent that made him want to reach out and touch—it took a strong effort of will to remain unaffected by her nearness.

'Car rules,' he said, passing her a bottle of water and hoping she hadn't noticed him looking at her. 'Seat belt on at all times. No eating in the car. And absolutely no attempts to change the music.'

Melissa peeked at his face to see if he was joking.

Apparently not. With uncharacteristic meekness she tugged at the seat belt—the seat belt, however, seemed to have firm ideas of its own, and refused to budge.

'I can't—' she started to say, and with an impatient shrug he leaned across to help her.

Melissa immediately froze. Her first thought was that he was much...much *larger* than she'd thought he was—the second was that if she moved just an inch she'd be touching him, and there was something terribly tempting about the thought. Then there was the smell of his aftershave... Woody, with a slight hint of citrus, it teased at her nostrils as he released the seat belt from where it was snagged behind her seat.

'Here—it's free now,' he said.

He moved away from her, apparently completely unaffected by her proximity. Oh, well, maybe her three-hundred-rupee perfume and demure clothes just didn't do it for him. Despite herself, she felt a little miffed. Sure, he was a hotshot executive and all that, but she would have liked him to take just a *little* interest in her as a woman. And her own reaction to him was annoying—she wasn't usually the swooning-over-a-hot-man type. Then common sense reasserted itself. Samir was undeniably gorgeous, and there was absolutely nothing to be ashamed of in finding him lust-worthy. As long as she restricted herself to a purely aesthetic appreciation of his hotness she'd be fine.

Samir put the car into gear, his lips thinning. The tiny gasp that Melissa had let out when he'd leaned over her hadn't escaped him, and he was regretting his offer of a lift more than ever.

Melissa was wrong about his reactions—one look at her long, tanned brown legs and her slim but curvy figure and everything male in him had responded enthusiastically. Being older and more experienced, he was just a great deal better at concealing his reactions.

They were both silent as the car sped through nearly empty streets all the way past Dadar and Chembur, and over the creek at Vashi. The sky was beginning to lighten, and the city looked as if it had just been through an extensive makeover. It was a wonder the amount of difference the lack of traffic and pollutants made.

They were nearly at the Pune expressway when Melissa finally spoke.

'Can we stop for a bit?' she asked.

Samir gave her an impatient look. 'I'd like to get on the expressway before traffic builds up,' he said. 'Can you hold on till we get to the first toll? There's a food plaza there, and it's only around an hour off.'

'I'm hungry,' she said in a small voice.

She'd missed dinner the night before, and the hostel breakfast service only started at seven in the morning. It was all very well for Samir, she thought resentfully. He probably had a retinue of cooks who would have a piping hot breakfast on the table even if he decided to leave home at four a.m.

Unwilling to explain that she was actually feeling light-headed with hunger, she said, 'And I need to use the loo. Right now.' *Ha*—that wasn't something he could argue with.

It didn't look as if he was fooled, but he pulled into a burger joint.

'D'you want anything?' she asked, and he shook his head.

'I'll wait outside,' he said.

'I'll be quick,' she promised, and darted into the restaurant.

The queues were long, and after almost an hour in the car Melissa found that she was feeling distinctly dizzy—her ears were buzzing, and by the time she got to the head of the queue she knew she was in no state to order.

'You can go ahead,' she muttered to the woman behind her.

'Oh, thanks,' the woman said gratefully—she had several kids in tow, and they had been bouncing with eagerness to order their second round of burgers. Then she looked a little more closely at Melissa. 'Are you feeling all right?' she asked.

Melissa had just enough time to shake her head before black spots started dancing in front of her eyes.

Samir finished sending out a couple of urgent e-mails on his smart phone and looked up, thinking that as they'd stopped anyway a coffee might be a good idea.

The restaurant had plate-glass windows on three sides, and just as he was about to start towards it he saw Melissa sink gracefully into the arms of the middle-aged woman standing next to her. He took the next few steps at a run, bursting into the restaurant just as the woman helped Melissa to a sofa.

'What's happened to her?' he asked, his voice harsh, and the woman looked up in undisguised relief.

'Oh, are you with her? Thank heavens. I didn't know what to do! I think she's just feeling a little faint. Rishu, give me that soda! And the rest of you kids, go and sit with Vishal Uncle. I'll be with you in a minute.'

The kid she'd addressed gave up the drink without

a peep, though he looked rather upset. Melissa was trying to sit up now, and the woman held the paper cup to her lips.

'Thanks,' Melissa said after a few sips. 'Sorry about this.'

'No worries,' the woman said comfortably, straightening up. 'I'll be right over there in case you need help,' she told Samir. 'I think she's OK now, but a check-up might be in order once you guys get home.'

Melissa thanked her again, and gave Samir an awkward look once the woman went away.

'I'm so sorry,' she said. 'This hasn't ever happened before.'

He was frowning. 'Do you feel OK otherwise? Should I take you back to Mumbai? That woman was right—you need to see a doctor.'

But Melissa was already shaking her head. 'There's no need,' she said. 'I think I'll be fine once I eat something.'

His frown deepened. 'Did you have breakfast?' he asked abruptly, and she shook her head. 'Dinner last night?'

Feeling hideously embarrassed, she shook her head again.

'Why not? What time did you leave work?'

'Nine-forty,' she muttered. 'The hostel curfew is at ten on week-nights, so I had to rush back. And I forgot that I was out of instant noodles.'

'We'll talk after I get some food into you,' Samir said grimly. The interested onlookers in the restaurant waved him to the head of the queue and he came back with a chicken burger and a milkshake.

Melissa took the burger, but shook her head at the

milkshake. 'Lactose intolerant,' she explained before biting into the juicy bun. The rush of flavours had her feeling a little sick for a few seconds, but the nausea soon receded and she tore enthusiastically into the burger.

'I'll get you another one,' Samir muttered, rejoining the queue. It took him a little longer this time, but he came back with another burger, a soft drink and a coffee for himself.

'So did you have lunch yesterday?' he asked conversationally.

Melissa paused mid-bite. 'I did,' she said cautiously. 'At least I think I did. Yes, of course! I remember. Dubeyji ordered a plate of *pav-bhaji*, and I shared it with him.'

'You *do* know that you're allowed time off for meals, don't you?' he asked. 'And that the agency won't shut down if you leave early enough to have dinner?'

She laughed. 'Yes, of course,' she said. 'This must be the first time I've missed dinner because of work. It's just that I hadn't originally planned on going to Goa, and I had a bunch of stuff to finish before I could go.'

'So essentially it's my fault?' Samir said.

Melissa said, 'Oh, no!' before she realised he was teasing her. Blushing hotly, she buried her face in her paper cup of soda.

'That's better,' he said. 'Finally, you have some colour in your cheeks.'

'I can't have colour in my cheeks. I'm too brown,' she retorted.

'Rubbish,' he said, and lightly patted her arm, sending a little tingle through her, all the way down to her toes. 'Tell me when you're feeling better and we'll leave. No hurry.'

'I'm good to go,' she announced, bouncing to her feet.

Samir put a steadying arm around her. 'Careful, don't jump around,' he said. 'We can't have you collapsing again.'

'I won't,' she protested, intensely conscious of the strong arm around her waist.

He didn't let her go till he'd handed her into the passenger seat of the car. Even then he waited till she was properly belted in before he went around to the driver's seat and got in.

'I need you to let me know if you're feeling the slightest bit unwell,' he said. 'And I'm relaxing the no food in the car rule—you can have what you want as long as you don't collapse again.'

In spite of her cynicism about rich playboys Melissa felt rather touched by Samir's awkwardly expressed concern. It had been a while since someone had cared enough about her to fuss. Even if the fussing was being done in an off-hand, ultra-macho kind of way.

Samir connected his MP3 player to the car's music system before they drove off. Melissa had assumed he'd be into rock or heavy metal, but surprisingly most of the tracks were *ghazals* or Bollywood oldies.

She hummed along to some of her favourite songs— she had a sweet and unexpectedly strong voice, and Samir found himself listening more to her than to the original song playing through the car speakers. She seemed so completely unselfconscious that he felt himself relaxing a little. It was a surprisingly liberating change, being with someone who didn't have an agenda either to impress him or to get information out of him.

'Who do you keep texting?' he asked as he watched her type out her third or fourth message since she'd stepped into the car. 'You're like a stenographer on steroids, the way you keep hammering into that phone.'

The second the words were out of his mouth he realised that he'd let himself relax a bit too much. Making personal remarks to someone he hardly knew was completely uncharacteristic of him—no wonder she was staring at him as if he'd grown a third eye in the middle of his forehead like Lord Shiva.

'I'm sorry,' he said immediately. 'None of my business—forget I asked.'

Melissa laughed, showing a perfect set of teeth, small, white and very even.

'I'm texting a friend back at the hostel,' she said. 'We just passed the turn-off for that new amusement park that's been built here. One of the girls is coming next weekend with her latest boyfriend—she wanted to know how long it would take to get here.'

'Won't it be more suitable for kids?'

'No, there are rides for adults as well. And the tickets are quite expensive—it's a rather cool place for a first date. For regular people, I mean.'

He raised his eyebrows. 'As opposed to *irregular* people like me?'

Refusing to be embarrassed, Melissa said, 'You know what I mean. If you took a girl out for a date you'd probably go to the theatre, or to a restaurant in a five-star hotel. The guys my friends date don't even own cars—they don't have many places to take a girl to.'

'Where does *your* boyfriend take you?' Samir asked, half jokingly and half because he wanted to know for sure that she was unattached. This asking questions thing was pretty addictive—especially when the other person was as cool about it as Melissa.

'I don't have a boyfriend,' she said, but there was something rather weird in the way she said it, as if she was mocking herself.

Samir wouldn't normally have given himself credit for being perceptive, but instinctively he knew he needed to change the topic.

'Do you like your job?' he asked, and she gave him a startled look.

'Yes,' she said cautiously, and then, 'Why? Is there any chance I mightn't have it any longer?'

This time Samir looked startled. 'Not that I know of. I'm not making any changes in the agency struc-ture—not for now at least. And when I do it definitely won't be at your level.'

'Too junior?' she asked, giving him a cheeky wink. 'Or is my salary not big enough to dent the profit fig-ures?'

It probably wasn't, but Samir could hardly say so without sounding impossibly condescending. He hes-itated for a second, and she let him off the hook by jumping to another subject.

'I just found a pack of candy in my purse,' she an-nounced. 'I'd forgotten I had them. You want one?'

Samir shook his head.

'They're nice,' she persisted. 'Tamarind and sugar.'

He took his eyes off the road for a second and glanced at the small packet in her hand. 'I haven't seen that stuff in years,' he said. 'They used to hand them out on flights when I was in college—I used to stuff my pockets full of them.'

'Does that mean you want one, then?'

'Yes, please. But you'll have to unwrap it first. I can't take my hands off the wheel.'

She took a sweet out of its wrapper and waited for him to take it from her. They were near Lonavla now, and at a rather tricky section of the road. There was no way Samir could let go of the wheel, and the candy had begun to melt in Melissa's palm.

'This is going all sticky,' she warned, and then, feeling very daring, 'Should I pop it in your mouth?'

He nodded, and she immediately wished she hadn't been quite so forward. He parted his perfectly sculpted lips a little and she leaned across to pop the sweet into his mouth. The candy stuck to her fingers for a few seconds and finally he sucked it off, the feel of his lips and tongue incredibly erotic against her skin.

Pulse racing, Melissa sat back and shot him a covert look. He was as unruffled as ever, but there was a slight smile playing about his lips. Until that instant she hadn't thought of him as someone she could actually get involved with. There were so many reasons, but right now she couldn't think clearly about them. All she could think about was how easy it would be to lean a little closer to him, breathe in the heady scent of his cologne, drop a kiss on his lips when he next turned to speak to her...

And probably make him drive the car into a road divider and kill them both. She sighed. Having a pragmatic side was all very well, but it did have a bad habit of popping up and ruining her best fantasies. So, all right, perhaps trying to seduce him while he was driving wasn't a good plan.

She stole another look at Samir. He had the kind of good looks that grew on you. The first time she'd seen him she'd thought he looked gorgeous, but rather cold—not her type at all. But the more time she spent with him, the more she noticed things—like the way his smile reached all the way up to his eyes when he was amused, and how he pushed his unruly hair off his forehead in an unconsciously sexy gesture every few minutes.

At around the end of the expressway Samir pulled out an electronic tablet and handed it to Melissa. 'I've plotted the route on this—the car's GPS isn't terribly reliable in this part of the world. Will you keep an eye on it to make sure we're on track?'

Melissa looked at him in horror. 'Don't you know where you're going?' she asked.

He laughed. 'Goa,' he said. 'We'll get there eventually. Sooner rather than later if you're a good navigator.'

She proved to be an excellent navigator—though more than once Samir found himself getting distracted by the way her hair fell across her face as she pored over the map, and the way her brow wrinkled up with concentration.

Even the first time he'd met her he'd thought that she had lovely eyes, but it was only now that he noticed the flawlessness of her dusky complexion and the near perfect shape of her lips. Her slim figure curved enticingly at all the right places, and in the few seconds he'd held her after she fainted he hadn't been able to help thinking how soft her skin was, and how right she felt in his arms.

'We'll be in Kolhapur in another hour or so,' Melissa said, effectively breaking into his thoughts. 'Are we stopping there or going straight on?'

'We could stop for lunch,' Samir said. 'There's another burger place on the highway, and a couple of coffee shops as well.'

Melissa wrinkled up her nose. 'I had two burgers for breakfast,' she said. 'I don't think I can look one in the face for a while. Can we go somewhere else? I've often seen Vegetable Kolhapur on restaurant menus—would it be a kind of speciality here?'

'Along with Kolhapuri *chappals*,' Samir agreed solemnly.

Melissa made a face at him. 'I wasn't planning to buy footwear. But do let's stop somewhere in the city.'

It would add another hour to the drive at least, but Samir complied. After Melissa's fainting fit his attitude towards her had changed. Not normally indulgent towards other people's whims, he found himself unaccountably wanting to fall in with whatever she wanted.

They chose a small restaurant in the centre of the city—the food was spicy, and not really to his taste, but it was worth the delay just to see Melissa savour the meal. Unlike the perpetually dieting women Samir normally dated, she genuinely enjoyed her food, just about stopping short of licking her fingers after polishing off everything on her plate.

'Dessert?' he asked after she was done. 'There's ice creams and *gulab jamun*. Or, no, you can't have the ice cream if you're lactose-intolerant. *Gulab jamun*?'

It was the first time anyone had actually remembered she was lactose intolerant—people who'd known her for years, including her own sister-in-law, continued to ply her with milkshakes and ice cream every time they met. Maybe he just had a good memory, but she couldn't help feeling a little flattered.

'*Gulab jamun,*' she said.

Samir watched her as she dug a spoon into a *gulab jamun*, golden syrup gushing out of the round sweet. It was a messy dish to eat, and she paused a couple of times to lick the syrup off her lips. His eyes were automatically drawn to her lush mouth and the way her little pink tongue ran over its contours. She was the first woman he'd met whose simplest gesture ended up being unconsciously sexy. Or, then again, maybe he was just turning into a horny old man.

'How old are you?' he asked abruptly.

'Twenty-four,' Melissa said, and her brow furrowed up as she polished off the last bit of *gulab jamun*. 'Why?'

Why, indeed? She looked so young that for a second he'd wondered if she was underage.

'I was thinking about the ad you wrote,' he said. 'I'd assumed it was written by an older woman—someone with kids.'

'Oh, that,' she said, looking embarrassed. 'I spent a lot of time with my sister-in-law after my nephew was born. She didn't have anyone else to help her with the baby.'

'Still, it was a very insightful piece of work. I'll be surprised if it doesn't win something.'

Feeling more and more embarrassed, Melissa said, 'Has Brian been brainwashing you?'

Samir laughed, his eyes crinkling up at the corners in a particularly attractive way. 'He happened to mention it a few times. But I don't get easily influenced by other people's opinions. Are you done? We should leave if we want to get to Goa before it's dark.'

He put a hand under her elbow to guide her out of the restaurant and Melissa felt all her fantasies come rushing back in full force. Of course he was probably just being polite. Or he was worried she'd keel over and faint once again, and he'd have to carry her out on his shoulder. Either way, her insides were doing weird things at his touch, and the temptation to touch him in return was immense.

She tried to kill the fantasy by imagining his reaction. Shock? Embarrassment? Then she remembered the feel of his lips on her fingers as he'd taken the sticky candy from them, and she couldn't help thinking that maybe, just maybe, he'd reciprocate. Bend down and kiss her. Tangle his big strong hands in her hair and tip her head back to get better access to her lips…

'Melissa?'

Brought back to earth with a thump, she realised he was holding the car door open for her.

'Sorry,' she said, sliding into her seat quickly.

'You're a complete daydreamer, aren't you?' he asked, looking rather amused as he got into the driver's seat. 'What were you thinking about?'

Ha—wouldn't you like to know? Melissa felt like saying. Maybe some day she'd actually be confident enough to come back with the truth when a man like Samir asked her a question like that. Unfortunately, as of now, she was less than halfway there.

'Just stuff,' she said after a pause.

'Random stuff?'

'Oh, very random.' He'd sounded a bit sceptical, and she felt she needed to justify herself. 'As random as Brownian motion—you know, that thing they show you in school…dust motes being tossed around by invisible molecules…my mind's a bit like that.'

He gave her a long look, and she shook her head, laughing.

'Sorry, sorry. Rambling a bit there.'

'Just a bit,' he said, but his lips quirked up at the corners as if he was trying hard not to smile.

Melissa had a nasty feeling that he knew exactly what she'd been thinking about. She concentrated on her phone for a bit, replying to the various texts that had come in while they were at lunch. When she looked up they were on the highway again, going down a rather lovely stretch of road with sugarcane fields on both sides and rolling green hills on the horizon.

'Look at the bougainvillaea down the centre of the road—aren't they beautiful?'

Samir hadn't noticed the bougainvillaea other than as an unnecessary distraction—at her words, though, he gave them a quick glance.

'They're OK, I guess,' he said. 'Though they seem to be planted in any old order. White for a few hundred metres and then miles of pink, with a couple of yellows thrown in.'

'I thought that was the nicest thing about them,' she returned. 'They look as if they've just sprung up, not as if someone planned—' She stopped short as she took in Samir's less than interested expression. 'Sorry,' she said. 'The driving must be stressful, and here I am babbling about bougainvillaea.'

'And now you're making me feel guilty about being a grumpy old git,' Samir said wryly. 'I'm sorry—I'm not very good at noticing things.'

'I'm the opposite,' Melissa said, mock-mournfully. 'I notice everything. My head's chock-full of all kinds of unnecessary junk.'

'It'll all come in handy some day,' Samir said. 'You'll be brilliant if you're on a quiz show, one day, and they show you a picture of a road and ask you to identify it.'

The good stretch seemed to be over now, because the next turnoff they took was onto a road that barely deserved the name. It was pretty much a long stretch of potholes connected by little strips of tar, and Melissa winced as the car bounced up and down.

'Sorry,' Samir said, putting a brief steadying hand on her knee as they went over a particularly bad crater.

Even through the frayed denim of her cut-offs Melissa could feel the warm strength of his hand, and she began to feel a lot more positive about the state of the road. *Every cloud...et cetera, et cetera*, she thought, an involuntary grin coming to her lips.

Beginning to enjoy herself thoroughly now, she let the next crater bounce her sideways so that she landed on his shoulder. 'Oops,' she said. 'You need to drive more carefully, Samir.'

Samir gave her a sideways look but didn't say anything. That last bounce had been deliberate, he was sure of it, but she seemed to be doing it for fun. He was used to women saying and doing things to win his approval—Melissa was something else altogether. She was definitely as attracted to him as he was to her, but she was treating the whole situation as a bit of a joke.

'I'm rolling the windows down,' she announced when they came to a stretch where, wonder of wonders, there was an actual repair crew busily laying a new layer of tar on top of the existing apology for a road. 'I love the smell of fresh tar.'

She didn't wait for his permission, and Samir wondered what she'd have said if he told her he was allergic to dust and tarry smells. He wasn't, but if he had been she'd probably have found that funny as well, he thought resignedly.

'Did you notice how the colour of the soil changes between states?' she was asking. 'It was brown while we were in Maharashtra, then it turned black near the Karnataka border—and in Goa it's brick-red.'

Samir shook his head. 'I wouldn't notice something like that even if there were mile-high signs telling me about it.'

Melissa didn't say anything, but it was clear she thought that not noticing anything sounded incredibly boring.

He gave her a quick smile. 'Though I *do* notice that you have a dirt smear on your cheek,' he said, stroking the offending item lightly with the back of his hand. 'That comes from having your nose stuck out of the window.'

'Touché,' Melissa said and grinned as she rubbed the smudge off. 'I've always wanted to say that to someone, only I've never met anyone swanky enough to speak French to.'

'I might be swanky, but I can at least speak Hindi,' Samir remarked. 'You're jabbering away in English all the time.'

'In the agency? That's because poor old Dubeyji almost had a heart attack when I tried speaking to him in Hindi. Apparently my grammar's all wrong, and I sound terribly rude.'

'You sound terribly rude even when you're speaking English,' Samir murmured.

She punched him lightly in the arm. 'Ouch, way too musclebound,' she said, pretending to nurse the knuckles on her right hand. 'You should go easy on the gym—live life a little. You'd make a much nicer punching bag if you were flabby.'

'What a nice thought,' he said, laughing. 'But I think I'll stick to my gym routine. And you might want to concentrate on that map—there's a town coming up and I've no idea whether to go through it or around it.'

'You have reached your destination,' the smug voice-over on the map informed them a few hours later.

'Except that we're in the middle of freaking nowhere,' Samir muttered.

After telling them to take a right turn towards the Uttorda beach the map had carefully led them to a cul-de-sac, with the beach on one side and a grove of coconut trees on the other.

A man passed by them, whistling cheerfully, and Melissa rolled down the window. 'Is there a hotel nearby?' she asked him in Konkani.

'Lots,' the man said. 'This is Goa—not the Thar desert. Any particular one that you might be looking for?'

Melissa consulted the name on the map and told him.

'You'll need to go back the way you came for a kilometre or so,' he said. 'Turn right at the big purple house and you'll see the signs for the hotel.'

'Well, at least it got us this far,' Samir said in resigned tones as he switched off the tablet a few minutes later. 'Though I wish our friend back there had given clearer directions—every third house here is purple. It didn't occur to me earlier—you're Goan, aren't you? Don't you have family here?'

'They all live very far away,' Melissa said. 'Um, should I call Devdeep or someone who's already arrived and get proper directions?'

'You'd need to explain where we are first,' Samir said. 'Let's do the old-fashioned thing and ask a real live human being.'

The next 'real live human being' they met fortunately knew the area well, and within ten minutes they were pulling into the hotel grounds.

'Thanks once again,' Melissa said once they'd arrived. She was feeling unaccountably shy, and automatically reverted to formality. 'You didn't have to give me a lift, but you did, and I had a great time.'

For a few seconds Samir looked down at her, his dark eyes mesmerising in their intensity. Then a hostess bustled up to them with a tray of welcome drinks and the moment passed.

'I'll see you around, then,' Samir said, taking his room keys from the bellboy and slinging his bag over his shoulder. 'Some of the other guys are already here—you could call them and catch up maybe.'

Was that a subtle way of telling her not to expect to hang around with *him*? Melissa felt absurdly upset at the thought as she watched him stride away.

Just as he was about to step out of the lobby, he turned around. 'Melissa?'

'Yes?' she said.

'Make sure you eat your meals on time, OK?' he said, smiling a crooked little smile. 'No fainting when you're called up to receive the award.'

'OK,' she said.

It was only when she reached her room and looked into the mirror that she realised that she was still smiling goofily.

'Idiot woman,' she told her reflection crossly. 'It was fun, but the trip's over now. You'll be lucky if he pays any attention to you at all after this.'

Her reflection looked back at her just as crossly, and she gave it a wry grin.

'I know. I liked him too. But he's my boss—I can't chase after him. Time for a cold shower now, OK?'

She moved away from the mirror, her good humour at least partly restored. She'd decided a couple of years back not to take men too seriously, and so far she'd managed to stick by it.

Wandering into the bathroom, she hummed softly under her breath as she turned on the taps. *Eek*, the cold water was really, *really* cold. Maybe a lukewarm shower would do just as well without giving her pneumonia.

By the time she was done with ironing an impossibly crushed pair of shorts, tucking her hair under a shower cap and actually going ahead and taking a shower, it was past six. It took her a few seconds to give her hair a brushing and pull on a yellow spaghetti strap top over the neatly ironed shorts. Once she was done, she gave herself a quick look in the mirror and headed off to the beach.

There was an enthusiastic game of cricket in progress between Devdeep and a couple of other guys from

Mendonca's and a bunch of youngsters from another agency. Pretty much the entire Mumbai advertising fraternity seemed to be in Goa, either infesting the beach or helping the state economy along by drinking larger quantities of beer and *feni*.

'Join us!' one of the younger cricket players in the group yelled out to Melissa.

'You're supposed to play volleyball on the beach, not cricket,' she yelled back. 'Losers!'

'Leave her alone—girls can't play cricket,' one of the surlier members of the team grunted.

'Oh, can't they?' Melissa said, promptly kicking off her sandals and joining them.

The sand felt good under her feet—it had been a long while since she'd gone barefoot. Mumbai had its fair share of beaches, but they were crowded and often dirty.

'You can field,' the surly man said. 'Just don't get in the way of the other fielders.'

Melissa didn't say anything—just waited till the luckless batsman hit a ball in her direction. She moved across the sand like a guided missile, leaving Mr Surly and the others gaping as she caught the ball in mid-air and whirled around to knock down a wicket. Clearly unused to running in the sand, the batsmen were only halfway down the crease—they didn't stand a chance.

'Out,' she said with satisfaction. 'I think I'll bowl next, thank you.'

There was a second of stunned silence, and then 'her' team started cheering madly. The bowler was the man who'd first called out to her, and he relinquished his place to her gladly. He was a nice-looking chap, with curly hair and an impish grin, and Melissa liked him immediately.

'Down here for the ad fest?' he asked as he handed over the ball.

Melissa nodded.

'I'm Akash,' he said. 'Would you like to catch up later? Figure out which of our entries is likely to get a gold in the festival?'

'Akash, stop hitting on the bowler,' one of the other players said.

'Yeah, Akash, there's no way she'd want to be seen with a loser like *you*,' another chimed in.

Melissa gave the guy a saucy grin. 'I'll tell you once the game is over,' she said.

She wasn't in the least attracted to him, but it made sense hanging out with a bunch of people her own age rather than hanging around and hoping Samir would come and find her.

CHAPTER THREE

AFTER THIRTEEN HOURS behind the wheel, every muscle in Samir's body felt stiff—he was supposed to be at a 'networking' session, but it sounded so incredibly boring that he'd made a flimsy excuse and escaped to his room.

Once there, he changed into running shorts and a dry fit T-shirt before slipping on his running shoes. A run would make up for the gym session he'd missed in the morning. Hopefully it would also get him tired enough to stop thinking about Melissa's lissom body.

Used to running on Tarmac, or on the jogging track at the Mumbai race course, Samir avoided the beach. The lane outside the hotel had a fair bit of traffic, and he turned off into a by-lane as soon as he could. There was much less traffic here, other than the occasional cow or motorcycle, and he was able to build up a decent pace.

Running always helped clear his head, and he was able to think a little more rationally about his reaction to Melissa. She was an attractive woman, but he'd been seeing her around the office for weeks now and had never turned to give her a second look. Maybe it had been the effect of being thrown together with her for several hours—yes, that had to be it, he decided. And her fainting fit in the morning had aroused his protective instincts.

The sun was on the verge of setting when Samir glanced at his watch. He had been running for forty-five minutes—a little short of his normal hour, but perfectly respectable. He was opposite one of the public entrances to the Uttorda beach, and he slowed to a walk.

He felt strangely reluctant to go back to the hotel. It had been only a couple of years since he'd started actually running the companies his family owned, and he wasn't yet used to the automatically deferential way the teams treated him. It was especially noticeable in Mendonca Advertising, because as a rule advertising people were a lot less respectful of hierarchy—Brian had been treated more like a well-loved uncle than a boss.

Maybe the rumours that he was planning to downsize accounted for it. People like Devdeep were desperately trying to prove that they were creative and revenue-focussed at the same time, like a modern-day David Ogilvy and Jack Welch rolled into one. And others, like Dubeyji, the elderly man who managed their Hindi advertising, were openly resentful. If you wanted to run a company successfully you couldn't keep everyone happy—Brian had tried, and in the process almost run the agency into the ground.

Green coconut water would be good, if he could find someone selling it, he thought as he made his way to the beach. There was a small stall right at the entry to the beach, and he paid for a coconut, sipping the delicate water through a straw as he walked towards the sea. There was a game of cricket in progress—and while the teams seemed to have very little regard for the rules of the game, they were evidently having the time of their lives.

Something vaguely familiar about one of the women playing caught his eye, and he automatically slowed down. She was slim, brown-skinned, with endless legs and flyaway hair, and he felt a jolt of recognition hit him as she turned to laugh at something one of the other players was saying.

In the next second Melissa caught sight of Samir, and she tossed the bat to the next player and came towards him.

'I just got run out,' she said, making a face. 'I'm brilliant at bowling and fielding—batting's not so good, though. Where were you? Jogging?'

'Running,' he said.

She probably didn't care if he'd been running or sprinting or playing hopscotch, but it seemed important to make the distinction. Jogging sounded like the kind of thing you did when you were forty and over the hill. Of course, to someone Melissa's age thirty might seem just as ancient.

She was looking at his shoes now, inspecting them as carefully as if she meant to buy them from him. 'You have proper running shoes,' she stated, sounding surprised. 'Everyone I know uses everything interchangeably—tennis shoes and football studs and running shoes.'

'Or they just run around barefoot,' Samir said, before he could help it.

Even covered in sand, her feet were very pretty, the nails painted a bright turquoise and a little silver anklet around one ankle. He'd been trying to keep his eyes off her legs and her small, pert breasts jiggling around under her yellow top, but her bare feet were pretty sexy as well.

Melissa made a face. Her spontaneous reaction when she'd seen Samir had been to come across to him—she'd forgotten what a sight she must look, with her muddy denim shorts, windswept hair and bare feet.

'I didn't bring proper shoes,' she said. 'And it was a spur-of-the-moment thing, joining these guys—I was planning to go and splash around in the sea, so I wore beach slippers.'

'You can still do that,' Samir said. Out of the corner of his eye he spotted Devdeep, abandoning his wicketkeeper role to come towards them, and he wanted to escape. 'Come on—race you to the water.'

He won, of course, but she came a close second, retaliating by running into the water and splashing him while he stopped by the edge to take off his shoes and socks.

'Just you wait,' he said, grabbing her around the waist and swinging her bodily into the next wave.

Their actual physical contact was brief—his hands touched her waist for a few seconds, and then she was back on her feet, spluttering and laughing. For a few more seconds their eyes met—then a massive wave came rolling in, almost knocking Melissa off her feet, and the moment was lost.

When the water receded Melissa discovered that her pavement store spaghetti strap top had taken the opportunity to turn completely transparent. Given that it was pale yellow, and that she'd chosen to wear a neon pink bra under it, the whole effect was a little B-grade Bollywood.

Samir was keeping his eyes studiously averted from her chest—great, that showed he was a gentleman—perversely, though, Melissa wanted to know if she had any effect on him at all. The flicker of interest she'd seen on the drive in had been so slight that she might have completely imagined it.

'Oops,' she said, looking down at herself. 'Need some help, here. I can't go back to the beach looking like India's answer to *Baywatch*. And no one handy to be rescued either.'

At that, Samir laughed. It wasn't a boastful comparison—in spite of her slim frame Melissa's bust offered fair competition to the world's most admired bathing beauties. He was having a hard time pretending to be indifferent.

'I can pretend to drown, if you'd like,' he offered. 'In the excitement you could slip away unnoticed.'

'It'd be more useful if you gave me your T-shirt,' she said, eyeing the beach apprehensively. The cricket game had wound up and the boys were heading purposefully towards the water.

Samir looked around and assessed the situation in a glance.

'Here you go,' he said, yanking the shirt over his head in a single fluid movement and tossing it to her. 'I've been running in it for an hour, though, and it's a mess. Not to mention the salt water.'

Melissa grabbed the shirt instinctively, but for a few seconds couldn't help gawking at him. His body more than lived up to expectations—in running shorts and nothing else he was all muscular chest and six-pack abs, and he looked like her favourite Bollywood star, only more real. When he frowned at her, she hastily pulled the shirt on.

Far from being 'a mess', the shirt smelt of clean male sweat and salt water, and the sudden intimacy made her hormones go into overdrive. She had to look away for a few seconds to get her unruly pulse under control. The shirt was big on her, flapping damply around her thighs, but at least she no longer looked like Silk Smitha.

The boys were nearer the water now, and even though she was decently covered Melissa couldn't help wondering how she'd explain Samir's suddenly shirtless self and her own in-the-sea costume change.

'Maybe we should take a walk down the seashore,' Samir suggested, 'and head back to the hotel after the sun sets?'

'I think that's a good idea,' Melissa said, hoping her dusky skin concealed the rush of colour to her cheeks.

'Have you spoken to your relatives yet?' he asked as they walked a little farther down the beach.

He was feeling intensely aware of her nearness and the unconsciously sexy picture she made in her tiny denim shorts with her damp hair tumbling over her shoulders. He could understand the Portuguese sailors who'd landed on the Goa coast centuries ago and then stayed, beguiled by the beauty of the Goan women they'd met there. It was a fanciful thought, but maybe one of Melissa's ancestors had been among those women.

'I didn't carry my phone onto the beach,' Melissa said, and it took him a few seconds to connect her reply with the rather banal question he'd asked a few seconds earlier.

'You could go and meet them if you want,' he said. 'I have a car booked, but I'm not likely to use it. There's some stuff that's come up at Maximus that I need to sort out.'

'Thanks,' she said. 'I'll let you know if I manage to get in touch with them.'

She had no intention of doing anything of the sort, but there was no point getting into a lengthy and possibly boring explanation of how things actually stood between her and her family.

'Looks like someone's decided to get married on the beach,' Samir said a few minutes later, touching her lightly on the arm.

Melissa turned to look. It was a rather impressive tableau against the setting sun—the bride in a perfectly stunning off-the-shoulder wedding gown, with a train that dragged along the sand, and the more casually dressed groom in a white linen shirt and pale dress jeans. The only other people with them were a bridesmaid, a priest and a photographer. The photographer and the priest were Indian; the couple and the bridesmaid could have been American or European—it was difficult to tell.

It had been two years, Melissa thought, but she still hadn't got over that initial jolt whenever she saw a blond male in his twenties. The groom wasn't Josh, but for a second she'd thought he was, and her heart-rate had tripled. Even now she couldn't help stopping to look, just to make sure that it wasn't him.

'I don't think we should stare,' Samir prompted. 'It's a rather private moment, don't you think?'

By then Melissa had got her wits about her, and she managed to retort, 'It's not very private if they've decided to get married on a public beach, is it? It's like deciding to hold a Kuchipudi performance on Flora Fountain and then getting offended if people don't pay for tickets.'

'Kuchipudi? Why Kuchipudi?' Samir was saying in bemused tones when the bridesmaid came running across to them.

'Hey, guys…if you've got a minute…Brenda and Mark just got married, and it'd be lovely if you could come across and share some champagne. Oh, I'm Sarah by the way—so nice to meet you!'

Sarah was definitely American, and from the sound of it had been at the champagne for a while now. It was difficult to refuse the invitation without sounding completely churlish, and Samir shrugged and smiled as they followed her to where the bride was trying to settle down on a plastic chair without completely ruining her dress.

Both she and the groom looked so completely happy that for a second Melissa's breath caught in her throat. This was what *she'd* hoped for once. Mark even looked a bit like Josh—she hadn't been completely delusional in the few seconds when she'd mistaken one for the other.

'He proposed when we were in Agra,' Brenda told them. 'Right in front of the Taj Mahal.'

OK, so it wasn't a very original place to propose, but Melissa couldn't help feeling touched. She took the glass of champagne Sarah was offering her and smiled. 'So getting married in India was a spur-of-the-moment thing?'

'Yes—actually, we've just exchanged vows. There'll be a proper legal ceremony when we go back.'

'So how about you two, then—are you a couple?'

While the question had been addressed to both of them, it was clear by the way Sarah was leaning towards Samir that it was his answer she was interested in.

'No, we just work together,' he said, but already he was drawing back from her, his expression becoming formal and shuttered off. 'We should leave,' he said in an undertone to Melissa.

'Why? You just got here. Have another drink before you go,' Sarah urged.

She'd not taken her eyes off Samir, and Melissa felt a second's atavistic urge to lean across and claw the other woman's eyes out. The impulse didn't last for more than a second, but it left her feeling more than a little shaken. Granted, Samir in his current bare-chested state looked like the answer to every single woman's prayer, but he was still her boss—where had that momentary surge of possessiveness come from? Luckily Samir was too focussed on getting away to notice her temporary confusion.

'D'you want your shirt back?' she couldn't help asking wryly as they got away from a visibly disappointed Sarah. 'I think you're more of a temptation to the opposite sex than I am.'

To her surprise, Samir flushed. 'Is your top dry now?' was all he said.

'Dry enough. I won't get arrested for indecent exposure at least,' she said, pulling his T-shirt off and handing it back to him. They walked on in silence for a bit, and then Melissa said, 'It was rather sweet, wasn't it? Those two deciding to exchange vows on the beach?'

Samir shrugged. 'I give that marriage one year,' he said. 'Proposing at the Taj Mahal, getting married in

Goa—its unreal. Once they're back in Chicago and squabbling about who gets to do the washing up they'll come back to earth.' Melissa gave an involuntary little giggle and Samir frowned. 'Something funny?'

'You're like the hero of a romance novel,' she said. 'Tall, brooding and cynical. All you need is a murky past and a scar on your forehead.' Like a romance novel hero, he was also sexy as hell—but she prudently didn't say that.

'Brooding and cynical?'

He sounded thoughtful, and Melissa gave him an apprehensive look, wondering if she'd gone too far.

Evidently not, because after a pause he asked, with genuine curiosity, 'Is that what the heroes in romance novels are like?'

'All of them,' she assured him. 'And they don't believe in love *ever*—until the very last chapter. My neighbour in the hostel is a romance novel junkie—she buys them by the dozen.'

'And you borrow them from her?'

'Sometimes,' Melissa said and laughed. 'No, actually I borrow them often—I'm just trying to pretend that I'm the highbrow type. I used to laugh at the plots at first, but they're actually quite addictive.'

'Right…' Samir said.

His phone pinged and he took it out of his pocket to look at the display.

'Sorry, I need to make some calls. I'll see you later—will you be able to get back to the hotel by yourself?'

A little startled by the abrupt brush-off, Melissa retorted, 'I'll try. I'm sure I can manage to find it.'

He didn't reply, still staring at his phone, and, feeling annoyed and just a little hurt, she marched off towards the hotel.

* * *

'It's one long jamboree,' Devdeep said. 'They'll announce the actual awards tomorrow.'

They were at the pre-awards cocktail party, and Melissa had been stuck with Devdeep and another colleague at one end of the room while Samir stood talking to a group from another agency at the other end. Luckily the event was in the same hotel they were booked into—at a pinch she could always develop a killing headache and escape to her room.

Melissa involuntarily looked across at Samir. He looked bored, as if he found the drinking and the locker room jokes tedious and a little immature.

Devdeep followed the direction of her eyes. 'Bit arrogant, isn't he?' he said, evidently expecting Melissa to agree with him. 'Doesn't make the slightest effort to mingle—probably thinks he's way too important to hang with small fry like us.'

'He might just be shy,' she suggested, realising how completely stupid she sounded as soon as the words were out of her mouth. Samir was to shy what Godzilla was to a garden lizard.

'You drove down with him, didn't you? Did you find out anything—his plans for the agency, that kind of stuff? Now that Brian's gone we can really catapult this agency into the big league, as long as Samir is willing to invest in it.' At her blank look, Devdeep's eyebrows flew up. 'You didn't ask him a thing? God, I wish I'd known he was driving you here; I'd have briefed you properly. What *did* you talk about, then?'

Bougainvillaea, she felt like saying. *And whether Kolhapuri chappals were invented in Kolhapur.*

'We…um…didn't talk much,' she said instead. 'He was concentrating on the road.'

Shivani, the other colleague with them, intervened. 'Devdeep, you're such a nerd,' she said. 'The guy's super-hot—I'm sure Melissa had better things to talk to him about than your stupid plans for world domination.'

At that point Samir looked across and caught Melissa's eye. Immediately, she felt her face grow warm, though she knew he couldn't have heard a word of their conversation.

'You're blushing,' Shivani said with satisfaction. 'Which means I'm right.'

'Nonsense,' Melissa retorted, but by now her ears were burning with embarrassment. 'Besides, he's way out of my league.'

'Yes, of course,' Devdeep said, evidently under the impression that he was rescuing Melissa from an uncomfortable conversation. 'Look at him—he's rich and good-looking. He could date anyone he wants!'

'Thanks, Devdeep,' she said drily.

He looked a little taken aback. 'I didn't mean…'

'No, of course you didn't.' She sighed.

Devdeep was right—no one sane would imagine that Samir was the slightest bit interested in her. And with all the dumb things she'd said about romantic novels he would probably avoid her as if she was the latest variant in bird flu.

Getting up, she said, 'I think I'll take a stroll outside. I need some fresh air—this place stinks of cigarette smoke.'

Once outside, she hesitated a little before going up to the reception desk. It was too early to go back to her room, but she didn't fancy hanging around in the lobby all alone—maybe there was a library or somewhere she could hang out until it was time for dinner.

When Samir came out of the bar a few minutes later she was deep in conversation with the concierge, discussing the relative merits of a game of billiards and a visit to the hotel's overpriced gift shop.

Samir stood watching her silently for a few minutes. Utterly unconscious of his presence, she made a charming picture as she politely scanned the list of guided tours that the concierge was thrusting on her. She was wearing a rather demure long-sleeved black dress, but her hair tumbled down her back in loose curls. The only make-up she had on was lip gloss and kohl around her eyes. The kohl emphasised the doe-like beauty of her brown eyes, and her mouth was pink and lush.

For a few seconds Samir imagined pressing his own lips onto hers. Then he came to his senses with a jerk. He'd followed her out to apologise for his earlier brusqueness at the beach, and he'd intended to say his piece and go back to the party. Standing by and gazing at her like a lust-ridden college kid was so far off the agenda it wasn't funny.

Melissa turned just then and caught sight of him, a lovely smile breaking out across her face. At the same moment, Samir noticed that the deceptively demure dress had a plunging neckline, and his already racing pulse-rate responded excitedly.

'I've been driving these people crazy,' she remarked *sotto voce* as she came up to him. 'They can't deal with anyone who doesn't want to go to the spa or go sightseeing.'

Samir was about to reply when he realised that Melissa had gone very still, staring at a man who had just entered the lobby.

The man was dark-skinned and in his late twenties, and he was staring back at Melissa as if he couldn't believe his eyes. Then, in a few quick steps, he crossed to her and grabbed her wrist, barking out something in Konkani. Samir whirled around, but something in Melissa's expression stopped him from intervening.

'What are you doing here?' the man demanded, almost shaking Melissa. 'And who's the guy?'

'My boss,' she said. 'Let me go, *men*, you're making a scene.'

Her Goan accent had suddenly become more pronounced, and her eyes were flashing with rage. As soon as she said the magic 'boss' word, though, the man released her arm, looking embarrassed.

Melissa sighed.

'Samir, meet my brother Michael,' she said. Then she elbowed Michael and said a few rapid sentences in Konkani. Probably something like, *Stop being a boor and be polite to my scary boss or he'll sack me*, because Michael held out a hand to Samir with a passable imitation of a polite smile.

'Welcome to Goa, *men*,' he said. 'Are you here for work?'

'No, he's here to look at the coconut trees,' Melissa said tartly. 'Of course we're here for work. How are Cheryl and the kids?'

'They're fine,' he said awkwardly. 'Justin still talks about you—asks about his Melly Aunty.'

He didn't look angry any longer, Samir noted—just upset and confused. Evidently there was a lot wrong here.

'And how's…' Melissa didn't complete the sentence, but Michael understood her.

'Dad's fine,' he said. 'Though his blood pressure's been on the high side. Come and see him, Melissa. It's been such a long while…. I can't believe you're here in Goa and didn't even tell me.'

It was clear that Melissa didn't want to reply, and Samir came to the rescue. 'We should be joining the others,' he said in what he hoped was a suitably authoritative tone. 'Maybe you could catch up with your brother some time tomorrow, Melissa?'

Michael looked as if he wanted to say something, but he didn't get a chance—Melissa gave him a hug and said, 'He's right. There's heaps of things to do—mustn't dawdle. I'll call you, Mickey *dada*. Sorry, Samir.'

Samir took the cue, and after giving Michael a quick nod turned and strode away towards the hotel lobby. Melissa scurried after him, and after a few minutes he shortened his stride so that she could keep up.

'Thanks,' she said as they entered the hotel.

Michael was still standing where they had left him, his expression puzzled and a little hurt, and Melissa was feeling dreadfully guilty. Not guilty enough to go back and have a proper conversation with him, but enough to want to be out of his sight.

Samir looked around. It was only seven, and there was an hour before dinner started. 'Do you want to go and wait in the bar till dinner begins, or would you like to go back to your room?'

'Bar,' Melissa said gloomily. 'Though I won't be very good company. I wish I drank. I'd like to get completely sloshed.'

She looked so ruffled that Samir impulsively put an arm around her and gave her an affectionate squeeze.

It was a perfectly innocuous gesture—brotherly, even—Melissa could only blame her own overactive hormones for her instant reaction. Trying not to be obvious by pulling away abruptly, she stayed absolutely still until he let go of her.

Seemingly unconscious of the upheaval he'd caused in her mind, he asked, 'Family problems?'

'The family has problems with me,' she said. 'So, yes, I suppose you could call it family problems.'

He waited till she was sitting down with a glass of juice in her hand before he said, 'Want to talk about it?'

'I wouldn't want to bore you,' she said. 'It's not such a big deal.'

But clearly it was—her voice was wobbly and her eyes looked suspiciously damp.

Samir put a hand lightly over hers. 'I don't get bored easily,' he said.

'My dad disowned me a couple of years ago,' she said tightly. 'Struck my name out of the family Bible and all that. Michael was pretty upset with me as well, but he's come around. Cheryl's level-headed—she must have talked some sense into him.'

'What happened—a guy?'

Melissa grimaced. 'Predictable, isn't it? My dad flipped out. It wasn't even anything terribly serious— just a teenage crush—I'd have lost interest if he hadn't made such a fuss.'

Samir frowned. Something didn't sound quite right. 'He threw you out of the house because you had a crush on a guy?'

'No...not exactly. I was going through a rebellious

phase, and… Well, I overstepped the mark quite a bit. Anyway, let's talk about something else; my love life isn't exactly the most thrilling topic.'

'Neither is mine,' Samir said, his voice deadpan. 'So that leaves politics and the economy. At this rate we'll soon be reduced to talking about the weather.'

In spite of herself, Melissa laughed. 'Storms are brewing in North Goa,' she said. 'That's where my folks live.'

'What was he like?' Samir asked abruptly.

There was something vaguely unsettling in the thought of Melissa having had a relationship serious enough for her to have broken ties with her family. Evidently the man was no longer in the picture—maybe they'd broken up afterwards.

'I don't want to talk about it,' Melissa said, shaking her head firmly. 'I need to take my mind off him, and my brother, and… Oh, what the heck? I think I'll have a drink after all.' She beckoned to a waiter and ordered a vodka with orange juice.

'Are you sure you can handle that?' Samir asked, eyeing the way she glugged it back with misgiving.

Melissa laughed. 'I come from a family of hard drinkers,' she said. 'My grandmother could probably drink you under the table. Turning teetotal was my way of rebelling.'

Many rounds later, Samir had to acknowledge that Melissa had inherited her grandmother's capacity for strong liquor. Not a heavy drinker himself, he was beginning to feel the effect of the vodkas. Melissa, on the other hand, was looking just the same—maybe just a tad more bight-eyed and chatty than she had been at the start of the evening.

'One more?' she asked, tapping Samir's empty glass with her finger.

He shook his head ruefully. 'I'm done,' he said. 'Any more and they'll have to carry me out of here.'

'Bo-ring,' she said. 'Come on, Samir, don't be a wuss. I was hoping you'd take me dancing after this.'

'Sorry—too old,' he said. 'Why don't you go with that Akash guy who was trying to chat you up so desperately?'

'Ah, so you noticed?' Melissa said. 'He's cute, but he's not really my type. Too chirpy. I like cynical brooding types.'

She was giving him a frankly assessing look, and Samir wondered if he'd got his initial reading wrong. Maybe she *was* drunk after all. Whatever the reason, the way she was looking at him was enough to make any red-blooded male lose his head.

Hurriedly, he got to his feet, reminding himself why he couldn't touch her. She was young, probably drunk, and she was an employee—there was no way he could pull her into his arms and kiss her senseless the way he wanted to. Better to leave before things got out of hand.

'I'm going to bed,' he said when she gave him an inquiring look.

'Ooh, good idea,' she said, sliding off the bar stool. 'I'll come with you.'

All right, so she was definitely drunk. For a few seconds he thought he'd heard her wrong. Then he thought he'd misunderstood—but clearly he hadn't.

'Melissa,' he said as she followed him down the winding path that led to his cottage. 'Your room's the other way; it's in the main part of the hotel.'

'Of course it is,' she said, laughing at him. 'But I'm not going there. I'm coming with you.'

She was feeling reckless—a combination of alcohol and the euphoria of being back in Goa. It had also been a long while since her last relationship had broken up. In the dim light of the bar Samir looked every inch a sex god, and resisting temptation seemed downright stupid.

'Look, I don't think this is a good idea,' he said. 'We've both had too much to drink, and…'

'And we shouldn't do something we'll regret tomorrow?' Melissa wrinkled her nose. 'Samir, if you wrote your own ads they'd be so full of clichés you'd have to pay copyright to the greetings cards company.'

'Melissa…'

'Shh,' she said and, leaning up, she kissed him full on the mouth.

Her lips were inviting, warm and lush against his, and then there was her pliant body, pressed provocatively against his. Involuntarily, Samir found himself returning the kiss, his arms coming up to pull her closer.

They were almost at the cottage, and later he couldn't remember opening the door or switching on the lights. But he did remember carrying her to bed and undressing her. And drinking in the sight of her near perfect body spread out on the bed before making wild, passionate love to her all night long.

CHAPTER FOUR

'AND THE AWARD for the best copy goes to...'

There was a long pause, and Melissa thought she'd keel over and die if they gave it to someone else.

'Mendonca Advertising for their ground-breaking, story format ad for India's most popular brand of baby soap. Come on, let's hear it for them!'

The hall burst into applause as Samir went on stage to accept the award. 'I know this isn't the Oscars, so I'll keep it short,' he said, smiling around at the audience.

Melissa noticed that several of the women immediately sat up and began preening.

'I've taken over at Mendonca Advertising only very recently. The people who really deserve the award are Brian Mendonca, the man who set up the firm, Devdeep Dutta, for a superb pitch that got us the account, but most of all Melissa D'Cruz, the talented young copywriter who wrote the ad for us.'

The applause wasn't overwhelming, exactly, but it was loud, and it went on till Melissa and Devdeep had accepted the award and returned to their seats.

'Nice of him to mention Brian,' Devdeep said in an undertone.

'He could hardly *not* mention Brian,' Melissa said

tartly. 'The agency still carries his name. Anyway, the ad was done long before Samir arrived on the scene.'

'Congrats, guys,' Samir said, coming to stand next to them. 'Very well deserved.'

Melissa gave a polite smile, pretending not to be affected by his nearness. She'd sneaked out of his room early in the morning before he woke up, and had spent the rest of the day avoiding him. There was the awkwardness, of course, of having practically thrown herself at him—her seduction skills were pathetic, and she hadn't even had the excuse of being properly drunk… not that it had seemed to matter to Samir…he'd responded pretty enthusiastically—but it wasn't just awkwardness. It was also that he was her boss, and one-night stands were sensible only if you were never going to see the person again.

He was looking at her now, and Melissa flushed automatically. The previous night had been…memorable. Samir was phenomenal in bed, and she'd been pretty vocal with her appreciation. So vocal that the memory of some of the things she'd said was making her cringe in embarrassment now. He probably thought she was a complete slut.

'You left,' he said in a low voice, once Devdeep had moved off. 'Why? I tried calling you, but your phone was switched off and you weren't in your room.'

'I went parasailing,' she said. 'My phone was in my room.'

'Parasailing?' he said thoughtfully. 'That's a new one. I don't think anyone's used *that* as an excuse to walk out on me before. Was I that bad?'

He seemed more amused than angry, and Melissa felt a rush of relief. 'You were spectacular, and you know it,' she said frankly. 'It's just that I thought I'd save us both an awkward morning-after.'

Samir reached out and touched her face lightly, and she felt her body automatically quiver with longing.

'I'd have preferred it if you'd stayed,' he said.

The simple statement went a long way towards calming her down.

'I wasn't sure,' she said. 'This isn't the kind of thing I do normally. I was in a bit of a reckless mood after meeting Michael, and I thought a one-night stand would be a good way to take my mind off things. Well, it worked!' she added defensively at the incredulous look in his face.

'Happy to help,' he said drily. 'Why did you do a runner, then?'

'You're my boss. Sleeping with the boss is never a good idea. I kind of forgot that bit in the heat of the moment last night.'

Samir stayed silent. He'd expected her to be shaken up, even embarrassed. Being told that he'd been a temporary diversion to take her mind off her more serious problems was a bit of a facer.

As if she'd read his mind, Melissa said, 'I don't make a habit of this. Yesterday was a bit of an aberration.'

'An aberration you don't want to repeat?'

'Um, yes. I mean, no, I don't want to repeat it. It was great, but it'll only become awkward with me working for you. People would figure it out and think I was sleeping with you to boost my career.'

OK, this was coming out all wrong, and Samir was looking clearly irritated, his perfectly sculpted mouth tightening with annoyance. And staring at his mouth was making her think of all the things that very same mouth had done last night, and she was going all hot and cold at the memory.

'You have a point,' he was saying now. 'Your career could do with a bit of a boost—being a copywriter with a tiny ad agency can't be where your ambitions end, can it?'

Melissa's eyes widened. Granted, his ego must have taken a bit of a beating when she'd told him that she didn't want to sleep with him again, but he was being insulting now.

'Look, there's no need to turn nasty,' she said, getting to her feet. 'I'm flattered that you think I'm ambitious enough to sleep with you because you're a big dude in the advertising world, but it isn't true. I slept with you because you've got a good body and sexy eyes, and ever since I met you I've been wondering what you'd be like in bed. Best way to get you out of my system.'

She put her rather cute little nose in the air and walked off before Samir could think of a suitable response.

Staring after her, he was surprised to find himself laughing. He'd never been put so firmly in his place before, and he found his respect for Melissa going up several notches. He'd reacted stupidly when she'd come out with that line about boosting her career, but it had triggered off a set of memories that he'd spent the last ten years trying to bury. Definitely not her fault, and he'd apologise as soon as he possibly could.

The one thing he knew was that he'd make sure he was more than a simple one-night stand for Melissa— she was worth fighting for.

Melissa's heart was pounding rather hard as she walked to the other end of the poolside garden where the award ceremony was being held. Her little outburst at Samir might mean that she'd shortly be out of a job, but she found she didn't care about that as much as she did about the thought of not seeing him again. She'd been lying about having got Samir out of her system—if anything, that one night with him had left her wanting far, far more.

A vaguely familiar-looking group of people near the bar smiled at her—with some effort she recognised her cricket teammates from the previous day's game on the beach.

Akash was waving to her. 'Congratulations,' he said, coming up to her and giving her an extravagant hug. 'I was trying to get your attention earlier, but you were completely engrossed in whatever Mr Razdan was saying to you. I do hope you managed to swing a better salary—you deserve it.'

For one horrified moment Melissa thought he meant that she deserved a higher salary for having slept with her boss. Then she realised he meant the award, and said, 'It didn't occur to me to ask for more money.'

'You should ask him now. There are a dozen other agencies here who'd hire you on the spot at double the pay. Actually, my boss has already been asking about you.' He gave her an engaging grin. 'She comes to these award dos to sniff out the talent. Saves her having to pay a headhunter. Interested?'

'What's she like to work for?'

Akash shrugged. 'A bit hormonal. Fundamentally OK, though. And you'd have brilliant colleagues like me to work with if you joined.'

Oh, dear—she'd really have to figure out a way of telling Akash she wasn't interested. The cricket game on the beach seemed to have given him all kinds of ideas.

She was trying to think of a polite way of giving him the brush-off when she saw his gaze shift to over her shoulder.

'The guy doesn't leave you alone for a minute, does he?' Akash muttered. He scribbled something on the back of a napkin and thrust it at her. 'Here—call me once Svengali's gone. I'll set up something with Maya.'

'New conquest?' Samir asked, once Akash was gone. 'Or is he launching a takeaway service?'

'Funny joke,' Melissa said, wrinkling up her nose. 'Not. He was offering me a job.'

Samir didn't seem to have heard what she'd said, and Melissa began to feel a little annoyed. Okay, maybe she wasn't in the big league, exactly, but it was pretty flattering being head-hunted by someone as well known as Maya Kumar.

She'd recognised the name the second Akash had mentioned it. Maya was a legend in Indian advertising circles, having quit as the creative director of a multinational advertising firm to set up her own company. Ten years later she was running one of India's most successful agencies, and Melissa found the thought of working for her rather exciting.

'I came to check if you'd like to go out for dinner,' Samir was saying. 'Unless, of course, you've already made other plans?'

'I have,' she said shortly, and added, as his eyes automatically shifted to where Akash was standing with a group of friends, 'I'm meeting Michael and Cheryl.

Thought it was time to try and do some patching up.'
There had been no real need to tell him that, but she'd
hate him to think that she'd jump straight out of his
bed into a flirtation with another man.

He looked surprised. 'You sure about this? I thought
you wanted to avoid your brother.'

'I can't avoid him for the rest of my life. And I really want to see my nephew.'

'I can drop you,' Samir offered. 'Wherever you're
meeting them. And hang around if you need moral
support.'

He really seemed to have missed the point of a one-
night stand, Melissa thought in exasperation. Moral
support was *so* not part of the deal. It didn't help that
he was looking especially hot today, in a tailored jacket
worn over an open-necked shirt and jeans that fitted
his long legs and lean thighs like a second skin. Nor
that the hotel had quoted her a perfectly outrageous rate
for a cab to Panaji, where she was meeting Michael.
A week's salary for a ride in a smelly old cab versus
a *gratis* trip to Panaji and back in Samir's top-of-the-
range roadster—she could be forgiven for giving in.
Still, it was better to make some things clear.

'What I said earlier, about getting you out of my
system…'

'You meant it. I know. And I'm sorry I said what I
did—put it down to my ego not being used to a bruis-
ing.' He gave her a quick smile. 'We'll stick to being
just good friends, OK?'

Impossible to tell whether he was serious or not, but
Melissa decided she didn't care. It was only by exercis-
ing super-human self-control that she was sticking to
her self-imposed no touching policy with Samir. There

was no point inflicting further torture on herself by refusing a simple lift.

'Let's go, then,' she said, giving him a sunny smile in return.

They were halfway to Panaji, and Melissa was just beginning to relax, when Samir spoke.

'Are you meeting your father as well? Or just your brother's family?'

'Just my brother,' Melissa said and sighed. 'I don't think I'm up to the strain of meeting my dad just yet.'

'He seems quite a tyrant. What does he do?'

'He owns a restaurant in North Goa,' she said. 'We all used to chip in: my mom, me, Michael and Cheryl— even my nephew used to hang around there the whole day. And when I finished college I started working there full-time. My dad was getting older, and we'd expanded a bit—he needed all the help he could get.'

Samir shot her a quick look. She sounded wistful, and a little sad, as if she wasn't quite as blasé about being cut off from her family as she pretended to be.

'Your mother?'

'She died six years ago,' Melissa said.

The words were matter-of-fact, but he could tell she was not over it yet.

'A road accident.'

'I'm sorry,' Samir said.

Melissa shrugged. 'It was quick—that was a mercy. She didn't suffer much.'

Unlike her family, Samir thought, trying to imagine how tough it would have been for Melissa, losing her mother while still in her teens. She was staring out of the window unseeingly now, and he swiftly steered the conversation so that she started talking about her nephew. That cheered her up almost instantly, and by the time he dropped her off at Panaji, she was smiling again.

He was deep in thought as he drove towards the waterfront. The Mandovi River passed right by Panaji, and after he'd parked the car he found a little restaurant that overlooked it. It was the first time in a long, long while that he'd been involved enough with a woman to worry about her. Not used to analysing his own feelings, he tried to tell himself that it was the natural result of the rushed relationship they'd had. One day they'd hardly known each other, the next they were having wild, passionate sex. And now they were acting out a 'just friends' charade that was a positive insult to his status as a red-blooded male.

Samir's phone rang when he was halfway through his dessert.

'Can you come and pick me up?' a quiet voice asked.

Immediately he knew something was wrong.

'Where?' he asked, and she named a popular store on the main street.

'I'm standing outside,' she said.

She looked positively woebegone when he drew up in front of her.

'Everything OK?' he asked gently, seeing how close to tears she was.

'Justin didn't recognise me,' she said. 'My own nephew. And Michael didn't tell him who I was because he was worried he'd go home and tell Dad. They sneaked out to meet me like I'm some kind of fallen woman or something. Michael kept saying that I should go and meet our parish priest—apparently he's the only person Dad discusses me with.'

She was practically shaking with rage, and once they were out of the tiny city Samir pulled up to the side and held out his arms. Melissa glared at him for a few seconds, as if he was personally responsible for the mess her life was in. Then, with a half suppressed sob, she crept into his arms.

Her body was soft and yielding against his, and because she wasn't crying any longer, just holding on to him for comfort, he felt no guilt in tipping up her face after a few minutes and kissing her. He'd meant the kiss to be gentle, but she seemed to go up in flames as soon as his lips touched hers.

'Hey…' he said softly as her fingers fumbled eagerly at his shirt buttons. 'Maybe we should get back to the hotel.'

For a few seconds she didn't seem to have heard him, and then she gave a shaky little laugh and drew away from him. 'You're right,' she agreed. 'Before the morality police catch up with us.'

She didn't say anything about having got him out of her system, he noted with satisfaction as he started the car.

'You're the first man I've been with after Josh,' Melissa said abruptly after a few minutes.

Samir glanced across at her. He'd thought as much after the previous night—she wasn't inexperienced, exactly, but it was evident that she didn't sleep around. Why she would want to give the impression that she did was something else altogether.

'So the one-night stand thing…?'

'Was just me trying to prove to myself that I could do casual sex if I wanted to.' She made a funny little grimace. 'Didn't work.'

Samir couldn't help laughing at her expression. 'You know what? I'm glad it didn't,' he said. 'At the risk of sounding impossibly old-fashioned, I must admit that I don't really approve of casual sex. And I'd like us to be more than a one-night stand.'

Melissa wrinkled her nose. 'What? Like a proper relationship?'

'Something like that.' They had stopped at a traffic light, and he leaned across and kissed her bare shoulder, making her shiver in reaction. 'Don't think about it right now, though.'

The light changed, and they were moving again, so Melissa didn't ask why not. Instead, she asked, 'Were you in a relationship before this?'

The way she said 'relationship' was incredibly cute—rather like a precocious child trying out a new word—and Samir smiled involuntarily. It was one of the most attractive things about Melissa: the little flashes of naiveté that showed between the chinks of her self-assured, woman-in-charge-of-her-own-sexuality persona.

'Not a serious one,' he said. 'But I was dating someone for almost year.'

Her eyebrows flew up. 'You spent a *year* with someone you weren't serious about?'

He shrugged. 'We thought it would work out initially. And it was convenient to have someone to bring along to social dos.'

'It sounds awful,' Melissa said frankly. 'And before that?'

'Before that I had a very intense fling with a journalist. That time we were both clear it wasn't going to last.'

'You're an even bigger disaster than I am,' Melissa said. 'The L word didn't happen ever? Even when you were in college?'

He was silent for a few seconds, and then he said, 'It did happen. Not when I was in college, but very soon after I graduated. Turns out I picked the wrong person.'

'She met someone else?'

He shook his head. 'No, just changed her mind about me. But it was a long while ago. Tell me about the guy you were with—why was your father so against him?'

As soon as the words were out of his mouth he wished he hadn't asked. Her face clouded over again, and she bit her lip.

'Josh was Australian—that was one thing. And he was definitely not serious about me; it was just a holiday romance as far as he was concerned.'

Samir hesitated a little. He'd shifted the conversation away from his own botched-up love life because he hated talking about the one period in his life when he'd let another person control him emotionally. He hadn't, however, wanted to make Melissa relive what had probably been a more traumatic experience—in his case at least his family had been kept out of it. Now he could hardly change the topic again without seeming callous, so he searched around for a question that would show he was listening without being overly intrusive.

'How did you meet Josh?' he asked finally.

'He came into the restaurant when I was doing the lunch shift. He was a travel writer, and he was in Goa to do some background research for his new book. I was used to foreigners—our restaurant had got good reviews on quite a few travel websites and we got dozens of tourists coming in every day. Josh was different. He'd been in the country only for a few weeks, but he seemed totally at home—like he was born here. We got talking, and…well, before I knew it I'd agreed to help him out with his research. I speak Konkani, and even a little Portuguese, and he needed someone to translate when he interviewed the locals.'

Samir felt a totally alien emotion sweep over him— it took him a few seconds to realise that it was jealousy. Melissa's voice had taken on a wistful tone that he'd never heard before, and he had a mad urge to hunt Josh down and smash his face in for him. Because he'd quite obviously hurt Melissa—not to mention messing up her relationship with her family.

It took some effort keeping his voice neutral as he asked, 'Your father didn't stop you from dating him?'

'He didn't know for a long while,' Melissa said. 'Josh used to flirt with me a little, but I didn't take it seriously at first. Then we started spending more time together—he showed me the work he'd already done on the book, and it was amazing. He wrote really well. You could visualise each sentence. I think I fell for his writing first. My dad found out I was having an affair with Josh just a week before he was due to leave India. I didn't want to miss those last few days with him and I refused to listen to my dad. Just packed up a bag and moved into Josh's place. He'd paid the rent for a full quarter, so after he left I had a place to stay for a while. My dad refused to let me into the house.'

'How did you end up in Mumbai, then?'

'I called Aunty Liz. She's Brian's wife, and she's a kind of cousin several times removed. I've always been close to her, and I thought she could help me get a job outside Goa. I majored in English literature—it's a pretty useless qualification, but I write pretty well. Brian offered me a copywriting job, and it seemed like the perfect solution.'

'Are you still in touch with him?'

'With Brian?' Melissa asked, looking puzzled.

For an instant, Samir felt like shaking her.

'Oh, you mean Josh. Well, yes—he e-mails me sometimes, but we're just friends now. I'm over him, if that's what you're asking.'

It was exactly what he was asking, and the casual way in which she said she was over Josh was more believable than if she'd protested vehemently.

'I don't know if I was really in love with him either,' she said after a while. 'It was all so mixed up. I didn't mind working in the restaurant, but a part of me had always wanted to escape. Then there was something glamorous about dating a foreigner—especially a writer. Maybe I just got a little carried away, trying to prove that I was an independent woman with a life of my own.' There was another little pause, and then she said, 'Or at least that's what I tell myself now. At the time I was pretty besotted with him. I even hoped he'd take me with him when he left India.'

'You were pretty young,' Samir said easily. 'Most people get carried away the first time they fall in love.'

'I guess,' Melissa said, adding silently to herself that 'most people', however, didn't run away from their families—or ignore the opposite sex for two years after the relationship ended and then suddenly decide that they wanted to have a casual relationship with the first man they found attractive.

Twisting her hands together in her lap, Melissa felt suddenly very close to tears. She'd thought she'd moved on—become a different person from the confused, heart-sore and rebellious girl who'd left Goa two years ago. Meeting Michael and Cheryl had brought it all back, and she didn't feel anywhere near as confident about her choices as she had earlier.

Especially after Michael had put a hand over hers and said, in his quiet way, 'Dadda and me didn't behave right with you, Melly. You'd never have left us if Mamma was still there.'

He was right, and that made it all so much worse. She'd whisked her hand out from under his and announced tightly that she needed to leave. Then she'd called Samir, wanting—no, *needing* his quiet strength by her side. And he'd been wonderful, encouraging her to talk without prying unnecessarily or turning judgemental. Not in the least like Josh, who'd hated any kind of emotional outburst—especially when it had to do with her family.

They were at the hotel now, and Samir pulled into the parking lot. Immediately the atmosphere between them changed, and Melissa felt a shiver of anticipation run through her. Samir came around to open her door and she automatically went into his arms as soon as she got out of the car. It felt like coming home as she inhaled the now familiar smell of his aftershave and pressed even closer to his hard, muscular body.

He was perfect, she thought as a wave of lust swept over her. Strong and gentle and wildly exciting all at the same time—she'd been crazy to think that a single night with him would be enough.

The kiss was slow this time, and unexpectedly sensuous, and when his lips finally left hers Melissa found herself clinging on to him for support.

A little breathlessly, she asked, 'Your room or mine?'

CHAPTER FIVE

'MOVE IN WITH YOU?' Melissa looked a little taken aback. 'Isn't that a bit drastic? We only met a couple of weeks ago.'

'It's the practical thing to do,' Samir said. 'I'm at serious risk of dying of frustration.'

It was a week since they'd returned from Goa, and they'd managed to spend only one afternoon together. Melissa's hostel had a curfew, and Samir was working crazy hours as he tried to get Mendonca's finances into shape before he handed it over to a new business head and moved back to Maximus. Sure, they saw each other in the office, but that wasn't enough—after spending their last few days in Goa almost exclusively in bed, it was torture having to pretend that they were just colleagues.

The thought of actually going back to the same house and sleeping—or staying awake—in the same bed was so incredibly tempting that the practicalities didn't strike Melissa for several minutes.

'What if it doesn't work out?' she asked. 'We might get tired of each other, or you might find out that I'm such a slob you can't bear having me around in your house.' Another thought occurred to her, and she went on without giving him a chance to interrupt. 'I'd have to give up my room in the hostel. There's no way I'll get it back later.'

'You won't need it later,' Samir said. 'Look, let's give it a shot. If it works—great. If not, we'll part ways, and I swear I'll help you find a place to live that's even better than your too-good-to-be-true hostel. I want us to be together.'

He was leaning forward a little as he spoke, and although his words were ordinary enough Melissa felt an automatic little thrill run through her in response to the simmering desire in his eyes.

'What about people at the agency finding out?'

Samir shrugged. 'Half of them have already guessed,' he said. 'And the rest don't need to know anything other than that you're my girlfriend.'

He was right, and the only reason Melissa still hesitated was because she knew that she was getting into murky waters here. A quick, no-holds-barred fling was what she'd wanted. But, like the lady in her favourite washing powder ad, she'd got a lot more than she'd expected. A heartbreakingly good-looking boyfriend. A complicated decision to make.

Sneaking a quick look at Samir, she wondered why it felt so tough. Sure, Brian and Liz would probably be horrified if she moved in with Samir, but her other friends wouldn't care much. It was more that she herself wasn't sure it was the right thing to do.

Perhaps if she'd met him a few years later she'd have been panting to move in with him. But right now her plans included rising up the agency ranks to make creative director, writing the perfect novel and travelling around India in her spare time. By train, because she was still flight-phobic. Men figured in her plans, but in the relative scheme of things they were at the same level of importance as the ad breaks on a movie channel.

Samir, however, showed signs of wanting to be the main feature film—worse, if she didn't get a grip on her life that was exactly what he'd end up being. It wasn't that she didn't like him. She did—a lot. But falling for him would clearly be a bad idea. He moved in completely different circles from her—his friends were socialites and high-flying executives, and Melissa knew she'd feel deeply uncomfortable with them.

Also, his lifestyle was as different from hers as a Bollywood star's was from the man who ran the corner *vada-pav* stall. He'd never commuted by bus or local train, and he'd looked surprised and a little disbelieving when she'd told him that she actually preferred public transport to whizzing around in an air-conditioned car. And he hated eating out at the little roadside joints she favoured. Small things, but they all added up to make the practical side of her brain think that their living together might not be idyllic. In spite of the red-hot sex.

Then again, the practical side of her brain hadn't had much of a say in the decisions she'd made since she'd met Samir.

It was difficult thinking things through while Samir was still watching her, his expression inscrutable. Probably he thought she was a right ninny, dithering around instead of saying anything. Wishing she was the organised type—the kind of person who could draw up a mental list of pros and cons and decide in a minute— she frowned as she tried to concentrate.

What other people thought didn't really matter. Nor

did it really matter whether she liked his friends or he liked hers. What mattered was whether she wanted to move in with him or not. And the more time she spent with Samir, the more she felt she wanted to.

It wasn't just that he was spectacular in bed—the more she got to know him, the more she liked him as a human being. His aloof, sometimes overly serious work persona concealed a genuinely warm, fun side that she'd got to know over the past couple of weeks. And, unlike Josh, he seemed to be as keen on her as she was about him. She couldn't help the warning bells that went off in her head every time she found herself getting a bit more involved with Samir, but she could decide to ignore them.

'Don't over-think it,' he was saying softly now, his hand moving persuasively up her thigh. 'Just go with the flow.'

God, she'd always hated that expression, but when Samir said it, it sounded positively enticing. Not to mention the way his hand was making her feel. *Impulsive* and *wanton* were the words that came to mind as she said, 'When should I start moving my stuff?'

'Maya Kumar's offered me a job,' Melissa announced two weeks later.

Samir looked up from his computer and frowned. 'The one that guy was speaking to you about? Ashish, or whatever his name was.'

'Akash,' Melissa said. 'Yes, that one. She's giving me a sixty percent pay-hike and she's also given me the option of working from home. What d'you think?'

'It's your decision,' Samir said slowly. 'Sixty percent is good, but we'd be able to match that here. And

I'll be out of Mendonca and on to my next project in a few months—do you still want to leave?'

Melissa plonked herself into the chair opposite Samir. 'We've talked about this,' she said. 'It'll look really weird, you giving me a pay-hike when everyone knows I'm your girlfriend.'

She'd moved into Samir's plush flat a week ago, giving the agency staff enough food for gossip for the next year at least. Other than Dubeyji, the elderly Hindi copywriter, no one had openly expressed disapproval, though Devdeep had taken to addressing her in a terribly stiff and formal way.

Samir shrugged. 'I don't particularly care what they think,' he said.

'Neither do I,' Melissa said honestly. 'But I'd feel much better getting a raise by changing jobs than...'

'Than sleeping with the boss,' Samir said in resigned tones. 'I know. You've mentioned it a few dozen times already. Go ahead, then.'

Melissa hesitated a little. In the office they tried to keep their conversations as formal as possible, and she wasn't sure if her next question was strictly professional. 'Are you upset with me?' she ventured finally.

Samir looked genuinely surprised. 'No, of course not,' he said. 'You're excellent at your work, and you've got a better offer at a better firm—it's natural you'd want to move.' He glanced at his watch. 'I have a meeting in Bandra—need to rush. Should I leave the car for you?'

'No, I'll take the bus,' Melissa said absently. 'Or, actually, if you're going to be home late I'll go visit Brian and Liz.'

'Keep the car and driver with you, then,' Samir said as he got to his feet. 'I'll ask Kash to book me a cab.'

Melissa knew better than to argue—Samir genuinely didn't get that she preferred walking or public transport to being driven around in his car. It was one of the many things they didn't agree on, and she hadn't got around to talking to him about it. Which would be because she'd spent every spare moment these past two weeks in bed, having wild, delicious sex with Samir—talking hadn't really figured very high on the agenda.

Her mouth automatically curved up at the corners at the thought, and Samir gave her an inquiring look.

'Planning something devilish?' he asked. 'I don't trust you an inch when you get that look in your eyes.'

'I'll tell you when you get home,' she said saucily. 'Off you go to your meeting now.'

She was terribly tempted to lean across and kiss him—he was near enough for her to smell the woody scent of his aftershave, and it could make her go dizzy with longing if she let it.

That was one of her reasons for quitting, she told herself. It was difficult staying focussed on work when he was around. Only once he was out of the room and she'd gone back to her desk she had to admit to herself that it wasn't the only reason. Nor even the main one. Maya Kumar was very different from Brian, but she had one big thing in common with him—she valued Melissa's work.

Melissa tried to imagine Brian's reaction if she'd quit when he was in charge. He'd have used every trick in the book to hold her back, and he'd have succeeded because she'd have known he wanted her to stay. But

Brian had retired, and Samir didn't really care about the agency.

Sighing, Melissa opened up her laptop and began typing out her resignation.

Liz had insisted that she stay for dinner, and it was almost ten when Melissa got back to Samir's apartment complex. It was a tall building in central Mumbai, and he had a massive three-bedroom flat that took up all of one floor—even the bathrooms were larger than the hostel room that Melissa had been living in for the past year. In spite of the scale, the flat had an impersonal look about it, as if it had been designed by an interior decorator as a showcase bachelor pad rather than an actual home.

Samir was still in his office clothes, and he was poring over a sheaf of papers heaped up on the dining table.

'Still working?' Melissa asked, and he leaned back in his chair, running a tanned hand through his already rumpled hair. His jaw was covered with stubble, and he managed to look unkempt and incredibly hot at the same time.

'There's a new deal coming up,' he said. 'A small media company that we might pick up a stake in.'

She crossed the room to him and put her hands on his shoulders. His body was warm and strong under her hands, the muscles flexing as he stretched. Unbidden, her hands started straying over his body—until he pulled away and said, 'I'll finish this in half an hour and be with you, okay?'

Somehow even the dismissal sounded like an invitation, because his dark eyes were dancing wickedly up at her.

'Did you have dinner?' she asked primly, and he shook his head.

'Kamala's son isn't well, apparently—she left a message with the security guard. I'll grab some fruit and cereal in a bit.'

'When?' Melissa asked in disbelief. 'It's ten o'clock. And no one eats fruit and cereal for dinner. Unless they're ill or on a totally weird diet.'

Kamala was the cook, and usually as punctual as clockwork—Samir was clearly incapable of managing without her.

He was still absorbed in work, and all he said was, 'I'm used to eating late. Don't worry about it.'

Melissa wrinkled her nose as she left the room. It was unlikely Samir would eat at all—and going by the last two times he'd brought work home it would be midnight before he came to bed. She gave her reflection in the mirror a rueful look. She'd spent a frantic few minutes in the car fluffing up her hair and redoing her make-up. Pretty much a wasted effort, as Samir hadn't even looked at her properly.

For a mad moment she considered changing into something skimpy and trying to vamp him into bed. Mentally, she reviewed her night wardrobe—teddy bear pyjamas, two striped nighties and a pair of exercise shorts that she normally paired with a tattered T-shirt. Hmm…not much scope for seduction there. Besides, she wasn't sure she had the required *oomph* for a grand seduction scene, even if she'd possessed a suitably titillating wardrobe. She'd lucked out with

Samir that first time in Goa, but after that he'd handled all the seducing that needed to be done.

Regretfully giving up the plan, Melissa wandered into the kitchen. Perhaps cooking the poor man dinner was a better idea, she thought, opening the fridge and peering inside. There was very little food in it—from what Melissa could figure Samir's cook bought just enough for two or three meals at a time. Whipping up a cordon bleu meal with two tomatoes, a handful of droopy beans and a capsicum would be next to impossible. Oh, well, Samir would have to manage with a simple pasta dish instead.

Luckily the freezer yielded a pack of frozen chicken, and there was a jar of olives at the back of the store cupboard. Suspiciously turning it around to check the expiry date, Melissa was relieved to find that it was a year away.

She found herself humming under her breath as she put a pot of water on to boil and started chopping the vegetables. One of the things she'd missed most in the hostel was access to a proper kitchen—after so many years of working in her father's restaurant she was a more than competent cook. Samir's kitchen might be poorly stocked, but the equipment was state-of-the-art. The interior designer had evidently pictured Samir in celebrity chef mode—actually, the more Melissa thought about it, Samir in a chef's hat and an apron would look pretty hot.

'What on earth are you doing?' Samir asked, appearing quite suddenly at the door.

Melissa gave a little yelp of alarm, almost dropping the pot of boiling pasta on the ground. 'You startled me!' she said once she'd safely drained the pasta and put the pot in the sink. 'Didn't anyone teach you not to creep up on people like that?'

'I wasn't expecting you to be here,' Samir said, frowning. 'What's that stuff?'

'Boiled worms and slug juice,' Melissa said crossly. She'd gone out of her way to cook him a decent meal, and he was acting as if he'd found her going through his wallet.

'I don't expect you to cook for me,' he said. 'I told you I'd have managed just fine with cereal.'

'It's not a big deal,' she muttered. Evidently the genius who'd said that the route to man's heart was through his stomach hadn't met Samir Razdan. He sounded positively put out—as if she'd transgressed some unwritten rule by cooking him a meal.

'Thanks anyway,' he said.

She poured the pasta sauce she'd made earlier over the spaghetti and he took the plate from her. Melissa watched as he took a bite.

'Hey, this is good,' he said, sounding surprised. 'Much better than the stuff Kamala turns out.'

'My dad runs a restaurant, remember?'

'Yes of course—I'd forgotten. So you're quite the little Tarla Dalal, aren't you?'

It was said in an indulgent way, but Melissa decided he was being unnecessarily patronising.

'Not really,' she said, turning away to clear up the kitchen counter. 'If I was Tarla the spaghetti would have been pure vegetarian, and you'd not have eaten more than two bites. Tell me if you want some more, otherwise I'll put this lot in the fridge and go to bed.'

He could move as silently as a panther when he

wanted to—Melissa gasped as she felt his hands come up to span her waist.

'Aren't you coming to bed with me?' he murmured, nibbling gently at the nape of her neck.

He knew exactly where the sensitive spot was, and she squirmed helplessly in his arms, finally managing to gasp out, 'Go and finish your dinner.'

'I will…I will.' He turned her around to face him, dipping his head to drop a light kiss on her lips. 'Why so stroppy today?'

Melissa raised her eyebrows. 'You clearly have different standards for yourself and for other people,' she said. 'If I'm stroppy, you're the Grinch. Samir, stop it!'

His mouth came down on hers, warm and sexy and tasting of tangy spaghetti sauce. Melissa resisted half-heartedly for a few seconds, then gave in and let him have his way. Grinch or not, he kissed like a dream— no point wasting a kiss just because she was a little upset with him.

'Still stroppy?' he asked when he finally raised his head.

Melissa shook her head. 'No, just very thankful I didn't put garlic in the pasta.'

He laughed at that, his amazing mouth curving up at the corners. 'You're really something,' he said, and there wasn't the slightest hint of anything patronising in his voice.

'I am,' she agreed solemnly. She was over her temporary fit of annoyance. 'Actually, I'm almost perfect. I write well, I'm very intelligent, I can cook, I'm quite pretty…'

'And incredibly modest as well,' Samir agreed as he moved away to pick up his plate.

'Yes, that too,' she said. 'Hurry up and finish eating now. I want to go to bed.'

He gave her a slow, heart-stopping smile, and she blushed furiously but stood her ground.

'Hmm…' he said. 'I'll be done in a minute—just taking another helping. I'm hungrier than I thought I was.'

She waited while he emptied the rest of the pasta onto his plate, then took the pan from him and rinsed it under the tap. Something had just struck her, and it made a lot of small, rather puzzling incidents fall into place.

'You don't like the thought of me settling in here too thoroughly, do you?' she asked, and his eyes flew up to meet hers immediately, a wary look in them.

'I don't know what you mean,' he said.

Melissa gave him a long, assessing look. 'Oh, I think you do,' she said cheerfully. 'You asked me to move in with you on impulse, because we were both pretty much dying of frustration, and now you're not sure you did the right thing. And every time I do something, like rearrange your CDs or cook you dinner, you start getting worried.'

Samir looked incredulous. 'What would I be worried about?'

'Now that I'm not too sure of,' Melissa admitted, giving him a sunny smile. 'Like I said, I'm very intelligent, but in this case I don't have enough data to go on. Maybe you're worried that I'll become a fixture here and when you're sick of me you won't be able to turf me out. Or that you'll get so used to having me around that you'll be heartbroken when I decide to leave. Or that Kamala will stop working for you because I've taken over the kitchen.'

'Or that little green aliens will come down and take over the planet,' Samir said, laughing. 'You have a really active imagination, Melissa.'

'And now you're acting all superior and patronising because you know I'm right,' Melissa said firmly.

'Melissa…'

'You might as well admit that I'm right.'

'You're not,' Samir said, exasperated. 'Stop being childish. I might be a little stand-offish at times, but there's a lot going on in my life. It doesn't have anything to do with you.'

'Does too.'

Goaded beyond endurance, Samir reached out and grabbed Melissa by her shoulders. She went utterly still as soon as he touched her, her eyes seeming to grow larger as she looked up at him. Torn between wanting to shake her and kiss her senseless, he ended up attempting the latter. She made a strangled little sound as his mouth fastened on hers but she was anything but reluctant, going by the way her arms went around him and her body moulded itself to his.

'You're a big bully,' she said breathlessly when he finally let her go. 'And you know I'm right.'

'A bully, am I?' he asked, looking pointedly at her arms, which were still twined lovingly around him.

'Yes,' she confirmed, leaning up to press a little kiss onto his mouth. 'A gorgeous one, but a bully all the same. No, *don't* do that again.' Determinedly, she wriggled out of his grip. 'I'm not going to be kissed into agreeing with you. Come on, Samir, be serious for a minute.'

He laughed, charmed back into good humour by the kiss and by her uniquely pragmatic way of looking at things.

'Think about it,' she urged. 'Aren't you a little uncomfortable with having let me into your life so easily?'

Samir leaned back a little, exhaling slowly. Melissa was right. He'd wanted her to move in, and he wanted her to stay, but there was still a part of him that was deeply uneasy about sharing his life with another human being.

'Only because I've had a bad experience in the past,' he said finally. 'It's not about you. I wouldn't have asked you to come and live with me if I didn't want you to be part of my life. What's funny?'

It had gone as quickly as it had come, but he knew he hadn't been mistaken about the flash of amusement he'd seen in her eyes.

'Sorry,' she said quickly. 'I told you in Goa—you look like the hero of a romance novel. And now you tell me you have a tortured past. And then you say things like "It's not about you". You're just too in character to be true.'

'Glad to be so entertaining,' he said, trying to keep the wryness out of his tone. 'I'm sure the way you regularly cut me down to size is good for my soul.'

'I'm sorry,' she said, suddenly contrite. 'I don't know what happened to you, and I've no right to make fun of it. God knows I've got a messed up past myself.'

He pushed a hand through his hair, the gesture so unconsciously sexy that Melissa's breath caught in her throat. It would be very easy to fall in love with Samir—she'd spent the past few weeks consciously guarding against it. Telling herself repeatedly that this was a short-lived thing had helped. So had determinedly seeing the funny side of things that could otherwise be upsetting or hurtful.

'It wasn't anywhere as exciting as what happened to you,' Samir said. 'In retrospect, I'm rather embarrassed about it—but I was very young then. I fell madly in love with a woman everyone except me knew was interested in me only because of my money.'

Some of her puzzlement must have shown in her face because he said, 'I inherited a fair bit from my grandparents. And I had a bright career ahead of me.'

'How did you find out?'

He smiled briefly. 'I was going through a self-discovery phase pretty soon after we got engaged. I thought I'd switch careers, do something I enjoyed. Trouble was, the stuff I enjoyed wasn't high-paying. And I wanted to use most of the money I'd inherited to go and live in Europe for a few years—she was out of the door the minute she realised I was actually serious.'

'What was it that you wanted to do?' Melissa asked curiously. So far he hadn't given the impression of being particularly passionate about anything—definitely not to the extent of giving up his expensive lifestyle. He worked very hard, but it didn't look as if he enjoyed that much either—it was difficult to think of him wanting to go off and follow a dream at any age.

'Ah, that's another story,' he said, taking her hand and switching off the kitchen light as he led her out of the door. 'Anyway, as it turned out I changed my mind and took up a corporate career instead.'

'So if your girlfriend had stuck with you she'd

have got all your lovely money after all,' Melissa said. 'Sounds like there's a moral in there somewhere.'

'She married a richer guy,' he said. 'So all in all I think it worked out well for her. And, Melissa…?'

They were inside the bedroom now, and she turned towards him at the suddenly serious note in his voice.

He touched her face gently—a fleeting caress that somehow had more feeling in it than all that they had shared earlier. 'If I've been shutting you out at times, it's because I've got used to being alone. Not because I don't trust you, or because I think you're like Shalini in any way.'

Melissa nodded. 'And, for the record, I'm not trying to push you into anything either. I know you're not in the market for a serious relationship right now and neither am I. Whenever we decide to call it quits we'll be able to do it without a fuss.'

The conversation had become a lot more serious than she'd intended it to. Served her right for nagging at him just because he hadn't been enthusiastic about his home-cooked spaghetti dinner. The next time he worked late she'd just hand him a takeaway menu.

Trying to lighten things up a bit, she added, 'But while I'm living here you'll have to get used to me invading every part of the house. Kitchen and CD rack included.'

Samir turned and caught her into his arms. 'You can invade what you damn well please,' he said, the words warm against her mouth. 'Just as long as you come back to my bed every night.'

CHAPTER SIX

'DON'T FORGET ABOUT the dinner tonight,' Samir warned Melissa as she got out of the car in front of the agency. 'I've got meetings at Maximus the whole day—I'll send the car for you and meet you directly at the party.'

The last time they'd planned to go out for dinner Samir had come home to find Melissa sitting at her laptop in a tattered pair of pyjamas, happily humming under her breath as she worked on her latest writing project. The minor fact that they had a reservation at one of the most exclusive restaurants in town had completely slipped her mind.

This time, though, it was hardly likely she'd forget the party, Melissa thought as Samir drove off. It was a kind of milestone in their relationship, because it was the first time she'd be meeting any of Samir's family—the dinner was at his cousin's home to celebrate her fifteenth wedding anniversary.

'Nervous?' Neera asked later as Melissa grabbed the bag with her evening clothes and headed off to the women's room to change.

Melissa grimaced. 'A bit,' she said. 'Samir's cousin is a total socialite. Not quite gossip column material, but she does a lot of fundraisers with NGOs and charities. I've never met that kind of person before—I'm dreading it.'

'You'll be fine,' Neera said comfortably. 'Just be confident and be yourself. What are you wearing?'

It was easy, telling her to be herself, Melissa thought resentfully. Neera wasn't the one who'd have to go meet a bunch of notoriously bitchy South Mumbai socialites, most of whom would look down their pedigree noses at her. And, while Samir hadn't mentioned it, she knew that more than one woman had nursed hopes of hooking up with him—a lot of those pedigree noses had been put out of joint when she'd appeared on the scene.

She pulled the dress she was planning to wear out of the bag and showed it to Neera. 'Does it look OK?' she asked. It was beige with a black trim and a deceptively simple cut that flattered Melissa's slim figure, making her look taller and curvier at the same time.

Neera wrinkled up her nose. 'It's nice enough, but it's a little dull. Why aren't you wearing the orange dress you bought when we went shopping together to Bandra? That looks great on you—really makes you stand out.'

'I don't want to stand out tonight. I want to blend in,' Melissa retorted. There were several reasons why she'd chosen the beige over the orange—it looked classier, for one, and though it was cheaper it was a far better brand. Export surplus that sold at one fourth of the retail price—but hopefully no one at the party would know that.

When she came out of the cubicle a few minutes later, Neera nodded in approval. 'It looks a lot better with you in it,' she said. 'I wish I had a bust like yours.

And a waistline like yours, for that matter. Come here and let me help you with your make-up.'

Ten minutes later she was ready to go, and she slipped her feet into nude pumps as she waved to Neera and hurried out of the office and into the waiting car. 'Mrs Kaul's place in Malabar Hill,' she told Samir's driver.

'Do we pick *sahib* up on the way?' the driver wanted to know.

Melissa shook her head. 'No, he's probably already there. He's hitching a ride with a friend.'

Except that he wasn't—when she reached Priyanka Kaul's plush flat she was told that Samir hadn't yet arrived.

'He messaged me to say that he's running a little late,' Priyanka said in her perfectly modulated voice. 'But it's so lovely to see you. Let me introduce you around to a few people so that you don't get bored. Everyone knows Samir, and they're dying to meet you.'

As far as Melissa was concerned, she could think of nothing worse, but there was no way she could wriggle out of the introductions without being impossibly rude to her hostess.

'So you've actually moved in with Samir?' one of the women asked. She was skinny to the point of emaciation, and had evidently been smoking continuously for a while as the ashtray in front of her was loaded with cigarette butts. 'That's pretty unusual, isn't it? Even in this day and age.'

'Oh, it's very common for advertising agency folk,' another woman said. 'I did a few weeks in an ad agency once when I was really bored. Pretty promiscuous, I thought. Half the women were living with someone or the other. Though I must say most of them had grotty little flats in God-forsaken places like Chandivali and Vasai. Samir's place must be heaven in comparison.'

'Where did you live before you hooked up with Samir?' the first woman asked.

'Colaba,' Melissa said shortly. She didn't explain about the working women's hostel.

Colaba was as nice as you could get in South Mumbai, and the woman looked a little disappointed. She'd probably hoped to hear that Melissa had lived in cockroach-ridden paying guest accommodation miles out of town.

Priyanka came up in time to hear the last bit of the conversation. 'I was so excited when I heard about you,' she said. 'One of my closest friends stays in the same apartment block as Samir, and she told me first. Then, of course, when Samir called next he told me he had a new girlfriend.'

'And a very pretty girlfriend too,' Priyanka's husband said, coming to stand next to her.

'Thanks, Anil,' Melissa muttered, feeling stunned. She'd always thought of Mumbai as being large and anonymous—it had never occurred to her that people she didn't even know might be talking about her and Samir. No wonder Samir was more conscious of appearances than she was.

'Samir's mother will be on the phone with Priyanka as soon as the party's over,' Anil said. 'We're actually more her generation than yours, and she keeps checking in with us about how he's doing. Samir's not the most communicative of sons.'

His mother? Melissa hadn't realised that Samir's mum even knew she existed, let alone that she was keeping track of the parties she attended and calling up people to ask about her afterwards. Priyanka was frowning at Anil now—evidently he wasn't supposed to have shared that last titbit.

'I wonder what's keeping Samir?' she asked, glancing at her watch. 'He said he'd be here by eight-thirty.'

'It's Janmashtami,' Melissa said. 'There are *dahihandis* set up all across town and the traffic's bad. He must have got stuck at Worli after he got off the sea link.'

'There's always something or the other happening in this city,' one of Anil's friends said. 'It's terrible the way they hold up everything just because of some archaic festival. It's barbaric, the way they make human pyramids to knock down that ridiculous pot of curds. And all for some piddly cash prize.'

'Ah, but the prize isn't piddly by common man standards,' a third man said.

He was thin and wiry, and his wire-framed spectacles gave him a permanently cynical expression. Vikas Kulkarni—that was his name, Melissa remembered. He was the only person in the group other than Priyanka and Anil that Samir had ever mentioned to her. Evidently a bit of a non-conformist, he gave the rest of the group a slow smile that Anil at least appeared to find intensely annoying. 'And, as for being barbaric, wasn't it one of *you* who was raving about breaking *piñatas* in Mexico?'

The man who'd originally called the festival barbaric flushed and was about to say something when Priyanka broke in, 'Oh, but it's not the same thing at all—is it, Vikas? I can't imagine why people would want to spend months practising for something like the *dahi-handi*.'

'It's rather fun, actually,' Melissa said. 'Last year a group of us joined an all-girls team and we used to practise three days a week.'

She didn't add that practising had been far more fun that the actual Janmashtami celebrations—the *pandals* had been packed with people and one of the girls had been groped in the crowd. Oh, and they hadn't won anything because the team had been able to form only five tiers of the pyramid. Other girl *govinda* teams were able to do six, and male teams went up to seven and eight.

There was a second's silence—they all looked as shocked as if she'd confessed to soliciting customers at Kamathipura on weekends, Melissa thought, trying to stifle the fit of giggles that threatened to overcome her. Even Vikas, the spectacled non-conformist, looked a little taken aback.

'Did you win?' Priyanka's thirteen-year-old daughter asked interestedly.

Damn kids—they always came up with questions one didn't want to answer.

Melissa shook her head. 'We weren't good enough,' she said succinctly.

'It's about participating, Nysa, not winning,' Priyanka said in reproving tones.

Vikas winked at Nysa. 'Remind her she said that when you appear for your board exams,' he said, and everyone laughed.

Priyanka grimaced. 'One can tell you don't have kids, Vikas,' she said. 'You're such a subversive influence.'

Nysa sidled up to Melissa. 'Mum says you write ads?' she asked. 'And you won an award at the festival?'

Melissa nodded. Priyanka and Samir didn't look like each other at all, but there was a strong resemblance between Nysa and him—a throwback to a previous generation, perhaps.

'I read some of your ads,' Nysa said. 'They're, like, quite cool. Though I didn't like the baby one that much—the one that got the award.'

Melissa smiled. There was something rather endearing about the girl.

'Samir Uncle says that's because I'm not part of the target audience,' Nysa went on. 'Sounds weird. Target audience. Like you're at rifle class or something. That's my target audience—boom-boom.'

OK, this was surreal. Samir had discussed her ads with his cousin's daughter. What was she, a specialist subject for their next family quiz show? Trying not to show her annoyance, she smiled dutifully at Nysa's joke.

'D'you want to see around the house?' Nysa asked. 'You haven't been here before, have you?'

'Yes, sure,' Melissa said. It would be better than standing around trying to be polite to a bunch of people she devoutly hoped she'd never have to meet again in her life.

The house was large and furnished with the most impeccable taste—it still felt like a home, though, and not like a museum, and Melissa felt some of her initial hostility fade. People's spaces said a lot about them. Samir's flat screamed 'keep your distance', but this one invited you in, made you feel welcome.

'And this is my room,' Nysa said, throwing open a dark blue door at the end of a passageway.

As expensively furnished as the other rooms, it was still a typical teenager's cluttered mess, with boy band posters on the walls and clothes strewn extravagantly over every possible surface. What caught Melissa's attention, though, was a big drum set that occupied half the room.

'This is yours?' she asked, and immediately wished she hadn't. Who else's would it be—Priyanka's? No wonder teenagers thought that adults were as thick-headed as turnips.

'Yes,' Nysa said and added gloomily, 'Mum got the door soundproofed. She wanted me to learn the violin.'

Melissa couldn't help grinning at that—though she didn't blame Priyanka, really. With her waif-like build and waist-length hair Nysa would look perfect in a white floaty dress on a concert stage.

She stepped into the room and shut the soundproof door behind her. 'May I?' she asked, gesturing towards the drumsticks that Nysa was fiddling with.

Nysa's 'You *play*?' was almost as incredulous as Priyanka's reaction to her *govinda* skills.

'You bet I do,' Melissa said, pulling up a stool and grabbing the sticks before Nysa could change her mind. 'My brother taught me—I took his place in the college band when he graduated.'

My God, it felt brilliant, getting her hands on the drums again. Even better than being back in a proper kitchen and almost as good as sex. And it was amazing the way the old beats came back to her, though it had been four years since she'd last played on stage.

When Samir arrived ten minutes later Melissa was

still holed up with Nysa. 'Happy anniversary,' he said, leaning down to hug his cousin. 'And congratulations on the new project—I believe everyone's completely blown away by it.'

Priyanka had just put together a massive fundraiser for the launch of a new medical charity, and it had been a spectacular success.

Samir's eyes automatically scanned the room for a familiar slim figure. 'Priyanka, where's Melissa?' he asked. He hadn't checked if she'd reached the party OK—for a second all kinds of horrifying scenarios crossed his mind.

Priyanka looked up from the designer arrangement of silk flowers he'd given her. 'Oh, she's around,' she said. 'I think Nysa took her to show her round the house. Such a sweet girl.'

'Who? Nysa?' Samir asked, grinning because he knew who she meant.

Priyanka shuddered. 'Nysa's a nightmare right now,' she said. 'Going through one of those teenage phases. I meant Melissa—she's so sparky and confident—I'm completely in love with her.'

'And she is going to tell your mother she approves, I believe,' Vikas murmured as he came up to Samir. 'I think you should prepare for some serious pressure from the female half of your family.'

Samir groaned. His mother had graduated from wanting to choose a bride for him to eagerly gathering information about every woman he dated in the hope that he'd finally settle down and give her the grandchildren she wanted.

'I approve too, by the way,' Vikas said.

Samir frowned. Vikas was notoriously picky and

difficult to please. 'What exactly has Melissa been doing since she got here?'

Vikas put his head to one side, rather like an inquisitive sparrow. 'Wellll,' he drawled, ticking off the points on his fingers, 'she's managed to deal with your bitchy ex-admirers over there without bursting into tears or clawing their eyes out. And she put a bunch of people in their place when they sneered at *dahi-handis*. She's corrected my English twice—once when I said "keep" instead of "put" and once when I said "improvise" when I meant "improve". And now she's gone off to play drums with Priyanka's daughter, I believe. I went inside to use the washroom and the door to that kid's room isn't as soundproof as our hosts would like to believe. Nysa's not bad at the drums, but she's still learning. I'll eat my best tie if it's her playing right now.'

Luckily Vikas didn't have to perform the threatened gastronomic feat, because when Samir pushed open the door to Nysa's room Melissa was banging out a hard rock rhythm while Nysa gazed at her in awestruck admiration. Her cheeks were glowing with the effort, and her flyaway hair had come loose and was tumbling around her shoulders.

'Oh, you're here,' she said, pausing mid-beat and looking up at him, evidently conscience-stricken at having abandoned the party. 'I'm so sorry. I lost track of the time a little.'

Samir had a sudden impulse to sweep her off her feet and kiss her—she looked so naturally lovely. But Vikas and Nysa were looking on interestedly, so he contented himself with dropping a chaste kiss on her brow and putting an arm around her as he shepherded her to the door.

Melissa found the rest of the evening surprisingly enjoyable. Vikas was clearly a bit of a trendsetter among Priyanka's friends, and because he'd taken an abrupt liking to Melissa the others started treating her less like an interloper. Samir didn't speak much, but she was conscious of his quiet strength by her side all along.

'Wasn't as terrible as you thought it would be, right?' Samir asked later as they drove home.

Melissa shot him a startled look, and he laughed.

'You're pretty easy to read,' he said, putting a hand on her knee and sending an automatic little thrill up her thigh. 'Relax—they all loved you.'

Really? she felt like saying. *What about the two women I met at the beginning?* They'd still looked at her as if she was some kind of cheap slut when she left.

'As far as I'm concerned it's more important what I thought of them than what they thought of me,' she announced. 'I liked Vikas, and your cousin and Nysa. Didn't really care for the rest.'

That was so typical, Samir thought, half amused and half exasperated. He was conscious that he'd wanted to see if she'd fit into his circle—it was important that she did if they were to have any kind of future together. She'd done amazingly well, keeping up a light, easy conversation without being sycophantic or intimidated. Trust her to have a completely different take on the situation, though.

When they got home Melissa brushed her teeth and went to bed while Samir was checking the mail that had come for him during the day. It had been a long day, and she was a little upset, and frankly feeling rather stupid. Of *course* he was more worried about her making some dreadful faux pas in front of his friends than he was about whether she liked them or not. She'd been dumb to think that her opinion would matter to him in the slightest.

Feeling hot tears prick at her eyelids, she blinked them back. It wasn't the end of the world, being at cross purposes with a boyfriend. She should be used to it by now—it had happened before. But Josh hadn't given out confusing signals like Samir did—he'd just not been in love with her.

Samir hadn't said he was in love with her either, but it was clear he was serious about their relationship. Introducing her to his cousin and his friends had made it seem as if he wanted to take things to the next level—as far as Melissa was concerned, though, she'd be happier if they first made up their minds about each other before they got other people involved.

Only Samir hadn't asked her. He'd evidently expected that she'd be overjoyed at the thought of being his official girlfriend rather than staying tucked away in an airtight corner of his life.

Wondering if she was being madly unreasonable, Melissa squeezed her eyes tightly closed and rubbed at her forehead with her knuckles. No, she decided, opening her eyes again. He needed to talk things over with her before he went off making one-sided decisions and subjecting her to being assessed by his family.

Samir came into the bedroom, and she turned towards the wall and pretended to be asleep.

CHAPTER SEVEN

THE NEXT DAY was a Sunday, and Melissa woke up at six-thirty to the sound of bells ringing in a nearby church.

She lay in bed and listened to the chimes die away. It had been over a year since she'd last gone to church, she realised. When she'd first come to Mumbai she'd gone with Liz to a church in Colaba almost every Sunday. Then slowly inertia had crept in and she'd started going less often, then stopped altogether.

There was a large church near Samir's apartment complex—maybe she'd try going there one Sunday. Samir was Hindu, of course, and from what she could make out not particularly religious. But he'd studied in a Catholic school for some years, and in the course of a general conversation she'd figured out that he knew more about Catholic customs than Hindu ones. Maybe he'd want to come with her to church. Or maybe not.

She turned to look at Samir. He was still fast asleep, one hand possessively clasping her hip and the other pillowing his cheek. His breathing was even and his face was smooth and untroubled. Clearly he'd gone to sleep the second his head hit the pillow instead of staying up half the night obsessing about a relationship that was going nowhere.

He sighed and shifted a little closer, automatically seeking the warmth of her body. It would be so *easy* to stop bothering about the complicated stuff and just let things happen.

Slowly, she slid out from under Samir's arm, putting it on a pillow instead. He didn't seem to mind in the least, and she smiled grimly. She was probably equally replaceable when he was awake, only he hadn't realised it yet.

After she'd brushed her teeth and washed her face she felt much better. Best of all she'd regained some of her sense of humour—enough to be able to laugh at herself and her silly problems. It wasn't the end of the world, liking someone more than they liked you—high school was full of such tragedies. Or at least it was for other people. Melissa herself had had a pretty good time in school. It was when she was all grown up that her man problems had begun.

Humming to herself, she went into the kitchen and started investigating the shelves. She'd found a wonderful little store that delivered provisions, and the kitchen was now beautifully stocked. As usual, just being in the kitchen made her mood lift up several notches. Now all she needed was a nice calorie-rich breakfast to get her back to being a hundred percent normal.

'Something smells nice,' Samir said, putting his head around the kitchen door after ten minutes. 'What're you making?'

'Pancakes,' she said and added wickedly, because she knew how particular he was about eating healthily, 'loaded with sugar and butter and refined carbs.'

'Oh, well, I'll just have to spend an extra half-hour in the gym,' he said. 'Or you could help me burn those calories in a more fun way...'

Melissa skipped neatly out of the way as he reached for her. 'Keep your hands to yourself,' she said, rapping him on the knuckles with a wooden spatula. 'I'm busy.'

The doorbell rang just as he was about to grab her around the waist, and he paused. 'Will you go and answer the door?' he asked.

'Absolutely not,' Melissa said. 'I'm not wearing a bra.'

Samir thought it over. 'Neither am I,' he said. 'So as excuses go...'

He dodged the dishcloth that Melissa threw at his head and went off laughing to open the door.

Five minutes later he was back. 'It's my financial consultant,' he said, making a wry face. 'I completely forgot I'd made an appointment to go over my portfolio. I'll try and finish as fast as I can.'

'Take your time,' Melissa said, waving a spatula at him. 'And ask your financial consultant if he'd like some pancakes.'

'It's a she,' Samir said, giving her the quirky smile he reserved for when he was pulling her leg. 'I'm surprised at you, Melissa, making gender-based assumptions like that. She won't have pancakes—I don't think she's eaten any carbs for the last decade or so. Save my share for me, OK?'

Once the pancakes were done, Melissa wandered into the TV room with her plate and put the TV on. As usual it took her a little while to figure out the various remotes for the satellite dish, the TV and the home theatre system, and when she finally did get the TV on and tried switching channels it insisted on playing one regional language channel after another. Another minute's tussle got her onto the satellite TV menu, and with a sigh of relief she chose a popular Hindi movie channel.

It was playing an old movie, set in Kashmir, with the obligatory *shikaras* on a lake being rowed by pink-cheeked damsels in traditional Kashmiri costumes. A sucker for old-fashioned romances, Melissa settled down with her stack of pancakes to watch the lead pair coo lovingly at each other. *Ooh*, they were so *sweet*, in their horrendous clothes and bright make-up. It had been a while since she'd watched an old movie—there was only one TV in the hostel, and people preferred chick-flicks and action movies to vintage Bollywood.

She was completely engrossed in the movie when the channel was changed abruptly. Melissa swung around to see Samir holding the remote.

'Hey, I was watching that!' she said indignantly as she grabbed at the remote.

Samir held it away from her, easily fending her off with one hand.

'It's an awful movie,' he said. 'Really, really terrible.'

It probably was, but that wasn't the point—he hadn't even bothered to ask her before changing channels. Granted, it was his home, but that didn't give him the right to be high-handed about every damn thing.

'I like it,' Melissa said, and when he didn't give her the remote she got up and went to the TV to change the channel manually.

'Melissa...' he said, and the slightly strained note

in his voice made her stop in her tracks. 'Look, I *really* don't want to watch that movie.'

'O-kay,' she said slowly. 'Is there a particular reason, or are you just Bollywood-phobic?'

He hesitated, and then shook his head as if to clear it of cobwebs. 'Something like that,' he said. 'But if you want to watch it don't let me stop you. I can always go somewhere else and read a magazine.'

Hmm…fifty-year-old movie or thirty-year-old boyfriend? Not much of a choice, really—especially not when Samir was looking so incredibly hot. His hair was still damp from the shower, and it was falling over his forehead in sexy spikes, and he smelt amazing.

Wishing she'd had just a little more practice at being seductive and alluring, she said, 'Or we could do something together.'

He raised an eyebrow. 'Play chess?'

'I was thinking Scrabble,' she said solemnly, and he laughed, coming up to her and running the backs of his fingers down the side of her face very, very slowly.

She shivered with anticipation as his hand slipped lower, to the neckline of her dress, and she gasped aloud as he finally gave up toying with her and pulled her ruthlessly into his arms.

It was much later, when they were having lunch, that Melissa asked, 'Why didn't you want to watch that movie? It was like you couldn't bear to look at the screen.'

He was silent for almost a minute, and Melissa began to wish she'd stayed off the topic. Then he said slowly, 'It was the location. The movie was shot in the town I used to live in as a kid. We had to leave the valley after militants razed the area—we were one of the few families lucky enough to escape alive.'

Melissa stared at him. 'I didn't know,' she said awkwardly. She'd been reading about the insurgency in the valley for years—the newspapers were full of it—but this was the first time she'd met anyone who'd been personally affected.

Samir shrugged. 'No big deal,' he said. 'Like I said, we were lucky to get out of there alive. Lots of people we knew didn't make it.'

There wasn't much she could say to that, and she stayed silent. It was ironic, she thought. There she'd been, obsessing about how little Samir knew and understood her, and it turned out she knew even less about him. If someone had asked her which state he was from she'd probably would have said Punjab—she didn't know enough about Hindu surnames to be able to place people by state. She'd not really thought about it much, other than once idly remarking that his colouring was typically North Indian—fair skin with dark but not quite black eyes and hair.

'I didn't have you pegged as a Hindi movie buff,' Samir said when the silence had stretched on long enough to be unnatural.

'I'm not,' Melissa said, shaking her head vigorously. 'I just like soppy movies. I'd watch them even if they were in Swahili. I'm thinking of writing a book about them one day.'

'Seriously?'

'Well, I might. There's a guy who's written one about Hindi blockbusters—it's pretty good. But there's something else I'm working on right now. If I ever find a publisher for that, I'll start working on this one.'

'What's the first one? A cookbook?' he asked.

He hadn't meant to sound patronising, but she seemed to gravitate to the kitchen whenever she was free and it was a natural assumption. It was only when her expression changed that he realised that he'd upset her.

'Not really,' she said. 'Anyway, it's at a very basic stage—I've a long way to go.'

Samir hesitated a little. He'd picked up on the way Melissa reacted to some of the things he said, only he didn't know which particular statement would set her off. Yesterday it had been what he'd said about his friends liking her, today it was her book... If it had been any other woman he'd have written her off as being over-sensitive and too high-maintenance to bother with. But Melissa didn't really say anything or create a scene. It was just by the way her lovely mouth turned down at the corners and a crease appeared between her eyebrows that he knew she was upset, and he'd begun watching her face like a hawk for the tell-tale signs.

Right now she seemed to be over her annoyance, so he let the subject slide. 'What do you want to do in the afternoon?' he asked.

Melissa jumped to her feet. 'Let's go to the art gallery near Flora Fountain,' she said. 'There's a new artist holding an exhibition there who's supposed to be really good.'

Samir grimaced. He didn't mind buying the occasional piece, recommended by a more knowledgeable friend, but given a choice he'd rather spend the afternoon getting a root canal done than wandering around an art gallery.

He didn't protest, though, and even feigned some enthusiasm as he followed Melissa out of the door. Another first for him, he thought. After Shalini he'd never bothered putting what a woman wanted to do ahead of what he wanted himself. And it would have been staggeringly easy to distract Melissa. For all her feistiness, a few kisses were usually enough to turn her into putty in his hands.

'I can see that your girlfriend is quite the dominatrix,' Vikas Kulkarni murmured when they bumped into him at the gallery. 'And you might want to watch out for that artist dude. He seems quite taken with her.'

Vikas was right, Samir realised as he looked across the room. The artist was ignoring a well-heeled couple who were on the point of buying one of his paintings in order to earnestly explain something to Melissa. Muttering an oath under his breath, he strode across to the two of them. Putting up with Melissa's whims was one thing. Allowing her to be chatted up by a skinny, long-haired artist was quite another.

The man looked up in alarm as Samir came up to them. 'I was just telling Melissa the thought behind this painting,' he mumbled defensively.

Samir surveyed the painting. From what he could see it was a set of random splodges of paint. Presumably it had some deep meaning, but as far as he was concerned it was a waste of a perfectly good piece of canvas. Melissa seemed entranced by it, though, because she kept on standing in front of it even when the artist went off to attend to the couple who were now getting decidedly impatient.

'If you really like it I'll buy it for you,' Samir said finally.

Her eyes widened. 'But it costs over a hundred thousand!' she exclaimed after looking at the price tag. 'The guy must be smoking something—pricing it so high.'

'It's a brilliant investment,' Vikas said, strolling up to them. 'Shekhar will be big in a couple of years. You've got a good eye for art, kiddo. This is the best piece in the show.'

'Let's buy it, then,' Samir said, trying not to show his annoyance at the interruption, and impressed in spite of himself. If Vikas said the piece was good, it definitely was, and he couldn't help feeling proud of the way Melissa had homed in on it.

Melissa looked tempted for a few seconds, but then she shook her head firmly. 'I've no place to hang it,' she said. 'It's huge. I could put it up in your place for as long as I'm there, but afterwards I'd have to stick legs on it and use it as a cot.'

Vikas gave a suppressed snort of laughter and Samir finally lost his temper. 'Let's go, then,' he said crisply. 'I don't see the point of hanging around and wasting everyone's time if we're not planning to buy anything.'

Melissa waited till they were back in the car park opposite the gallery before she said tentatively, 'Are you upset?'

Samir glared at her. 'I'm not upset,' he said. 'I'm flaming furious. What possessed you to start babbling about putting legs on a canvas in front of that old gossip Vikas? You made me look like an absolute fool.'

She was staring at him, her eyes wide. 'All I meant was that whenever we split up I won't have any place to put that painting!'

'*When* we split up. It's not even *if* for you, is it? God knows I've done enough to try and make it work—

asking you to move in with me, introducing you to my friends, letting you have your way with all your little whims and fancies. But *nothing* convinces you to try and give us a fighting chance!'

'I didn't know you *wanted* us to have a fighting chance!' she protested, her eyes turning bright with unshed tears. 'Stop shouting at me, Samir. I don't even know what I've done wrong.'

Samir shut his eyes for a second and rubbed at his forehead. 'All right, let's start from the beginning,' he said. 'I'm sorry I yelled at you. All I'm trying to say is that it's hurtful when you just assume that we don't have a future together.'

Hurtful? Melissa turned that thought over in her mind carefully, too surprised to stay upset. She hadn't imagined that anything she said or did would have the power to hurt Samir. Apparently, she'd been wrong.

'I thought it was…safer,' she said after a bit. 'We started off thinking it would be a holiday fling kind of thing, and then it got more serious. I wanted to make sure I didn't read more into it than you wanted me to.'

Samir took her hand. 'That was partly my fault,' he admitted. 'But I've never met anyone like you before. I've been trying to figure things out as we go along.'

'That makes two of us,' Melissa said, giving him a watery smile. 'Maybe we should just try talking a little more from now on? Just a thought.'

'It might work,' he said, but when she started to reply he stifled the words against her lips. 'Not right now, though,' he whispered, his warm breath mingling with hers. 'I can think of more exciting ways to make up.'

* * *

The next Monday morning, when Samir walked into the Mendonca Advertising office, he found Melissa busily clearing out her desk. For a second an icy hand clutched at his heart. Then he remembered that she was changing jobs. She'd be joining Nexus, Maya Kumar's agency, next Monday—she was taking this week off to relax.

'I'll miss seeing you around,' he murmured as he bent over her on the pretext of helping her put some of her things into a carton.

She blushed and said softly, 'I'll miss you too. But at least I won't get distracted when I'm supposed to be working.'

The thought that he had the ability to distract her was hugely pleasing, he realised, barely able to stop a smile from spreading across his face. The weekend had been pretty amazing, once they'd sorted out their misunderstanding, and he knew Melissa had been quite as blown away by it as he was.

'Are you coming to my farewell lunch?' she asked. 'Devdeep's asked me a dozen times through the morning.'

'I guess so,' he said. 'Where are they holding it?'

'The Parsi café opposite the office,' she said, and added quickly as she saw him frown, 'Don't ask them to change the venue, please. That's where they've always held agency celebrations—it's a bit of a Mendonca tradition. And Brian's coming too.'

The restaurant was run by a pair of elderly, slightly wacky Parsi brothers who'd known Brian for years. In spite of its grungy appearance the kitchen was as hygienic as the average five-star restaurant, and the food was a dozen times better. Though most of Melissa's colleagues seemed more interested in the bottles of ice-cold beer than in the food.

Melissa shook her head as Brian offered her a bottle. 'I don't like the taste,' she said. 'But you go ahead. I'm so thrilled you could make it, Brian!'

'He wouldn't have missed your farewell party for the world, *dikra*,' said Cyrus, the older of the two brothers, as he leaned over her shoulder to plonk a plate of mutton *dhansak* in front of her. 'And if he'd still been running that agency of yours I bet a million rupees you wouldn't have left.'

'Shh,' Melissa said, casting an agonised look at Samir, but he seemed more amused than offended.

Darius, the other brother, chimed in. 'Melissa, forget this whole agency rubbish and come and work with *us*. We'll make this the best restaurant in town.'

'What do you mean by that? It's already the best restaurant in town,' Cyrus huffed, but he gave Melissa an affectionate look. 'Not that you wouldn't be a whiz at running this place, Melly. We're both getting a bit too old to manage it.'

'Speak for yourself,' Darius muttered.

Melissa stood up and hugged both of them in turn— she couldn't help it. 'I'll come here for lunch every Saturday,' she said. 'And the day you give me a stake in the restaurant I'll quit my job and come and join you.'

It was amazing, the way she developed a rapport with all kinds of people, Samir thought, feeling a little glow of pride as he watched Melissa. He himself found it easy to establish working relationships with most people, but he was close only to his own kind—the people who had been to the right schools, who spoke with the right accent.

Brian leaned across the table. 'I can't believe you're letting her go,' he said. 'That girl's a star.'

Samir looked back at him, his good mood evaporating immediately. 'I have my reasons,' he said evenly. 'And I told you when I took over, Brian: I'm a businessman, not an ad man. I'm here to get the financials into shape before I hand over to someone who knows how to run the place.'

His annoyance with Brian persisted when on the way home Melissa said, 'It was so good to see Brian again.'

'It was hardly a surprise,' he said stiffly. 'I don't suppose he has much to do—he must have been looking forward to this lunch for weeks.'

'You don't like him much, do you?' Melissa said slowly.

Samir shrugged. 'He's all right. To be honest, I'm a little irritated by the way he kept telling me that I shouldn't have let you leave. He knows perfectly well that there were personal reasons behind the decision. And left to himself he'd have run the agency into the ground—each and every one of you would have been out of a job.'

'But he didn't let that happen, did he?' Melissa said. 'He sold the place to Maximus even though he hated the idea.'

'He made a pot of money in the deal,' Samir snorted. 'Though, knowing how impractical he is, he'll probably give most of it away.'

'We're squabbling again,' Melissa said, suddenly conscience-stricken. 'And I was so sure we wouldn't, after that talk we had.'

Samir laughed. 'It's natural to squabble,' he said. 'The same way it's natural for me to feel a bit jealous of Brian. I know you wouldn't have changed jobs if he was still in charge.'

Completely disarmed by the admission, she leaned across and hugged him, narrowly missing sending the car into a ditch.

'Whoa—careful,' he said, putting an arm around her and giving her a brief hug.

'You're amazing,' she said. 'Have I told you recently how amazing you are?'

Samir grinned. 'Not recently enough,' he said. 'Looking forward to the new job?'

Melissa nodded. 'I am. I won't be working directly with Maya, of course—she's way too senior—but she was so encouraging at the interview that I can't wait to join.'

This time Samir didn't voice it, but he felt a little left out in her enthusiasm for the move. He'd been a bit surprised at her decision to change jobs—especially when the hours at her new place were likely to be so much longer.

'What are you planning to do this week?'

'Work on my book project, mainly,' Melissa said. 'I won't get much time once I start the new job, and Maya said she wanted to take a look at it. I'd like to do another round of edits before I show it to her.'

Samir frowned. 'Is that a good idea?' he asked. 'She's your new employer, and at least at the beginning you should come across as being fully committed to your job. I mean, writing a book isn't the same as writing copy for ads—she might think you're not concentrating on what she's employing you for.'

'I didn't think of it that way,' Melissa said. 'It came

up in the interview and she wanted to tell me about an opportunity to do a short story for a magazine.'

Maya Kumar had actually been very encouraging— she'd asked to see samples of Melissa's work, and she'd actually read the stories and given her feedback on them. Melissa found she didn't feel like telling Samir those details, though. Evidently, he didn't think her important enough for someone like Maya to be interested in her work, and anything she said would only come out sounding as if she was trying to blow her own trumpet.

'I still think you should keep the book thing a little low-key for now,' Samir said. 'But it's great that she's interacting with you directly, given how senior she is.'

'Yes, it's brilliant,' Melissa said, unable to keep the sarcasm out of her voice.

Samir looked up immediately. While Melissa was supremely confident about her copywriting abilities, she could get incredibly touchy and secretive about her book. Every time he'd tried discussing it with her he'd found himself inadvertently treading on her toes. He needed training from Maya on how to handle the topic, he thought wryly. She'd evidently hit exactly the right note—Melissa seemed to have elevated her to fairy godmother status.

'I'd like to read your book some time,' he said, trying to backpedal out of the mess he'd got himself into. 'You haven't even told me what it's about.'

'You wouldn't like it,' she said. 'I'm writing it from a completely feminine point of view.'

'I think I can handle it,' he said, but she was already shaking her head.

'Anyway, it's not complete yet. I don't want anyone to see it until I'm happy with what I've done.'

Anyone other than Maya Kumar, evidently, Samir thought, but he didn't say anything. There was no point getting Melissa upset, though he was now feeling very curious about the book. He didn't pretend to be a literary critic, but he knew good writing when he saw it. So far he'd only seen Melissa's advertising work, which was uniformly excellent, but he knew that being a superb copywriter didn't necessarily mean you'd make a good author.

Melissa's book could be brilliant, but it could equally well be trash—and she herself didn't seem confident about it. Hopefully he'd be able to convince her to let him read it soon so that he could form his own opinion.

They were almost home, and there was a brief pause as Samir negotiated a complicated three-point turn to get the car into the apartment complex.

'Dreadful planning,' he muttered as the car shot across the road at right angles to oncoming traffic. 'It's a wonder there hasn't been a car crash here yet.'

'My cabbie always goes straight down the road and takes a turn at the signal,' Melissa said, her lips curving into a smile. 'He says that only careless rich people can afford to take the risk of getting their bumpers dented here.'

Samir, who'd got used to her chatty friendships with everyone she met, grinned. 'So did you tell him that your boyfriend's one of those careless people?'

'Of course not,' Melissa said in her best shocked tones. 'That would have ruined my street cred completely!'

CHAPTER EIGHT

THE LANDLINE WAS ringing when Melissa let herself into the flat, and she dragged her cartons in and dumped them by the door before she went to answer it. Samir had dropped her by the lift and gone to park the car, and Kamala had taken the day off, so there was no one else in the flat.

'Hello?' she said.

There was a brief pause before a woman's voice said, 'Hi. Could I speak to Samir, please?'

'He isn't at home,' Melissa said. There was something vaguely familiar about the voice, but try as she might she couldn't place it. 'Can I take a message?'

'No, that's all right. I'll call him on his cell phone later. Is that Melissa?'

'Um, yes,' Melissa said warily. If this was one of Samir's ex-girlfriends she really didn't want to get into a conversation with her.

'I'm Bina,' the woman said. 'Do tell Samir I called, OK?'

'I will,' Melissa replied, wondering if she was supposed to know who Bina was.

She'd sounded pretty authoritative, actually—not like an ex, more like an older cousin, or Samir's boss or something. Only, if she was his cousin or his boss wouldn't she have called him on his cell?

Giving up on figuring it out, Melissa went back to the living room to fetch her cartons.

'The more I think about it, the more I realise how much I'll miss you at work,' Samir said when he came in a few minutes later.

'You'll get over it,' Melissa said unsympathetically. 'One of those spreadsheets you keep slogging over will suddenly show that Mendonca's making a profit and you'll be so excited that you'll forget all about me. And, in any case, aren't you going back to Maximus in a couple of months?'

'Well, I'll miss you for those couple of months,' he said. 'And you're completely wrong about the spreadsheets—Mendonca's already showing profits. Devdeep's doing a good job, and it helps that Brian's not around, taking on commissions for peanuts and then giving away most of the money to noble causes.'

Melissa was about to spring to Brian's defence when he took the wind out of her sails.

'Though I must say in all the years I've been working I haven't come across anyone who's as genuinely generous as Brian is.'

Melissa's brows flew up. 'Wow, that's a complete volte-face,' she said. 'Did the lift man slip you a tolerance pill on your way up?'

Samir shrugged. 'He's still a terrible businessman,' he said. 'A guy like Brian would be better off running an NGO.'

Feeling suddenly contrite about the bitchy way she'd reacted, Melissa made an apologetic face. 'Sorry,' she said. 'Volte-face is another one of those swanky phrases I've never used before in real life.'

'At least you'll not get bored with me until you've had a chance to use your entire French vocabulary,' he said lightly.

Melissa ran across the room to him. 'I'll never get bored of you, and I'll miss you at work too,' she said, in a rare burst of candour about her feelings for him. 'I'll be thinking about you all the time.'

Samir swung her off her feet effortlessly and strode towards the bedroom. 'We'll need to make sure we make the best use of the time we have at home,' he said, depositing her carefully on the bed. 'We wouldn't want you getting bored when you think about me.'

It was a while before she remembered the phone call. 'Someone called for you,' she said, pulling away and frowning in an effort to recall the name. 'Bina.'

Samir groaned. 'On the landline?'

'Well, yes. She'd hardly have called you on my cell.'

'You don't know my mother,' Samir said grimly.

Hang on—his *mother*? Melissa stared at him. 'That was your mum? But…she sounded so young! And she didn't *say* she was your mum.'

'She wouldn't.' Samir's smile was wry. 'She's been dying to talk to you ever since she found out about your existence. And anyway she always introduces herself by her first name. She works for a European embassy and she's picked up some of their ways.'

Melissa digested that carefully as Samir swung his feet over the side of the bed and stood up. To her surprise, he didn't reach for his phone immediately. Instead, he opened his wardrobe and pulled out a set of tennis clothes.

'Think I'll go and play tennis for a bit,' he said.

'Why? Didn't you get enough exercise?' Melissa asked waspishly before she could stop herself. Who did he think he was? A world class tennis player?

Samir laughed. 'I did…I did. I just feel like some fresh air.' He hesitated a little. 'Would you rather that I don't go?'

'Aren't you going to call her back first?' Melissa asked, and when he gave her a blank look, said, 'Your mum?'

He sighed. 'I'll call her. Not right now, though.'

Knowing she should let it go, Melissa couldn't help asking, 'What if she calls again?'

'Tell her that you gave me the message and I said I'd call her back.'

The front door of the flat closed behind him with a firm thud, and Melissa was left staring after him. There had been something definitely odd about the way Samir had reacted, she thought. Come to think of it, he hardly talked about his immediate family—she knew he had a younger brother, and now she knew that his mum worked in an embassy. There had been that one time when he'd told her about their escaping to Delhi when the trouble was at its height in the valley, but other than that he didn't seem to talk about them at all.

On impulse, she picked up her phone and typed 'Bina Razdan' into a search engine. Her jaw dropped at the number of hits thrown up.

'She works for a European embassy' had been an understatement, implying that she had some kind of clerical job—from what Melissa could see, Samir's mother was a pretty senior diplomat.

It was the first time Melissa had tried to find out more about Samir's family than what he'd voluntarily told her, and she mentally contrasted the picture on the internet of Bina in a silk sari and pearls talking to a powerful politician with her own mother.

Theresa D'Cruz had been a regular mum, wrapped up in her kids and their studies. She'd helped out in her husband's restaurant, and she'd used to sing in the church on weekends. If you'd asked her if she wanted a career, she'd have thought you were pulling her leg.

Trying to imagine what it would be like to have a high-flying diplomat for a mum, Melissa wondered who had picked up Samir from school and helped him with his studies, done the hundred little things mothers were supposed to do.

Then she shook herself. Bina having a career didn't automatically mean that she was a bad mum. In any case, Samir had spent the first ten years of his life in Kashmir—his mum had probably been at home then. And it looked as if his father was a pretty rich businessman—they must have had a luxurious life even after they'd moved to Delhi, because she remembered Samir telling her that his father had moved most of his investments into the capital city when the trouble in the valley escalated.

Slipping off the bed, Melissa went into the bathroom for a quick shower before changing into running shorts and a T-shirt. Time she went and got herself some fresh air as well, she thought. Samir's apartment had a very well-equipped gym attached, but Melissa preferred jogging on the track that ran around the building.

It was almost dark when she hit the track, and it took her a while to settle into a rhythm. There was hardly anyone in downstairs—Melissa had discovered that most of the neighbours spent their evenings either in front of the TV or eating out at expensive restaurants. One would have expected the place to be eerily silent, but it was actually quite the opposite.

Like most of the new high-end apartments in central Mumbai, Samir's building occupied former mill land. The mills were long gone, but the tenements that had housed the mill workers were still there. Most of the workers were now drivers or cleaners for the rich people who lived in the buildings, and Melissa still found the divide between the rich and the not so rich very unsettling.

It was the first day of the annual Ganpati festival, and the nearest set of tenements had set up a huge marquee where people were in the process of installing a seven-foot-high clay idol of the elephant-headed god. Music blared out from loudspeakers, people were dancing on the roads outside, and a troupe of drummers was enthusiastically giving the dancers their money's worth.

Melissa automatically found her feet hitting the ground in time to the drums. Maybe this could be the next big thing after Tai Chi and Pilates, she thought, grinning to herself—running to the beat of the *dhol*. For a few minutes she was tempted to go out onto the street and watch the Ganpati being hauled into place, but she knew that she'd need to be properly dressed to do that. *Kameez* over jeans at the very least, if not a proper *churidaar kurta* or a sari.

She was still thinking about the Ganpati festival

when she rounded a corner and heard a very familiar voice. So Samir hadn't gone to play tennis after all—or if he had he'd ended the game early. He was standing in the car park and speaking into his cell phone. Melissa automatically slowed down, but he was standing with his back towards her and didn't see her.

'*Why* did you call Melissa?' Samir was saying heatedly into the phone. 'Mum, I need you to stay out of this—please. It's very early days, and I haven't made up my mind yet.'

His mother was obviously saying something, and it sounded as if he was cutting her short.

'No, you can't come down to Mumbai right now. Let me figure things out first, OK?'

Figure *what* out? Melissa was standing stock-still now, her face very pale. She could no more have stopped herself from eavesdropping than she could have stopped breathing.

Samir's voice had softened now.

'I'll try and come down to Delhi next week. Yes, I miss you too. I've just been very busy… And it'll be great to see Dad as well.' There was another pause, and then he said, 'God, you're such a *woman*!' But he sounded indulgent now, not annoyed. 'It's difficult to describe her like that. She's very pretty, and she's bright—not the academic type, really, but feisty and street-smart.'

There was yet another pause.

'I don't know if I'm in love with her, Mum.'

Melissa bit her lip. *Of course* he didn't love her. What had she expected? That he'd confess to having been secretly in love with her since the second he'd clapped his eyes on her?

His mother was evidently still firing questions at him, because he went on.

'I haven't met her family, except for her brother. Seemed a nice enough chap—typical middle-class Goan, runs a restaurant with his dad and plays drums for a local band in his free time. Her mother's dead.'

It wasn't said in a callous way at all, but his last words still cut deep. She hadn't talked about her mother with Samir except the one time he'd asked about her. It wasn't something she spoke about much.

She started walking again, picking up speed as she tried to get away from Samir's line of vision as quickly as possible before he turned around and saw her. *Her mother's dead. Typical middle-class Goan.* Both true, and logically there was no reason for her to be upset. What he *hadn't* said was, *Not our kind of people*, though the implication had come through loud and clear. It matched up with what she'd found out about his family—they were leagues ahead of hers, both in terms of social status as well as wealth and power. Things she'd never ever given importance to because they hadn't directly affected her before.

Her footsteps slowed again once she'd put enough distance between herself and Samir. She felt bewildered and heartsore. Ever since Samir had told her that he was doing his best to make it work between them she'd relaxed her guard and let herself believe that they had a future together. Evidently she'd been fooling herself. Perhaps what had got Samir riled up after their trip to the art gallery was her stubborn insistence that theirs was a short-term affair—presumably the length was something that *he* wanted to dictate.

It was the first time that someone she cared about

had made her feel that she was *lacking* in some way. She'd been the youngest in her family—not pampered, exactly, but always valued. Michael and her father had been quietly indulgent during her teenage years, and when Michael had got married, Cheryl had become the older sister Melissa had always wanted. Until, of course, Melissa had ruined everything by taking up with Josh.

For a few seconds Melissa missed home so badly that it was like a physical pain. In spite of the past two years being rocky, she knew that her father and brother loved her deeply. Michael had been calling regularly, and he'd dropped enough hints for her to figure out that her father had been keeping track of her through Liz and Brian ever since she'd left Goa. Maybe that was what she needed to do, she thought—go back and make peace with her 'typical middle-class Goan' father, and come to terms with her own identity.

Reinventing oneself was all very well, but in the instant that she'd heard Samir describe Michael she'd known that if she had to choose between turning into a snooty rich bitch lookalike to stay with Samir or remaining her regular self and doing without him, she'd choose the latter. However much it hurt.

Still feeling a little shaky, and definitely not confident enough to go back upstairs, she veered off the jogging track and went to sit on a bench in one of the little artificial gardens next to the swimming pool.

Think, she told herself sternly. She'd already admitted to herself that somewhere along the line she'd fallen in love with Samir. Well, that couldn't be undone now—but what she *could* do was make sure Samir never figured it out. Which meant she'd either have to put on a front all the time, or leave as soon as she possibly could.

Her heart twisted within her at the thought of leaving, and she wondered if she wasn't jumping to conclusions. Maybe Samir just needed some time—there was nothing to say that he wouldn't decide to continue with their relationship. After all, he'd just told his mother that he hadn't made up his mind yet. Miserable as the hope was, it buoyed up her spirits temporarily, and she got up to go back to the flat.

Once Samir had finished his call, he headed back towards the tennis court, hoping to get a game in before dinner. He was lucky—one of his neighbours had just come to the court and was looking for a partner. The man was a lot older than Samir, but he was very fit, and the game was close.

'Great game,' he said after shaking Samir's hand. 'I thought I saw your wife around here a while back. Does she play as well?'

About to tell him that Melissa wasn't his wife, Samir held back and just said, 'No, she's never learnt.'

Mumbai was reasonably progressive, but he didn't want more people than necessary knowing that they weren't married. They would have some explaining to do if they actually *got* married, but that was something he was sure he could handle. He pulled himself up short before that particular train of thought could go any further—*could* they actually get married? Had he really been thinking that?

He took a deep breath. The conversation with his mother had unsettled him more than he wanted to admit. She'd always been unusually perceptive, and evidently she'd sensed that Melissa meant more to him than any of the girls he'd dated before. It wasn't something he'd allowed himself to think about much.

Melissa challenged him in ways no woman had before—sometimes making him question his whole approach to life and the way it should be lived. On the other hand, with her easygoing, undemanding ways, she was also incredibly easy to live with. And then there was the sex. Mind-blowing was an understatement, and he needed to be sure it wasn't clouding his judgement in other things.

When he got back to the flat Melissa was in the kitchen, looking very busy.

'Where's Kamala?' he asked.

'Kamala's taken the day off for Ganpati,' Melissa said. 'She told you a couple of days back.'

'We could have gone out,' Samir said, leaning against the doorjamb. 'We still can, actually. Let that stuff be and go and get ready.'

Melissa didn't look up from her chopping and marinating. 'It'll spoil,' she said. 'And I don't like eating out.'

Something was wrong—her voice sounded different and she still wasn't looking at him. 'We'll go to a Goan place,' he promised. 'Come on, Melly, you're starting a new job from Monday—you need to relax a little.'

'I find cooking relaxing,' she said.

Samir shrugged, beginning to feel annoyed. If she was upset about something, she'd have to come out and tell him what it was—he hated guessing games. 'Well, all right,' he said, turning away to go into the living room. 'Don't make anything very spicy, though.'

Melissa stared at the pan where she'd been carefully combining spices. She'd planned to make chicken *xacuti*, and there were six red chillies in the masala, waiting to be ground up into paste. Sighing, she turned the stove off.

'Let's go out,' she called after Samir. 'But not a Goan place, please—the ones in Mumbai are rubbish. Let's go to one of the places *you* like.'

'I was thinking I'd go to Goa for a couple of days,' she said over dinner. 'See my dad. I've left things to fester too long. I was looking at Brian and Cyrus and Darius today—they suddenly seemed so old...and Dad's the same age as Brian.'

'Are you sure?' Samir asked, his eyes warm and concerned. 'Last time you met Michael you came back looking an absolute wreck.'

'I've spoken to him since then,' Melissa said. 'I overreacted, I think, that time I met him. They didn't want Dad to know I was in town because he would have been upset I didn't go and see him.' With a flash of her normal spirit, she added, 'Though unless they thought I'd grown telepathic I don't know how they expected me to figure that one out.'

Samir smiled at that, but still came back to the topic once they were home. 'Should I come with you?' he asked. 'If you think your dad will be upset if he knows we're living together I can stay out of the picture, but at least you'll know I'm nearby if you need me.'

'I think I'll be okay,' she said. 'And it's something I need to do on my own. But thanks for offering to come with me. It...it means a lot.'

'Any time,' he said softly and leaned across to kiss

her, his lips warm as they lingered on hers. It was a slow kiss, but it set her veins on fire, and she clung to him when he finally tried to draw away.

CHAPTER NINE

MELISSA TOOK THE overnight train to Goa—this time luckily the tickets were easy to get. Samir had tried to talk her into taking a flight, but her fear of flying was still too strong for her to attempt it alone.

Michael was at the station to meet her, and he put his arms around her and hugged her when she got off the train. 'It's good to see you, *men*,' he said. 'Dad's looking forward to seeing you too.'

Her father looked older and frailer than when she'd seen him last, but he was evidently very pleased to see her. She'd wondered how he'd manage the conversation about their two-year-long estrangement, but after a while she realised that he wasn't planning to talk about it at all. He seemed happier pretending that she'd been away for work.

'Brian told us about the new job,' he said. 'This boy you're with now—Samir—he's Hindu, isn't he?'

'Yes, Dadda,' Melissa said, heaving an inward sigh. Some things about her father hadn't changed. Presumably no one had told him that Samir and she were living together or he'd have disowned her all over again.

'If you get married will he convert?'

'I don't know,' Melissa said. 'I don't think we'll get married, Dadda. It's not that serious.'

Her father grunted. 'You be careful,' he said. 'Don't let people take advantage of you. And no need to tell them about what happened earlier.'

He sounded like a medieval father whose daughter had been raped by invaders, Melissa thought, torn between anger and amusement. Evidently he thought that her chances in the marriage market had dwindled after she'd run away with Josh.

The more time she spent with her family, the more the differences between her and Samir were underscored. She tried to imagine bringing Samir to her home. He'd probably be bored out of his wits—the conversation in their family revolved around food and films, mostly, and Samir wasn't interested in either. Then, of course, he'd have the option of hanging out with Michael and his mates from the band. Or with her father and the parish priest.

Her lips curved up in an involuntary smile. To be fair to Samir, he'd probably do both without even once indicating that he wasn't exactly enthralled by the company or the conversation. Only he'd be dying to get back to Mumbai, or at least to a more hip and happening part of Goa. Melissa's smile faded. In spite of the strong resistance her heart was putting up, her brain seemed to be coming up with more and more reasons why her relationship with Samir wasn't going to work.

The rest of her visit was peaceful enough, though it dragged a little—especially in the morning, when her nephew was in school and everyone else was busy in the restaurant preparing for the lunch crowd. She tried helping them, but she'd lost the rhythm of working in a large kitchen and, though no one said anything, she soon realised that she was in the way.

'I got this out of the safe for you,' her father said, handing her a small blue box on the day she was packing to leave.

Melissa opened the box to see a pair of heavy gold bangles that had belonged to her mother.

'Dadda…' she said, suddenly overcome. Her mother had worn those bangles to church every Sunday, and when she was very young Melissa had thought that her mother wouldn't be allowed in if she didn't wear them.

'She'd have wanted you to have them,' her father said heavily. 'I spoke to the Father, and he told me to look within my heart and think what my wife would have wanted me to do for my children. She would never have let you go away.'

So the parish priest had some sense after all, Melissa thought. No wonder Michael had tried to make her meet him when she was last in Goa.

'Thanks, Dadda,' she said.

She didn't have it in her heart to be resentful about the way he'd treated her. Parents were human as well, and who was to say he hadn't been right? Maybe if she'd listened to him and given Josh up she'd have been much happier. But she'd never have moved to Mumbai, and she wouldn't have met Samir… Probably by now she'd be married to Savio, who ran the neighbourhood grocery store and had always had a crush on her. She thought of Savio and his curly hair and sweaty hands and suppressed an involuntary shudder. Some things about the move to Mumbai had definitely worked out for the better.

'I'll come back and visit you soon,' she said, giving

her father an awkward peck on his withered cheek. He nodded, and she picked up her bag and gave Justin and Cheryl a hug. 'I'll see you guys soon too,' she said.

When her train pulled into CST she automatically looked around for Samir, even though he'd told her he had an important meeting and wouldn't be able to come to the station. His driver was there, though, and she handed her bag to him and followed him out to the station car park.

Her phone rang as soon as she was in the car.

'Hey, there,' Samir said, and she felt her pulse quicken at the sound of his voice. 'Had a good trip?'

'The best,' she said. 'But I'm happy to be back.'

'Can't wait to see you,' he said, and his voice was a husky promise. 'I'm sorry I couldn't be there to pick you up, but there's a minor crisis at work. I'll get home as soon as I can this evening.'

'See you soon, then,' she murmured, mindful of the driver's being within earshot. 'Bye.'

It didn't take her long to unpack, but it took a lot longer to figure out where to put her stuff. The clothes were easy—they just went into the wardrobe in the master bedroom that Samir had cleared out for her. The problem was with the books and CDs she'd brought back from Goa with her.

There were quite a lot of them, she realised, staring at the heap on the bed. She'd left most of her stuff behind in Goa when she'd left with Josh, and she'd assumed her father had got rid of it when he'd done the whole disowning-his-only-daughter thing. As it turned out, though, Cheryl had carefully stored everything away, and in a fit of nostalgia that she was now regretting Melissa had carted almost all of it back to Mumbai.

She padded into the media room to examine the bookshelves there. Most of Samir's books were glossy hardcover editions of popular books on management and advertising. There were a few tomes on art, and the odd novel. Everything looked so perfect that Melissa wondered if the interior decorator had chosen the books as well as the bookshelves. There was no way her tattered collection of largely second-hand paperbacks would be welcome on those shelves. And there were no closed bookshelves or spare cupboards in the room—presumably they wouldn't have fitted in with the decor.

It was when she was investigating a small cupboard over the bar in the living room that she found the photo albums. The complete impersonality of Samir's flat had been bothering her for a while. There were no pictures or souvenirs, or anything that suggested a home rather than a hotel room. The albums had evidently been there for a while, and she dragged them off the shelf carefully and dusted them by clapping them together.

Sneezing as a cloud of dust rose up around her, she got off the chair she'd been standing on and inspected the albums. The older one had pictures of Samir as a young boy, standing solemnly with his parents on the shores of a lake, blowing out candles on a birthday cake almost as large as himself, and playing cricket with a bunch of equally small and solemn-looking friends.

The second album appeared to be exclusively filled with pictures from a single holiday. It was at least six or seven years old, and Samir looked young and carefree as he posed for the camera. The pictures were mostly taken in Greece and Italy, and Samir seemed to have gone there with two other men his age. One of the men looked vaguely familiar, and after peering at the picture for a while Melissa realised that he was Vikas Kulkarni, the rather cynical-looking man she'd met first at Priyanka's party, and then at the art gallery.

'Searching for something?'

Samir's voice came from behind her, startling her so much that she almost dropped the album.

'Or generally snooping around?'

His tone was light, but there was an edge to his words that she couldn't fail to miss.

'Snooping around,' she said gaily, getting to her feet. 'Only you're not much of a Bluebeard, are you? This is the only cupboard I found with anything remotely interesting in it.'

'I'd forgotten I still had those,' Samir said, glancing at the albums. 'God, we were such a bunch of losers.' The photo he was looking at had the three men posing in completely ridiculous attitudes in front of the Parthenon.

'I don't know—I think it's a cute picture,' she said. 'You were pretty hot. In a boy-band kind of way.'

'As opposed to my current manly appearance?' he asked, raising his eyebrows as he took the albums from her and returned them to the shelf.

The tight expression had left his face, and he looked almost relaxed now. A four o'clock stubble darkened his jaw, and his shoulders looked even broader than usual in a well-cut formal shirt. He was right—there wasn't the merest hint of 'boy' in him now.

Feeling her mouth go dry with longing, Melissa hastily averted her gaze from his perfect shoulders and the even more perfect body attached to it.

'That's right—as opposed to your current old man

appearance,' she said. 'Such a pity I missed out on your best years.'

'I'm not so upset about it,' he said gravely. 'You were probably in kindergarten then. I'd have been hauled up for child abuse.'

Melissa laughed, and looked curiously up at the albums before he shut the cupboard door.

'What about the girlfriend, then? Shivani…no, Shalini. How come she's not in any of the pictures?'

'Because she wasn't with us on the holiday, Einstein,' Samir said.

He seemed perfectly relaxed, and Melissa ventured a second question. 'So what was she like?'

Samir shrugged. 'Pretty. Bone-lazy. And as hard as nails.'

Melissa wrinkled her nose. 'Doesn't sound very appealing,' she said. 'Of course you could be prejudiced because she dumped you.'

'Very likely,' Samir said.

But he didn't seem to be really paying attention to what she was saying. Instead, he was looking at her, his dark brown eyes fixed on hers so intently that she blushed and fell silent.

'Did I happen to mention I missed you?' he asked finally, his voice low and scorching hot.

Trying to sound as casual as possible, she said, 'You did say something.'

His eyes glittered a little as he moved closer. 'And…?'

'And…well, of course it's natural, you getting a little lonely rattling around in this big old flat…' Her voice trailed off in an undignified squeak as a large, warm hand clasped her waist, and Samir swung her up into his arms.

He'd carried her into the bedroom when he stopped abruptly and said, 'Bloody hell, what happened to the bed?'

Melissa peeked over his shoulder and gave a gurgle of laughter. 'I got some of my old stuff back from Goa—I was looking for a place to put it, and that's why I opened the cupboard.'

But Samir was already striding purposefully towards the guest room. 'You can tell me all about it later,' he promised. 'Right now I've got more important things on my mind.'

Afterwards, Samir propped himself up on one elbow and gently traced a line down her arm, making her shiver with delight. One part of her brain was admonishing herself, though—it had been only a few minutes since they'd made love and here she was, going up in flames at his touch all over again. Shameless or what?

'I got you something,' he said, and she looked up in surprise.

He reached across and took a rectangular box out of the pocket of his discarded trousers.

'A watch,' she said, taking it out and smiling up at him. 'Thanks, Samir, it's lovely.'

And it was, with a delicate rose-gold strap and a mother-of-pearl dial studded with little diamonds. She wasn't sure if the diamonds were real, never having seen any close up. Goodness knew how much it had cost.

'I was thinking we should take a few days off and go on a holiday,' he said. 'Somewhere nearby, perhaps—Krabi or Koh Samui.'

'That's in Thailand.'

He smiled. 'Yes, but not the terribly touristy part. The beaches are great.'

Melissa thought hazily that she wouldn't care if they *were* touristy. She'd never been outside India, really—a childhood holiday to Nepal *so* didn't count.

For a few seconds she daydreamed about having Samir all to herself for five days—maybe even a week.

Then reality sank in. 'I can't go,' she said. 'I'm starting a new job, remember? I can't saunter in and ask for leave the day I join.'

Samir shrugged. 'It's not such a big deal. Tell them you'd already made plans and you couldn't cancel. Anyway, there won't be much work right now while the Ganpati festival's on.'

She shook her head regretfully. The thought of a holiday with Samir was incredibly tempting, but she knew she couldn't mess round with Maya.

'I can't. And anyway, I'm phobic about flying, remember?'

'That won't be a problem if you're with me,' he said, so confidently that she had to smile.

'I still can't come.'

Samir shrugged. 'Maybe in a couple of months, then,' he said, but it was clear that the idea had already lost some of its charm for him.

A couple of months.

She'd had a lot of time to think on the way back from Goa, but she'd still not made up her mind about staying or leaving. The one thing she was sure about was that she wasn't going to mould herself into a Stepford wife in order to make Samir propose to her. If needed, she'd do the opposite and make sure he understood exactly what he was getting into.

'What time are you getting back home tomorrow?' Samir asked, interrupting her thoughts. 'You'd better get in early—it's the last day of the festival and there'll be hordes of processions on the roads, taking the idols to immerse them in the sea.'

'I was planning to go and watch the *visarjan* at Marine Drive,' Melissa said. 'It's pretty amazing.'

Samir groaned. 'Mel, of all the crackpot ideas to have! D'you know how crowded it gets? Anything could happen!' He stopped short, realising that he sounded horribly like someone's fussy maiden aunt. 'It's not like you're even celebrating Ganpati Puja,' he continued after a brief pause. 'Why would you want to go for the *visarjan*?'

'Because it's interesting,' she told him firmly. Then she relented a little. 'There's a friend of mine who lives near Churchgate—we'll go to his place if it gets too bad.'

'Who's we?'

'Me and Neera and a couple of others. You can come along if you want.'

That last was clearly an afterthought, and Samir grimaced. 'No, thanks. I'll get home early and work from home for the second half of the day. You can take the car and driver.'

'I won't need them,' she said. 'We'll take a cab.'

'I'd feel safer if you had the car with you,' Samir said, frowning. Melissa came to him and gave him a conciliatory hug.

'Of course you would,' she said. 'But I don't need the car and I can take care of myself.'

'I know you can,' Samir said, pulling her closer. 'It's just that I like taking care of you as well.'

'Then come with me,' she whispered. 'Leave the car behind and mingle with the hoi polloi for once.'

The words were out of her mouth, said in her best temptress tones, before she knew what she was doing. Insisting on going for the *visarjan* was just another way of emphasising the differences between them; she hadn't *meant* to ask him to come along.

Samir hesitated only for a second before saying, 'All right, I will. In any case I won't be able to work if I'm worrying about what exactly you're up to.'

Damn, she hadn't expected him to actually agree. In spite of herself, though, Melissa felt a little thrill go through her. If he was willing to do something so out of character, just for her sake, surely that meant he cared? Then she gave herself a brisk mental shake and told herself not to be silly. If he cared he'd have told her. He wasn't exactly in *purdah*, was he?

'Where shall I meet you?' she asked. 'Don't bring the car anywhere near Marine Drive—the roads will be blocked for kilometres all around.'

'I don't think I'm really comfortable hanging around if Samir's going to be here,' Neera said. 'It's OK for you—he's your boyfriend and you don't work at Mendonca's any more. But he's my boss, and I'm sure he thinks we're mad, coming out to watch the *visarjan*.'

This was something that Melissa hadn't anticipated. Finally, she'd managed to convince Neera to come with her, but the rest of the gang from Mendonca's had dropped out. Worst of all, Samir had been right—the crowds were terrible and, unless you were actually with one of the *puja* committees, it was impossible to get anywhere near the part of the beach where the immersion was happening. There were cops everywhere, and without her usual gang around it was really no fun. The previous year, they'd accompanied one of the smaller Ganpatis actually into the sea, and it had been amazing. Being a bystander was not a patch on it.

'I think I'll head back,' Neera muttered. 'I've got to meet the rest of the guys, and I promised my mum I'd be home early.'

With her last supporter gone, Melissa acknowledged defeat. 'It was much better last year,' she said despondently.

Samir heroically refrained from saying *I told you so*—but her disappointment was contagious. Also, he suspected that it had been more fun the previous year because she had been with friends, and he knew he was responsible for their not being around this year.

'Maybe you should have just gone with your friends,' he said, putting the thought into words.

'Maybe,' Melissa agreed, giving him a rather lopsided smile. 'You wouldn't have had to slum it then.'

Samir sighed. 'That's not what I meant,' he said. 'If we're together, we can't live in a bubble, can we? It's just a question of adjusting a little.'

'But we're adjusting all the time,' she said slowly. 'You didn't want to come here, and you're hating every minute of it, only you're too polite to say it. And it's the same for me. I had to make an effort every single minute at that party at Priyanka's house. The only time we're together and happy is when we're in bed.'

'That's not a bad start, is it?' Samir said teasingly, but Melissa refused to smile.

'If we're together just for the sex—' she started to say, but Samir interrupted her.

'I'm in it for a lot more than the sex, Melissa,' he said. 'But I don't think this is the place to discuss it.'

It definitely wasn't—they were in one of the lanes leading off Marine Drive, but the music and drumbeats were as loud as if they were right on the beach with the Ganpatis and their worshippers. Also, some of the stragglers from the processions were giving them curious looks.

'Let's head back, then,' Melissa muttered.

Lost in thought, she stepped out of the lane right into a mass of people. Probably it was because she was walking in a direction opposite to the flow of people, or because she was still a little shaky after the conversation with Samir, but she felt herself lose her balance and trip. The procession kept moving—perhaps no one noticed her—and in an instant she found herself knocked into the path of a truck carrying a massive Ganesha.

There was time only for her to give one terrified scream before Samir's strong hands pulled her out of harm's way.

'Of all the careless…' He was very pale, and she noticed dispassionately that his hands were shaking as he half dragged, half carried her into a nearby doorway. 'Are you hurt?'

'No,' she said, leaning against a pillar to catch her breath. 'Just a little bruised.'

And more than a little shaken, though she didn't tell him that. For an instant, with the Ganpati looming above her, she'd thought she'd be crushed under it. So much for her enthusiasm about the *visarjan*—she'd never be able to see a clay idol again without thinking of the day she'd almost got herself killed.

'Thanks,' she said, smiling at him wanly. 'I don't think anyone else even noticed I'd fallen.'

He brushed her thanks away impatiently. 'Are you sure you're OK?' he demanded. 'You're as white as a sheet.'

'So are you,' she retorted without thinking, and he laughed grimly.

'You're back to normal, at least,' he said. 'God, Melissa, you really know how to keep things lively.'

A dozen confused retorts ran through her mind, but before she could say anything the skies opened up in a perfect torrent of rain. It was the tail-end of the monsoon season, and it had been cloudy all afternoon.

'Great,' Samir said with water streaming down his body. 'What a lovely end to the day.'

He was laughing, though—properly laughing this time—and after a few seconds Melissa joined in.

Samir held out his hand to her. 'Let's go home,' he said. 'And don't you dare suggest walking back—we're taking a cab.'

'There's something about the rain and sex,' Melissa mused later on in the evening. 'Maybe it's all those old Bollywood movies with the leading ladies dancing in the rain in clingy white saris.'

'Or under waterfalls,' Samir said, lightly running his hand up her leg. 'Waterfalls were pretty big in those days.'

'Hmm…' Melissa gave in to the pleasurable sensations his hands were evoking and stretched like a cat, pressing her body even closer to his. 'Pity I don't own a chiffon sari.'

'Cotton *kurtas* can be pretty sexy too,' Samir said, smiling as he remembered what had happened in the afternoon.

They'd barely made it to the bed before collapsing in a tangled heap of wet limbs. Their damp clothes were still strewn around the living room and the passage that led to the bedroom—at some point they'd need to be picked up and put in the washing machine...

'All good, Mel?' he asked, and they both knew he wasn't talking just about right now.

Melissa gave a little sigh and pulled away, sitting up with a sheet tucked around her. 'We need to talk,' she said and prodded him with an elbow. 'Go and get some clothes on. It's very distracting, you sitting there without a stitch on.'

Ten minutes later they were sitting across from each other at the dining table, both fully clothed.

Melissa looked directly at Samir. 'It won't work,' she said.

Samir took a deep breath. He'd expected her to say something like that ever since their argument on Marine Drive.

'Why do you think that?' he asked. 'We've had a few ups and downs, but that's normal.'

'The ups and downs are normal,' she said. 'But that's not it. I don't fit into your world, and I don't think you want to fit into mine.'

'When you say you don't fit into my world...'

'It's all so artificial!' she said. 'You've got to be careful about what you say, and people are more bothered about how much money you make and what brands you wear than what kind of a person you are.'

'That's not true,' he said quietly. 'You just need to be yourself. But whenever we meet a friend of mine you seem to go out of your way to say something outrageous. Like what you said to Vikas at the art gallery. I'm not ashamed of the relationship we have. I'd like it to be a lot more than just sex, that's all.'

Put like that, it sounded very logical, and Melissa began to feel terribly guilty. Belatedly, it occurred to her that Samir had known these people for years, and the way she'd behaved reflected badly on him and his judgement.

Her shoulders sagged in defeat. 'It's not about your friends or mine, really,' she admitted. 'That can always be worked out. It's *us*. We have fun together, and the sex is great, but we don't really...*connect*. I still know hardly anything about you, and you don't seem particularly interested in knowing about me—though of course that doesn't stop me from babbling out my life's secrets at every opportunity.'

Realising that she'd lost the thread of what she'd wanted to say, and also that she wasn't sounding as calm and collected as she'd planned, she ground to a halt.

'I *am* interested in whatever you tell me,' Samir said quietly. 'I'm just not very good at expressing myself. And if there's anything you'd like to know about me, you only have to ask.'

'But that's just it—I *have* asked, and you always clam up!'

'Like what?' Samir's patience was wearing thin now. 'Ask me again. Ask me whatever you want!'

'What were you planning to give up your career to do?' she blurted out. OK, it wasn't the most important thing she needed to know, but it *had* been bothering her. He looked a little puzzled, and she clarified. 'You told me that Shalini split up with you because you wanted to go off to Europe and work on something that wasn't likely to pay much. What was it?'

His brow cleared. 'That…' he said. 'It was a bit of an impractical plan, really. I was crazy about cars—vintage cars especially—and the idea was to buy a bunch of old cars, work on them and set up a dealership. Also drive them in rallies and stuff like that.' He shrugged. 'What can I say? I was only twenty-two.'

'It doesn't sound that impractical,' she said. 'There's a museum like that in Goa, and I think they're doing pretty OK.'

Samir shrugged. 'Shalini didn't think so,' he said, and his mouth twisted for a few seconds in memory of that long-forgotten hurt. 'What else did you want to know?'

'You mentioned having to leave Kashmir. I can understand you not wanting to talk more about that,' she added hastily. 'But you don't talk about your parents much, or even your brother. At first I thought you weren't very close to them, but from what Priyanka said that's not true.'

Samir sighed. 'I'll tell you all about them,' he said. 'Soon. I promise. Is that it? Or is there something else that's bothering you?'

There was, but it was very nebulous, and she certainly couldn't tell him about overhearing his side of his conversation with his mother. He was still looking at her, however, and finally she said, 'I keep getting the feeling that you're assessing me, somehow. As if you're trying to figure out whether I'm good enough for you or not.'

The last thing she'd expected was for him to go on the offensive, but he raised his eyebrows and said, 'And aren't *you* doing exactly that yourself? You've practically made a catalogue of everything that's wrong with me.'

'It's not the same thing—' she started to say.

He interrupted her ruthlessly. 'It's exactly the same thing,' he said. 'Neither one of us is perfect. But I still think we can make it work.'

He got up and came around the table to put his hands on her shoulders, bending down to nibble gently at her neck. In spite of herself, she squirmed against him with pleasure and he laughed softly.

'And if it doesn't work, at least the sex is great,' he said. 'That's a good reason to stay together, don't you think?'

The doubts crept back that night as she watched Samir sleep, his head pillowed on one arm, while the other was casually flung across her. She'd let him talk her into staying, but she wasn't at all sure that their relationship would last. Great sex was all very well, but they couldn't spend all their waking hours in bed. Other problems were waiting to happen.

She hadn't brought up their different religions because that was something that would matter only if they planned to get married. It bothered her, though. Samir was borderline atheist, and though she wasn't exceptionally devout herself, she *was* a believer. Also, he'd been raised Hindu, which meant his family mightn't take kindly to his marrying a Christian.

Samir stirred slightly in his sleep, his arm tightening possessively around her, and Melissa bent down and pressed a kiss onto his perfectly sculpted lips. Some things about him were perfect, even apart from his startling good looks and prowess in bed, and that was what made the decision so difficult.

In spite of her carefully guarded independence she'd come to depend on his quiet strength—she knew he'd never let her down if she needed him. And he had an irreverent streak in him that perfectly matched her own rather wacky sense of humour, and he always managed to tease her out of a bad mood. He was honest and straightforward, and a genuinely good person, and at the same time he was sizzling hot and pretty near irresistible to women. She would have had to have superwoman powers to stop herself from falling in love with him.

The breaking point came a few days later, when she figured out that Samir expected her to accompany him to a party that the Maximus top brass were holding on Friday.

'But I'm working,' she said. 'You said it yourself— it's a new job, and I can't take things easy.'

'Mel, the party starts at eight,' Samir said. 'Surely you'll be done by then?'

'I'll be done with my office work,' she said. 'But there's that short story Maya asked me to do for a magazine—that's due by Saturday morning.'

'Finish it today, then,' Samir said impatiently. 'How long is it supposed to be? One thousand words?'

'A little more than that,' Melissa said, and hesitated.

'I've actually finished it already. I just need a quiet evening to polish it up a little.'

Maya had lined up a book contract for her that would go through if the publisher liked the story, and she was on tenterhooks. She hadn't told Samir, though, instinctively feeling that he wouldn't understand. Or, worse, wouldn't think it important enough.

'Can't you do that between today and tomorrow?'

'It's…um…difficult to work when you're around,' she said.

The first two times she'd tried to sit down to write he'd cajoled her into bed. After that she'd scheduled her writing for when he wasn't at home.

'I won't disturb you,' Samir said tightly. 'Get the work done and keep Friday free.'

Melissa stared at him, feeling very torn. The party evidently mattered to Samir, and though she didn't want to attend it in the least she'd have gone if not for the short story. The solution he was suggesting didn't work for her. She wanted to let the story be for two days and then come back to it on Friday. Right now she was finding it difficult to be objective—she might ruin it completely by over-editing it.

Samir picked up on her hesitation and said quietly, 'Right, I guess that means it's a no, then. All the best with your story.'

'You haven't even asked to read it,' she blurted out.

'This is the first time you've mentioned it since you told me that you'd been asked to write it,' Samir said. 'If you want me to read it I'm more than happy to.'

Melissa didn't say anything, and Samir went out of the room before he could say anything he'd later regret.

He'd come to respect Melissa's individuality, but to-day's behaviour seemed plain selfish by any standards.

His lips curved up in a mirthless grin. Most of his earlier girlfriends would have jumped at the opportunity to be seen with him in public. Melissa, however, seemed to see it as an imposition.

It was on impulse that he picked up his phone and dialled a number that he hadn't accessed for a while now.

After a largely silent dinner, Melissa said quietly, 'I'll come with you.' She'd thought the whole thing over, and decided that she was being rather immature. Unless she explained to Samir why her writing was so important to her she couldn't expect him to understand—he wasn't clairvoyant. And if the party was important, she owed it to him to go. Whether she enjoyed it or not, he was providing her with a lifestyle that was light-years beyond her means, and so far she'd done very little to show her appreciation.

Samir looked up. He was already regretting the hasty phone call he'd made, but what was done couldn't be undone. And maybe it would help bring Melissa to her senses.

The brusqueness of his tone as he replied was a measure of how uncomfortable he was with the situation, but Melissa didn't know him well enough to realise it. 'It's all right. I don't need you to come,' was what he said.

'But I want to,' Melissa said, hoping her nose wouldn't grow longer. As whoppers went, that was the biggest one to come out of her mouth in a while. 'I've figured out how to manage the work thing.'

'I wish you'd told me earlier,' Samir said. 'The thing

is, it's kind of mandatory to bring a partner along, and once you said no I had to invite someone else. My secretary's already put her name down on the invitee list.'

He knew Melissa would assume it was an ex-girlfriend he'd invited, and in a sense it was true. Rita and he had dated for a while, but then she'd met Vikas Kulkarni and fallen head over heels for him. Their marriage had broken up recently, and as in most divorces friends had been forced to take sides. He'd been slotted into the Vikas camp. Privately, he thought that Rita and Vikas would get back together, and part of the reason he'd asked her to the party was so he'd get an opportunity to talk some sense into her.

Melissa's eyes were wide with disbelief, but her voice was as light as any practised socialite's when she said, 'Oh, OK. I assume you didn't find it too difficult to find a replacement, then?' Only a slight quiver in her lips betrayed how upset she was.

For a few seconds Samir was tempted to call Rita and tell her the party was off. She'd understand, and it would get rid of the betrayed look in Melissa's big brown eyes. Then suddenly anger kicked in. She had no business looking at him like a wounded deer, given that it was *her* unreasonableness that had landed them in this situation in the first place.

'No, it wasn't difficult at all,' he said, and his voice was as cold as ice. 'Replacements are always available.' It was probably his evil genius that prompted him to add, 'Maybe that's something you should keep in mind.'

There was a long pause, and then Melissa said quietly, 'I've been thinking about it for a while, actually.'

For a few moments she thought Samir would melt

and take her into his arms, and she could go back to
pretending that everything was great. But he didn't say
anything and he didn't move towards her.

Quite suddenly she couldn't take it any more. Getting to her feet, she said, 'I'd better go and get writing.
See you around.'

CHAPTER TEN

'I'M SO SORRY.' The matron didn't look sorry in the least. 'You told us you were moving out for good. Your room was allotted to someone else the very next day. And the waiting list has some twenty names in it—it'll be at least a year before you can get a room again.'

Melissa put her name down anyway, but her shoulders slumped as she walked out. The working women's hostel wasn't ideal, but it was cheap, clean and safe, and it had been her home for two years. The other options were significantly less appealing—either she could find someone who took in paying guests, or she could move to the suburbs, where rents were lower. Leaving Samir's flat had been an impulse decision—she hadn't really thought out where she would go. Right now she was occupying the spare room in Liz and Brian's flat, but she couldn't stay there indefinitely.

As she was leaving the hostel one of the girls she knew slightly caught up with her. 'No luck with Matron?' she asked sympathetically.

Melissa shook her head. 'She's got a waiting list as long as her arm.'

'One of my friends has found a place, and she's looking for someone to share it with her,' the girl said.

'Do you want to check it out? You'd get along well, I think.'

It was one of those things that clicked immediately. The studio flat was tiny, but new and clean, and there was a direct bus from right in front of the building to Melissa's office. And Rohini, the girl she would be sharing the flat with, was plump and cheerful, with a wacky sense of humour.

'I was supposed to be sharing this place with my boyfriend,' Rohini confided as she locked the flat door behind her. 'Then he decided to go back to his wife—which was a bit of a surprise, seeing as I didn't know he was married in the first place. And there I was, stuck with a lease that had only my name on it and a rent I couldn't afford. How about you? Any ex-boyfriends or stalkers I should know about?'

Melissa shook her head, smiling slightly. 'Couple of ex-boyfriends, but they're not likely to bother you. One of them isn't even in the country.'

Rohini put her head to one side, looking a lot like an inquisitive bird. 'And the other one?'

The other one. For a second, the memory of Samir's tense, angry face swam in front of her eyes and she felt a physical pain in the region of her heart.

'The other one wasn't important,' she said, smiling slightly at Rohini. 'So, when can I move in?'

'Today, if you like,' Rohini said. 'Or tomorrow. You decide. The quicker you start paying your share of the rent the better, as far as I'm concerned.'

And the quicker Melissa moved out of Liz and Brian's flat the better. They'd been wonderful, but she couldn't impose on them any longer.

Liz was a little tearful when she moved out, but

Brian looked relieved—he'd missed his peaceful routine and having Liz's full attention.

Between her job and her writing, Melissa managed to stay so busy that she hardly had time to think. The nights were toughest, and she lay awake for hours while Rohini slept like a baby. In the mornings she pretended that she'd had a proper night's sleep, but she had a feeling she wasn't fooling Rohini one bit. The thought that she'd made a colossal mistake was eating away at her, and it took all her will-power not to answer Samir's calls or try to contact him herself.

It still hurt when she thought back to the morning she'd left Samir. She'd waited in the bathroom the morning after their row until she'd heard the front door shut behind him. Then she'd scrubbed her face, come out of the bathroom, and made several valiant attempts to write him a note.

An hour later she'd been out of tissues, and had had nothing to show for it other than a few torn up sheets of paper. So much for her skills as a copywriter, she'd thought wryly. Perhaps she should tell Maya Kumar that she'd been hired on false pretences. Giving up on the note, she'd put all her things into the two suitcases she'd brought with her and, carefully pulling the door shut behind her, she'd taken a cab to Liz and Brian's apartment.

On the surface, there had been no real reason to leave—when Liz had asked her what had happened, she'd just told her that things weren't working out rather than explain that she'd refused to go to a party with him, and he'd taken someone else. End of story. And, of course, he'd told her that replacements were easy to find—probably true, given that it had hardly taken him ten minutes to find another companion. But that had been all. Any other woman would have laughed it off and done her best to charm him back into a good mood.

It was the depth of hurt she'd felt that had surprised her. If she'd felt that bad about him going to a simple party without her, she'd have been devastated if he'd actually left her for someone else. And the way things had been going it had become very likely he'd leave her—sooner if not later. Leaving of her own accord had seemed to be the only option.

It was only after she'd moved out that doubt began to gnaw at her. Pride had kept her from answering his calls or calling him herself, but she couldn't help wondering if she'd completely misjudged the situation. Maybe he'd been upset with her because he cared? But if he cared he wouldn't have given up so easily— he'd have come after her, not just dialled her number a few times.

'You OK?'

Rohini was standing just behind her and looking so ludicrously concerned that Melissa had to laugh.

'Yes, of course,' she said, though it was an effort plastering a cheerful smile on her face. 'Let's go—we'll miss the movie otherwise.'

It was a mercy Rohini was such good company without being inquisitive, Melissa thought later, as she struggled to follow the plot of the movie. It would have been torture getting through the past couple of weeks without her.

For an instant she thought she saw a glimpse of Samir in the audience, and her heart-rate tripled. Then the man turned, and she realised she'd been tricked by a chance resemblance.

* * *

'Brian, I just need to know where she lives now.'

'Maybe if you ask her…?' Brian said, peering up at Samir hopefully.

Samir shook his head in exasperation. 'She refuses to answer my calls,' he said. 'It's been three weeks.'

Brian shook his head. 'If she's not taking your calls, I can't tell you, can I? And when I was your age, if my girlfriend had walked out on me I wouldn't have waited three weeks before trying to figure out where she was.'

Samir passed a hand over his face. 'I had to go to Delhi,' he said briefly. 'My father wasn't well.'

His father had suffered a mild heart attack the day after Melissa left, and Samir had had to leave for Delhi at about an hour's notice. Even now his mother had agreed to his returning to Mumbai only because his younger brother had come over from the US to be with his parents.

The past few weeks had been tough—while the heart attack itself hadn't been serious, the doctors had discovered a lot of other health issues, and his father had been hospitalised for over a week. Keeping his distraught mother calm had been an uphill task, and all the while he hadn't been able to stop thinking about Melissa.

For the first few days he'd tried calling her almost every day, and messaging her when she didn't take his calls. He hadn't mentioned his dad's illness because that would have been playing a sympathy card. She'd replied to his texts, saying briefly that she was sorry she'd walked out without telling him but she'd made up her mind—she wasn't coming back.

'I can pass on a message or a letter if you'd like,' Brian offered.

Samir shook his head. 'No, I'll figure it out. Thanks anyway, Brian.'

'Did you read the story Melissa wrote for that magazine?'

Samir nodded. He'd picked up a copy of the magazine when his father had been in the hospital. It was very simply written and incredibly moving without being in the least soppy—about a young girl who'd lost her mother when she was ten, and then spent the next seven years of her life searching for her in other people. Her laugh, the curve of her neck, the fall of her hair... Then finally, when she was seventeen, she'd looked into the mirror and found her mother staring back at her. Not normally a very sensitive person, Samir had found his eyes had been damp by the time he'd finished reading it.

'It was brilliant,' he said. 'She's got real talent.'

He sat with the older man for a while, talking about advertising and the recent changes at Mendonca's.

It was when he was getting up to leave that Brian cleared his throat and said, 'She thinks you don't care about her.'

Samir stared down at him in surprise, and Brian continued hurriedly.

'She didn't say anything to me—I couldn't help overhearing when she was speaking to Liz. She said that it made more sense to leave of her own accord before you threw her out.' At Samir's thunderous expression, Brian said, 'Well, that's what she said. I was pretty sure she was barking up the wrong tree, but I don't like interfering in these things.'

* * *

Before he threw her out. Why would she think he'd do anything of the sort?

Samir's hands clenched into fists as he left Brian's flat. Clearly he'd made an even bigger hash of things than he'd thought he had. He thought back to what he'd said the night before Melissa left. He'd made that ill-advised crack about replacements, but he didn't think just that would have made her think she needed to leave. And he'd fully intended to apologise, but when he'd got back home from work the next day she was gone.

He'd had to leave for Delhi almost immediately afterwards, and it had only been after several attempts to contact Melissa that he'd admitted to himself how much he cared about her. It had taken another week for him to realise that she'd carved her way into his heart—if this wasn't love, he didn't know what was. He thought about her practically every minute of the day, and her absence was like a physical ache.

And when he'd come home the house had seemed so empty without her that he'd had a second's mad impulse to go and find her and not come back until she agreed to come home with him.

It had been stupid, not telling Melissa that he loved her and wanted to marry her, but he hadn't known it himself. Thinking back, the only conclusion he could come to was that he'd been appallingly selfish. He'd known from the day he'd met Melissa that she was special, but he hadn't ever let her know. Instead, he'd bided his time, trying to figure out if their relationship would work, throwing her into one situation after another to see if she'd fit into his social circle.

No wonder she'd felt he didn't value her enough, and finally that he didn't deserve her.

Picking up his cell phone, he dialled her number yet again, not thinking for a minute that she'd answer.

He almost dropped his phone in surprise when her soft voice said, 'Hello?'

'Hi, Melissa, it's Samir,' he said stupidly.

'Yes, I know, your name comes up on the screen.' Her voice was cool and controlled, but her knees were shaking so badly that she had to sit down.

'You doing OK?' he asked.

His voice managed to be low and gentle and sexy all at the same time, and Melissa blinked back sudden tears. She'd not realised quite how much she missed him until she heard him speak.

'All good,' she said. 'I'm sorry I didn't take your calls earlier—I've been a bit…um…confused, I guess.'

'I need to meet you,' he said. 'Please, Melissa.' She hesitated, and he said urgently, 'Just for a short while. We can't leave things like this, sweetheart—we need to talk, and not over the phone.'

He was right—they *did* need to talk. Only she wasn't sure if she could face him without breaking down and telling him exactly how unhappy she'd been since she'd walked out on him almost a month back.

'We can meet,' she said slowly. 'But I don't want to come to your place. After work some day would be best.'

'Today? I'll pick you up around six.'

Melissa had a deadline for a shampoo ad, and another for an ad for super-crunchy peanut butter. In the state of mind she was right now she'd probably write about crunchy hair and extra-lather peanut butter…

Sighing in defeat, she said, 'OK, then. Do you know where it is?'

'I'll find out,' he said. Before he rang off he added, 'Mel? I've really missed you.'

Me too, she thought as she put the phone down. *Me too.*

She was staring vacantly into her screen when Maya walked by.

'Searching for inspiration?' she asked drily.

Melissa sat up in alarm. Maya was a wonderful person to work with most of the time, but the one thing you absolutely could *not* do was slack off at work. In the short time Melissa had worked with her she'd seen grown men turn into weak-kneed jellyfish when Maya raised her perfectly plucked eyebrows at them.

'No, I was just…' she started to say, but Maya wasn't listening.

Leaning over, she slid the briefing document for the shampoo ad out from where it was currently serving as a coaster under Melissa's bottle-green coffee mug.

'Concentrate,' she said. 'If you're PMSing, pop some medication, and if it's a boyfriend he's probably not worth it.'

At six-twenty, after having dashed off two lyrical pages on strawberry-scented shampoo and one more on the health benefits of peanut butter, she stood on the pavement outside her office. Maya was wrong, she thought. Samir was totally worth it. But she could have done with some of Maya's inner strength, she thought as she hungrily watched Samir cross the road to come to her—she was in imminent danger of turning into a helpless little puddle of need.

When he was finally standing in front of her she had

to take a deep breath so that she didn't show him quite how affected she was by his proximity. He looked good enough to eat, she thought, drinking in the sight of him in an open-necked denim shirt and perfectly cut beige chinos. He was thinner, his sculpted cheekbones a little more prominent than they had been, and there was a haggard look in his eyes that she wanted to kiss away.

'Hey,' he said softly, touching her cheek. 'It's so good to see you.'

A whiff of his woody cologne teased at her nostrils, and the temptation to lean closer was immense. Once again she felt deeply thankful that she'd suggested meeting in a public place.

'It's good to see you too,' she said as graciously as she could, doing her damnedest to channel Maya Kumar. Strong, smiling, with a core of steel. She gave a yelp of alarm and jumped backwards as he bent his head to brush his lips lightly against her cheek. Okay, now she was channelling Chihuahua, not Maya, and passersby were giving her funny looks.

'Should we find some place we can sit down?' he asked, his lips curving up in his trademark half devilish, half little-boy way.

'There's a small restaurant a little way down the road,' she said, a little breathless. 'Not swanky, but we can talk there.'

She turned and started walking towards it, hoping she didn't trip and fall flat on her face in her agitation. The worst part was not knowing *why* he was here—perhaps all he wanted to do was have a civilised conversation before they called it quits on their relationship. Then again, maybe not. The way he'd looked at her suggested that he wanted to do a lot more than just talk—his dark eyes had smouldered into hers in true romantic hero style. Though this time she'd been too rattled to tease him about it. Instead, she'd lowered her head and done her best to memorise the cracks in the pavement.

Samir fell into an easy stride by her side. 'Congratulations on the story,' he said. 'I just finished reading it. I don't know what to say, Melissa—it was brilliant. I had no idea you could write so well.'

It was ridiculous to feel so pleased. She knew that. Trying to sound as nonchalant as possible, she said, 'Thanks. All credit to Maya, though—she put me in touch with the magazine. Left to myself, I'd have decided the story wasn't good enough to send anywhere.'

'I'm glad you met Maya, then,' he said. 'Though I still haven't forgiven her for stealing you away from Maximus.'

'From Mendonca's,' she corrected. 'We're here—the red door is the place we need to go. It serves the best Indian-Chinese food in the city.'

They stepped into the unassuming little restaurant and found an empty table in a corner.

Samir waited while the server plonked two menus in front of them and wandered off, and then asked bluntly, 'Why did you leave? Was it because I invited someone else to that party?'

Melissa bit her lip. 'No,' she said. 'That wasn't it. I just thought it wasn't working any more.'

'Why?' he asked, leaning forward. 'We might have had a few issues, but we could have worked those out. What was so bad that you had to leave?'

'Sir—order?'

Samir looked up in exasperation, but the little waiter

refused to budge. The restaurant managed to keep its prices low by keeping the turnover high—one thing it absolutely didn't encourage was people dawdling around, occupying tables and staring into each other's eyes without ordering anything.

'Ask for either the chilli chicken or the Idli Manchurian,' Melissa prompted. 'And a diet soda for me.'

'Idli Manchurian?' he said in disbelief. 'What is that?' As was usual with Melissa, the conversation was slipping off into a direction he hadn't planned.

Melissa gave him a lopsided grin. 'Idlis rice cake, sliced up, dipped in cornflour, fried and tossed in Manchurian gravy.'

'I wasn't really asking for the recipe.'

'Oh, it tastes great,' she said. 'Though there's enough garlic in it to ward off an invading army of vampires.'

Samir shuddered. 'We'll have the chilli chicken,' he told the waiter. 'And two cans of soda.'

He gave Melissa a wry look once the boy had zipped off into the kitchen. 'This isn't exactly the right place for an uninterrupted conversation, is it?'

No, that's why I chose it, Melissa thought. 'I'm sorry,' she said out loud, more Aunty Liz than Maya Kumar this time. 'But there are no fancy places around here. We'll have to make do with this.'

Samir was about to reply when the boy waiter returned with a large bottle of soda and two glasses which, going by the state of his sleeves, he had just rinsed in the sink.

'Soda,' he announced proudly, and Samir sighed.

'Thank you,' he said, pushing the bottle across to Melissa.

'So I was asking.'

'Chilli chicken dry or with gravy?' his nemesis asked, popping out of the kitchen.

'Dry,' Melissa called out, suppressing an involuntary giggle as Samir sank his head into his hands in exasperation.

'Spicy or medium spicy?' the boy asked.

Samir gave him a look, and he promptly vanished back into the kitchen, saying as he went, 'Medium spicy better for you, I think.'

'You know what? Let's cut to the chase,' Samir said. 'I've been a self-centred pig and I've probably ruined my chances with you, but I just need you to answer one question.'

Melissa looked at him, her eyes wide.

'Is there any way you would consider marrying me?'

Her answering gasp was loud enough to make diners at the other end of the restaurant turn around to stare at them.

'Of all the…' She was sputtering in anger now, but Samir was leaning back, his dark eyes dancing with amusement.

'I'll take that as a yes,' he said. 'If it was an unequivocal no you'd have been much nicer to me. Come on—let's go.'

He was on his feet already, and before she knew what was happening she was standing next to him, still clutching her bottle of soda.

'We won't be needing that chilli chicken after all,' Samir informed the diminutive waiter as he put a five-hundred-rupee note into his hand. 'Madam has some really important work to do.'

The boy flushed with pleasure as he pocketed the money, and Samir swept her out of the restaurant.

'But…where are we going?' Melissa asked, thoroughly confused now.

'Some place where I can propose to you properly,' Samir said. They were already in his car, and he turned to look at her, his eyes warm with suppressed desire. 'And some place where I can kiss you the way I want to.'

'Hang on,' Melissa said.

Samir turning all masterful on her was an incredible turn-on, but she needed to know what was happening.

'A month back you weren't sure you wanted to be with me. Then I walked out, and you suddenly want to marry me?'

'I always wanted to marry you,' he said, starting the car and turning onto the road. 'I just wasn't sure it was the sensible thing to do.'

'What's changed then?' she asked.

Samir shrugged. 'Nothing major,' he said. 'Except that I've figured out I can't live without you.'

The words were said in such a matter-of-fact way that for a second she thought he was being flippant. Then she saw that his hands had tightened on the steering wheel so hard that his knuckles had turned white. It must have taken considerable effort for him to say that, she realised, especially since he was normally so restrained. And he hadn't said the words, but the implication that he was in love with her was pretty loud and clear—people didn't say they couldn't live without you if they were only mildly fond of you.

And, come to think of it, she was finding it pretty hard to live without him as well.

'Let's go to your flat,' she said, her voice sure and steady for the first time that evening.

She was having a bit of an epiphany, she realised. She'd got it wrong all along—fooled by Samir's apparent coolness into thinking that he didn't care for her. But now that she thought back she realised that right from the beginning he'd been the one trying to make the relationship work, while she'd fought her feelings at every step. They'd been at cross purposes all along.

They were both silent till they were inside the door—then Samir pushed it shut behind them and took her into his arms, the raw hunger on his lips matched by the passion on hers.

It was a while before he released her, saying raggedly as he pushed a hand through his hair, 'God, I love you so much. I was crazy to think this was just about the sex—I want to spend the rest of my life with you, Mel.'

'So do I,' Melissa said, putting up a hand to caress his face and stealing a quick kiss before she went on. 'Spend the rest of my life with *you*, I mean, not myself.'

The rest of what she'd meant to say was lost as he crushed her lips under his in a kiss that managed to be hot and hungry and wildly passionate all at the same time. A little moan escaped Melissa's lips as she finally abandoned herself to the tide of sensation that was sweeping over them both.

Much later, he said softly, 'I was all kinds of fool to say what I did about replacements. I should have known better—I was just so worked up about you refusing to come with me that I let my mouth run away with me.'

Melissa gave the offending mouth a consoling kiss. 'I wasn't thinking straight either,' she said. 'I'd overheard you talking to your mum a few days before that, and I thought you felt I wasn't good enough for you. You even said you weren't in love with me.'

Samir frowned. 'When did I say that?'

'The day your mother called on the home phone and I spoke to her. You called her back from the car park— I'd gone for a jog, and I couldn't help hearing you. You said you needed to sort things out with me...'

His brow cleared. 'That was a long while back,' he said. 'I already knew I didn't want to let you go, but I hadn't got around to figuring out that I was in love with you. We hadn't discussed marriage. And my mother tends to get a little ahead of the situation at times. When things didn't work out with Shalini she was perhaps even more upset than I was.'

Seeing that Melissa looked puzzled, he went on.

'She lost a lot of her family in a militant strike around the time we left Kashmir. So it's her dream to have a large family again—both her sons married, lots of grandchildren, the works. If she'd known things were even remotely serious she'd have had us kidnapped and taken to the nearest registry office before we could change our minds. But I promise you—the second I get a ring on your finger, she'll be the first person I'll tell.' He bent his head and planted a little row of kisses on her shoulder. 'And you'll need to speak to your dad as well.'

'He'll want us to have a church wedding,' she said. 'And bring up our kids as good Catholics.'

'If the priest doesn't mind performing the ceremony I don't mind,' Samir said. 'As for the kids—they can grow up and decide what they want to be.'

'Very permissive,' Melissa said teasingly, but a great load was off her shoulders.

Samir wasn't done yet, though.

'There was another thing I wanted to tell you,' he said. 'I mayn't have come across as being very supportive of your career or your writing. Maybe I was a little jealous of the time you were spending away from me. But I'll back you every step of the way from now on. You've got real talent, and you deserve every possible bit of support I can give you.'

Melissa nestled a little closer to him. 'Even if I bunk off your incredibly boring office dos to write?' she asked.

'Even if you do that,' he said. 'I'll probably bunk off them as well and stay home to watch you.' His expression turned serious, and he cupped her face in his hands, tipping it up so that he could look directly into her eyes.

'I love you,' he said. 'Corny as it may sound, I'll love you till the day I die.'

'In some situations corny is good,' she said, and she met his gaze squarely. 'I love you too, Samir. And I'd love to marry you, and grow old and cranky with you, and have several kids.'

The last bit came out all muffled against his lips, and Melissa gave up the attempt to outline the path she wanted the rest of their lives to take. She loved him, and he loved her back, and right now that was all that mattered.

EPILOGUE

THE WEDDING WAS in Goa, in a little church near Melissa's childhood home. They'd had a big Hindu wedding first in Delhi, followed by a register office ceremony, but to Melissa exchanging their vows in the church she'd gone to for all her growing up years was the most important of the series of ceremonies.

'You look beautiful,' Cheryl said, carefully adjusting Melissa's veil. 'I'm so glad you decided to wear your mamma's wedding sari.'

The sari was made of lovely white brocade, and Melissa had insisted on wearing it instead of an elaborate wedding gown of the kind popular in the current generation. A single perfect strand of pearls gleamed at her throat—they were one of Bina Razdan's many gifts to her brand-new daughter-in-law. With her silky hair piled up in a chignon, Melissa looked like a graceful young queen.

'I wish Mamma could have been here,' Melissa said softly as her sister-in-law gave the veil a final tweak and stepped back to admire her handiwork.

Cheryl bent down and gave her a hug. 'I'm sure she can see you,' she said. 'And that she thoroughly approves of that gorgeous man you're marrying.'

Melissa's father was waiting for her at the door of the church, and as they slowly walked down the aisle Melissa's eyes sought out Samir's. He looked incredibly handsome in his dark formal suit, and his eyes lit up as she reached him. Cheryl was right, Melissa thought with a sudden rush of pride. He *was* gorgeous—and, better still, he was all hers.

'Have I told you yet how much I love you?' he whispered as they took their places in front of the parish priest.

'Many times,' Melissa whispered back. 'But I have short-term memory issues—you'll need to keep telling me every so often.'

'Shh…' Melissa's father said, smiling at them fondly.

He'd taken an abrupt liking to Samir, and that had helped heal things further between him and Melissa. It was as if the whole episode with Josh and the two years after that had never happened at all.

The ceremony was performed by the young parish priest who'd encouraged Melissa's father to reach out to her. In his early thirties, and almost as good-looking as the bridegroom, he was attracting languishing stares from the younger female members of the congregation—his attention, however, was solely focussed on the couple in front of him.

When he said, 'You may now kiss the bride,' there was a mixture of sighs and gasps from the audience.

Melissa suspected that if they hadn't been in a place of worship people would have whistled and stamped their feet. Then Samir's lips came down on hers, and for a few seconds she forgot about audience reaction as the world closed in to accommodate just the two of them.

When they broke away a minute later her cheeks were flushed and her heart-rate twice what it had been when she'd entered the church. 'Not fair,' she muttered under her breath, and Samir smiled at her, his expression so openly and radiantly happy that she felt her heart miss a beat.

'I love you,' he said once again, and though he kept his voice low it was strong enough to be heard by the people in the front pew. 'She has short-term memory issues,' he explained to the priest, who had paused to grin broadly at them. 'I need to keep reminding her.'

'Welcome to the family,' Samir's father said, beaming as he raised a toast to them at the lunch that followed the wedding.

His mother gave them a lovely smile, and Melissa thought for the nth time since she'd met Samir's parents that she'd been so completely off the mark when she'd thought that they wouldn't accept her. Ever since she'd met them they'd gone out of their way to make her feel she was part of the family. So much so that she'd had to be careful not to offend them when she'd insisted on doing the preparations for the wedding herself and refused the ridiculously expensive gifts they'd tried to thrust on her.

'Congratulations,' Vikas Kulkarni said. 'Could I have the honour?'

Michael had arranged the music, and the members of his band had now loosened their ties and were playing popular Goan dance numbers.

'Can you dance?' Melissa asked suspiciously.

In her experience most non-Goan men hadn't mastered the art of dancing with the opposite sex—they either flung their arms around enthusiastically and stamped on their partner's toes or stood stock-still and tapped their feet to the music, presumably expecting their partners to gyrate around them Bollywood style. Neera was currently dodging a partner of the second category and giggling over a drink with one of Samir's Maximus colleagues.

'My ex-wife forced me to go through an entire year of Latin ballroom dancing classes,' Vikas said as he expertly swung her onto the dance floor. 'Good music, by the way, Melissa. Michael's done an amazing job.'

'Thanks,' Melissa said. 'Though I think a couple of Samir's relatives are absolutely scandalised by my band party family.'

Vikas glanced over at the relatives in question. 'Oh, I wouldn't bother about them, if I were you,' he said dismissively. 'Sour-faced bunch of prunes. Just remember their faces and snub them royally if they volunteer to be godparents to your babies. Samir's parents are in love with you, and so are his friends. Even his brother's bowled over.'

Melissa laughed, hoping he was right. Bina had confided to Melissa that she'd always had a secret yen for a church wedding herself, and she was thrilled to be part of one. Right now she was being whirled around the dance floor by one of Melissa's cousins, while Samir's father looked on with an indulgent smile. He'd completely recovered from the heart attack, but he still needed to take things slowly—Bina was trying to convince him to retire and hand over the business to Samir's brother to run.

Melissa's eyes met Samir's, and for a second she forgot to move, forcing Vikas to steer her abruptly out of the way of a couple doing the *bhangra* to a peppy Konkani number.

'I can see I've lost you.' Vikas sighed in her ear, and she blushed vividly. 'But before you rush off to your loving husband could you be a darling and introduce me to that lovely flatmate of yours?'

Sadly, Vikas and Rita hadn't reconciled, in spite of Samir's best efforts—Rita was now seeing someone else, and Vikas was revelling in his new-found bachelor status. Melissa took him across to Rohini, whose eyes promptly lit up. There were clearly some serious sparks going on there, and Melissa left them to get on with it as she headed back to Samir.

'I've been thinking for a while, and I've now made up my mind,' Melissa announced later as they got into the car to leave for their honeymoon.

Samir looked at her in mock alarm. 'Statements like that make me very nervous,' he said. 'What exactly have you decided, Melly?'

'Today is quite definitely the happiest day of my life,' she said. 'I was trying to choose between today and the day you asked me to marry you. But today is better.'

'It is,' Samir said, brushing his hand gently against her collarbone and making her shiver with longing. 'But I'd like to think that we have even better days ahead of us.'

'Fabulous honeymoon sex,' she said, wrinkling her brow as she pretended to concentrate very hard. 'Setting up house together.'

'Our first child,' Samir supplied.

'Second child.'

'Third... Actually, no, our first child's graduation day.'

'His wedding.'

'Grandkids.'

Melissa began to laugh. 'We seem to have it all mapped out,' she said. 'Our own version of happily-ever-after.'

'Everything might not turn out exactly the way we think it will,' Samir said, turning to smile his trade-mark heart-stopping smile. 'But the happily-ever-after bit—that's non-negotiable.'

'Completely,' she agreed. 'Though I *would* like the bit about fabulous honeymoon sex to turn out the way I've imagined it.'

And it did.

* * * * *

A sneaky peek at next month...

MODERN tempted™

**FRESH, CONTEMPORARY ROMANCES TO TEMPT
ALL LOVERS OF GREAT STORIES**

My wish list for next month's titles...

In stores from 17th January 2014:

❑ No Time Like Mardi Gras – Kimberly Lang

❑ The Last Guy She Should Call – Joss Wood

In stores from 7th February 2014:

❑ Romance For Cynics – Nicola Marsh

❑ Trouble On Her Doorstep – Nina Harrington

Available at WHSmith, Tesco, Asda, Eason, Amazon and Apple

Just can't wait?

*Visit us
Online*

You can buy our books online a month before
they hit the shops! **www.millsandboon.co.uk**

0114/31

Hot reads!

These 3-in-1s will certainly get you feeling hot under the collar with their desert locations, billionaire tycoons and playboy princes.

**Now available at
www.millsandboon.co.uk/offers**

Join our *EXCLUSIVE* eBook club

FROM JUST £1.99 A MONTH!

Never miss a book again with our hassle-free eBook subscription.

★ Pick how many titles you want from each series with our flexible subscription

★ Your titles are delivered to your device on the first of every month

★ Zero risk, zero obligation!

There really is nothing standing in the way of you and your favourite books!

Start your eBook subscription today at www.millsandboon.co.uk/subscribe

The World of Mills & Boon

There's a Mills & Boon® series that's perfect for you. There are ten different series to choose from and new titles every month, so whether you're looking for glamorous seduction, Regency rakes, homespun heroes or sizzling erotica, we'll give you plenty of inspiration for your next read.

By Request

Back by popular demand!
12 stories every month

Cherish™

Experience the ultimate rush of falling in love.
12 new stories every month

INTRIGUE...

A seductive combination of danger and desire...
7 new stories every month

Desire™

Passionate and dramatic love stories
6 new stories every month

nocturne™

An exhilarating underworld of dark desires
3 new stories every month

For exclusive member offers go to
millsandboon.co.uk/subscribe

Which series will you try next?

Wholesome, heartfelt relationships

4 new stories every month

Only available online

Awaken the romance of the past…

6 new stories every month

The ultimate in romantic medical drama

6 new stories every month

MODERN™

Power, passion and irresistible temptation

8 new stories every month

True love and temptation!

4 new stories every month